Lucas Davenport returns in the most harrowing and unexpected Prey novel yet—the story of a congenial man, and his most uncongenial obsession . . .

CHOSEN PREY

Art history professor James Qatar's hobby was taking secret photographs of women. At night when he was all alone he'd dream about them and indulge his fantasies. Then one day his fantasy went too far. Now it's Qatar's turn to become an obsession—of Davenport's. And for both men there's no turning back.

"BRUTAL, UNRELENTING ACTION."
—*Los Angeles Times*

"A HEART-STOPPING CLIMAX."
—*Richmond Times-Dispatch*

"A REAL RUSH, YOU'LL LOVE IT."
—*Lancaster Intelligencier Journal*

"NEW TWISTS AND SURPRISES."
—*The Charleston Post and Courier*

Titles by John Sandford

DEAD WATCH
DARK OF THE MOON

RULES OF PREY
SHADOW PREY
EYES OF PREY
SILENT PREY
WINTER PREY
NIGHT PREY
MIND PREY
SUDDEN PREY
SECRET PREY
CERTAIN PREY
EASY PREY
CHOSEN PREY
MORTAL PREY
NAKED PREY
BROKEN PREY
INVISIBLE PREY

THE NIGHT CREW

The Kidd Novels

THE EMPRESS FILE
THE FOOL'S RUN
THE DEVIL'S CODE
THE HANGED MAN'S SONG

CHOSEN PREY

JOHN SANDFORD

BERKLEY BOOKS, NEW YORK

THE BERKLEY PUBLISHING GROUP
Published by the Penguin Group
Penguin Group (USA) Inc.
375 Hudson Street, New York, New York 10014, USA
Penguin Group (Canada), 90 Eglinton Avenue East, Suite 700, Toronto, Ontario M4P 2Y3, Canada
(a division of Pearson Penguin Canada Inc.)
Penguin Books Ltd., 80 Strand, London WC2R 0RL, England
Penguin Group Ireland, 25 St. Stephen's Green, Dublin 2, Ireland (a division of Penguin Books Ltd.)
Penguin Group (Australia), 250 Camberwell Road, Camberwell, Victoria 3124, Australia
(a division of Pearson Australia Group Pty. Ltd.)
Penguin Books India Pvt. Ltd., 11 Community Centre, Panchsheel Park, New Delhi—110 017, India
Penguin Group (NZ), 67 Apollo Drive, Rosedale, North Shore 0632, New Zealand
(a division of Pearson New Zealand Ltd.)
Penguin Books (South Africa) (Pty.) Ltd., 24 Sturdee Avenue, Rosebank, Johannesburg 2196,
South Africa

Penguin Books Ltd., Registered Offices: 80 Strand, London WC2R 0RL, England

This is a work of fiction. Names, characters, places, and incidents either are the product of the author's imagination or are used fictitiously, and any resemblance to actual persons, living or dead, business establishments, events, or locales is entirely coincidental. The publisher does not have any control over and does not assume any responsibility for author or third-party websites or their content.

CHOSEN PREY

A Berkley Book / published by arrangement with the author

PRINTING HISTORY
G. P. Putnam's Sons hardcover edition / May 2001
Berkley mass-market edition / May 2002

ISBN: 978-0-425-18287-1

BERKLEY®
Berkley Books are published by The Berkley Publishing Group,
a division of Penguin Group (USA) Inc.,
375 Hudson Street, New York, New York 10014.
BERKLEY® is a registered trademark of Penguin Group (USA) Inc.
The "B" design is a trademark belonging to Penguin Group (USA) Inc.

PRINTED IN THE UNITED STATES OF AMERICA

25   24   23   22   21   20   19   18   17   16   15   14

For Beryl Weekley

CHOSEN
PREY

JAMES QATAR DROPPED his feet over the edge of the bed and rubbed the back of his neck, a momentary veil of depression falling upon him. He was sitting naked on the rumpled sheets, the smell of sex lingering like a rude perfume. He could hear Ellen Barstad in the kitchen. She'd turned on the radio she kept by the sink, and "Cinnamon Girl" bubbled through the small rooms. Dishes tinkled against cups, fingernail scratches through the melody of the song.

"Cinnamon Girl" wasn't right for this day, for this time, for what was about to happen. If he were to have music, he thought, maybe Shostakovich, a few measures from the Lyric Waltz in Jazz Suite Number 2. Something sweet, yet pensive, with a taste of tragedy; Qatar was an intellectual, and he knew his music.

He stood up, wobbled into the bathroom, flushed the Trojan in the toilet, washed perfunctorily, and studied himself in the mirror above the sink. Great eyes, he thought, suitably deep-set for a man of intellect. A good nose, trim, not fleshy. His pointed chin made his face into an oval, a reflection of sensitivity. He was admiring the image when his eyes drifted to the side of his nose: a whole series of small dark hairs were emerging from the line where his nose met his cheek. He *hated* that.

He found a set of tweezers in the medicine cabinet and carefully tweezed them away, then took a couple of hairs from the bridge of his nose, between his eyebrows. Checked his ears. His ears were okay. The tweezers were pretty good, he thought: you didn't find tweezers like this every day. He'd take them with him—she wouldn't miss them.

Now. Where was he?

Ah. Barstad. He had to stay focused. He went back to the bedroom, put the tweezers in a jacket pocket, dressed, put on his shoes, then returned to the bathroom to check his hair. Just a touch with the comb. When he was satisfied, he rolled out twenty feet of toilet paper and wiped everything he might have touched in the bedroom and bathroom. The police would be coming around sooner or later.

He hummed as he worked, nothing intricate: Bach, maybe. When he'd finished cleaning up, he threw the toilet paper into the toilet, pressed the handle with his knuckles, and watched it flush.

ELLEN Barstad heard the toilet flush a second time and wondered what was keeping him. All this toilet flushing was less than romantic; she needed some romance. Romance, she thought, and a little decent *sex*. James Qatar had been a severe disappointment, as had been all of the few lovers in her life. All eager to get aboard and pound away; none much concerned with her, though they said they were.

"That was really great, Ellen, you're great—pass me that beer, will ya? Ya got great tits, did I tell you that . . . ?"

Her love life to this point—three men, six years—had been a pale reflection of the ecstasies described in her books. So far, she felt more like a sausage-making machine than the lover in the Song of Solomon: *"Your breasts are like two fawns, like twin fawns of a gazelle that browse among the lilies. Until the day breaks and the shadows flee, I will go to the mountain of myrrh and to the hill of incense. All beautiful you are, my darling, there is no flaw in you."*

Where was that? Huh? Where was it? *That's* what she wanted. Somebody to climb her mountain of myrrh.

James Qatar might not look like much, she thought, but there was a sensual quality in his eyes, and a hovering cruelty that she found intriguing. She'd never been pushy, had never pushed anything in her life. But as she stood with her hands in the dishwater, she decided to push this. If she didn't, what was the point?

Time was passing—with her youth.

Barstad was a fabric artist who did some weaving, but mostly made quilts. She couldn't make a living at it yet, but her quilting income was increasing month by month, and in another year or two she might be able to quit her day job.

She lived illegally in a storefront in a Minneapolis warehouse district. The front of the space was an open bay, full of quilting frames and material bins. The back she'd built herself, with salvaged drywall and two-by-fours: She'd enclosed the toilet and divided the rest of the space into bedroom, sitting area, and kitchen. The kitchen amounted to a tabletop electric stove and a fifties refrigerator, with a bunch of old doors mounted on sawhorses as countertops.

And it was all just fine for an artist in her twenties, with bigger things ahead. . . .

Like great sex, she thought—if he'd ever get out of the bathroom.

THE rope was in his jacket, balled up. Qatar took it out and pulled his hand down the length of it, as though to strip away its history. Eighteen inches long, it had begun life as the starter rope on a Mercury outboard motor—one end still had the rubber pull-handle. The rope had been with him, he thought, for almost half his life. When he'd eliminated the tangles, he coiled it neatly around the fingers of his left hand, slipped the coil off his fingers, and pushed it carefully into his hip pocket. Old friend.

Barstad had been a brutal disappointment. She'd been nothing like her images had suggested she'd be. She'd been absolutely white-bread, nothing but spread-your-legs-and-close-your-eyes. He couldn't continue with a woman like that.

The postcoital depression began leaking away, to be replaced by the half-forgotten killing mood—a fitful state, combining a blue, close-focused excitement with a scratchy, unpleasant fear. He picked up his jacket and carried it into the living room, a space just big enough for a couch and coffee table, hung it neatly on the back of a wooden rocking chair, and walked to the corner of the makeshift kitchen.

The kitchen smelled a little of chicken soup, a little of seasoned salt, a little of cut celery, all pulled together by the hum of the refrigerator and the sound of the radio. Barstad was there, with both hands in dishwater. She was absently mouthing the words to a soft-rock tune that Qatar didn't recognize, and moving her body with it in that self-conscious, upper-Midwest way.

Barstad had honey-blond hair and blue eyes under pale, almost white eyebrows. She dressed down, in Minnesota fashion, in earth-colored shifts, turtlenecks, dark tights, and clunky shoes. The church-mouse clothes did not completely conceal an excellent body, created by her Scandinavian genes and toned by compulsive bicycle-riding. All wasted on her, Qatar thought. He stepped into the kitchen, and she saw him and smiled shyly. "How are you?" she asked.

"Wonderful," he said, twinkling at her, the rope pressing in his hip pocket. She'd known the sex hadn't been that good—that's why she'd fled to her dishes. He bent forward, his hands at her waist, and kissed her on the neck. She smelled like yellow Dial soap. "Absolutely the best."

"I hope it will get better," she said, blushing. She had a sponge in her hand. "I know it wasn't everything you expected. . . ."

"You are such a pretty woman," he said. He touched the side of her neck, cooing at her. "Such a pretty woman."

He pushed his hips against her, and she moved her butt back against him. "And you are such a liar," she said. She was not good at small talk. "But keep it up."

"Mmmm." The rope was in his hand.

His fingers fit over the T of the handle; he would loop it over her chin, he thought, so that it wouldn't get hung up by the turtleneck. He would have to pull her over, he thought; get a foot wedged behind hers and jerk hard, backward and down, then hang her over the floor, so that her own weight would strangle her. Had to watch for fingernails, and to control the attitude of her body with his knees. Fingernails were like knives. He turned one foot to block her heels, so that she would trip over it when she went down.

Careful here, he thought. No mistakes now.

* * *

"I know that wasn't too great," she said, not looking back at him. A pink flush crawled up her neck, but she continued, doggedly, "I haven't had that much experience, and the men . . . weren't very . . . good." She was struggling with the words. This was hard. "You could show me a lot about sex. I'd like to know. I really would. I'd like to know everything. If we could find a way to talk about it without being too, you know, embarrassed about it."

SHE derailed him.

He'd been one second from taking her, and her words barely penetrated the killing fog. *But they got through.*

She wanted what? To learn about sex, a lot about sex? The idea was an erotic slap in the face, like something from a bad pornographic film, where the housewife asks the plumber to show her how to . . .

He stood frozen for a moment, then she half-turned and gave him the shy, sexy smile that had attracted him in the first place. Qatar pushed against her again and fumbled the rope back into his hip pocket.

"I think we could work something out," he said, his voice thick. And he thought, silently amused: Talk dirty—save your life.

JAMES Qatar was an art history professor and a writer, a womanizer and genial pervert and pipe smoker, a thief and a laughing man and a killer. He thought of himself as sensitive and engaged, and tried to live up to that image. He kissed Barstad once more on the back of the neck, cupped one of her breasts for a moment, then said, "I've got to go. Maybe we could get together Wednesday."

"Do you, uh . . ." She was blushing again. "Do you have any sexy movies?"

"Movies?" He heard her, but he was astonished.

"You know, sexy movies," she said, turning into him. "Maybe if we had a sexy movie, we could, you know . . . talk about what works and what doesn't."

"You could be really good at this," he said.

"I'll try," she said. She was flaming pink, but she was determined.

QATAR left the apartment with a vague feeling of regret. Barstad had mentioned that she had to go to the bank later in the day. She'd gotten enrollment fees for a quilting class, and had two hundred dollars in checks she'd wanted to deposit—and she had almost four hundred dollars in cash, which she would not deposit, to avoid the taxes.

The money could have been his; and she had some nice jewelry, gifts from her parents, worth maybe another thousand. There was some miscellaneous stuff, as well: cameras, some of her drawing equipment, an IBM laptop, and a Palm III that, together, could have pulled in a couple of hundred more.

He could have used the cash. The new light topcoats for the coming season were hip-length, and he'd seen the perfect example at Neiman Marcus: six hundred fifty dollars, on sale, with a wool lining. A pair of cashmere sweaters, two pairs of slacks, and the right shoes would cost another two thousand. He'd been only seconds away from it. . . .

Was sex better than cashmere? He wasn't sure. It was quite possible, he mused, that no matter what Barstad was willing to do in bed, she would never be as good as Armani.

* * *

JAMES Qatar was five feet, eleven ten inches tall, slender and balding, with a thin blond beard that he kept closely cropped. He liked the three-days-without-shaving look, the open-collar, striped-shirt, busy-intellectual image. He was fair-skinned, with smile lines at the corners of his mouth, and just a hint of crow's-feet at the corners of his eyes. He had delicate hands with long fingers. He worked out daily on a rowing machine, and in the summer on blades; he would not ever have thought of himself as a brave man, but he did have a style of courage built on willpower. He never failed to do what he wanted to do, or needed to.

The smile lines on his face came from laughing: he wasn't jolly, exactly, but he'd perfected a long, rolling laugh. He laughed at jokes, at wit, at cynicism, at travail, at cruelty, at life, at death. Years before he'd cornered a coed in his office once, thinking that she might come across, thinking that he might kill her if she did, but she hadn't. She'd said, instead, "All that laughing doesn't fool me, Jimbo. You've got mean little eyes like a pig. I can see the meanness."

On her way out, she'd turned—posing her coed tits perfectly in profile—and said, "I won't be coming back to class, but I better get an A for the semester. If you read my meaning." He'd let out his rolling laugh, a little regretfully, peered at her with his mean eyes, and said, "I didn't like you until now. Now I like you."

He'd delivered the A, and considered it earned.

QATAR was an art historian and associate professor at St. Patrick's University, author of *Not a Pipe: The Surfaces of Midwestern Painting 1966–1990,* which had been favorably reviewed in *Chicken Little,* the authorative quarterly of late-postmodern arts; and also *Planes on Plains: Native Cubists of the Red River Valley 1915–1930,* which the reviewer for the Fargo *Forum* had called "seminal." He'd begun college as a studio artist, but switched to art history after a cold-eyed appraisal of his talents—good, but not great—and an equally cold appraisal of an average artist's earning potential.

He'd done well with his true interests: blond women, art history, wine, murder, and his home, which he'd decorated with Arts and Crafts furniture. Even, since the arrival of digital photography, with art itself.

Art of a sort.

The school provided computers, Internet connections, video projectors, slide scanners, all the tools required by an art historian. He found that he could scan a photo into his computer and process it through Photoshop, eliminating much of the confusing complexity. He could then project it onto a piece of drawing paper and draw over the photo.

This was not considered entirely proper in the art community, so he kept his experiments secret. He imagined himself someday popping an entire oeuvre of sensational drawings on a stunned New York art world.

It had been just that innocent in the beginning. A dream. His historian's eye told him that the first drawings were mediocre; but as he became more expert with the various tools in Photoshop, and with the pen itself, the drawings became cleaner and sharper. They actually became *good.* Still not good enough to provide a living, but good enough to engage his other enthusiasms. . . .

He could download a nude from one of the endless Internet porno sites, process it, print it, project it, and produce a fantasy that appealed both to his sense of aesthetics and to his need to possess.

The next step was inevitable. After a few weeks of working with appropriated photos, he found that he could lift the face from one photo and fit it to another. He acquired an inconspicuous Fuji digital camera and began taking surreptitious pictures of women around campus.

Women he wanted. He would scan the woman's face into the computer, use Photoshop to match it, and graft it to an appropriate body from a porno site. The drawing was necessary to eliminate the inevitable and incongruous background effects and the differences of photo resolutions; the drawings produced a *whole*.

Produced an object of desire.

Qatar desired women. Blond women, of a particular shape and size. He would fix on a woman and build imaginary stories around her. Some of the women he knew well, others not at all. He'd once had an intensely sexual relationship with a woman he'd seen only once, for a few seconds, getting into a car in the parking lot of a bagel shop, a flash of long legs and nylons, the hint of a garter belt. He'd dreamed of her for weeks.

The new computer-drawing process was even better, and allowed him to indulge in anything. *Anything*. He could have any woman he wanted, and any way. The discovery excited him almost as much as killing. Then, almost as a by-product, he'd discovered the power of his Art as a weapon.

Absolutely.

His first use of it had been almost thoughtless, a sociology professor from the University of Minnesota who had, years before, rejected his interest. He'd snapped her one day as she walked across the pedestrian bridge toward the student union, unaware of his presence. Theirs had not been a planned encounter, but purely accidental.

After processing the photo, and a dozen trial sketches,

he'd produced a brilliant likeness of her face, attached to a grossly gynecological shot from the Internet. The drawing had the weird, sprawling foreshortening that he'd never gotten right in his studio classes.

He mailed the drawing to her.

As he prepared to do it, it occurred to him that he might be—probably was—committing a crime of some kind. Qatar was not unfamiliar with crime, and the care that comes with the dedicated commission of capital offenses. He redid the drawing and used a new unhandled envelope, to eliminate any fingerprints.

After mailing it, he did nothing more. His imagination supplied multiple versions of her reaction, and that was enough.

Well. Not quite enough. In the past three years, he'd repeated the drawing attacks seventeen times. The thrill was not the same as the killing—lacked the specificity and intensity—but it was deeply pleasurable. He would sit in his old-fashioned wooden rocker, eyes closed, thinking of his women as they opened the letters. . . . And thinking of those others as they fought the rope.

He'd met Barstad because of the drawings. He'd seen her at work in a bookstore; had attracted her attention when he purchased a book on digital printing. They'd talked for a few minutes at the cash register, and again, a few nights later, as he browsed the art books. She was a fabric artist herself, she said, and used a computer to create quilt patterns. The play of light, she said, that's the thing. *I want my quilts to look like they have window light on them, even in a room without windows.* The art talk led to coffee, to a suggestion that she might pose for him.

Oh, no, she'd said, I wouldn't pose nude. That wouldn't be necessary, he said. He was an art professor, he just wanted some facial studies that he could print digitally.

She agreed, and had, eventually, even taken off a few of her clothes: her back turned to him, sitting on a stool, her glorious back tapering down to a sheet crinkled beneath her little round butt. The studies had been all right, but it was at home, with the computer, that he'd done the real drawings.

He had drawn her, wined her, dined her, and finally, on this bleak winter afternoon, fucked her and nearly killed her because she had not lived up to her images he had created from her photographs. . . .

THE day after the assignation with Barstad, the low stacked-heels of Charlotte Neumann, an ordained Episcopalian priest, author of *New Art Modalities: Woman/Sin, Sin/Woman, S/in/ister,* which, the week before, had broken through the top-10,000 barrier of the Barnes & Noble online bestseller list, and who was, not incidentally, the department chairperson, echoed down the hallway and stopped at his door. A tall ever-angry woman with a prominent nose and a single, dark, four-inch-long eyebrow, Neumann walked in without knocking and said, "I need your student budget line. This afternoon."

"I thought we had until *next* Wednesday?" He posed with a cup of coffee held delicately in both hands, his eyebrows arched. He'd left the steel-blue Hermès silk scarf looped around his neck when he'd taken off his coat, and with the books behind him, the china cup, and the scarf framing his face, he must've been a striking portrait, he thought. But it was wasted on Neumann, he thought; she was a natural Puritan.

"I've decided that we could avoid the confusion of last year by having them in my office a week early, which will give me time to eliminate any error," she said, leaving no doubt that she used the term "error" as might a papal inquisitor: "Last year" Qatar had been two weeks late with the budget.

"Well, that's simply impossible," Qatar said. "If you'd given me any notice at *all* . . ."

"You apparently didn't read last week's departmental bulletin," she snarled. There was a light in her eye. She'd caught him out, she thought, and he'd soon get a corrective memo with a copy for his personnel file.

"*Nobody* read last week's departmental bulletin, Charlotte," Qatar snarled back. He'd been widely published and was permitted a snarl. "Nobody ever reads the departmental bulletin because the departmental bulletin, is, in the words of the sainted Sartre, *shit.* Besides, I was on periodic retreat on Thursday and Friday, as you should have known if you'd read the memo I sent *you.* I never got the bulletin."

"I'm sure it was placed in your mailbox."

"Elene couldn't find her own butt, much less my mailbox. She can't even deliver my paycheck," Qatar said. Elene was the departmental secretary.

"All right," Neuman said. "Then by tomorrow. By noon." She took one step backward, into the hallway, and slammed the door.

The impact ejected Qatar from his office chair, sloshing coffee out of his cup, across his fingers, and onto the old carpet. He took a turn around the office, blinded by a red rage that left him shaking. He'd chosen the life of a teacher because it was a high calling, much higher than commerce. If he'd gone for commerce, he'd undoubtedly be rich now; but then, he'd be a merchant, with dirty hands. But sometimes, like this, the idea of possessing an executive power—the power to destroy the Charlotte Neumanns of the world—was very attractive.

He paced the office for five minutes, imagining scenarios of her destruction, muttering through them, reciting the lines. The visions were so clear that he could walk through them.

When the rage subsided, he felt cleaner. Purified. He poured another cup of coffee and picked it up with a steady hand. Took a sip, and sighed.

He would have taken pleasure in throttling the life out of Charlotte Neumann, though not because she appealed to his particular brand of insanity. He thought he might enjoy it the way anyone would whose nominal supervisor enjoyed small tyrannies as Neumann did.

So he would get angry, he would fantasize, but he would *do* nothing but snipe and backbite, like any other associate professor.

She did not engage him—did not light his fire.

THE next day, passing through Saks, he found that the cashmere sweaters had gone on sale. There wasn't much cold weather left, but the cashmere would wear forever. These particular sweaters, with the slightly rolled neckline, would perfectly frame his face, and the tailored shoulders would give him a nice wedgy stature. He tried the sweater on, and it was perfect. A good pair of jeans would show off his butt—he could have the legs tailored for nine dollars a pair at a sewing place in the Skyway. A champagne suede coat and cowboy boots would complete the set . . . but it was all too expensive.

He put the sweater back and left the store, thinking of Barstad. She *did* engage his insanity: He could think of Barstad and the rope and find himself instantly and almost painfully erect. Blondes looked so much more naked than darker women; so much more vulnerable.

The next day was Wednesday: Perhaps he could buy them after all.

He would take the rope.

BUT on Tuesday evening, still thinking about Barstad and the rope, feeling the hunger growing, he was derailed again. He arrived home early and got a carton of milk from the refrigerator and a box of Froot Loops from the cupboard, and sat at the table to eat. The *Star-Tribune* was still on the table from the morning; he'd barely glanced at it before he left. Now he sat down, poured milk on the Froot Loops, and folded the paper open at random. His eye fell straight down the page to a small article at the bottom: The two-deck headline said "Woman Strangled/Police Seek Help."

> *The body of an unidentified woman was found Sunday in the Minnesota state forest north of Cannon Falls by a local man who was scouting for wild turkey sign. A preliminary investigation suggested that the woman had been dead for a year or more, said Goodhue County medical examiner Carl Boone.*

"Shit." He stood up, threw the paper at the kitchen sink. Stormed into the living room, hands clenched. "Shit, shit."

Dropped onto a chair, put his hands on his head, and wept. He wept for a full minute, drawing in long gasping breaths, the tears rolling down his cheeks. Any serious art historian, he felt, would have done the same. It was called sensitivity.

After the minute, he was finished. He washed his face in cold water, patted it dry with paper towels. Looked in the mirror and thought: Barstad. He couldn't touch her for the time being. If another blonde disappeared, the police would go crazy. He would have to wait. No sweaters. No new clothes. But maybe, he thought, the woman would come through with some actual sex. That would be different.

But he could still feel her special allure, her blondness. He could feel it in his hands, and in the vein that pulsed in his throat. He wanted her badly. And he would have her, he thought.

Sooner or later.

2

THE WINTER HADN'T been particularly cold, nor had there been much snow; but it seemed like months since they'd last seen the sun. The streetlights still came on at five o'clock, and with the daily cycle of thaw and freeze, the dampness rose out of the ground like a plague of ghouls.

Lucas Davenport peered through the café window, at the raindrops killing themselves on the vacant riverside deck, and said, "I can't stand any more rain. I could hear it all day on the windows and roof."

The woman across the table nodded, and he continued. "Yesterday, I was up in the courthouse, looking down at the sidewalk. Everybody's in raincoats and parkas. They looked like cockroaches scuttling around in the dark."

"Two more weeks 'til spring," said the woman across the table. Weather Karkinnen finished a cup of wild rice soup and dabbed at her lips with a napkin. She was a small woman with a minor case of hat hair, which she'd shaken out of a hand-knit watch cap with snowflakes on the sides. She had a crooked nose, broad shoulders, and level blue eyes. "I'll tell you what: Looking at the river makes me feel cold. It still looks like a winter river."

Lucas looked out at the river and the lights of Wisconsin on the opposite shore. "Doesn't smell so good, either. Like dead carp."

"And worms. Eagles are out, though. Scavenging down the river."

"We ought to get out of here," Lucas said. "Why don't we go sailing? Take a couple of weeks . . ."

"I can't. I'm scheduled eight weeks out," she said. "Besides, you don't like sailing. The last time we were on a big boat, you said it was like driving an RV."

"You misremember," Lucas said. He waved at a waitress and pointed at his empty martini glass. She nodded, and he turned back to Weather. "I said it was like driving an RV across North Dakota at seven miles an hour. Except less interesting."

Weather had a glass of white wine, and she twirled it between her fingers. She was a surgeon and had the muscled hands of a surgeon. "What about this woman who was strangled? Why don't you help with that?"

"It's being handled," Lucas said. "Besides, I—"

"It's been a while," Weather said, interrupting. "When did they find her? Last weekend?"

"Last Sunday," Lucas said. "Takes time."

"A week, and what've they got? Anything? And she'd already been dead for eighteen months when they found her."

"I dunno. I don't know what they got. You know I knew her folks?"

"No, I didn't."

"They came to see me when she disappeared, asked for

help. I called around, talked to some people. Half of them thought she'd split for the Coast, the other half figured she was dead. Nobody had any idea who did it. All they knew was that she was gone, and it didn't look like she'd planned to go. . . . Other than that, we had zip. Nothing."

"So why not get in it? It's the kind of case you enjoy. You get to figure something out. It's not some jerk sitting in the kitchen with a can of Schlitz in his lap, waiting for the cops to bust him."

"I don't want to fuck with somebody trying to do a job," Lucas said. He scrubbed furiously at an old scar that ran down his forehead and across an eyebrow onto a cheek. He was a large man, heavy-shouldered, dark-complected—almost Indian-dark—but with sky-blue eyes. He moved uneasily in his chair, as though it might break under his weight. "Besides, knowing her folks makes it tougher. Knocks me off center. Makes me feel bad."

"Oh, bullshit," Weather said. "You're moping around looking for sympathy. Maybe you oughta call what's-her-name. She'd probably give you some sympathy."

Lucas deliberately misunderstood the reference to "what's-her-name." "Or a pot. If she didn't give me sympathy, she could give me a pot."

Weather's voice went dangerously quiet. "I didn't mean *that* one."

Of course she hadn't, but Lucas could play the game too. "Oh," he said, and tried his charming smile. But his charming smile hardly ever came off: His eyes could be charming, but his smile just made him look hard.

Romantic relationships were like gears in an old pocket watch, Lucas thought, looking across the table at Weather. They were always turning, some of the gears small and fast, others bigger and slower. The biggest of his life, his relationship with Weather, was lazily clicking around to something serious.

They'd once been headed for marriage, but that had come undone when Weather had been taken as a hostage by a crazy biker because of a case Lucas had worked on. There'd been an ambush, and the biker had been killed. Weather had . . . gone away; had left her wedding dress hanging in Lucas's bedroom closet. They'd been apart for a couple of years, and now they were seeing each other again. They'd been in bed for two months, but nothing had been *said*. No final commitments yet, no ultimatums or we-gotta-talk's. But if something went wrong again, that would be the end. There could be no renegotiation now, not if there were another breakdown. . . .

Lucas liked women. Most of them, with a reasonable number of exceptions, liked him back. Enough had liked him well enough to keep a couple of gears spinning at a time. The summer before, he'd had a quick, enjoyable fling with a potter. About the same time, an old college girlfriend had been going through the breakup of her long-term marriage, and he'd started talking to her again. *That* hadn't ended. There'd been no dating, no sex, nothing but talk: But Catrin was the gear wheel that most concerned Weather.

Lucas kept telling her that there was no need to worry. He and Catrin were friends, going way back. Old friends. "Old friends worry me more than new potters," Weather had said. "Besides, the potter's a child. You couldn't date a child for long."

The potter was eight years younger than Weather, whose baby alarm was now booming like Big Ben.

The waitress came with the martini—three olives—and Lucas turned back to the river. "Oh, man, look at that."

Weather looked: A seventeen- or eighteen-foot Lund open fishing boat was chugging by, the two occupants bent against the rain. "They're going *out*," Weather said.

"Walleye fishermen," Lucas said. "They're all crazier than a shithouse mouse. Or would it be mice?"

"Mice, I think." She smiled a crooked smile under her crooked nose, but her eyes had gone serious, and she said, "So why don't we get pregnant?"

Lucas nearly choked on an olive. "What?"

"I'm gonna be thirty-nine," she said. "It's not too late yet, but we're pushing it."

"Well, I just . . ."

"Think about it," she said. "No emotional commitment is necessary, as long as I'm inseminated."

Lucas's mouth worked spasmodically, no words forming, until he realized that she was teasing. He popped the second olive and chewed. "You're the only person who can do that, pull my chain that way."

"Lucas, every woman you know pulls your chain," Weather said. "Titsy pulls it about once every three minutes."

Titsy was Marcy Sherrill, a homicide cop. A woman with a fine figure, Lucas thought, who deserved a nickname more dignified than Titsy. "But I always see her coming," he said. "I *know* when she's doing it."

"Besides, I was only pulling your chain on the last part," Weather said. "If you're not going to do anything with the Photo Queen, I think we should start working on some kids."

The Photo Queen was Catrin. "Catrin and I are . . . friends," Lucas said. "Honest to God. You'd like her, if you'd give her a chance."

"I don't want her to have a chance. She's had her chance."

"So look," he said, flopping his arms. "I've got no problem with the kid thing. If you want to get . . ."

"If you say 'a bun in the oven,' or something like that, I swear to God, I'll pour a glass of wine in your lap."

Lucas swerved: ". . . if you want to get pregnant, we can work something out."

"So it's settled."

"Sure. Whatever."

"What's this *whatever* shit? What's this . . ."

Lucas scrubbed at the scar. Christ, a minute ago he'd been idly musing about commitment.

THE rain dwindled to a mist as they drove back west toward the Cities. They made it to St. Paul just before nine o'clock and found a strange car in Lucas's driveway—an aging hatchback, dark, a Volkswagen maybe. Lucas didn't have any friends who drove Volkswagens. There'd been some bad experiences with people waiting at Lucas's door. He popped open the Tahoe's center console; his .45 was snuggled inside. At the same time, Weather said, "Somebody on the porch."

Two people, in fact. The taller, heavier one was pushing the doorbell. Lucas slowed, turned into the drive. The two people on the porch turned, and the big one walked quickly into the Tahoe's headlights.

"Swanson," Lucas said, and relaxed.

Swanson was an old-time homicide dick, a voluntary night-shift guy, a little too old for the job, a little too heavy. Not brilliant, but competent. The woman beside him was a short tomboyish detective from the sex unit: Carolyn Rie, all freckles and braids and teeth. An interesting woman, Lucas thought, and well worth treating with a poker face when Weather was around. She was wearing a leather-and-wool letter jacket, too large, without gloves.

"Swanson . . . Hey, Carolyn," Lucas said out the window.

"Got something you might want to look at," Swanson said. He waved a roll of paper.

INSIDE, Weather went to make coffee while the cops pulled off their coats. "Tell me," Lucas said.

Rie took the roll of paper from Swanson and spread it across the dining table. "Oh, my," Lucas said. It was a drawing, detailed, and nearly full-length, of a nude woman whose body was projecting toward the viewer, legs slightly spread, one hand pressed into her vulva. She was fellating a man who was mostly, but not entirely, out of the picture.

Weather picked up on the tone and came over to look. "Gross," she said. She looked closely at Rie. "Where'd you get it?"

"Back in November, a woman named Emily Patton was walking across the Washington Avenue Bridge, the covered part, going over to the university library on the West Bank. This was about six in the morning, still really dark, not many people around. She sees this drawing on one of the walls—you know what I'm talking about? Those inside walls where the students paint all their signs and put up posters and stuff?"

"Yeah, go ahead," Lucas said.

"Anyway, she sees this poster, and there are a couple more like it. The thing is, Patton recognized this woman." Rie tapped the face of the woman in the drawing. "She figured the woman would *not* approve, so she takes them down. There are three of them, and I personally think they must have been put up within a few minutes of Patton coming by, because I think somebody would have stolen them pretty quick. They were only Scotch-taped up."

"Any prints on the tape?" Lucas asked.

"No, but I'll come back to that," Rie said. "Anyway, Patton was embarrassed about it, and she didn't know what to ask the other woman—they were once in a class together, and she didn't know her all that well."

"What's her name?" Weather asked. "The woman in the picture?"

"Beverly Wood," Rie said. "So Patton eventually looks up Wood, this is a couple days later, and says, 'Hey, did you know that somebody posted some pictures of you?' Wood didn't know, so Patton showed her, and Wood freaked. She came to see us, with Patton. The thing is, she says, she never posed for any pictures like that. In fact, she'd only had, like, two sexual relationships in her life, and neither had lasted very long. The sex, she says, was all very conventional. No photographs, no drawings, no messing around naked."

"Sounds kinda boring," Lucas said.

"That's the point," Rie said. "She's not the kind of person who winds up in this kind of picture."

"Did you check the guys? The ex-boyfriends?"

"Yeah, we did," Rie said. "Both of them deny anything, both of them seem to be fairly nice guys—even Wood said so. Neither one of them has any background in art . . . and whoever did this, I mean, he seems to be pretty good. I mean, a pretty good artist."

They all looked again: He *was* pretty good, whoever he was. "No question that this is Wood? It could be pretty generic."

"Nope. That little bump on the nose . . . She's got that beauty mark by her eye. I mean, you've got to see her and talk to her. This is *her.*"

"Okay," Lucas said. He stepped back from the table and looked at Swanson. "What else? You say this happened back in November?"

"Okay. We checked it for prints and it came up absolutely clean, except for Patton's prints and a few that Wood put on them. So the guy who drew this knows that somebody might be looking for his prints. He's careful."

"Did you check Patton? And Wood?" Weather asked. "It could be a form of exhibitionism."

Rie batted the question away. "We were doing that . . . but you have to understand, we were not even sure that a crime had been committed. Anyway, we checked them. Or we were in the process of checking on them, but in the meantime, Patton and Wood had both talked about the situation, and the *Daily Minnesotan* got onto it. They sent this kid reporter over and . . . with Wood's permission, we gave them a little story. We thought the most likely guy to do something like this would be somebody in the art department, and maybe somebody would recognize the style. We got these."

Rie unrolled two more sheets of paper, both smaller than the first, and both creased, as though they'd once fit inside an envelope. One was a drawing of a woman masturbating with a vibrator. Another was a low-angle drawing of a nude woman leaning against a door, her hips thrust toward the viewer.

"These were mailed to two university students, one back in June, last year, the other one in late August or early September. Neither woman reported the drawings. One of them thought it was just a silly trick by one of her art friends, and actually thought the drawing was kind of neat."

"That would be the door drawing," Weather said, carrying cups of microwave coffee.

"Yeah. Not many woman would think the vibrator drawing was all that cool," Rie said. "Anyway, this woman"— she touched the masturbation drawing—"not only claims that she never posed for anybody, but nobody has ever seen her nude, not since she was in high school gym class. Nobody, male or female. She's still a virgin."

"Huh," Lucas said. He looked at the three drawings. There was no question that they'd been done by the same artist. "So we got a weirdo." Again he looked at Swanson. "And?"

"That strangled chick that got dug up last Sunday? Aronson? This was in her file; we'd found it in a desk drawer. To tell you the truth, I think most everybody had forgotten about it, except Del." Swanson rolled out another drawing. A woman was sitting astride a chair, her legs open to the world, her breasts cupped in her hands. The pose was marginally less pornographic than the first two, but there was no doubt that it'd had been done by the same hand as the other drawings.

"Uh-oh," Lucas said.

"We didn't know about the other drawings, because Sex was handling them," Swanson said. "Del saw them when he stopped to talk to Carolyn, and he remembered the drawing in the Aronson file. We pulled them just this afternoon, and put them together."

"A psycho," Rie said.

"Looks like it," Lucas said. "So what do you want? More people?"

"We thought maybe you'd like to come in, take a look."

"I'm a little tied up."

"Oh, horseshit," Weather said. She looked at Swanson and Rie. "He's so bored, he's talking about renting a sailboat."

And to Lucas: "It would certainly give you something to do until the sun comes out."

3

DEPUTY CHIEF/INVESTIGATIONS Frank Lester supervised all the nonuniformed investigative units except Lucas's group. He had the spread-ass look of a longtime bureaucrat, but still carried the skeptical thin smile of a street cop. When Lucas walked into his office the next morning, Lester gestured with a cup of coffee and said, "You got a hickey on your neck."

"You must be a trained investigator," Lucas said, but he self-consciously touched the hickey, which he'd noticed while he was shaving. "Did you talk to Swanson?"

"He called me at home last night, before he talked to you," Lester said. "I was hoping you'd come in." He was leaning back in his chair, his feet up on his metal desk. A dirty-gray morning light filtered through the venetian blinds behind him; a senile tomato plant wilted on the windowsill. "Are you gonna tell me about the hickey?"

Instead of answering the question, Lucas said, "You told

me once that when you sit with your feet up on your desk, you pinch a nerve."

"Goddamnit." Lester jerked his feet off the desk, sat up straight, and rubbed the back of his neck. "Every time I get a cup of coffee, I put my feet up. If I do it too long, I'm crippled for a week."

"Oughta see a doctor."

"I did. He told me to sit up straight. Fuckin' HMOs." He'd forgotten about the hickey. "Anyway, you and your crew are welcome to come in. I'll have Swanson brief you on the crime scene, get you the files and photos, all the stuff they picked up from Aronson's apartment. Rie's gonna bring in the woman in the other drawings. Isn't that weird, the drawings?"

"It's weird," Lucas agreed.

They both thought about it for a minute, the weirdness, then Lester said, "I'll talk to Homicide, and send Swanson and Black to you guys, and you can take the whole thing. We've got three current homicide cases and the Brown business. Without Lynette Brown's body, it's all circumstantial and the prosecutor's scared shitless. We still can't find the goddamn dentist who put that bridge in her mouth."

"I heard Brown hired Jim Langhorn." Langhorn was an attorney.

"Yeah. The rumor is, he called Langhorn, and Langhorn came on the phone and said, 'One million,' and Brown said, 'You got a client.' "

"If it really is Langhorn . . ."

"It is," Lester said.

"Then you're at least semi-fucked."

"I know it."

"Maybe you'll catch a break. Maybe somebody'll find a tooth sticking out of an egg carton," Lucas said. "You could do a DNA or something."

"Everybody thinks it's fuckin' funny," Lester said. He poked a finger at Lucas. "It's not fucking funny."

"It's a little fuckin' funny," Lucas suggested. "I mean, Harold Brown?"

Harold Brown was a rich do-gooder who ran a recyling plant with his dead daddy's money, turning old newspapers into egg cartons. The last thing he was suspected of recycling was his wife, Lynette. Homicide believed he'd thrown her body into the acid-reduction vat—a gold bridge was found at the bottom of the vat when it was drained—and that Lynette was now holding together several dozen grade-A eggs.

"No. It's not fuckin' funny," Lester said. "Ever since Channel Eleven found out about the bridgework, the TV's been on us like a coat of blue paint." Then he brightened. "And that's one thing *you* got going for you. Nobody but Swanson, Rie, Del, and you and me know about the drawings. None of the news pukes got it yet—that we've got another weird motherfucker roaming around."

"I hate to tell you this, but we might have to put the drawings on TV," Lucas said. "If we got two people coming in with drawings because they saw a four-inch article in the *Daily Minnesotan,* you gotta wonder—how many more are there?"

Lester leaned back and put his feet up on his desk, unconsciously crossing his ankles as he did it. He scratched the side of his chin and said, "Well, if you gotta. Maybe it'll take some heat off the Lynette Brown thing."

"Maybe," Lucas said. "You want me to talk to Rose Marie?"

"That'd be good."

On the way out, Lucas paused in the door and said, "You got your feet up."

"Ah, fuck me."

*   *   *

ROSE Marie Roux, the chief of police, was meeting with the mayor. Lucas left a message, asking for a minute of her time, and walked down the stairs to his new office. His old office had been a closet with chairs. The new one still smelled of paint and wet concrete, but had two small offices with doors, desks, and filing cabinets, along with an open bay for the investigators' desks.

When the space opened up, there'd been a dogfight over it. Lucas had pointed out that Roux could make two groups happy by giving him a larger office, then passing his old office to somebody who didn't have an office at all. Besides, he needed it: His intelligence people were interviewing contacts in the hallway. She'd gone along, and mollified the losers with new office chairs and a Macintosh computer for their image files.

When he walked through the door—even the door was new, and he was modestly proud of it—Marcy Sherrill was sitting in his office with her feet up on his desk. She was on medical leave, and he hadn't seen her in a week. "You're gonna pinch a nerve," he said, as the outer door banged shut behind him.

"I got nerves of steel," she said. "They don't pinch."

"Tell me that when you can't stand up straight," Lucas grunted, as he moved behind the desk. She was attractive, and single, but she didn't worry Weather: Marcy and Lucas had already been down the romance road, and had called it off by mutual consent. Marcy was a tough girl and liked to fight. Or had. "How're you feeling?"

"Not too bad. Still get the headaches at night." She'd been shot in the chest with a deer rifle.

"How much longer?" Lucas asked.

She shook her head. "They're gonna take me off the analgesics next week. That'll stop the headaches, they say, but I'll get a little more chest pain. They say I should be able to handle it by then. They think."

"Keeping up with physical therapy?"

"Yeah. That hurts worse than the chest and the headaches put together." She saw him looking her over, and sat up. "Why? You got something for me?"

"We're gonna take the Aronson murder. Swanson will brief us this afternoon. Black's gonna join up temporarily. We need to get Del and Lane to come in. The short version of it is this: We got a freak."

"You gonna bring me back on line?" She tried for cool, and got eager instead.

"Limited duty, if you want," Lucas said. "We could use somebody to coordinate."

"I can do that," she said. She got up, wobbled carefully once around the office, pain shadowing her eyes. "God-damnit, I can *do* that."

ROSE Marie's secretary called while Lucas and Sherrill were planning an approach to the Aronson case. "Rose Marie would like to see you *right now*."

"Two minutes," Lucas said, and hung up. To Sherrill: "So maybe the feds can give us a psychological profile of the artist. Get the drawings over to one of those architectural drafting places, with the super Xerox machines, and have them make full-sized copies. Overnight them to Washington. Call what's-his-name, Mallard. His name's in my Rolodex. See if he can run interference with the FBI bureaucracy."

"Okay. I'll have Del and Lane here at two o'clock, and get Swanson and Rie to move the files over and do a briefing."

"Good. I'm gonna talk to Rose Marie, then go run around town for a while, see what's happening."

"You know you got a hickey?" she asked, tapping the side of her own neck.

"Yeah, yeah. It must be about the size of a rose, the way people are talking about it," Lucas said.

Marcy nodded. "Just about. . . . So you gonna knock her up? Weather?"

"Maybe," he said. "Maybe not."

"Jesus. You're toast." Marcy smiled, but managed to look a little sad.

"You're sure you're okay?" he asked.

"I just wish I could get done with all this shit," she said restlessly. She meant the pain; she'd been talking about it as though it were a person, and Lucas understood exactly how she felt. "I'm only one inch from being back, but I wanna *be* back. Fight somebody. Go on a date. Something."

"Hey. You're coming back. You look two hundred percent better than you did a month ago. Even your hair looks good. A month from now . . . a month from now, you'll be full speed."

ROSE Marie Roux was a heavyset woman, late fifties, a longtime smoker who was aging badly. Her office was decorated with black-and-white photographs of local politicians, a few cops, her husband and parents; and the usual collection of twenty-dollar wooden plaques. Her desk was neat, but a side table was piled with paper. She was sitting at the side table, playing with a string of amber worry beads, when he walked in, and she looked at him with tired hound-dog eyes. "You stopped by," she said. "What's up?"

Lucas settled into her leather visitor's chair and told her about the drawings and the Aronson murder. "We're gonna take it," he said. "Lester is worried about the media and what they'll do. I'm thinking we might have to use them, and wanted to let you know."

"Feed it to Channel Three, make damn sure they know

it's a big favor, and that we're gonna need a payback," she said. She nodded to herself and repeated, almost under her breath, "Need a payback."

"Sure. So what's going on?" Lucas asked uncertainly. "You sound a little stressed."

"A little stressed," she echoed. She pushed herself onto her feet, drifted to her window, and looked out at the street. "I just talked to His Honor."

"Yeah, they said he was here." Lucas tipped his head toward the outer office.

"He's not going to run this fall. He's decided." She turned away from the window to look at Lucas. "Which means I'm history. My term ends in September. He can't reappoint me, not with a new mayor coming in a month later. The council would never approve it. He thinks Figueroa is probably the leading candidate to replace him, but Carlson or Rankin could jump up and get it. None of those people would reappoint me."

"Huh," Lucas said. Then: "Why don't you run?"

She shook her head. "You make too many party enemies in this job. If I could get through the party primary, I could probably win the general election, but I'd never get through the primary. Not in Minneapolis."

"You could switch and become a Republican," Lucas said.

"Life isn't long enough." She shook her head. "I tried to get him to go for one more term, but he says he's gotta earn some money before he's too old."

"So what are you going to do?" Lucas asked.

"What are *you* going to do?"

"I . . ." Lucas shrugged.

Rose Marie sighed. "You're a political appointee, Lucas, and I'll tell you what: The only likely internal candidate is Randy Thorn, and he won't reappoint you. He's a control freak, and he doesn't like the way we let you operate."

"You think he'll get it?" Lucas asked.

"He could. He's a damn good uniform chief. All that rah-rah shit and community contacts and brother-cop backslapping. He put on some combat gear last week and went on a raid with the Emergency Response Team. There're a couple of macho assholes on the council who like that stuff."

"Yeah. I'm not sure he's smart enough."

"I'm not, either. It's more likely that the new mayor'll bring somebody in from the outside. Somebody with no other local loyalties. Somebody who's big with the New York no-tolerance style. I doubt that any outsider would reappoint the current deputy chiefs. He'd want to put his own people in. Lester and Thorn are still civil service, and captains. If they don't keep their deputy-chief spots, they'll still have a top slot somewhere. But you're not civil service."

"So we're both history," Lucas said. He leaned back, interlaced his fingers behind his head, and exhaled.

"Maybe. I'm gonna start working on something," Rose Marie said.

"What?"

She waved him off. "I can't even start talking about it yet. I'm gonna have to stab a couple of people in the back. Maybe give a couple blow jobs."

"Not at the same time. You could pull a muscle."

She smiled. *"You're* taking this pretty well. Which is good, because I'm not. Goddamnit. I wanted one more term. . . . Anyway, I wanted you to know that we're probably on the way out."

"I was starting to have fun again," Lucas said.

"What about you and Weather?" Rose Marie asked. "Is she pregnant yet?"

"I don't know, but it could happen."

Rose Marie laughed, a genuine, head-back, chest-shaking laugh, and then said, "Excellent. That's really perfect."

"And if she is . . ." Lucas squinted at the ceiling, calculating. "You and I oughta be getting fired just about the time the baby arrives."

"Like you need the job. You got more money than Jesus Christ."

"I *do* need the job. I need *some* job," Lucas said.

"Then hang on. It's gonna be a ride."

AFTER leaving Roux's office, Lucas went back to Homicide, got an exact reading on where Aronson's body had been found, marked it on a map and Xeroxed the map, then walked over to the Fourth Street parking ramp and got into his Tahoe. On the way south, out of town, he passed within a block of Aronson's apartment, and remembered talking with her parents when she disappeared: trying to reassure them, when he felt in his cop heart that their daughter was already dead. They'd all been together at her apartment, her parents waiting for a phone call, from her, from anybody, and he remembered wandering around inside. . . .

Aronson's apartment had been in a six-story brownbrick prewar building south of the loop, and her mother had been waiting at the door when Lucas turned the corner on the stairs.

"Glad you could come," she'd said. He remembered that the apartment building hallways had smelled of paint, disinfectant, and insect spray but that Aronson's apartment had the odor of a Christmas sachet.

The place felt like murder. A crime scene crew had been through it, leaving behind a kind of random untidiness—a disheveled feel, if apartments can be disheveled. All the cupboard doors were open; all the chests and closets and boxes and files and suitcases, all cracked open and left. The general air of bleakness, of disturbance, of violation, was exacerbated by the light that flooded the rooms: The crew had pinned back the drapes to let in as much light as possible, and on the day of Lucas's visit, that light had been chilling.

Four rooms: living room, separate small kitchen, bedroom, and bath. Lucas had walked through, his hands in his pockets, peering at the debris of a short independent life: stuffed animals on the bed; an Animal Planet TV poster on one green plaster wall, showing a jaguar in a jungle somewhere; a plastic inflatable statue of The Scream; knickknacks on the shelves, with photos. Mostly people who looked like parents, or sisters. . . .

"Knickknack," he said aloud at the traffic out the window of the Tahoe. He'd taken from the apartment a feeling of loneliness, or shyness. A woman who arranged fuzzy things around herself so that she might feel some affection. He remembered looking in her medicine cabinet for birth control pills, and finding none.

THE grave site was on a hillside south of Hastings, according to his map; all the roads were clearly marked. He still got lost, missing a turn, trying to recover by cutting cross-country, stymied by a closed road. Eventually, he turned into a DNR parking lot that had been built to provide public access to a trout stream. Above the parking lot, the Homicide cops had said, halfway up the hill, and a hundred and fifty feet farther south. A triangle of old fallen trees was just below the grave site; the cops had used the trees as benches.

The woods were still wet from all the rain, and the hillside, covered with oak leaves, was slippery. He picked his way through the bare saplings, saw the triangle of downed trees, spotted the hole in the hillside and the scuffle marks where cops had worked around the hole. The rain was smoothing the dirt fill in the hole, and leaves were beginning to cover it. In two more weeks, he couldn't have found the spot.

He walked farther down the hillside, then up to the crest; there were houses not far away, but he couldn't see any. Whoever had put the body here had known what he was doing. The grave had simply been a bit too shallow, and a dog had found it, or coyotes. And then the hunter had come by, scouting for bird sign.

And that was all, except the sound of the wind in the trees.

On the way back to town, he called Marcy to tell her that he'd be running around town for a couple of hours, talking to his people, picking up bits and pieces.

"Afraid to leave them on their own?"

"I need time to think," he said. "I'm a little worried about giving those drawings to the movie people, but I can't see any other seams in the thing."

"That's probably our best bet," Marcy agreed.

Lucas spent the rest of the morning and early afternoon roaming the metropolitan area, working his personal network, thinking about the Aronson murder and about the possibility of losing his job and maybe having a baby or two. He touched the hickey on his neck.

Susan Kelly was a pretty woman, but she wasn't at Hot Feet Jazz Dance. Her dog was having a breast cancer operation and she wanted to be there when it woke up, her assistant said. Lori, the assistant, was also a pretty woman, if a little over the edge with the dancing. She grabbed one of the brass rails that lined one wall of the polished-maple practice floor, dropped her head to the floor, and told Lucas from the upside-down position that a creep named Morris Ware was back in action, looking for little girls to pose for his camera.

"Wonderful. Glad to hear it," Lucas said.

"You ought to chain-whip him," Lori said.

Ben Lincoln at Ben's Darts & Cues told him that two Harley clubs, the Asia Vets and the Leather Fags, were planning a paint-ball war on a farm south of Shakopee, and it could get rough; some of the Leather Fags were reportedly replacing the paint balls with ball bearings. Larry Hammett at Trax Freight said that somebody had dumped a ton of speed on local over-the-road drivers: "Half the guys on the road are flying; I won't let my daughter take the car out of the fuckin' driveway."

Lannie Harrison at Tulip's Hose Couplings and Fittings told him a joke: "Guy walks into a bar and orders a scotch-and-soda. The bartender brings it over, puts it on the bar, and walks away. Just as the guy is reaching for the drink, this little teeny monkey runs out from under the bar, lifts up his dick, dips his balls into the scotch-and-soda, then runs back under the bar. The guy is astounded. He calls the bartender over and says, 'Hey. This little monkey just ran out from under the bar . . .' And the bartender says, 'Yeah, yeah. Sorry about that. Let me get you another drink.' So he brings over a fresh scotch-and-soda and walks away with the old one. Just as the guy is reaching for the fresh drink, this little monkey runs out from under the bar . . .''

"Lifts up his dick and dunks his balls in the scotch-and-soda," Lucas said.

"Yeah? You heard this?"

"No, but I'm familiar with the form," Lucas said.

"Okay. So the guy calls the bartender back and says, 'The little monkey . . .' And the bartender says, 'Listen, pal, you gotta watch your drink. I'll give you one more fresh one.' And the guy says, 'Well, what's the story about the goddamn monkey?' The bartender says, 'I only worked here a couple of weeks. But you see that piano player over there?' He points to a guy at a piano and says, 'He's worked here for twenty years. He can probably tell you about it.' So the guy gets his new drink and goes over to the piano player and says, 'You know that little teeny monkey that runs out from under the bar and lifts up his dick and dips his balls in your scotch-and-soda?'

"The piano player says, 'No, but if you hum a couple of bars, I can probably fake it.' "

AT a southside sweatshop, where illegal Latinos embroidered nylon athletic jackets with team insignias, Jan Murphy told him that a noted University of Minnesota athlete had gotten a job at a package-delivery service. Unlike the other messengers, who drove small white Fords, the athlete's company car was a Porsche C4.

"A kid's gotta have wheels, this day and age. And who knows, maybe he only handles special deliveries, really important stuff," Lucas said.

"Oh, that's right," Murphy said, pointing a pistol finger at him, "Mr. Four-Year Letterman, right? Hockey? I'd forgotten."

At The Diamond Collective, Sandy Hu told him that nothing looked better with a little black dress than a black pearl necklace and matched tear-shaped black pearl earrings, on which she could give him a special police discount, four payments of only $3,499.99 each.

"Why didn't you just make it four payments of $3,500?"

" 'Cause my way, it keeps the price under the magic $14,000 barrier."

"Ah. Well, who would I give it to?" Lucas asked.

Hu shrugged. "I don't know. But you see a hickey like the one on *your* neck, you try to sell the guy something expensive."

She hadn't heard anything new about anybody; she *had* heard the monkey balls joke.

Svege Tanner at Strength and Beauty said that over the weekend, somebody took twenty-five thousand dollars in cash from an apartment rented by an outstate legislator named Alex Truant. "The word is, Truant has a girlfriend here in the cities and they'd been dropping some big money at the casinos. With one thing or another, he was like way-deep over his head, so he got hired by the trial lawyers to carry some water for them. That's where the twenty-five came from."

"Who'd you hear this from?" Lucas asked.

"The girlfriend," Tanner said. "She works out here. Got an annual ticket."

"Think she'd talk to somebody?"

"Yeah. If somebody went to see her right away. Truant whacked her around when the cash came up missing. He thought she took it. She doesn't look so good with a big fuckin' mouse under her eye."

"Did she? Take it?"

Tanner shrugged. "I asked, she says *no*. She's the kind who if she stole twenty-five thousand on Monday, would come in Tuesday wearing a mink coat and driving a fire-engine-red Mustang. If you know what I mean."

"Not exactly a wizard."

"Not exactly," Tanner said.

"Got a phone number?"

"I do."

A shylock named Cole had retired and moved to Arizona. An old doper named Coin had been hit by a car while lying unconscious in the street, and was at Hennepin General, sober for the first time since he'd gone to an antiwar rally in the sixties; he didn't like it. An enormously fat man named Elliot, who ran a metal-fabrication shop but was mostly known for being enormously fat, had come down with prostate cancer, and was going to die from it. Half-Moon Towing was bankrupt and the bad-tempered owner, who collected guns, blamed the city council for cutting him out of the city towing contracts.

Routine, mostly. A few notes, a few melancholy thoughts about finding a new job. But who else would pay you to have this kind of fun?

LUCAS made it back to the office and found Marcy waiting with Del and Lane; plus Rie from Sex, and Swanson and Tom Black from Homicide. The start of virtually every homicide investigation—other than the ordinary ones, where they knew who the killer was—began with paper, the details lifted from the murder scene, with interviews, with the reports from various laboratories. Swanson and Black had been pushing the routine.

"The problem is, Aronson didn't have a boyfriend or a roommate, and the two ex-boyfriends we *can* find don't look real good for having done it. One of them is married and has a kid now, working his way through college, and the other one lives in Wyoming and barely seemed to remember her," Swanson said.

"She have a phone book?" Sherrill asked.

Black shook his head. "Just a bunch of scraps of paper with numbers on them. We checked them and came up dry. Woman in the next apartment said she heard a male voice over there a couple of times in the month before she disappeared. Never any kind of disturbance or anything."

"Look at the numbers stored in her cell phone?" Lucas asked. "Anything in her computer? She got a Palm Pilot or anything like that?"

"She had a cell phone, but there weren't any numbers stored at all. The e-mail in her computer was mostly with her parents and her brother. No Palm. We got her local phone records: She had lots of calls out to ad agencies and to friends—we talked to them, they're all women, and we don't see a woman for this—and then some random calls out, pizza, stuff like that. We never tried to reconstruct the pizza-delivery guys, and now . . . hell, I don't know if we could. It's been too long."

"What you're saying is, you ain't got shit," Del said.

"That's the way it is," Black said. "That's one of the reasons we always thought there was a possibility that she was still alive—we came up so empty. She didn't drag around bars. Wasn't a party girl. No drugs, didn't drink much. No alcohol at all in her apartment. She worked at a restaurant called the Cheese-It down by St. Pat's. I suppose she could have run into somebody there, but it's not a meat rack or anything, it's a soup-and-sandwich place for students. She freelanced ad work, designing advertisements, and did some Web design, but we couldn't get hold of anything."

Swanson was embarrassed. "We're not looking too swift on this thing."

Lucas parceled out assignments.

"Swanson and Lane: Take all those ad agencies and the restaurant. Find out who she was talking to. Make lists of every name you run."

He turned to Black, who had once been partnered with Marcy. "Marcy can't do a lot of running around yet, so I want you and her to work out of the office, get these three women in here, the ones who got drawings, and list every person they knew or remember having talked to before they got the drawings. No matter how slight the connection. When they can't remember a name, but remember a guy, get them to call people who would know him. I want a big-mother list."

To Rie: "I want you and Del to get copies of the drawings and start running them around to the sex freaks. This guy has a screw loose, but I wouldn't be surprised if he's shown a few of these things around. He's an artist, so maybe he's been out looking for a little appreciation. We want more names: all the possibilities that your friends can think of." He snapped his fingers. "Do you remember Morris Ware?"

"No."

"I do," Del said. He looked at Rie. "Might've been before your time. He takes pictures of children."

"He may be back in business," Lucas said. To Del: "Why don't you hang with me tomorrow. If we have time, we'll go look him up."

"All right."

"I see a couple of big possibilities for an early break," Lucas said. "The first one is, somebody knows him and turns him in. The second one is, we've got to figure he's had some contact with these women. If we get big enough lists, we should get some cross-references."

"But we need those big-mother lists," Black said.

"That's right. The more names we get, the better the chances of a cross. And the more people we can find who have gotten these drawings, the bigger the lists will be."

"What're you gonna do?" Marcy asked.

"Go talk to the movie people about some publicity," Lucas said. "We're gonna put the pictures on the street."

4

CHANNEL THREE WAS located in a low, rambling stone structure, a fashionable architect's attempt to put a silk purse on a corner that cried out for a pig's ear; Lucas had never liked the place. The building was a brisk crosstown walk from City Hall, and during the walk, Lucas thought for a moment that he'd seen a slice of blue in the sky, then decided that he'd been wrong. There was no blue; there never would be. He grinned at his own mood, and a woman he was passing nodded at him.

Lucas had a full-sized Xerox of the Aronson drawing in his pocket, along with partial copies of the other three drawings; in those three, the faces had been carefully scissored out. He met Jennifer Carey in the Channel Three parking lot, where she was smoking a cigarette. She was tall and blond and the mother of Lucas's only child, his daughter, Sarah. Sarah lived with Carey and her husband.

"Lucas," Carey said, snapping the cigarette into the street. A shower of sparks puffed out of the wet blacktop.

"You know those things cause cancer," Lucas said.

"Really? I'll have to do a TV show on it." She stood on tiptoe and kissed him on the cheek. "What's happening? Where'd you get the hickey?"

"That's it, I'm buying a turtleneck," Lucas said.

"You'd look like a French thug," Carey said. "I could kind of go for it. . . . So you're back with Weather?"

"Yeah. Looks like," he said.

"Gonna do the deed?"

"Probably."

"Good for you," she said. She looped her arm in his and tugged him along toward the door of the building. "I always liked that woman. I can't imagine how a little thing like a shooting came between you."

"She had the guy's brains on her face," Lucas said. "It made an impression."

"The brains? Or the incident? I mean, like a *dent?* Or did you mean impression, as a metaphor? Because I don't think brains would really—"

"Shut up."

"God, I love that tone," she said. "Why don't we get your handcuffs and find an empty van?"

"I got a story for you," Lucas said.

"Really?" The bullshit stopped. "A good one? Or am I doing your PR?"

"It's decent," Lucas said.

"So walk this way," she said. He followed her into the building and through a maze of hallways to her office. A stack of court transcripts occupied her visitor's chair; she moved them to her desk and said, "Sit down."

"This is a purely unofficial visit," Lucas said. He took the Xerox copy of the Aronson drawing out of his pocket.

"The best kind," Carey said. "What's that paper?"

"There are a couple of conditions."

"You know the kind of conditions we can accept. . . . Can we accept them?" she asked.

"Yeah."

"Then . . . gimme."

Lucas pushed the paper across the desk and Carey unfolded it, looked it over, and said, "She could lose a few pounds."

"She has," Lucas said. "Death will do that for you."

"She's dead?" Carey looked at him over the drawing.

"That's Julie Aronson. Her body—"

"Found her down south, I know the story," Carey said. She turned her lips down. "We've sorta hashed that over. Not that we can't use it."

"Hang on, for Christ's sakes. Goddamn movie people," Lucas said. "The thing is, several women have gotten drawings like this—three more that we know of. Two got them in the mail, and a third set was posted on a bulletin board over at the U. We got a freak."

She brightened. "You got more pictures?"

He gave her the other three. She looked at them one at a time, said, "Man," and then, "These might possibly make a story. It'd be better if we could interview the victims."

"I'd have to check. You won't get them today."

"Could we hold off until we get them? Until tomorrow? That'd really pump the story."

"No. If you don't want to use these today, I'll take them to Eight," Lucas said.

"No no no . . . this is fine," she said hastily. "The biggest thing we've got going tonight is a promo for a soap opera. We'll do the drawings tonight, and then if we could get interviews tomorrow . . . that might even be better. Carry the story longer."

"Good. And you've got to use them at both five and six o'clock. We want all the other stations screaming for them, scrambling around to catch up, playing them big at ten o'clock. We're really trying to plaster them around."

Carey was no dummy. She looked at him closely and said, "You could do that by calling a press conference. Why the exclusive for us?"

"Because you used to be my sweetie?"

"Bullshit, Lucas."

"Because we want you to owe us?"

"There we go. Why?"

"Another story's about to break out of City Hall, and there are some consequences that I'd like to . . . manipulate." He put a hand to his cheek and thought for a second. "That came out wrong."

"But it's probably right," Carey said. "Manipulate. What's the second story?"

"If I tell you, you can't bury the drawings under the other story. The drawings have gotta be prominent."

"Deal," she said. She looked at her watch. "But there's not much time. What is it?"

"The mayor's not going to run this fall," Lucas said, leaning forward, elbows on his knees. "One consequence is that Rose Marie is out—he can't reappoint her just before the election. I suspect a few other top people are gonna fall, too."

Carey stood up, reached toward the phone, stopped. "Who knows this?"

"The mayor's walking around City Hall right now, talking to his top people, maybe a couple of people on the council. Word will leak tonight."

"Okay." She picked up the Aronson drawing, held it vertically like a poster, and said, "You know, it's really pretty good." Then she folded it, businesslike, and said, "Get out of here. I'll get the police guy to come see you in twenty minutes about the drawings. I'll tell him I got them from an insider, but *not* you. You can be surprised—he won't know where it's coming from. I'll get the mayor myself."

"The Aronson picture . . . I mean, her ass is in it. I don't know if you show asses at five o'clock, but you've got to show enough that people get the idea of the style. Same with the others. . . . We need to find the guy who drew them."

"I think we can show an ass," Carey said.

"The more the better," Lucas said. "We need a little pop, a little shock. Some talk."

"You'll get talk," she said. "You can bet your ass on it."

BACK at the office, Lucas barely had time to get his coat off before the department's public relations officer called and said that the Channel Three reporter wanted to speak to him. "He says it's urgent. He's got a camera with him. You know what it's about?"

"I got an idea," Lucas said. "Send him down."

"The movies?" Marcy asked when Lucas hung up.

"Absolutely," Lucas said. "You want to take it? I got this goddamned hickey."

"Really?"

"Yeah. I'll just pass him on to you."

"Jesus, I gotta . . . I gotta . . . my hair looks like somebody peed on it. I gotta . . ." She dashed out of the office.

Del came in a step ahead of the camera. Lucas was shocked when the reporter asked about the drawings. "Where do you guys get this shit?" Lucas looked sideways at Del, who said, "Hey, I just met them in the hallway. I never said a word."

"I got sources," the reporter said with a sly smile. "You gonna give us something? We got most of it already."

"Sergeant Sherrill's handling it. We'd decided we might

talk to you guys tomorrow. I guess a day early wouldn't hurt, but the other stations—"

"Fuck the other stations," the reporter said. The cameraman was leaning against the wall, and appeared to have gone to sleep. Marcy came back five seconds later. Her hair looked neater and she had some color in her cheeks, either from cold water or slapping herself. And she'd unbuttoned one more button on her blouse; Lucas thought she looked terrific. The cameraman, sensing the presence of an unbuttoned blouse, woke up.

"What're we doing?" she asked.

"Whatever you want to do," Lucas told her. "You want to go with it?"

"Say yes," the reporter said. "We'll owe you big."

"I guess it wouldn't hurt," Marcy said, shrugging. "Sure I'll talk to you."

"So we got two favors owed to us on one story," Marcy said forty minutes later, as they sat in the bay area of the office watching a portable TV. Carey was on the City Hall steps, reporting that the mayor had confirmed that he wouldn't be running for reelection in the fall. Channel Three had led with a few shots from the drawings as a teaser—police fear killer-artist stalks Minneapolis women—and then cut to Carey with the exclusive from the mayor's office. From that report, she segued into the murder story:

"This major story breaks exclusively on Channel Three just as police officials are huddling on another nightmarish problem: A killer is stalking Twin Cities women, and before he strikes, he apparently lures them into posing nude."

Lucas sat up. "That's not right," he said to the television.

"Close enough for TV work," Del said.

The drawing of Aronson appeared on the screen, ass

included. "Julie Aronson was strangled eighteen months ago by a man who apparently had intimate knowledge of her."

"Gonna scare the shit out of the other women," Marcy said. "I mean, we're *gonna* get some attention. I better call them."

"That's what we wanted," Lucas said. "Attention." They watched as the Channel Three reporter came up, on tape, with the details, and then Marcy was on, with an explanation.

"Great blouse button," Del said, leering at her.

"Fuck you, it just fell open," Marcy said, flushing.

"No, no, don't say that," Lucas said. "That's great technique. If you hadn't thought of it, I would have suggested it, except I probably wouldn't have thought of it. But you know, it doesn't hurt to have a sexy cop talking to TV. Gives you some leverage, God help us all."

"Look at the way they framed you. Not just your face, but from the cleavage up," Del said. "That *is* really good."

"It just occurred to me that there've only been two women on the newscast," Marcy said. "And you've slept with both of them, Lucas. Was Carey better than me, or was I better?"

Del looked at Lucas and said, "Run."

THE two stories on Channel Three pulled all the other TV stations and both newspapers into City Hall. The mayor confirmed that he would not be running and Rose Marie outlined what was known in the Aronson case, correcting the impression that more than one woman had been threatened.

Rose Marie called as soon as she was off the air. "I assume that was you, pulling strings with Carey."

"Yeah. They owe us."

"Good. Talk to you tomorrow. I'm gonna go home and cry."

Lucas hung up, looked at his watch, then called Weather and suggested they get together for a late sandwich.

"I'll bring pajamas," she said.

"Yeah? You have any idea how old I am?"

"Not nearly as old as you're gonna be by midnight."

He was pulling on his jacket when the phone rang again. He thought it might be Weather with a quick call-back. "Yeah?"

"Lucas?" A man's voice.

"Yeah."

"This is Gerry Haack. You remember me?"

"Yeah, Gerry. What's happening?" Lucas looked at his watch again.

"I'm the lawn-care guy. I had that thing."

The thing with crystal meth and the rampage through the men's fine accessories department at Dayton's. "Yeah, yeah, what can I do for you?"

"You said I owed you, and I should call if I ever got anything. I got something."

"Yeah?" Weather would be walking out the door already. "What you got?"

"I'm not in the lawn business anymore, I'm working at the Cobra Lounge over in St. Paul. It's not the greatest place, but I'm trying to get back on my feet, you know—"

"That's great, Gerry. So, what you got?"

"You know this woman that got strangled? Aronson?"

"Yes."

"I just saw the picture on TV, but they didn't say anything about her selling it."

"What?"

"She was on the corner, man." Haack's voice dropped a half-octave and got cozy. Man-to-man.

"*What?* What're you talking about?"

"She was doing the hokey-pokey for money," Haack said.

"You know that for sure?"

"Yeah. I know a guy she dated a couple of times. Cost him a hundred bucks a time, nothing but blow jobs and straight fucking. Nothing kinky. They sit around here and talk about it at night."

"You say you know him?"

"Well, yeah. You couldn't ever tell him who let on. They'd kill me." Now his voice was nervous, as though he were having second thoughts about the tip.

"Nobody'll know," Lucas said. "What's his name?"

AFTER talking to Haack, Lucas stole another ten minutes to go back through the file on Aronson. Swanson noted that he'd searched state and national records on her and checked her fingerprints with the feds, and she'd come up clean. Still, if Aronson had been on the corner, somebody should have picked it up.

He'd worked himself into a fury by the time he arrived at the restaurant. "How in the hell can you have a criminal investigation going on for a year, and you don't know the chick is hustling?"

"It wasn't going on for a year. It was a halfhearted missing-persons investigation for a couple of weeks after she disappeared, and then it wasn't anything," Weather said. "And maybe she was an amateur. You said she'd never been arrested."

"But you gotta know that stuff," he said. "You gotta talk to enough people that you find it out. Now there's a question about these other women. Are they pros? One of them claims that she's still a virgin—not that anybody got out his flashlight and looked. If they're pros, then we've got a whole other problem than the one we started with."

"Is that bad, or is that good?"

He thought about it and said, finally, "Too early to tell. Actually, it might be good. If the guy is hitting on hookers, we've limited the number of people we have to look at, and I've got pretty good connections in the area."

"So twelve hours into the investigation, you're already a genius. And you look like you're enjoying yourself, pissed off as you are."

"Hmph." He remembered the mayor's announcement. "Did you watch any TV tonight?"

"No. Were you on?"

"No, but there were a couple of stories. . . . The thing is, I might be out of a job in a few months." He told her about it, and the unlikeliness that he'd be reappointed by a new chief.

"So if we do get pregnant, we won't have to find a nanny," Weather said.

"That's not exactly how . . . You're jerking my chain. This is serious."

"If you really want to keep the job, you can figure out a way to do it," Weather said. "But maybe it's time to try something else."

"Like what?"

"I don't know. Something else. You've done one thing all of your life. Maybe you could do something . . ."

He picked up her direction. "Kinder and gentler."

"Yeah. Maybe," she said. "You were sorta good at business." Lucas had briefly been the nominal CEO of a computer company that produced simulations for police 911 systems. He'd hired another guy for the job as soon as he could, and had gone back to the police department.

"Nothing I've ever done is as brutal as what corporate

execs do all the time," Lucas said. "I've never fired any-body. Never taken a perfectly innocent hardworking guy and screwed up his life and his family and his kids and his dog, because somebody needed to put an extra penny on the fuckin' dividend."

"Communist," she said.

LATER that evening, Lucas sat up in bed and sighed.

"Oh, go on," Weather said. She pulled a blanket up to her chin.

"What?" But he knew.

"Go on, see if you can find this guy. The one getting the blow jobs."

"Not much of a night for finding guys," Lucas said, his eyes drifting toward the bedside clock.

"Lucas, you've been twitching ever since we got in bed," she said.

"Del was gonna be out late," he said, tentatively.

"Then call him. I'm working tomorrow so I've got to go to sleep anyway. I won't if you keep twitching. Go."

Lucas pretended to struggle with the idea for a moment, then kicked back the sheet, crawled across her to reach the telephone on the nightstand, and called Del's cell phone. Del answered on the first ring. "What?"

"You awake?"

"I hope so. If I'm not, I'm dreaming that I'm standing in a puddle of slush at Twenty-ninth and Hennepin, with snow blowing down my neck."

"It's snowing?"

"Yeah. The snow pushed the rain right out of the pic-ture."

"I'm in bed with Weather. We're warm and naked," Lu-cas said. Weather reached beneath his chest and gave one of his nipples a vicious pinch. "Ow. Jesus Christ . . ." He bounced away from her.

"What?" Del asked.

"Never mind," Lucas said, rubbing his chest. "You know the Cobra over in St. Paul?"

"My home away from home," Del said.

"There's a guy who hangs out there, a Larry Lapp. Julie Aronson was playing his bagpipe at a hundred bucks a toot. That's what I'm told."

"Do tell. Want to look him up?"

"Yeah. Meet me there in half an hour," Lucas said.

"If you meet me there in half an hour, and you're really naked and warm in bed right now, you're a crazier fuck than I ever knew. It's bad out here."

"See you then," Lucas said.

As he dropped the phone on the hook, Weather asked, "Playing his bagpipe? Where do you guys come up with that trash?"

"That was really bad," Lucas said. "Pinching me. It still hurts."

"Aw. What are you going to do about it?"

He looked at the clock. He was ten minutes from the Cobra. "I'm gonna have to turn you over my knee," he said.

"Fat chance," she said.

THE weather was as bad as Del had said it was. A bitter winter wind was blowing the snow directly into the car's windshield as he headed north along the river, and created an illusion of a funnel; Lucas felt as though he were staring into the small end of a tornado. Ten minutes later, he spotted Del standing under a streetlight, and parked next to him.

"The place is cursed," Del said, as Lucas got out of his

Tahoe. Del was wearing his winter street outfit, an East German Army greatcoat with home-knitted mittens and matching toque. He was looking across the street at the Cobra. The place was a storefront with venetian blinds covering the windows, Busch and Lite signs in the window, and a gold-on-black sign that said "Cobra" and flickered from a bad fluorescent tube.

"Cursed? You mean Minnesota?"

"I mean the Cobra. I bet there've been ten businesses in there in the last fifteen years," Del said. "Nobody makes it."

"That snake place," Lucas remembered. "Is that how the Cobra got its name?"

"Yeah, I think so. I knew that guy who owned it, the snake place. Herpetology Grand. He said snakes were the coming yuppie pets, the next new thing. They were beautiful, clean, quiet, and they only ate once a week. Plus there was a big markup on them. He wanted me to invest; he was going to start a whole chain of them."

"What could possibly have gone wrong?" Lucas asked, as they crossed the street.

"You had to feed them live gerbils," Del said. "Turns out that yuppie women can't get tight with the idea of feeding live gerbils to big snakes. You know, as an everyday thing."

THE Cobra was as dim inside as out, a narrow entry past the bar with its red leatherette stools, a couple of tables in the back with a color TV, a shuffleboard bowling game, and what appeared to be a little-used dartboard. The smell of beer and peanuts and smoke. A unisex toilet in the back showed down a back hall, next to a lighted sign that said "Caution, Alarm Will Sound: Emergency Exit Only." Two customers sat at a table in the back, watching a Lakers game. A third huddled over the bar. Lucas pointed at a stool and said, "Beer?"

"You buy," Del said.

The bartender drifted over, pulled two beers, gave Lucas change on a five. Lucas laid his badge case on the bar and said, "We're cops. We're looking around for one of your regulars."

"Yeah?" The bartender was friendly enough. "I seen you on TV once or twice. You the Minneapolis guy?"

"Yeah. We're looking for Larry Lapp," Lucas said. "You know him?"

"Larry?" The bartender was surprised. "What'd he do?"

"Nothing, really. We need to talk about a friend of his."

"I wondered. He's a good guy. . . . He was here tonight, must've left two hours ago. He only lives two or three blocks away, I think, but I don't know where, exactly."

"Couldn't find him in the phone book," Lucas said.

"He's got an old lady, I think it's her house." He spread his hands apologetically. "All I know about her is that her name is Marcella."

Del nodded toward the back of the bar. "Any of those guys know him?"

The bartender looked. "Those guys?" He thought about it. "Yeah, maybe."

Lucas and Del collected their beers and walked to the back, where the two guys were watching the basketball game; they were painters, Lucas thought, still in paint-spattered jeans. Both were in their mid-twenties; one was wearing a Twins baseball hat and the other a Vikings sweatshirt with a plastic football on the chest. Lucas and Del watched the game for a minute, then Lucas said to the guy in the baseball cap, "We're police officers. We're looking for a friend of yours."

The two men looked at each other, then the guy in the baseball hat shrugged and said, "Who? What'd he do?"

"Larry Lapp, and he didn't do anything. We just need to talk to him about a woman he used to know."

"Oh, jeez . . . You're talking about that girl that got killed?" the Vikings fan asked.

They nodded, and Del asked, "You knew her?"

"Knew who she was," the Vikings fan said. "She was from the neighborhood, until her folks moved out-state somewhere. She knew some other kids from over here."

"I understand she was . . . seeing this Lapp guy," Lucas said, giving a little extra to the "seeing."

"Oh, man, I don't think so—and you could get Larry in big trouble with his wife, talking that way," the guy said. "Him and this girl went back a long way, you know, to junior high or something. They weren't doin' nothing, but Marcella ain't gonna believe that if you go knockin' on her door."

Del said, "Mind if we sit for a minute?" and pulled around a chair without waiting for an answer. Lucas pulled one up for himself, leaned on the table, and said quietly, "We were told that this girl . . . might have been selling it. Hundred bucks a throw. Nobody's gonna get in trouble for talking about it, or even going with her—we're just trying to get some traction on the murder. Either of you guys ever hear anything like that?"

"That's bullshit," said the baseball cap, sitting back. "Whoever told you that is an asshole."

"Never heard nothing like that," the football-shirt guy said, shaking his head. "She was a nice kid. Shy. I mean, if she was selling it, she could've sold it to me, and she never offered or even let on that, you know, it might be possible."

The baseball cap said, "Same with me. We get a pro in here every once in a while, and it's not like you don't figure it out pretty goddamn quick."

"Look around," the football shirt said. They looked down the bar at the cheap stools, at the used booths sloppily cut into the new space, at the crap littering the floor. "You think you're gonna find a hundred-dollar girl working this place? Twenty-nine-ninety-five is more like it."

"This Lapp guy," Del said.

"You're gonna fuck him up if you talk to him with his wife around," the baseball cap said. "He has a troubled marriage."

"If you want, I could go get him," the Vikings guy said. "He's only two blocks from here."

"That'd be cool," Lucas said. "If I could get your names first . . . for the notebook."

"In case we decide to run for it?" the baseball cap asked. He grinned at Lucas.

"Well. For the notebook, you know."

LARRY Lapp was short and square, wore a heavy, short, square dark coat, and a Navy watch cap pulled down to his eyebrows. He followed the painters into the bar, nodded at the bartender, and continued back to the table where Lucas and Del were waiting. He nodded, quickly, and sat down, hands in his coat pockets. He had a flat, wide face and a day-old beard that looked like it was made of nails. "What's this shit about Julie?"

"We're trying to follow up on some information."

"If somebody told you she was selling it, that guy oughta be investigated, because he's full of shit," Lapp said. He was angry, his face tight and white despite the cold. "She was one of the nicest goddamn girls you could want to meet."

Lucas shook his head apologetically. "I'm sorry, we just heard . . . actually, we heard that you were the recipient of some of her favors, but that you'd had to pay."

"You *heard* this?" Lapp asked, his voice rising. "About *me?* How could you hear this about me? What'd you hear? Who told you this?"

"I can't tell you where the information came from, we just got it from one of our intelligence guys. . . . she said that Julie was selling, ummm, oral sex at a hundred bucks a time."

"Blow jobs?" Lapp whispered hoarsely. He looked from Lucas to Del, unbelieving, then at the two painters, and he said to the painters, "You know who they were talking to? That fuckin' Haack."

The baseball cap nodded judiciously and said, "Yup. Bet it was."

"Who's Haack?" Del asked. He looked at Lucas, then back at Lapp.

"Gerry fuckin' Haack," Lapp said. "He saw me in here a couple times with her—this must've been last year, right after he got out of jail—and the last time he said something about me getting a blow job from her. I told him to shut his mouth or I'd pull his fuckin' nose off."

"He's got a thing about blow jobs," the football-shirt said. "Always hearin' that this chick gives head or somebody was caught gettin' some head."

Lucas scratched his forehead. "Ah, shit."

Del asked Lapp, "What do you know about art?"

"Art who?" Lapp asked with apparent beetle-browed sincerity, and when Del started to laugh, said, "What?"

"Did you actually date Aronson?" Lucas asked.

"Hell no. I knew her way back when," Lapp said. He shook a brown cigarillo out of a cardboard box and lit it with a Zippo. He blew a stream of smoke and said, "We went to kindergarten together and the same schools up to eighth grade, and then they moved away. She came in here with a couple of other friends from the neighborhood, and that's when I saw her again. But we were doing nothing. Nothing. I'm happily married." The baseball cap guy snorted, and Lapp turned and looked up and said, "Fuck you, Dick, this is serious."

"Was she dating anybody that you knew of?" Lucas asked.

"Is this the first time you guys . . . I mean, how come

you don't know this shit already? She disappeared more'n a year ago."

"We never knew about the St. Paul connection," Lucas said. "We were just checking out a random tip."

"Well, she said she was going out with an artist guy—is that the art you meant?—I think maybe over where she worked or something. I think they were . . . in bed."

"Why do you think that?"

"Because he was taking these pills. She told me this, we were laughing about it." He looked at the baseball cap. "What do you call them? That new cholesterol drug? Lapovorin? Is that it? Anyway, she said he'd told her that the pills had weird sexual side effects. They made you come backwards."

"Come backwards?" Del asked. He seemed fascinated by the concept. "How can you come backwards?"

"Beats the shit out of me," Lapp said, leaking more brown smoke from the cigarillo. "But that's what she said. He said that he had to quit the pills, because instead of coming, he went."

Nobody laughed; this could be a serious problem. "What else did she say about him?" Lucas said, leaning forward. "Names or where he lived—"

"Nothing. He was older than she was. This was like two weeks before she disappeared."

"That's all? She was dating an artist and he was older than her."

"Actually, I might have seen the guy. . . ."

Lucas and Del looked at each other, and then Lucas said, "Where?"

"I was coming out of Spalonini over in Minneapolis. I went in there for lunch? There's this diner across the street."

"The Cheese-It. She worked there part-time," Del said.

"Yeah. I saw her coming out of there with a guy and she had her arm under his. Tough-looking guy, but kind of artistlike. You know, he had a buzzcut and a three-day beard, had this long dark wool coat all the way down to his ankles. Maybe an earring, I think. They walked on up the street."

"Would you recognize him if you saw him again?" Lucas asked.

Lapp thought for a minute, then said, "Nah. I just saw him for one second, from the side, and then from the back. I remember he was a cocky-looking sonofabitch. You know who he looked like? This stuck in my head. He looked like Bruce Willis in this movie where Willis was playing a boxer? Uh, something *Fiction*?"

"Pulp Fiction," Del said.

"Yeah, that's it. He looked like Willis in that movie, kind of fucked up, big shoulders. Dark like that, but a buzz-cut."

"But you couldn't pick him out?"

"If you had a lineup with Dick and George, here," Lapp said, waving at the Vikings guy and the baseball cap, "and a buzzcut who looked sorta like Bruce Willis, then I could pick him out. If you had six buzzcuts, then I couldn't."

"Goddamn good memory anyway," Del said. His voice may have carried a vibration of skepticism.

Lapp shrugged. "Just between you and me . . . maybe I *did* have a little thing about her. Nothing serious. Then she went away. . . . I just remembered. I remember remembering, if you know what I mean."

"How come you didn't call this in? We could've used the help," Del said.

Lapp shook his head. "I didn't think it would be important. I mean, I heard about it when you were looking for her, but it seemed like she just might've, you know, split."

"And there's his old lady," the baseball cap said, nodding at Lapp. "If he told you, he'd have to tell her."

They talked a few more minutes, and Lucas took Lapp's address and telephone number. Outside, on the sidewalk, Del said, "Lapp is right. Unless we get lucky with those lists, we ain't got shit."

"He's an artist and he's got a buzzcut and he takes Lapovorin. We can check pharmacies and make more lists."

"Buzzcuts are the fashion right now, and Minneapolis's got more artists than rats and every second guy on the street takes Lapovorin."

"But it's something. I can see him in my mind's eye now."

"Then you oughta stop down to one of them photo booths and have a picture taken before you forget," Del said. He yawned, looked up and down the street at the wind-whipped snowflakes slanting through the streetlights like shading in a cartoon. He slapped Lucas on the back and said, "See you in the morning. We'll look up some artists, or some fuckin' thing."

5

SHE'D MADE SOME kind of cheese dish with garlic. Qatar liked garlic when he was eating it, but an hour later, after another rugged round of sex, he could smell it in his own sweat, and in Barstad's sweat mingled with his; he touched his stomach and found it cool and wet.

The sexual education of Ellen Barstad might not be the lark that he'd assumed it would be, Qatar thought. He was in her bathroom again, washing. His penis had gone past the tingling stage: It hurt. This was their fourth time together, if the first unsuccessful bedding was counted. He was beginning to feel the pressure.

The second time together, they had watched a pornographic movie and then tried some of the more modestly deviant practices. The third time, they had moved on. Nothing truly advanced, Qatar thought, though it was as advanced as he'd ever managed.

This time, Barstad's wrists were tied to the head of the

bed with two of his old, too-wide neckties. "James," she called. She was waiting.

"Good God," he said under his breath. He knew the tone. His face seemed a little pale, a little drawn, in the bathroom mirror. He didn't have another one in him, he thought. He turned the water off and went back to the bedroom. Barstad lay flat on the bed, her legs spread slightly, her arms over her head; her eyes were half closed, her face slack. The woman seemed to have no limit.

"Could I get a drink of water before the next one?" she asked.

"My dear, I don't think there will be a next one, not today," he said. "I feel like I've been pushed through a wringer."

A wrinkle appeared on her forehead. "What's a wringer?"

"You know, for wet clothes."

"What?"

She'd never heard of a wringer, Qatar thought. Too young. He looked down along her body: It was perfect. Everything that he had always thought he'd wanted.

Except.

He was beginning to suspect that what he'd always wanted wasn't sex; that his particular streak of insanity— he called it that, was comfortable with the word—needed resistance, maybe even a little *disgust.* An hour earlier, he'd been looking down at the spinal groove in the back of her neck. His hands had ached for her neck. He'd almost done her then—would have, if he'd had the rope. The next time, he'd bring it.

Over the next couple of days, before they got together again, he would think about it, he would see if the killing passion returned. And maybe the thing with Aronson's body would blow over. She was long dead; there could be no clues—they hadn't found anything else. . . .

* * *

ELLEN Barstad watched him thinking about her. Maybe she *was* pushing too hard—but once she got into it, she found it hard to stop. There were so many . . . her girl-friend called them "pickles." Little interesting variations, like crazy quilting: You do this and then you do that. Qatar, on the other hand, was basically like all the men she'd known: He just wanted to bang away, and then nap until he could get up again, and then bang away some more. She wanted to try this and then that and then the other thing, to see how it all felt. Was there anything wrong with that? She thought not.

Qatar was being a prig about the whole thing. Maybe, she thought, it was time to find somebody younger. Actually, if she could find somebody completely unformed, maybe a seventeen-year-old, somebody who'd actually be grateful . . . After all, this wasn't that difficult, was it? All of it was in the books.

"So you're going home?" Barstad asked.

"Yes. I'm really busy. I've been here for two hours."

"I thought we were going to do the Ping-Pong paddles again today."

He had to laugh. "Slipped my mind," he said. Then: "It's all right to slow down, Ellen. We're not on a time clock."

"I suppose," she said, disappointment in her voice. She rubbed her feet together. "You sure you don't want a little suck?"

"Ellen . . ." He really did hurt; but how often do you get this kind of offer? Sometimes, he thought, you've got to go with common sense. "Okay. But you *must* take it easy."

WHEN he got home two hours later, thoroughly used, he turned on the television and went into the kitchen for some

Froot Loops. He was eating and reading a two-week-old copy of *The New Yorker* when he heard the television announcer talking about drawings and murder and that the images might not be appropriate for children.

He knew what they were, even without looking or listening. He didn't want to believe it; he pushed to his feet so abruptly that milk sloshed out of the bowl onto the magazine.

In the living room, he caught the sight of one of his drawings in the fraction of a second before the cameras cut away, like the quick flash of a queen of hearts in a riffled deck of cards. The reporter was saying something, but he couldn't seem to make out the words. Then the camera cut away from the reporter, and one after another, a set of his images flashed on the screen, finally ending with a drawing of Aronson.

". . . police looking for the artist who drew these sexually charged images . . ."

He stood unbelieving, aghast. He'd never let Aronson take home any of the images. He'd shown her this one—it was sexy, but not pornographic—to impress her with his skills. He remembered throwing it aside in his office. He didn't remember seeing it again.

"She took it," he said aloud, to the television. "She stole it from me. It wasn't hers! It was mine!"

He would go to prison, he thought. Nobody would ever understand. He watched until the drawings went away, and the reporter—a slender blonde, he thought, who might be interesting—moved on to politics.

"Prison," he said. An announcement. His career in ruins. They'd lead him out of the building in chains: He could see it in his mind's eye, long rows of mocking former colleagues and their harridan wives, in a gantlet, and he'd walk down between them enduring their smirks and superior smiles. They would put him in denim shirts and jeans, with a number on his shirt, and he would be locked in a cell with some redneck who'd rape him.

He thought of suicide—really, the only way out. Jumping, he thought. The feeling of flying, and then nothing at all. But he was afraid of heights. He didn't even like to stand too close to a window.

A gun. Tighten the finger, and nothing . . . But that'd be really messy, and would destroy the side of his head. Too much. Hanging himself, that was out: He'd suffer. He could imagine the pain, clawing at the rope at the last minute, trying to pull himself up. . . . No.

Pills. Pills were a possibility if he had time to accumulate some. He could go to Randy. Randy could get as much as he needed, barbiturates. That'd be the way to go. Simply sleep, never to awake.

A tear rolled down his cheek as he thought about his mother's distress when his body was found. He dropped into the easy chair by the TV and closed his eyes, imagining it. And was suddenly touched by anger: The bitch wouldn't miss him. She'd sell all his furniture, and the wine, and the carpets. She'd cash his life insurance, pathetic as it was, and she'd keep it all. He could see it plainly, as a vision: the inventory of his belonging, the clothes going into the trash—into the trash!—the furniture carried away on trucks and even pickups.

Anger swelled in his heart, and he pushed himself out of the chair and paced back to the kitchen, sobbed. Pounded a fist into the other palm, then stuffed his knuckles into his mouth and bit until he felt the skin break. She'd take it as a victory: She'd outlasted him.

Well, fuck her. Fuck her. He shouted it at the walls: "FUCK HER."

So what to do? He sat down again, stared at the box of Froot Loops. He'd enjoyed making his drawings and he'd known right from the start that he'd be in trouble if he were found out. So he'd been secretive. He still had some of the images stored on the computer at school, but he could get rid of them.

He sighed, and calmed himself. Things weren't completely out of control. Not yet. He'd have to get busy, get cleaned up, just in case.

His mind skipped back to his mother: bitch. He couldn't believe her pleasure at his suicide. Couldn't believe it. There wasn't any doubt about it: The clarity of his vision carried the unmistakable scent of the truth. They hadn't had much to say to each other for five years, but she could show him enough loyalty to regret his passing.

More tears gathered at the corners of his eyes. Nobody loved him. Not even Barstad—she just wanted the sex.

"I'm alone," he said. His hand hurt, and he looked down at his knuckles. They were bleeding, badly; how had that happened? He was bewildered by the blood and pain, but he could also feel the anger gathering. "I'm all alone."

6

THE SKY WAS churning, but it was neither snowing nor raining when Lucas made it down to City Hall. He'd had too much coffee, and he stopped at the men's room; Lester, the deputy chief for investigations, was facing into a urinal when Lucas stepped inside and parked next to him. "What do you think about the mayor?" Lester asked.

"Gonna be some changes," Lucas said.

"Don't see any way that Rose Marie'll be reappointed," Lester said gloomily. "I'll probably get stuck out in the weeds somewhere."

"So quit, get a state job, and double-dip. Two pensions are better than one."

"I sort of like it here." Lester shook a couple of times, zipped up and walked over to a sink, and turned on the water. "What are you going to do? Stay on?"

"That'd be tough," Lucas said. "A little depends on who gets the top job."

"I'll tell you what, there's a lot of calculation going on today," Lester said. "People standing around talking. The bullshit machine is running overtime."

"Always happens," Lucas said, zipping up and moving to the next sink. "How many chiefs you been through?"

"Nine," Lester said. "Rose Marie was the ninth. But it was a lot easier to make the change on the first four or five, when I was sitting in a squad with a flashlight and a doughnut."

DEL and Marcy were waiting in the new office. "Swanson and Lane are over at the Cheese-It, trying to find somebody who might have seen Aronson with Bruce Willis," Marcy said. She handed Lucas a photograph of the actor. "We downloaded a picture of Willis from the net, and we're gonna have it redrawn, and sort of generalized, with the long black coat. Put it out in the papers."

Lucas snapped the photo with his fingertip and said, "That's good. Get it going. How about the lists?"

"We got Anderson to set up a computerized sorting program. We type in lists for each woman and push a button and it finds matches. So far, we don't have any. But we do have something else."

"What?"

"We have nine women calling in—count 'em, nine—saying they got these drawings in the mail."

"Nine?"

"Over three years. Five of them saved the drawings. I've got a couple of squads running around right now, picking up the drawings, and four of the women are coming in this afternoon to talk to me and Black. We're probably gonna have to go out for the others. They can't get away from their jobs so easy."

"If we got nine, then there are probably twenty more," Lucas said.

"We're also getting a little more media space than we thought. There hasn't been much good crime news lately, so CNN and Fox picked up on the drawings from the local stations last night, and they're showing them every fifteen minutes all day."

"So I can go home and take a nap?"

"No. You and Del are going to six ad agencies. Gonna look in the art department for buzzcut guys with long dark coats. Also, you got a call from a Terry Marshall—he's a sheriff's deputy from over in Menomonie, in Wisconsin. Dunn County. He's hot to talk. And a guy named Gerry Haack who wants you to call back right away."

Del said, "I've got the list of ad agencies. We can walk to them."

"Let me make the calls, and we'll go," Lucas said.

HE called Haack first. "What?"

"You told those guys who I was," Haack screamed. The scream was followed by two rattling *whack*s, as though Haack had banged the receiver against a wooden wall. "They're gonna kill me. I'm gonna lose my job."

"I didn't tell them anything," Lucas said bluntly. "I asked if Aronson was on the corner, and they said no. Then they asked who told me that, and when I wouldn't say, they guessed. And guess who they thought of first?"

"Goddamnit, Davenport, you gotta tell them I wasn't the one. They're gonna pull my nuts off," Haack shouted.

"You've been hanging out with the wrong people," Lucas said. "Your speeder friends might pull your nuts off, but these guys, they're not bad guys. They might give you a little shit, but that's about all."

"Goddamnit, Davenport."

"And Gerry . . . if you call back, make sure you know what you're talking about, okay? This worked out, no problems. They even gave me a little help. But bad information is usually worse than no information, because we waste time chasing it. Think you can remember that?"

"Goddamnit . . ."

Lucas hung up, looked at the slip for the Dunn County cop, and poked in the number. A woman answered on the first ring. "I'm returning a call from Terry Marshall," Lucas said.

"I'm afraid he's gone for the day," the woman said. "Who's calling?"

"Lucas Davenport. I'm a deputy chief over in Minneapolis."

"Oh. Okay. Terry's on his way there now. I think he's looking for you."

"You know what it's about?"

"Nope. I just got a note. Says if I need to get him, call your office, he expects to be there by noon unless there's a problem with the snow. He's driving."

"There's snow?"

"Around here there is; it looks like a blizzard. You can see it on the radar all the way to Hudson. . . . Must be past you guys."

"Yeah, it's past here. . . . I'll keep an eye out for your guy." He dropped the phone on the hook and went to get Del. As they were leaving, Marcy got off the phone and said, "I just talked to Mallard in Washington. He says the shrinks are looking at the drawings and pulling on their beards, but don't expect anything before tomorrow."

Cool spring day, the air damp, walking across town, looking at all the muddy cars, eighty-thousand-dollar Mercedes-Benzes that resembled melting mudbergs, and at the women with their red noses and cheeks and plastic boots. "Kind of interesting, having Marcy as a coordinator,"

Del said, as he hopped over an icy puddle at a corner curb.

"Could be chief someday, if she works things right," Lucas said, hopping after him. "If she's willing to put up with some bullshit."

"Hate to see her go for lieutenant," Del said. "She'd wind up stuck away somewhere, property crime or something. They'd start pushing her through the rounds."

"Got to do it, if you want to go up," Lucas said.

"You didn't do it," Del said.

"Maybe you didn't notice, but I never went up until I pulled a political job out of my ass," Lucas said.

THE six ad agencies took the rest of the morning; hip, smart people in sharp clothes, all with a touch of color, the people looking curiously at the cops. Lucas, in his straight charcoal suit, felt like a Politburo member walking in a flower garden. They showed pictures of Willis in *Pulp Fiction*, and got shaking heads at four of the agencies, raised eyebrows at two others. They looked at the possibilities presented by these two agencies, without any personal contact, and agreed that they were possible but unlikely.

One was a kid, the right size and shape, but probably too young—his personnel jacket said he was twenty-two, a summer graduate of the University of Minnesota–Morris. His winter coat was a dark blue hip-length parka, and his boss had never seen him in anything else. "Never in a topcoat," she said. "He's pretty *country* for a topcoat."

Lucas nodded. "So thanks," he said.

"What should I do?" she asked. "If he's being investigated . . ."

"Don't do anything," Lucas said. "Wouldn't be right; the chances of his being involved in anything are pretty slim."

Outside, Del said, "Didn't Aronson come from out there somewhere? Like Morris?"

"No, she was from Thief River," Lucas said.

"That's out there."

"Del, Thief River is about as close to fuckin' Morris as we are to fuckin' Des Moines, for Christ's sakes."

"Excuse my abysmal fuckin' ignorance," Del said.

The second possibility was the right age, and he had a dark topcoat, but the hair and body shape were wrong. The agency chief said the man never had a buzzcut, always the ponytail. They thanked him and left.

"This sucks," Lucas said.

"Be nicer if we were walking around in the summer," Del said. "I'll run them both, but they don't feel so good." He looked up at the gray sky and said, "I wish the sun would come out."

"Maybe in April."

THEY walked back to City Hall through the Skyways, shouldering through the lunchtime rush and the human traffic jams around the food courts. Lucas got an apple at the courthouse cafeteria, and Del got a tuna-fish sandwich and a Coke. At the office, Marcy, who was talking to a severe-looking young woman, looked up and said, "The Dunn County guy is here. I put him in your office. And we got those pictures made. You say yes, and we send them out."

Lucas took a picture from her. The artist had deftly generalized Willis's features, emphasized the buzzcut and added the long coat. "Good," Lucas said. "Send it."

Terry Marshall was ten or fifteen years older than Lucas, in the indeterminate mid-fifties to early sixties, with a lean, weathered face, brown hair showing swatches of gray, and a short brush-cut mustache. He wore round steel-rimmed glasses that might have made someone else look like John Lennon. Marshall didn't look anything like Lennon; he looked like something that might have eaten Lennon. He was sitting in Lucas's guest chair reading the paper. When Lucas pushed through the door, he stood up and said, "Your girl out there told me to wait here."

For all his wolfish appearance, he seemed a little embarrassed, and Lucas said, "As long as you didn't go through my drawers."

Marshall grinned and said, "Let it never be said that I spent any time in your drawers. Is that girl a secretary, or what? She pushes people around."

"She's a cop," Lucas said. "She does push."

"Ah." Marshall sat down again as Lucas settled behind his desk. "I thought she seemed, I guess . . ." He stopped, looking confused.

"What?"

"She seemed like she might be . . . I don't know. Handicapped, or something."

"We had a guy up here running around shooting people last fall. We caught him in a gas station—it was on TV."

"I remember that," Marshall said.

"Before we caught him, the guy shot Marcy with a hunting rifle. Right through the rib cage from about fifty feet. She got off a couple of rounds as she was down—helped us pin down the car and break the whole thing. But she was pretty messed up."

"Jeez." Marshall leaned forward to look at Marcy through the office window. "She gonna be all right?" There was concern in his voice, and Lucas liked him for it.

"In a while. She's getting pretty antsy already, that's why we've got her in here."

"Never been shot myself."

Marshall seemed to think about that for a minute, and Lucas, just a little impatient, said, "So, what can I do for you?"

"Ah, yeah." Marshall had a beat-up leather briefcase by his foot, and he picked it up, dug through it, and pulled out a legal portfolio. "This file is for you. Nine years ago, we had a young girl—nineteen—disappear. Name was Laura Winton. We never found out what happened to her, but we think she was strangled or smothered and dumped out in the country somewhere. We never did find the guy who did it."

"You think . . ."

"The thing is, he was pretty clever," Marshall said. "He apparently hung around this girl for a week before he killed her. He killed her on Christmas day, during Christmas break at the university. She lived on a street full of older houses that are all cut up into apartments as off-campus student housing. . . . You know what they're like."

"I know. I lived in the same kind of place myself when I was a kid."

Marshall nodded. "Anyway, he hung around her for about a week, and not a single one of her housemates ever saw him. When he killed her, he did it when they were all gone—she had three housemates, and all three were gone for Christmas."

"Why wasn't she gone?"

"Because she was a hometown girl," Marshall said. "She was the older of two daughters and she had two younger brothers, and when she moved out of her house to go to the university, the other daughter got the bedroom to herself. It was just too much trouble to stay overnight when her own place was only a couple of miles away. So she went over to her parents' for Christmas morning, to open gifts and eat lunch, and then she went back to her apartment. As far as we know, nobody ever saw her again, except the killer."

Lucas leaned back. "Why do you think she was strangled?"

Marshall's Adam's apple bobbed, and he looked down at

his hands. When he looked up, there was a tightness around his eyes. Terry Marshall could be just as hard—mean—as he needed to be, Lucas thought; it was something you saw in longtime sheriff's deputies, even more than in big-city cops. "When she disappeared . . . there was no reason. There was no note; she was supposed to go back to her folks' the next day. She'd been sorting clothes for the laundry, apparently, when the killer showed up."

"If there was a killer . . ."

Marshall flushed, bobbed his head. "There was. The thing is, we brought in a crime-scene crew. There was nothing obvious, no big pools of blood or anything, no sign of violence except . . . she had this old carpet, a fake Oriental rug. They found her fingernails in it."

"Fingernails."

"Three of them. She was trying to pull herself away from somebody, clawing across this rug. Snapped her fingernails off. There was a little fresh blood on one of them, and we type-matched it. It was hers."

Lucas thought about it for a minute, then said, "I can see that. A strangulation."

Marshall nodded. "If you think about it, it fits . . . and she was going with a guy her housemates called 'the artist.' "

Lucas leaned forward again. "The artist?"

"Yeah. He met her at the Union, sort of picked her up. He told her he was an art student and that his name was Tom Lang or Tom Lane. She went out to meet the guy a couple of times, and her housemates had teased her about him—what he looked like, was he ugly, and so on. She said he was cute, blond, skinny, not very tall. She told one of the girls that he looked like a movie star."

"Not Bruce Willis?"

Marshall, puzzled, shook his head. "No, no. Like a guy named Edward Fox. He played the bad guy in a movie called *Day of the Jackal.*"

Lucas said, "The assassin? The guy trying to kill Charles de Gaulle?"

"That's the guy. I've seen the picture about a hundred times. And she said he rode a bike."

"A bike."

"A bike. That was what we got on him. That was it," Marshall said.

"He never drew a picture of her or anything?" Lucas asked.

"Not that we know of."

"Any forensics at all?"

"No. Not except for the fingernails." Marshall was floundering, and Lucas looked at him curiously.

"Did you know this girl?"

"Yeah, yeah, she was my niece. My sister's girl. She was like a daughter—I never had a kid, and I just . . ." He shook his head and stopped talking; her image was in his eyes, Lucas thought.

"Jeez. I'm sorry," Lucas said.

"Yeah, well . . ." Marshall came back from wherever he'd gone. "I just hope I haven't gone goofy. When I saw that thing on TV last night, there wasn't one thing that *didn't* sound like our guy."

Lucas leaned back in his chair. "I hate to tell you this, but we found a guy last night who might've seen him. He supposedly looks like Bruce Willis. Kind of stocky, buzz-cut hair, dark. We do think he might've met Aronson in a restaurant, like the guy picking up your niece in the Union," Lucas said. "Hang on a second. . . ."

He went to the outer office and retrieved Marcy's drawing of Willis, brought it back, and passed it to Marshall. "We found an old friend of Aronson's last night who might've seen the guy, just by accident. This is what we think he might look like."

Marshall looked at the picture for a moment, then up at

Lucas, shook his head, and said, "Just the opposite of what Laura told her housemates. Perfect opposite."

"Pretty much," Lucas said.

Marshall peered at the picture for another moment, sighed, and then said, "Maybe I'm on the wrong track. But there are a couple of other things there in the file. I've kept a lookout for women who might have been victims. We didn't have much to go on, so there are quite a few candidates—people drop out of sight all the time. There was a young girl here in Minnesota who disappeared about two years after Laura was killed: Linda Kyle. Came from Albert Lea and was going to Carlton College in Northfield. Anyway, she disappeared one day, never has been found. She was an art student and had been hanging around galleries up here in Minneapolis when she got bored. She'd had a couple of dates with a guy in the city, but none of her friends ever saw him. No suspects."

"Huh. None of her friends ever saw him. It's like a technique," Lucas said. Then: "I don't remember her. I don't remember the case."

"Not too surprising—seven years ago, and they never found anything, and she wasn't from here," Marshall said. "Then there's another one, three years ago, from New Richmond, Wisconsin, just across the St. Croix River."

"I know the town," Lucas said. He drove through it sometimes on the way to his cabin.

"A woman named Nancy Vanderpost, married but separated, twenty-two years old, and one day she disappeared. Hasn't been found. She'd been talking about going to Los Angeles and doing performance art. She also had a romance going on here in the Twin Cities, but they never identified the guy. She was living in a trailer home, and when they went in there was no sign of a struggle or anything, but they found . . . fingernails. Two broken fingernails. And they found her purse next to a couch, all of her clothes were there as far as they knew, and the main thing is, all of her insulin was there. She wouldn't have left that."

"The connection is the fingernails and the art in the Cities?" Lucas asked. "And the thing about nobody ever seeing who the woman is dating?"

Marshall nodded, his Lennon glasses opaque with reflected light, hiding his eyes. "One other thing, a guess. All the trailers in this trailer court are right next to each other. Ten feet apart. If her purse was in the place, then I think that's where the guy took her out of . . ."

"If somebody took her out."

"Yeah. If. If somebody did, he didn't shoot her, didn't beat her to death, didn't do anything that gave her a chance to scream, didn't get involved in any loud arguments, wasn't drinking, and didn't stab her to death. They brought the state crime lab in to look at her trailer, and there was no trace of blood at all. I think he strangled her. I think that's what the fingernails mean: These women are beating their hands on the floor."

"No drawings?"

"Only hers. She did drawing and music and dance and acting and poetry and journaling and photography and everything else, but I'm told she wasn't very good at any of it. Just sort of a . . . fucked-up soul, looking for something a little bigger than she was."

"Some kind of art guy," Lucas said.

"That's what I think," Marshall said. "I pushed it hard as I could from Dunn County, but there was nothing to go on, and there was always the possibility that she was in L.A., or that she'd had an insulin problem and had wandered off somewhere and died. There's all kinds of places around New Richmond where you could get lost."

"Her car?"

"Was parked in town. They found it the day after they went into her place."

"I see one difference between what you've got and what we've got," Lucas said. "Yours are all small-town kids, and ours isn't. Like maybe your guy is picking on kids who are a little naive. Aronson was living here in the Cities, and had been—"

"But the paper said she was originally small-town. Maybe it's an attitude that pulls him in."

"Maybe. . . ." Lucas got his feet up on his desk for a moment, thinking about it, and then said, "You heading back home?"

"I'd like to hang around this afternoon. It was snowing like crazy when I went through Hudson. I'm afraid they're gonna close the Interstate over the river. I'd like to see what you've got going. I know our part of the case backwards and forwards, and maybe something'll occur to me."

"You're welcome to hang out long as you want. Get Marcy to run that name—Tom Lang?—through the lists we're compiling. Maybe you should go over and look at Aronson's body—talk to the docs, see if she's missing any nails, or if there's any abrasions on her hands."

"What do you think about my list?"

"Interesting. Somebody's probably out there operating."

"Somebody always is," Marshall said.

DEL came back a few minutes after Marshall left and found Lucas staring at the ceiling of his office. Del said, "I ran those guys from the ad agencies. One of them doesn't pay his parking tickets. The other one has never talked to a cop, far as I can tell."

"Did you run them against the lists?" Lucas asked.

"Not yet. Marcy was entering stuff. . . ." Lucas had turned in his chair, his eyes drifting away as Del was talking. Del said, "Hey. What's up?"

"Huh?"

"Look like you've seen a ghost."

Lucas explained about Marshall. "I've been looking through his file. It's got a bad feel to it, Del."

"You think he's onto something?"

"I'm afraid he might be," Lucas said.

"He got anyplace we can go with it?"

Lucas pushed himself onto his feet. "Not right away. So let's go look up Morris Ware."

Del nodded. "That dickhead. I was hoping he'd moved to one of the fuckin' coasts with the rest of the perverts. Where'd you hear about him?"

Lucas pulled his coat on. "That Lori chick over at Hot Feet Jazz Dance, down on . . ."

". . . Lyndale. Yeah. Strange chick."

"I was over there a couple of days ago. She did one of those dance things where you hold on to a bar and stretch your leg over your head. I spent five minutes talking to her crotch."

"And her crotch said Morris Ware . . ."

". . . is back out on the street with his Brownie, looking for the young stuff again."

"Not surprised," Del said. "That's not something you get over."

Lucas asked, "Didn't Ware run with the art crowd, like from over at the Walker?"

"Yeah, for a while, I think. He did this book, *Little Women on the Edge,* or something like that. Like on the edge of puberty. It was supposed to be art, naked girls, but it had the smell of puke about it."

7

MORRIS WARE LIVED in a tidy two-story stucco house under the northern approach lanes for Minneapolis–St. Paul International Airport. A Miracle Maids van sat in front of the house, and a pink plastic Miracle Maids bin sat on the porch, next to the front door. The porch might have held a porch swing—there were hooks in the ceiling, and worn spots on the deck—but didn't. Both the back and front yards were surrounded by low dark-green chain-link fences. A clapboard garage sat astride the driveway behind the fence, and on the lawn, next to the driveway, a Macon Security sign warned against burglary: "Armed Response Authorized."

"Light in the window," Lucas said.

"Of course. It's almost two o'clock," Del said. "This fuckin' place."

"Not very cold, though," Lucas said, as they pushed through the front gate and headed for the stairs.

"Not for Moscow," Del said. "For any other place, this is cold."

A machine was whining inside the house. Lucas rang the doorbell, and they both heard a thump. A man's eyes appeared in the small window cut in the front door, and a second later, the door opened.

"Yeah?" The guy in the doorway wore white coveralls and a white paper hat that covered his hair. He was thin, slat-faced, with a two-day stubble.

"Minneapolis police," Lucas said. "We're looking for Morris Ware."

"Uh, Mr. Ware isn't here. We're the housecleaners."

"You're a Miracle Maid?" Lucas asked.

"Yeah. That's what I am." He sounded like he didn't believe it himself.

"Do you know where Ware'd be?" Del asked.

The man's eyes flicked to Del, lingered for a moment, and a rime of skepticism appeared. "Do you guys have any ID?"

Both Lucas and Del nodded automatically and flipped their IDs. "So . . ."

"I don't have an address or anything, but I do have a contact number. I think it's his office," the man said.

Lucas and Del waited on the porch while he went to get the number, and Del said, "I'm not sure he believes I'm a cop."

"You're too hard on yourself," Lucas said.

The housecleaner returned with the number. Lucas jotted it down and then said, "You don't have to call him and tell him we were here."

"Maybe I should just forget it entirely."

"Good policy," said Del.

Lucas called the phone number in, and a minute later got an address back. "It's off 280, off Broadway somewhere, in those warehouses," the dispatcher said. "You know where that Dayton's office furniture place is? Around there somewhere."

They took I-35 north, then 280, falling in behind a highway patrol cruiser. The cruiser cut a yellow light at Broadway, while Lucas eased into the turn lane. As they sat at the stoplight, waiting to make a left, a half-dozen teenagers in nylon jogging suits ran in a pack down a hill on the golf course across the highway.

"That's what you ought to do, get in shape," Lucas said.

"Life's too short to spend it getting in shape," Del said. "Besides, it'd ruin my credibility on the street."

MORRIS Ware's office was in a long line of low, yellow-painted concrete-block warehouse spaces that mostly held distributors of one kind or another. The address was obscure: They finally spotted it as a signless window between a pressure-hose distributor and something called "Christmas Ink."

The warehouse was fronted by a service street with diagonal parking. Lucas pulled in fifty feet past Ware's, and they both got out. As they did, a woman pulled in at Christmas Ink, walked around to the back of her minivan, and popped the hatch. She was struggling with a cardboard box when Lucas and Del walked up.

"Let me get that for you," Lucas said.

She stepped back and took them in. "Thanks."

The woman was in her fifties, with elaborate gold-frosted hair and electric-red lipstick. She wore a hip-length nylon parka and rubber snow boots. She waited until Lucas had the box out, locked the van, and led the way to the door of Christmas Ink.

Inside, a counter ran from wall to wall, and another

woman and two men sat at metal desks in the back peering at computer screens. A bookcase was stuffed with catalogs and directories; one wall was covered with holiday cards, with header signs that said "Memorial Day," "Mother's Day," "Father's Day," and "New Sympathy Cards from Leonbrook." The woman in the parka lifted a countertop gate, went through, said, "You can just leave it on the counter. Thanks again."

Lucas put the book on the counter and said, "We're Minneapolis police."

The woman said, "Yes?" and the three people in the back all looked up.

"We're looking for a guy named Morris Ware. We'd like to talk to him."

One of the men looked at the woman behind the computer screen and said, "Told you."

" 'Told you' what?" Del asked.

The man said, "We don't want any trouble with our neighbors. . . ."

Lucas shrugged. "There's no need for Mr. Ware to know we stopped in here."

The woman in the parka unzipped the coat and said, "There's some pretty peculiar goings-on over there."

Del asked, "Like what?"

One of the men said, "I was out back, hauling some trash to the Dumpster. This kid who works over there was hauling out some bags of trash. . . . When he went back in, I could see this light coming out of there and just caught a shot of this girl. She was naked."

"How old?" Lucas asked.

The guy shrugged. "Not very. I mean, old enough to do that kind of stuff, maybe. I mean, she had breasts and everything."

"But there have been some people going in there that

were too young," said the woman, who was taking off the parka. She tossed it at an office chair and said, "We don't know that anything was going on with them, but I've come here a couple of times in the morning and there were a couple of kids hanging around outside, waiting for those people to show up. They looked like orphan kids or something."

"You mean street kids?" Lucas asked.

"Yeah. They always look old," she said.

"Younger than eighteen?"

"We don't want to get involved in a huge hassle here," said the second man, who'd kept quiet.

"You never want to get in hassles, George," the second woman said. "We should have called somebody."

"I'm just trying to keep our head above water," he said.

"We still should have called."

"Younger than eighteen?" Lucas asked again.

"A couple of them looked like they were maybe fifteen, at the most," said the woman who had worn the parka.

Lucas said, "Please don't mention this to anyone, okay? And thanks. Del, let's go outside."

Outside, they turned away from Ware's window and walked back toward Lucas's car. "We can call Benton, he'd give us a warrant."

"Take an hour," Del said.

"So we go eat some black beans and rice. . . ."

"He won't talk, Ware won't. If we find anything. He'll get lawyers and they'll shut him up."

Lucas thought about it for a minute, then said, "Aronson isn't coming back to life, and if Ware's doing that child shit . . . We ought to put him in Stillwater regardless of Aronson. We can have the Sex guys find us somebody else who knows the city."

Del nodded. "All right. Let's go for the warrant." After a moment, he added, "I've been on the street for so long that sometimes I forget that there's something more than deals. You know?"

"Absolutely."

THEY spent an hour at a health-food place in Roseville, eating black beans with cheese, and drinking water faintly flavored with lemon, waiting for the phone call. They got it from an assistant county attorney named Larsen.

"I'd like to come along, but I'm stuck in court," she said.

"Next time," said Lucas.

On the way back to Ware's, Lucas mentioned to Del that Larsen would have liked to come. "I wonder why," Del said. "She gonna run for something? Get her picture taken?"

"I think she just likes the rush," Lucas said. "She's been along on a couple of entries."

JUST before four o'clock, a Chevy van with the entry team backed into a parking space between Christmas Ink and Ware's office while two squads moved into position to block the back door. Lucas and Del parked down the block again, walked down to Christmas Ink, and went inside. The woman who'd been wearing the parka was on the phone. One of the men had left, but the other man and woman were still at their desks.

"You're back," the man said. He didn't look happy.

"Is there any way to tell if your neighbors are home?" Lucas asked. "I mean, without calling them on the phone?"

The parka lady said, "I gotta go," into the phone, hung up, and turned to Lucas. "UPS delivered something ten minutes ago, and somebody was there. I've been watching."

"All right," Lucas said. He took his phone out of his pocket, called the van, and said, "Go when you're ready."

* * *

LUCAS and Del stood in the window with the Christmas
Ink people and watched the van unload. Carolyn Rie, the
Sex Unit cop, led the way in her letter jacket. A uniformed
cop followed just behind, carrying a sledge. Another uniformed cop and a computer specialist climbed out behind
them.

Rie tried the door handle, shook her head no, stepped
aside, and the uniformed cop lifted the sledge. As he
started his backswing, Lucas and Del opened the door at
Christmas Ink, and as the unmarked door at Ware's exploded inward from the impact of the hammer, they joined
the surge into the office.

The front was exactly that: a front. Only seven or eight
feet deep, it contained four chairs lined up against one
wall, and a metal desk with a red telephone. A door, closed,
led into the back. The uniformed cop didn't bother to try
the knob, but simply kicked it, and the door flew open.

The back room was huge: a warehouse space draped
with rolls of backdrop paper. A plush red couch was sitting
on one of the rolls; a brass bedstead with a king-size mat-
tress was pushed into a corner. A table held lamps, and two
floor lamps stood behind them. There were five strobes on
their light stands, two of them covered with soft-boxes,
and more lighting equipment sat on another side table.

A short, balding man sat on the couch, holding a camera
the size of a shoe box; he was frozen in place. Another
man, older, taller, wearing a crisp white shirt and gray
slacks, was walking briskly toward a desk full of computer
equipment. The computer cop yelled, "Hey, hey hey . . ."
and the man walked faster, reaching, and the computer cop
ran straight into him and pushed him away from the computer desk.

The man in the white shirt started screaming at the computer cop: *"Get away, get away, get away, this is all illegal this is all illegal get away . . ."*

Another man, who had been out of sight behind a lighting rack, walked to the back door and punched it open: Two cops stood there, and he turned back. "Hey, what's happening . . ."

Then the guy on the couch with the big camera stood up and said, "I'm leaving. I'm not even supposed to be here."

"Everybody shut up," Rie shouted. "We're Minneapolis police. You two guys . . ." She pointed at the man who'd tried the back door, and the man by the couch. "Sit. Just sit."

"I want to call my lawyer," the man in the white shirt shouted.

Lucas walked over to him. "How are you, Morris?" he asked. "You remember me?"

Ware looked at Lucas for a moment, then said, "No. I don't. I want my attorney, and I want him *now.*"

"Somebody give Mr. Ware a copy of the warrant," Lucas said. And to one of the squad cops from the blocking car: "Then take him out front and let him use the phone."

Rie got IDs on the other two men, Donald Henrey and Anthony Carr, as Ware was taken into the front room. As he went, he said to Rie, "You're all going down for this. This is the end of your jobs. This is the end. . . ."

The computer specialist pulled a phone line out of the back of Ware's sleek Macintosh, and checked the power cords that went out to peripherals. "Looks okay," he said. "We're isolated, but I'd rather not work on it until I can get it back to the shop."

Lucas nodded. "Whatever's best. The way he was going for it when we came in . . . gotta be something there."

One uniformed cop from the blocking squad watched the two men on the couch, while Rie, Larsen, Del, Lucas, and the two entry-team uniforms began taking the back room apart—pulling out drawers, looking under pillows, shaking out boxes. They found not a single photograph. They did find two dozen Jaz disks for the Macintosh.

Nothing to look at.

Finally, Lucas asked Henrey, the man with the big camera, "What're we going to find on the disks?"

"I don't know," he said. He sounded depressed. "I'm just hired to shoot. Nothing illegal. I won't shoot anything illegal."

"Does anything illegal get shot in here?"

"I don't know," he said. He turned the big camera in his hands. "I was just hired for one shoot."

"When? Now? Earlier? Later?"

Henrey looked at his watch. "Half hour. We were just setting up lights."

Lucas turned to Rie. "Maybe we ought to get Ware back in here. You could sit out front and be a receptionist."

She ticked a finger at him. "Not bad."

WARE came back with his escort, looked at Lucas, and snapped, "What?"

"Sit on the couch," Lucas said.

"My attorney is on the way," Ware said.

"Good. I suggest that you not say anything until he gets here."

"I won't. Nobody else better say anything, either," he said, looking at the two other men. "I'll sue for slander and get every nickel you've got. You better believe it."

Lucas crooked a finger at the man with the camera, who followed him into the front room. Rie was moving a chair behind the metal desk, ready to receive visitors.

To Henrey, Lucas said, "If we find child porn on those disks—child stuff is Ware's big thing—then you could wind up in Stillwater for a few years. You know how it goes."

"Listen, man, honest to God, I was hired," Henrey said earnestly.

"We understand that, and we'll take into account any help you give us. Give me just one thing that'll help."

"I gotta talk to a lawyer."

"One thing, buddy," Lucas said. "Just give me one thing. We might not need you an hour from now."

The guy looked around and said, "You better not be lying. Give me a note or something."

"We don't really have a lot of time to fool around."

"I'm not a bad guy, I'm just trying to make a living taking a few pictures. I usually do wildlife and nature."

"Yeah, well, that's cool."

Henrey sat head-down for a moment, and Rie looked at Lucas and winked. Then Henrey said, "I don't know about the child-porn thing. I heard that he does it, but it'd be stupid. It's death. There're plenty of places outside the States where you can do it all you want, and nobody cares."

"Ware is sort of a hands-on kinda guy," Lucas said.

The photographer winced and said, "Just one thing?"

"Just one."

He nodded. "But you gotta help me. . . . The thing is, sometimes when I've been here shooting, the actors—"

From Rie: "Actors?"

"Models, whatever. They sort of like to get their noses into it, and Morrie usually has a little coke around. I've seen him get it a couple times . . . go for it. It's not like I could go over and see what he's doing, but I think one of the power outlets behind his desk is a fake. I think he keeps a little stash in there."

Lucas slapped him on the back. "See? That was no problem. And if you're like an up-and-up nature guy, like you say . . . maybe we can deal. Okay? Now, I'm gonna put you back on the couch with Ware. Don't say anything to him."

Lucas brought Del out to the front, told him about the power outlets, then sent Henrey back to the couch and brought Carr into the outer room. Lucas sat him down where Henrey had been, and made the same pitch.

"Look, all I do is maintain his website," Carr said. "He's never bothered to learn how to do that. He puts his pictures on disks, gives me the index number, and I move them over to the Web and set up thumbnails. ErosFineArtPhotos.com."

"Any children on the site?" Lucas asked.

"No. Of course not," Carr said.

"Does he do kids?"

Carr looked uncomfortable. "I don't know. I don't see everything. I just move megabytes. I'm a moving guy."

Lucas nodded and said, "Listen, pal—you better get an attorney. If we find pictures of kids around here, you're gonna go down as an accomplice, and that means a couple of years in prison. You better think of ways to help us, and get your lawyer to cut a deal. . . . I mean, I don't want to sound like I'm threatening you, but this is serious shit."

Carr puffed up his cheeks and audibly exhaled. "If I don't have the money for a lawyer . . ."

"We'll get one appointed," Lucas said.

"Listen, I can probably tell you a couple of things. I never got involved in the photography at all, but Morrie once told me that sometimes he had 'special stuff.' "

"Special stuff."

"That's what he called it. He was, like, being important. He said he'd transfer it directly to a guy in Europe who puts it up on a website there." He twisted his hands around, as though he were playing cat's cradle. "I think . . . Morrie's a content provider. We got eight zillion websites without content, and Morrie provides it."

"There's not enough porno out there?" Rie asked.

"Yeah, there's a lot of stuff, but people are always looking for fresh stuff."

"Young stuff," Rie said.

"Yeah. Teenagers, anyway."

"I'll make you a deal right now," Lucas said. "Give me something, give me anything, and I'll help you out. I won't help you if I find out you've been dealing kid stuff, but if you're just getting paid by Ware to run his website . . . we can help."

Carr puffed his cheeks again, rubbed his hair, said, "Maybe I ought to see a lawyer."

Lucas shrugged. "That's absolutely up to you. But I'll tell you what, this offer may expire. If we find a bunch of stuff . . ."

"Aw, man . . ." He looked at Rie, then said, "I'm not a freak."

"Nobody said you were," she said.

To Lucas, mumbling, Carr said, "There's a possibility . . . that he ships stuff to an underground website in Europe—Holland, I think—called donnerblitzen451." He spelled it, then said, "You need some kind of code to get in. Putting in the wrong code too many times may wipe the site. Maybe your guys can do something with it."

"Donnerblitzen like the reindeer," Lucas said.

"Yeah. Four fifty-one like the Ray Bradbury book, *Fahrenheit 451*," Carr said. "Four fifty-one is supposed to be the burning point of paper, so I think that's Morrie's little joke. If you put the wrong number into the website—more than a couple of times, anyway—it burns."

"Why would he do that?" Lucas asked. "If somebody found it by mistake . . ."

"How are you gonna find donnerblitzen451 by mistake? It's not a public facility—it's his. It's his warehouse, I think. You put a high-res photo file in there, somebody wants something special, you go to your warehouse, you order it sent, the site sends out the file, the recipient prints it. . . . There's no way to get back to Morrie. He has a photo negative for ten minutes. After he develops it, he scans it, he burns the neg, and the picture is nothing but a bunch of numbers somewhere in Europe."

"That's interesting," Lucas said. "But you don't know the code to get in."

"No, but I've seen the setup before, and I think it's booby-trapped. If you try to get in, you better know what you're doing, or the place is gonna burn." He nodded, as if turning over the problem in his mind. "I've given the whole thing some thought. Tried to figure out what the code was—tried to catch him going out to the site. I even thought about installing a keystroke recorder in his computer, but . . . I never did."

"All right, this helps," Lucas said. "If you let on to Ware for one minute what you told us, our deal is off. And you still better get a lawyer."

WHEN Lucas was done with Carr, he sent him back to the couch and said to Rie, "We need to get the code for that website before we turn Ware loose. If he gets five minutes with a computer, he can kill the site."

"How're we gonna do that?" she asked.

"Call the feds, I guess. They're supposed to have some big-deal computer forensics operation going on. Maybe they can help."

"You want to do that?"

"Yeah, I'll take care of it," he said. "And . . ." He turned his head at movement outside. "Hey—I think we've got customers."

A man and a woman had gotten out of an old Chevy and were walking toward the door.

"They'll see the broken door," Rie said.

"I'll get it." Lucas hurried over to the door and pulled it open, as though he were leaving.

The man was just stepping up onto the sidewalk, and stopped when he saw Lucas. "Hey. Is Morrie around?"

"Yeah. He's in the back," Lucas said. "Who're you?"

"We're the talent," the woman said. She was young, but her face was tough, touched with worry lines—a street kid. She looked straight at Lucas, challenging him. Maybe eighteen, Lucas thought. Maybe not.

"Come on in, talk to Carolyn," Lucas said.

The two stepped past Lucas, crowding into the small reception room. Rie, behind the desk, stood up as Lucas stepped back inside and pulled the door shut. The woman said to Rie, "We're the talent. Morrie said we're supposed to meet him here. We're a couple of minutes early."

"That's all right," Rie said. She held up her badge. "We're the police. Morrie's being raided."

The woman said, "Oh, shit," and pivoted, looking at the door.

"I'd just run you down if you got past me," Lucas said, leaning back against it.

"Fuckin' . . ." The word came out as a harsh grate, then swung up to a whine. "We haven't done anything."

"No, but we're asking people to cooperate. I'd like to see a little ID, a driver's license."

"I think we need a lawyer," the man said. He was in his late twenties, Lucas thought.

"You might," Lucas agreed. "And you'll get one. But first I want to see some ID."

Lucas took the man's license, read the name, and Rie noted it down. The woman said, "I don't drive."

"Oh, horseshit. You drove that car over here," Lucas said. "Give me your goddamn license."

The woman stared at him for a moment, then said, "Fuck this. Fuck this." She dug in her purse, found a license, and handed it over.

Lucas read her name off: "Sylvia Berne." Then: "Tell officer Rie what your birthdate is, Sylvia."

Berne muttered something, Rie said, "What?" and Berne muttered the date again. Rie looked at Lucas. "Is that what the license says?"

"That's what the license says," Lucas said. To Berne: "You gotta remember to call me when you turn eighteen. I'll buy you a malt."

Berne looked puzzled. "A what?"

"A malt. . . . Never mind." To Rie: "We'll need a statement from Ms. Berne. And get a juvie officer down here."

"Absolutely," Rie said.

Lucas asked Berne, "How many times have you done this?"

She shrugged. "A couple. Nobody gets hurt."

"Morrie never gave you a free sample of the pictures, did he?"

"Maybe," Berne said.

"I love you," Lucas said.

The man said, "What about me?"

"You better sit down," Lucas said. "I got a whole bunch of bad news for you."

TEN minutes later, Lucas arrested Ware on charges of abusing a minor and of creating child pornography, and Henrey for creating child pornography—Berne said he was the shooter at the last session—and the man who arrived with Berne for child sexual abuse. Carr was freed, but was told not to leave Minnesota.

"She's not a child," Ware snarled, gesturing at Berne. "Look at her, for Christ's sake. She's got tits out to *here*."

"Looks like a kid after you scrape off the abuse," Del said. To Lucas, he said, "I was fooling around behind the desk, and one of those power outlets looked a little strange. I took the cover off, and guess what? It's a little teeny little safe. There's a Baggie full of white powder inside. We gotta get the crime-scene folks down here."

Lucas looked at Ware. "Uh-oh," he said.

THE uniform cops took Ware downtown to be booked, and Lucas called Washington from his cell phone. He finally tracked down Louis Mallard at his home and said, "We need another favor."

"Jeez, you guys are running up a bill," Mallard said.

"Well, you know we're tracking this guy, the drawing guy."

"Yeah, yeah, quite the artworks."

"So we went out and busted a porno guy, hoping we can squeeze him on the sex scene around here . . . and we find out that he's probably got a child-sex photo warehouse over in Europe somewhere. Our source gave us the address for the site, but says the thing can probably be burned in about ten seconds. We need some hot-shit feds to track the site down, and then maybe get onto the cops wherever it is—our source thinks maybe Holland—and grab the servers before our man makes bail tomorrow."

"We can try," Mallard said. "Of course, it depends on what kind of cooperation we get. If it's Holland, we ought to be able to do something. We're fairly tight with the Dutch."

Lucas gave Mallard the details on Ware and the site address, and said, "Let me know."

"I'll call you tomorrow. And we ought to have something on the drawings first thing tomorrow morning."

LATER that night, Lucas and Weather walked down to Eau du Chien, a new French-American restaurant a block from the Ford Bridge in St. Paul. A waitress lit the white tapers on their table, they ordered Chardonnay and looked at the menus, and Weather asked, without taking her eyes off the menu, "Whatever happened to that engagement ring?"

"Gave it away," Lucas said absently, peering at his own menu.

Now she looked up, a wrinkle of vexation on her forehead. "Gave it away?"

"For charity. They had an auction, I got a tax write-off."

She said, "Lucas, this is serious. If you're pulling my leg . . ."

"It's in the chest of drawers, second drawer, in the box under my socks."

They looked at the menus for another moment, then Weather said, over the menu, "I've been thinking. We may be going at this whole thing a little too informally."

"You're scaring me," he said.

"I don't want to scare you. I just think we should Talk," she said.

"Ah, Jesus. Not that."

"What?" The wrinkle was back.

"Talk. I don't want to talk with a capital T. I want to get married and have a couple of kids and send them to parochial schools or wherever you think is best, but I really don't want to fuckin' hack through all the pieces ahead of time."

"I don't want to hack through all the pieces," she said. "I just want to have some kind of rational, up-front discussion. I mean, we haven't even formally decided to get married yet."

"Weather, will you marry me?"

"That's not what I was looking for, exactly," she said.

"Well, will you?"

"Well, yes," she said, the menu still open in front of her, like a book.

"Good. That's taken care of. Put the ring on. And tell me what the fuck Number Five is. That's not something with snails or clams, is it? Or from diseased geese?"

"Lucas . . ."

"Weather, I'm begging you," Lucas said. "Not right now. Not in Eau du Chien. We can go home, have a beer, get comfortable."

"You'll wave your arms around and rave," she said.

"I will not."

"You won't if we Talk here," she said.

"Goddamnit, Weather."

The waiter thought they were having a fight.

8

Lucas arrived at the office at nine o'clock, ragged after a long, intense evening. Marcy was shouting at somebody on the telephone. A bullet-headed man sat in a chair next to her desk, watching her talk. When she saw Lucas walk in, she shouted, "Gotta go," hung up, and said, "Where've you been?"

"Had to run Weather over to her place early, then bagged out there for a couple of hours. What happened?"

"You know the guy with the butch haircut and the long black coat who was seen with Aronson outside of Cheese-It?"

"Yeah?" Lucas's eyes drifted toward the bullet-headed man, who'd turned to look up at him.

"This is the guy," Marcy said. "Jim Wise. Walked in a half hour ago."

Wise stood up, and Lucas noticed that he had a black coat folded over his arm. "I saw the picture in the paper and I thought it had to be me," he said. "I was in there with her, and I had the coat, and my hair used to be cut shorter."

"Put the coat on," Marcy said.

Wise pulled the coat on, buttoned it, shrugged his shoulders, and looked at Lucas.

"Damnit," Lucas said. Behind Wise, Marcy rolled her eyes in exasperation. "How well did you know her?"

"Not very well. I've got a furniture business, Wise-Hammersmith American Loft. Maybe you've heard of it?" When Lucas shook his head, Wise continued. "We sell period furniture and accessories—lamps, art pottery, and so on. Anyway, Ms. Aronson did freelance ad work and we needed some good-looking ads cheap, to run in the trade magazines . . . and that's what I was seeing her about."

"Did she do the ads?"

"Yeah. Three of them. They're still running." He stooped, picked up a brown leather briefcase, and took out a magazine with a chair on the front cover. He opened it to a folded-over page and showed Lucas the ad—a photograph of an English-flavored arrangement of fruitwood furniture topped with a glass lamp, and overlain with an arty typeface. "The thing is, getting an ad done is a lot more complicated than it should be. You've got to get certain kinds of output and all that computer stuff—I don't understand it. We just paid her two thousand dollars, and she arranged for the photographer and did the digital stuff, and gave us disks with the ads on them, all to the magazine's specs. That was what it was."

"Did you see her more than the one time?" Lucas asked.

"Yeah, when she delivered them. The disks with the ads. Our store's down on Lake Street."

"Why'd you meet at Cheese-It? She lived downtown here."

"She worked there. She was up front about it—she was working until she got her feet on the ground—and suggested that I just stop in when I had a minute, and we'd talk. We wound up walking down to a coffee bar so I could sketch out what we wanted. We'd already put a special type font on our signs and business cards, and we wanted to keep going with that in the ad."

They talked for another three minutes, and Lucas was convinced: Not only was he probably the right guy, he probably had nothing to do with the killing. "I've got a guy I want you to talk to, if you have a few minutes. Give a statement," he told Wise.

"You think I'm okay? The whole thing was quite a shock. Seeing the picture in the paper."

"We'll pull the picture," Lucas said. "We'll say that you came forward voluntarily and . . . Whatever sounds good."

LUCAS called Sloan, who was the best interrogator on the force, took him aside, and explained what he needed. Sloan took Wise off to Homicide to make the statement. Lucas looked at Marcy and said, "Shoots that idea in the ass."

"Not only that, wait'll you hear what the feds have for us," Marcy said.

"Good news or bad?"

"One of each. Which do you want first?"

"Bad."

"You know that profiling stuff on the drawings? It's shit. You could get it out of a book. When I got finished with the FBI stuff, I knew less than when I started. It's like somebody sawed off the top of my head and poured in sawdust."

"Nothing?"

"He's probably between twenty-five and forty and has some formal education in the arts."

"Ah, man. What's the good news?"

"The Dutch cops grabbed Ware's computer site in Holland. The forensic computer people traced it, and it was early morning in Holland already, and they called over there and the cops busted the place. They're doing something that copies all the files out, I don't know what, but they say there are huge files that gotta be pictures. Hundreds of them."

"Has Ware made bail yet?"

"Hearing's right now. The county's asking for a lien on his house."

"Who's his attorney?" Lucas asked.

"Jeff Baxter."

"All right. We want to talk to him, soon as he gets out of the hearing. In fact, I'll walk on over there and see if I can catch him."

"Too bad about the drawings," Marcy said.

"Yeah. . . ." Lucas pulled at his lip for a moment, then said, "There's an art guy over in St. Paul. Supposed to be a big name. He's a painter. I don't know anything about him except that I called him one time. There was a question about a painting, and he just told me the answer right off the top of his head. A guy over at the U says he's a genius. Maybe if we asked him to take a look . . ."

"What's his name?" Marcy asked.

Lucas scratched his head. "Uh, Kidd. I can't remember his first name, but he's supposed to be pretty famous."

"I'll run him down," she said. "What're you doing the rest of the day?"

"Talk to Baxter and Ware, if I can. Think about it. Read all the paper. Goddamnit, I wish Wise had run for the border instead of coming in here. We woulda had him in a day."

"Two problems: He wasn't there, and he didn't do it."

"Yeah, yeah. But you know what this does? That guy from Menomonie—this puts his whole theory back in play. A skinny blond guy who looks like some other movie star, not Bruce Willis."

"Edward Fox. The guy in *Day of the Jackal.*"

"Yeah. I'm gonna have to look at it again—get a feel for the guy."

JEFF Baxter, a thirty-something criminal attorney with reddish-blond hair, a pale Nordic complexion, and a prominent English nose, was leaning against a wall outside a courtroom, reading papers in a green file folder. He saw Lucas coming and raised a hand.

"How's it going?" Lucas asked.

"Slow season. It's all this rain," Baxter said. "Nobody's gonna stick up a 7-Eleven in this weather."

"Right. When's the last time you defended a 7-Eleven guy?"

"I'm talking in theory," Baxter said. He pushed away from the wall. "Is this just a random, friendly encounter, or did you come over looking for me?"

"Look, you're defending Morrie Ware?" Lucas asked.

"Yeah. Your guys just finished throwing the book at him. I'm not sure how good a case it is." Baxter was a good attorney and could smell the smallest molecules of a possible deal.

"However good it is, it got better in the last couple of hours," Lucas said. "The Dutch cops grabbed Ware's website in Holland, and I suspect it is chock-full of little children playing with their wee-wees."

"Ah, fuck. You know for sure there're kids?"

"Not yet. The feds are handling that end of it. But Morrie's a scuzz-bag, whatever they find."

"Yeah, well . . . just between you and me, if I ever caught him standing next to one of *my* kids, I'd stick a gun in his ear. But he *does* get a lawyer."

"That's why I'm talking to you," Lucas said. "Ware may be able to help us on another, unrelated case. We'd want somebody to pick his brain . . . and we can probably deal down the cocaine problem."

"What other case?"

"The Aronson murder."

"The guy in the black coat?" Baxter asked. "I saw his picture."

"Wasn't him," Lucas said, shaking his head. "He came in this morning. Didn't even need an attorney."

Baxter made a farting noise with his mouth.

Lucas grinned. "Yeah, yeah. Anyway, we need to talk to Ware about what he knows about sex freaks in the art community. Since he *is* one, we thought he might know some more."

"You don't think he's involved . . ."

Lucas shook his head. "No reason to think so. We're just looking to talk, and we can probably deal on the cocaine."

"We'd want it to go away. Entirely," Baxter said. "It's small-time, anyway."

Lucas shrugged. "I can ask, I can't promise. There's no way anybody's gonna deal on the kid-porn stuff."

"Yeah, I know."

"So long as you know it's not part of the deal. And you tell Ware: If he bullshits us, we'll stick the coke charge right down his throat, along with everything else. If we push the little girl we picked up harder, I think we can get a few more names. I think we can bring in a few more kids who'll say that Ware feeds them cocaine in exchange for sex and pictures."

"So I'll talk to Morrie," Baxter said. He looked at his watch. "He's downstairs, getting his clothes."

"Gotta be quick. Like this morning. Like right now. We've got big problems with the Aronson thing."

"Maybe it's worth more than you're offering?"

Lucas shook his head. "Nah. It's unlikely that he can

give us *anything*. He's just a shot in the dark. You better settle for talking down the coke charge."

They chatted for another minute, then Lucas headed back to his office, and thought about skinny blond men killing skinny blond women.

Marcy said, "I talked to that artist. He sounds sorta . . . funky." In Marcy's vocabulary, "funky" was usually desirable. "He said he could stop by this afternoon."

"Excellent."

"What're you doing? Just gonna wait for Ware?"

"Yeah, and read the file that the Menomonie guy brought in. Maybe there's something in it."

Going through the file from Menomonie, Lucas began making a list. The three missing women all had several things in common with Aronson. They were all blondes, all in their twenties, all three had some involvement with art—and specifically, he decided, painting. All three in the Menomonie files had taken art classes shortly before their deaths. There were no classes listed in Aronson's file, but since she was young and in the arts, she almost certainly had taken some not long before. All of them, he thought, either lived in, or recently had lived in, small towns. But the small towns were scattered all over the place, and might not mean anything except that small-town women were a little more vulnerable than big-city kids. And it might not even mean that.

His list:

• Look at art teachers at the schools they attended; check for criminal records involving sex.

• If the teachers don't pan out, get class lists and look at students.

• Go back ten years, look for small blondes reported

as missing anywhere in southeastern Minnesota or western Wisconsin.

What about the drawings? The guy who killed Aronson, if he was the same guy who did the drawings, seemed to be under some compulsion to draw the women. There were no drawings listed in the Menomonie files . . . but that didn't mean there weren't any. He may have retrieved them after he killed the women.

He was still going through the file, page by page, when Marcy stuck her head in the door and said, "Ware's attorney called. They don't want to talk until they get the deal on paper from the county attorney. That's going on now, and they'll be over as soon as they're done."

"All right."

He went back to the file, and when he looked up again, out through the office window, he saw Marcy talking to a man in a scarlet ski jacket and faded jeans. The man had broad shoulders, like a gymnast's, and a nose that looked like it'd been hit once or twice too often. He was an inch or two shorter than Lucas, but Lucas thought that he might have a couple extra pounds of muscle.

Lucas recognized him from somewhere, a long time ago. As he watched, the man parked a hip on Marcy's desk, grinned, leaned over and said something to her, and she laughed. The artist? He walked over to the door.

"This is Mr. Kidd," Marcy said when Lucas stuck his head out of his office. "I was just coming to get you."

"I saw you dashing for my door," Lucas said dryly. He and Kidd shook hands, and Lucas said, "I know you from somewhere, a long time ago."

Kidd nodded. "We were at the university at the same time. You were a hockey jock."

Lucas snapped his fingers. "You were the wrestler. You

pushed Sheets's head through the railings in the field house, and they had to call the fire department to get him out."

"He was an asshole," Kidd said.

"What kind of asshole?" Marcy asked.

"He was gay and predatory," Kidd said. "He was pushing a kid from upstate who sorta leaned that way but didn't lean toward Sheets. I warned him once." To Lucas: "I'm amazed you remember."

"Who was he? Sheets?" Marcy asked. Lucas noticed that she was looking at Kidd with a peculiar intensity.

"Assistant wrestling coach," Lucas and Kidd said at the same time.

"They kick you out?" Marcy asked Kidd.

"Not right away," Kidd said. "The NC-Double-A's were coming. When those were over, they pulled my scholarship and told me to go piss up a rope."

"You were everybody's hero for a while," Lucas said. Kidd said, "Glory days," and Lucas said, "Thanks for coming over."

"Marcy told me about the drawings," Kidd said. "We were just going to take a look. . . ."

"So let's look."

KIDD handled the drawings carefully, Lucas noticed, like real artworks; stopped once to rub the paper between his fingers. He laid them out one at a time on a conference table, taking his time. Twice he said, "Huh," and once he tapped a drawing with his index finger, indicating something about an oversized foot.

"What?" Marcy asked.

"The foot's wrong," Kidd said absently.

Lucas watched him examine the drawings, and finally, impatiently, asked, "What do you think?"

"He wants to go back to the womb," Kidd said.

"Any womb," Marcy said, adding, "Somebody said that in a movie."

Kidd looked up at Lucas. "Marcy told me about the FBI profile—that he's between twenty-five and forty and has a formal arts education. How many thousands of people would that include?"

"Too many to count," Lucas said. He asked again, "What do you think?"

Kidd didn't reply immediately, but instead turned over three of the sheets and looked at them again. Finally, he said, "He's a porno freak."

"That's a keen observation," Marcy said. "I'll write that down in my Big Book o' Clues."

"I mean a photo-porno freak," Kidd said. "Most of these bodies were drawn from pornographic photographs and the heads were added later. It'd be no problem with a computer program like Photoshop. Kids do it all the time— take the head off a movie star, stick it with a piece of porn, and try to pass it off as a real photograph."

Lucas and Marcy looked at each other, and then Marcy said, "You mean . . . I mean, how, I mean . . ."

"Look at these," Kidd said, unrolling one after the other. "What's one glaringly obvious thing you can tell about the bodies?"

"The drawings are all sorta gross," Lucas said. "They're not like art."

"Actually, some good art is fairly gross," Kidd said. "But that's not what I'm talking about. What I'm talking about is, none of the women have nipples showing."

Marcy said, "Nipples?"

"God, I love the way you said that," Kidd said, glancing down at her.

Lucas said, "Ah, Jesus," and Marcy nailed Kidd with an elbow. "Just tell me."

Kidd said, "If you're an artist, especially an artist who does a lot of nudes—"

"Do you do a lot of nudes?" Marcy asked.

"No, I do landscapes mostly. I make exceptions sometimes." Again, the quick grin. "Anyway, if you do a lot of life drawing, and if you have the technical background, you can pretty much look at anyone and draw that person nude." He looked at Marcy. "I can look at you, and I can see your shoulders and the shape of your breasts and the width of your hips, and since I know all those parts, I could do a pretty good drawing. But I couldn't know about the aureoles around your nipples, or the—"

"The what?" Marcy asked. Lucas thought she might have turned a little pink, and suppressed a smile.

"The aureole. I wouldn't know how big and distinct it was. I wouldn't know whether your nipples protrude or how big they are. With a guy, I couldn't tell how long his penis is or whether he's circumcised. Or how hairy his chest is . . . This guy probably didn't put in nipples because if he'd put in protruding nipples and the woman didn't have that kind of nipple, then it would obviously be a fake. But maybe he didn't think of toes. There are two or three places where you can see lots of toes, which are really pretty distinctive, though nobody looks at them. If I were you, I'd get these women in here and look at their feet."

"Ah . . . I see what you mean," Lucas said. He shuffled through the drawings. "None of these drawings—"

"None of them have the kind of specifics that individualize the body. That's especially striking since the faces are so individual," Kidd said. "I think the guy never really saw these women nude."

"So he's a photographer? He draws from photographs?" Marcy asked.

"I think he's an artist, but he's using photography. A straight photographer wouldn't draw this well," Kidd said.

"How hard would it be?"

"Not hard. You can take a photograph of somebody, scan it, find a porno shot on the 'Net—there are literally thousands of them, all ages and sizes and shapes and positions—and match them. Then you can eliminate the photographic detail using a Photoshop filter and produce something that almost looks like a drawing. Then you can project that image on a piece of paper, and draw over the projected image. It takes some skill. The FBI is right: This guy has had some training, I think. But not too much. That foot . . ."

He shuffled through the drawings until he found the one with a foot that looked wrong. "What's happened here is, the bodies extend away from you, so this woman's foot is relatively larger than the rest of her body. It's called foreshortening. I'm not sure, but I think that not only is the foot foreshortened, it's also distorted, and it's distorted in the way that things are when you use a wide-angle lens. If you use a wide-angle camera lens from up close, things at the edge of the picture are unnaturally wide. . . . This looks like a photographed foot to me."

"The woman who was killed did commercial art and design—ads and stuff," Marcy said. "We thought maybe somebody she met in the business."

"Uh." Kidd looked at the stack of drawings, then shook his head. "I don't think he's a commercial artist. If he took art classes, they'd be in fine art."

"What's the difference?"

"It's subtle. Commercial artists learn a lot of shortcuts, shorthand ways of doing things—they're paid to produce recognizable images, and to do it quickly. They're not struggling to get down something that's unique. These drawings look like the guy was trying pretty hard, and he really doesn't show any of the bag of tricks that a commercial artist has. When he doesn't get the noses right, he doesn't cheat by doing a shorthand nose, he fights it. He tries to get it right."

"So an artist."

"Not a very good one," Kidd said. "He doesn't know the anatomy that well. There are a couple of places where you've got an image that might come off a photograph." He went through the drawings again and found one with a woman who had one arm extended over her head. "See this one? There's no feeling of a joint where her shoulder is. It's just a silhouette like you might get from a photo, but it's an awkward one."

They talked for a few more minutes, working through the photos, and Kidd picked out two with fairly distinctive big toes. "Check these. I'd be willing to bet they don't match."

Jeff Baxter stepped into the office; Morris Ware trailed behind, looking stunned. Lucas looked past Kidd and said, "This is the right place."

"You've seen the paper from the county attorney?" Baxter asked.

"Not yet."

"If you say okay, they'll drop the coke charge. Morrie gives you full cooperation on anything he knows about the local sex scene that doesn't impinge on his current case."

Lucas nodded. "That's fine with me. Why don't you go into my office, and I'll bring another guy back to talk to you." He gestured to his office. "Right in there. We'll just be a minute."

Kidd was collecting his jacket, and Lucas said, "Thanks for coming. You told us more about the killer in ten minutes than the feds did in two days."

"Yet another reason to eat the FBI," Kidd said. And to

Marcy: "Speaking of eating, isn't there a cafeteria around here someplace? I don't know Minneapolis very well."

"Yeah, but the food is not exactly gourmet," she said.

"Better a cafeteria than starve to death."

"I could probably show you a better place," she offered.

Lucas thought Kidd's eyelids may have dropped a tenth of an inch as he said, "That'd be good."

"The guy comes over to catch a killer and winds up hustling my staff," Lucas said, bending his head back to talk to the ceiling.

"With a staff like this . . ." Kidd said.

"Yeah, yeah, yeah."

KIDD and Marcy left together—Kidd was asking, "Can I touch your gun?"—and Lucas, shaking his head at the ways of singles sex, called Sloan and asked him to come over. "We got that porno guy I was telling you about. He's gonna converse."

"I'll bring the tape deck," Sloan said.

Sloan was a narrow-faced man who tended to dress in shades of gray and brown, and always had, from his first day in plainclothes. He was one of Lucas's best friends, and for years had never seemed to change. But Lucas had noticed in the past few months that Sloan's hair was swiftly going white. Like most cops, Sloan had always been a little salt-and-pepper, but over the winter he'd gotten perceptibly older. The white seemed to emphasize the lines of his face and the narrowness of his stature. And the last time they'd talked, Sloan had remarked that he'd be eligible to retire in a couple of years.

Getting old.

Lucas stood in his office door, chatting with Baxter, while Ware slumped on a chair and picked at his cuticles.

He'd also aged after the long night in the lockup. Yesterday, his gray-on-black shirt and jacket had looked arty; today they looked drab. Then Sloan banged into the office and asked, cheerfully, "Everybody ready?"

Lucas nodded, and Sloan dragged an extra chair into the office, plugged in the tape deck, checked the cassette, and then recited everybody's names and the date, looked at Ware, and said, "Looks like you had a pretty bad night."

"Ahhhh," Ware said in disgust.

"It's a problem when somebody comes in late," Sloan said. "The courts just won't move themselves around to have round-the-clock bail hearings."

"I think it's absurd. You're supposed to be treated as if you're innocent until proven guilty."

"No," Sloan said. "You *are* innocent until proven guilty."

"That's right, that's right."

Baxter looked at Lucas and rolled his eyes. They both knew what Sloan was doing—he was getting on Ware's side. "Why don't you ask a question," Baxter said to Sloan. "We can have the blood-brother ceremony later."

Morris Ware listened to the story of the drawings, then looked at the drawings. "Very nice," he said, but he said it with a bored tone that sounded genuine.

"What?" Lucas asked. "They're not to your taste?"

"No, they are not," Ware said.

"You like the young stuff," Lucas suggested.

"I am not interested in bodies," Ware said. "I am interested in *qualities*—innocence, freshness, dawning awareness . . ."

"Let's cut the horseshit, Morrie," Lucas said. "Look at this guy."

Ware took the printed-out photo of the actor from *Day of the Jackal.* "Yes?"

"Who do you know in the sex-freak community who

looks like this—a guy with connection to the arts, who knows about computers and photography, is interested in blond women, who might like to *strangle* them?"

Ware looked over the photo at Lucas. "If I knew, it'd be worth a lot more than dropping this stupid cocaine charge."

"On the other hand, if you know and don't tell us, and we find out—that's accessory to first-degree murder. When a known child pornographer is charged with murder, sometimes the juries aren't too fussy about how strong the evidence is," Lucas said.

"I'm not— Fuck you."

Sloan eased in: the good guy. "Take it easy, Lucas, we want the guy to cooperate."

"Dickweed says he's not a pornographer," Lucas snapped.

Sloan held up a hand, then looked at Ware. "Let's forget the pornography stuff. Who do you know? That's the question."

Ware looked down at the photo again, then back at Sloan. "You know, this is a fashionable look among the art crowd—that languid, ascot-wearing, private-school look."

"So you know some people?"

"I could give you five or six names of people, um, in the art community who, um, also have an interest in nonconventional sexuality."

"Great," Sloan said.

"But I don't think any of them will be your man," he said.

"Why not?" Sloan had the ability to project eagerness for an answer.

Ware closed his eyes and tilted his head back. "Because I think I met your man. At a photography show at the Institute."

"The Institute of Art," Sloan said.

Ware nodded without opening his eyes. "But it was a long time ago—ten years, maybe. The fellow was maybe twenty-five, and he was looking at a series of nudes by Edward Weston. I can sometimes tell by the way people look at . . . pictures . . . that they are enthusiasts. He had the look—and by the way, he doesn't so much *look* like the man in your photograph as much as he shares an *air* with him."

"What'd he say?"

"He talked about how Weston did photographs that were as clean as fine drawings. He took a pencil from his pocket and used the eraser end to show how you could follow the line of the nude to make a whole new creation. There was a certain *frenzy* to it."

Sloan glanced at Lucas, then at Ware. "That's interesting. Do you remember his name, have you seen him since, know where he works, or what he does?"

Ware opened his eyes and looked at Lucas. "I never knew his name. I can't remember seeing him since that day. I don't know where he works. It was all too long ago. . . . But one thing struck me, given his enthusiasm. I don't know what it was, but something he said made me think that he was a priest. Or studying to be a priest, or something."

"Really?" Sloan's eyebrows went up.

"Something he said made me think he might be a priest," Ware said.

"A priest?"

"That's the only reason that it all stuck with me: He was a priest, and his *enthusiasm* was so clear."

"He was wearing a collar?"

"No, nothing like that. But if you were a priest and you were going to an exhibit of nudes . . . maybe you wouldn't wear the collar."

Sloan ticked it off on his fingers. "So he was an enthusiast, he had a *frenzy* about him, he compared the nudes to drawings . . ."

"One other thing. He was so obviously an enthusiast—and perhaps he saw it in me—that we walked along for a bit, looking at the photographs and talking, and I said something about women being endlessly fascinating. He shook his head and he said, 'Not endlessly. Not endlessly.' He looked at me, and I was a little frightened. Really—frightened."

Lucas said, interested, "Huh. In the middle of the day, in the museum, you were frightened."

"Yeah." Ware nodded. "Years ago, back in the eighties, there were rumors of Mexican snuff flicks. You know, some woman gets hauled into a warehouse, is raped and beaten, and then she's killed on camera. There were even a few flicks offered around, for collectors of that kind of thing. Pretty bad fakes, for the most part. But occasionally, you'd get somebody looking for one. Sometimes they were cops, sometimes they were reporters, sometimes they were curiosity seekers. Sometimes they were people who scared you. People who *really wanted* a snuff flick. I got a whiff of that from the priest."

"But you don't really know that he was a priest," Sloan said.

"Something he said . . ."

On another topic: "Have you ever seen anything like these drawings on the Internet?"

"Not really. Porn guys like photographs. They like specifics: You show them a clitoris the size of a chili pepper, they want you to blow it up as big as a zucchini. And they always want better color and better resolution. . . . They're crazy."

"Have you seen photographs that look like the bodies in these drawings?"

"Well, sure, the drawings . . . those are all pretty standard poses," he said.

"I mean specifically: photos that could have been used for these drawings."

Ware shook his head. "I couldn't tell you that. I'm not out on the Internet that much. You oughta ask Tony Carr."

Carr was the computer tech who'd been at Ware's when the door was kicked. "What about him?" Sloan asked.

"He knows all the sites. What he does is, he loots them, then he burns the images onto CDs and peddles the CDs. He's basically interested in money, not the porn, but he knows about every site out there."

"How about Henrey?" Lucas asked.

"He's just a hired gun. He's not particularly creative, and he's no good with lights—not good enough for product photography or anything hard, anyway. He can do boudoir stuff okay."

"So he's not much."

Ware shook his head. "He's a dummy."

MARCY had returned during the interrogation, and was at her desk when Lucas and Sloan finished with Ware. Lucas told Baxter that they might need to talk again; Baxter agreed, and escorted Ware out of the office. Sloan said he'd get back with a transcript for the file; he scrubbed Marcy's head with his knuckles, and left.

"Get anything?" Marcy asked.

"We need to talk to Anthony Carr again. You'll find him in the Ware file. Call him up and tell him to come in."

"All right. . . . Tomorrow?"

"Yeah, it's gonna have to be tomorrow. We're running out of time today. How was your lunch with Kidd?"

Marcy looked up at him, thinking, and then her eyes drifted past to a blank wall. After a couple of seconds, she nodded: "He's a pretty good guy. He's a hardass, though. He's one of those guys who's gonna do what he's gonna do and he doesn't care much about what anybody else thinks about it. He's a lot more of a hardass than you are."

"He's supposed to be a good painter."

"I called up a woman I know. Over at the Institute. She said Kidd paints six or eight paintings a year and gets maybe fifty thousand bucks each. He's in all the big museums. She asked me if I was going out with him and I said we'd been to lunch, and she sounded like she wanted to crawl through the phone and choke me. I think in that world, you know, the guy is *eligible.*"

Lucas said, "Huh. You gonna see him again?"

"I wouldn't be surprised. He kinda liked me."

"Did you let him touch your gun?"

"Not yet."

LUCAS took the Menomonie files home with him, meaning to look through them during the evening. Weather arrived a few minutes after he did, and they went for a walk along the river, enjoying the cold. Then they walked back to Lucas's house and ate small triangular sandwiches of cheese, onions, and sardines, with tomato-herb soup, at the dining room table. He told her about Jim Wise, the bullet-headed man who was not the killer; about Ware and his priest; and about Kidd.

"You think Marcy and this Kidd guy . . . ?"

"She likes the type," Lucas said. Then he asked, "How can a sandwich that stinks this bad taste so good?"

"It's a great mystery," Weather said. "So is Kidd a good-looking guy?"

"Not as good-looking as me."

"We could hardly expect that," she said.

"But . . . I don't know. Not bad-looking. Sort of beat-up. Big shoulders: Looks like he could pick you up, put you over his shoulder, and carry you right up to his nest in the tree. I suspect he gets laid a lot."

"Hmm. I'm feeling a little tingle myself," Weather said.

"Marcy did, for sure," Lucas said. He looked over his empty plate at hers. "You gonna eat that triangle?"

WEATHER helped him with the dishes, and afterward, they hiked a mile to a used-book store and hauled a dozen books back. While Weather paged through a book on human osteology, Lucas went back to the file from Menomonie. At the back, there were Xerox copies of perhaps thirty or forty photographs. Most of them were police photos taken in Laura Winton's apartment or in Nancy Vanderpost's trailer home by crime-scene crews. One set was mostly of a young woman, identified in notes as Winton, Marshall's niece. She was shown walking in the woods, and then standing on a sidewalk somewhere. There was a gap in the trees behind her, and Lucas thought it looked a lot like the Mississippi River Valley between Minneapolis and St. Paul, but there were no identifying landmarks, only a small semicircular stone wall.

He handed the photo to Weather. "Think that's around here?"

She looked at it for a long moment, then said, "Could be. Who is it?"

He explained, and she said, "Then it might be in Menomonie. There's a river and a big lake there, pretty deep valley. . . . Could be there."

"Feels like here."

He had to page back through the file to find the spot where he'd taken the photo out, and there was something about the pictures taken in the woods. Were the woods close by? Maybe they went with the stone wall photo, something that he walked by often enough to ring a bell. . . .

He paged through them again. Then he tumbled: "Holy shit."

Weather looked up, hearing a tone in his voice. "What?"

"These pictures . . . they look like the place where Aronson's body was found."

"What?"

"These pictures of Winton. They look like they're taken where Aronson was found. I went down there the other day." He went through them again. "Goddamnit, Weather, I think it's the same place."

MARSHALL might know something.

Lucas looked at his watch: twenty minutes to eleven. Still early enough. He went back through the file and found Marshall's business card, with a home phone number scrawled on the back. Marshall had said to call anytime.

He dialed, and the phone rang four times before a man answered, a harsh rasping cigarette voice, thick with sleep. " 'Lo?"

"Terry Marshall?"

"Yeah . . . who's this?"

"Terry, I apologize for calling you at this time of night, but this is Lucas Davenport, the deputy chief you talked to."

"Yeah, Chief, what's going on?"

"I've been reading your files, looking at the pictures in the back. Those pictures of your niece in the woods, where did those come from?"

"Just a minute, let me get my feet on the floor. . . . Uh, the pictures. We think, uh . . . *I* think that they might have been taken by the killer. When she came up missing, and the story got in the papers, the owner of a local drugstore called and said she'd left some film to be developed. We picked it up and got those pictures—her housemates said she'd gone on a hike with the guy, had been talking about a hike out in the woods. What's going on?"

"You don't know where this is?" Lucas asked.

"No, no, it's just woods."

"I'll tell you what, Terry, I may be going crazy, but I think these pictures were taken at the same spot that Aronson's body was found. There's something about them. The way the hill sits, the trees. I may be fucked up . . ."

A long moment of silence, then: "Oh, brother. I never went down to the site. I went to New Richmond, but not to the others."

"Think about this," Lucas said. "If you're a killer, and if you find one good spot, why go looking for another one?"

"A graveyard," Marshall said.

"That's what I'm thinking," Lucas said.

"You gonna look?" Marshall asked.

"I'll get something started as soon as I get in tomorrow."

"I'm coming up," Marshall said.

"No point in coming up tomorrow. I'll have to talk to the sheriff down in Goodhue and get some technical guys together. I don't see us getting down there until the day after tomorrow, at the earliest."

"I'll be there. Jesus. Jesus. Why didn't I look at that site? I looked at everything else. . . ."

"It's your file, man. Never would have come up without your file."

9

WEATHER LEFT EARLY the next morning, as she always did, driving out through a cold rain. Lucas thought early-morning operations were crazy—why get everybody up at five-thirty?—and was told that it had to do with nursing shifts. When she was gone, he cleaned up, got in the Tahoe, and drove south out of town to the hill where Aronson had been found.

He learned nothing. He walked the hillside in his rain suit, stood for a long time looking at the hole where Aronson had been found, but could find nothing else about the hillside distinctive enough to be sure.

"Feels right, though," he said to himself. He looked around. A graveyard? He felt a chill, and kept moving.

DOWNTOWN, the office was full of cops who didn't want to go out in the rain. Lucas had changed his rain suit for an umbrella, and was shaking it out when Anthony Carr, Ware's computer programmer, came by and took a look at the drawings. Marcy tried to embarrass him, but Carr wasn't embarrassed.

"I see so much of this shit that I can't remember what goes with who," he said. "*All* of it looks familiar."

"We have an art expert who says the drawings are probably made from projected images," Marcy said. "So the bodies would be *exactly* like the drawings. We'd like you to check around, see if you can match any of them."

Carr shrugged. "All right, I'll look. I can't promise. One time I tried to figure out how many of these pictures are out there, but I gave up after a while—but there gotta be hundreds of thousands of them."

WHEN he was gone, Lucas turned to Marcy and said, "Kidd ever call back?"

"Like it's any of your business," Marcy said.

"Please tell us," said Black, her former partner. Black had given up any effort at work, and was punching a lemon-colored Gameboy console with his thumbs. "If you don't, we'll start rumors that it was Carr who caught your eye."

"Asshole," Marcy said. To Lucas: "He did. We agreed that it might not be a bad idea to have dinner sometime."

"So it's a little indefinite," Lucas said.

"If you want to call getting picked up at seven o'clock tonight indefinite," she said.

"Be nice if the rain stopped. You know, big date and all," Lucas said.

"We can always find a place to get warm," she said.

He never won.

* * *

LUCAS talked to the Goodhue County sheriff. He promised he'd get permission to enter the property around the Aronson grave site.

"It's probably nothing," Lucas said. "But if it is something . . . it's gonna be ugly."

"Glad you called."

When he'd set up a rendezvous by the Goodhue grave site, Lucas called around until he found an engineering consultant who used ground-penetrating radar to look for pipelines, missing utilities, old cemeteries, and ancient campgrounds. The guy's name was Larry Lake, and he ran a three-man company called Archeo-Survey, Inc.

"Last time I worked for you guys, it took two months to get paid," Lake said. "I had to threaten to have your patrol cars attached."

"That's 'cause you didn't find anything and nobody wanted to be blamed for the bill when you didn't find anything. It was a pretty big bill."

"I'm a certified civil engineer, not a burger flipper," Lake said. "If I bring fifteen thousand or twenty thousand bucks' worth of equipment out in the rain, I need to get paid."

"I promise you," Lucas said. "You'll get the money in a week. If it pans out, of course, you'll be famous. Probably get on one of those forensic TV shows."

"You think?"

"It could happen."

THAT evening, Weather showed up with a big black leather Coach travel bag for her sixth consecutive sleepover. Lucas dropped *The Wall Street Journal* on the floor next to his chair and said, "I've figured it out. You hate me and you're trying to fuck me to death."

"In your dreams," she said. "The fact is, I'm gonna get

pregnant. You volunteered. The second fact is, I'm right around my fertile period and I'm trying to blanket it."

"Blanket it."

"Yes. So if you don't mind, bring yourself back to the bedroom. It'll all be over in a few minutes."

THE rain continued overnight, spitting against the windows, but by morning had changed from a steady pelting storm to a steady miserable drizzle. Weather left early, as usual, and Lucas got another hour of sleep before he climbed out of bed, cleaned up, and rolled out of the driveway in his Tahoe.

Del was waiting in his driveway, under the eaves of the garage, already dressed in a rain suit. His wife stood beside him, wearing a heavy sweater. "You guys be careful," she said. "The roads are slippery. Get some decent lunch somewhere. Eat something with vegetables, like a salad or something."

In the truck, Del said, "Jesus Christ—vegetables."

The drive to south Dakota County took forty-five minutes, a slow trip against rush traffic, "Money, Guns, and Lawyers" bumping out of the CD player, the wipers beating time. The roadside ditches were showing long strips of water, and Del told a story about a Caterpillar D-6 that once sank out of sight, was never recovered, and was presumably on its way to China after encountering a bog in weather just like this.

When they arrived, they found a green Subaru Forester parked on the shoulder of the road, with a magnetic door-sign that said Archeo-Survey, Inc. Just beyond were three sheriff's cars and a battered Jeep Cherokee. One of the cars had its light bar flashing out a slow-down warning. A half-dozen men in slickers turned to look at them as they pulled off the road.

"Cop convention," Del grunted.

Lucas parked, got out of the truck, walked around to the back, lifted the hatch, found his rain suit, and pulled it on. Del waited until he'd pulled the hood tight around his face, then they walked down the road to introduce themselves to the others.

"Don Hammond, chief deputy down here," said the largest of the cops. "These guys are Rick and Dave. You know Terry Marshall." Marshall nodded at Lucas; little flecks of rain speckled his steel-rimmed glasses, and he looked tough as a chunk of hickory. Hammond continued: "The sheriff'll stop out later. You sure picked a good morning for it."

"It's all I had," Lucas said. They all looked up at the sky, then Lucas asked, "Where's the radar guy?"

"He's up in the woods with his helper," Hammond said. "They're setting up reference points. We were waiting for you."

"What do you think? Bunch of bodies?" asked the deputy named Dave.

"I can't take the chance," Lucas said. "I'd say it's about one in ten."

"Good. We got, like, two shovels, and I got an idea who'd be using them."

"LARRY Lake?" Lucas asked. He was struggling up the steep hillside, slipping on the oak leaves, Del, Hammond, and Marshall trailing behind.

"That's me." Lake was a lanky man with an uncontrolled beard and aviator-style glasses. He wore a red sailing-style rain suit with green Day-Glo flashes on the backs and shoulders. His face was wind-tanned, and two pale blue eyes peered out from behind the glasses. He was standing beside a yellow metal box on a tripod, which was set up over Aronson's grave. As Lucas came up, he saw that the metal box housed a lens. "Are you Davenport?"

"Yeah."

"I better get paid. This is miserable."

"Yeah, yeah, yeah. How long is it gonna take?"

"I got my guy over there setting up the last of the reference pins, so we'll start the survey in ten minutes or so. I'm gonna get a cup of coffee first."

"How long is it gonna take after that?"

Lake shrugged. "Depends on how much you want surveyed. We could show you some of it in a couple of hours, a lot more this evening, more tomorrow . . . whatever you want. We could do the whole hill in about three days. We're using this grave as a center point. . . ." He touched his ear, and Lucas realized that what looked like a plastic tab near his mouth was actually a microphone. Lake, talking to the mike, said, "Yeah, Bill. Yeah, the cops came up. Just a sec." To Lucas and the others: "This'll take a second, then we'll go some coffee."

He looked through the lens on the survey instrument, sideways across the hill to where Bill was holding a red and white survey rod with a knob on top. Lake said, "Two forward, a half left. A half forward, one inch right. Two inches back, one half inch right. You're good—put in a pin. Yeah. Yup. Down at the truck."

AT the truck, Lake's assistant got a gallon thermos out of the Subaru and started pouring coffee into paper cups, as Lake explained what he'd been doing. "We set up four control points around the center, which is at Aronson's grave, so we've got a big rectangle laid out on the hillside. The next thing is, we stretch lines from the pins at the top of the hill to the pins at the bottom. Those lines are marked at one-meter intervals. Then we stretch another string across the hill, between the vertical lines, as a guide. We'll walk back and forth with the radar, along the string, and move down the hill one meter with every sweep. We can probably get you a fifty-meter-square block in about two hours."

"If there's a grave, how do you find it later?" asked Del.

"Our computer'll actually generate a map, to scale," Lake said. "If we find a possible site fifteen yards north and five yards east, it'll show on the computer plot, and then I'll just use the total station—"

"The total station's the box on the tripod," one of the deputies said.

"—I'll just use the total station to spot the center of the suspected site, and you guys—not me—start digging."

"How accurate is it?" Lucas asked.

"At that distance?" Lake looked up the hill. "A couple thousandths of an inch."

THE work was even more miserable than it looked. Lucas and Del, alternating with Hammond and Marshall, stretched a long piece of yellow string between the corresponding one-meter markers on the vertical strings of the survey box, so it resembled the letter *H*. The cross string had to go around trees, got caught in branches; whenever it got tangled, whoever went to untangle it inevitably slipped on the sodden leaves and slid in the mud down the hill.

Lake, in the meantime, walked back and forth across the hillside, straddling the yellow string, with two boxlike radar units hanging down from one shoulder. After the cops figured out the routine, the work went quickly, except for the falls. An hour into it, Lucas noticed that neither Lake nor his assistant ever fell down.

"How come?" Lucas asked.

"We're wearing golf shoes," Lake said. He picked up his feet to show Lucas the spikes.

"You've done this before," Del said.

"Once or twice," Lake said.

LAKE had expected some results in two hours, but the rain, the falls, the jumble of trees stretched the two hours into three. When they'd run the last line between the bottom points of the survey box, Lake said, "Let's throw the gear into the truck and run into town. Find a café."

"How long will it take you to process?" Lucas asked.

"We'll dump the information into the computer on the way into town. We'll pull up some preliminary results right there."

They went to the High Street Café in Cannon Falls, took over the round booth by the window, and dragged some chairs around the open side. A half-dozen coffee drinkers sat down the length of the breakfast bar, farmers waiting out the rain. They made no attempt not to stare as Lake produced a fifty-foot extension cord, got a waitress to plug it in, and started the computer. "Data looked pretty good going in," Lake muttered. "It's not like we came up dry."

"Can you actually see bodies?" asked Marshall.

"No, no. Nothing like that. What we see are soil changes. They'll look like grave shapes."

"Trouble is," his assistant chipped in, "sometimes you see a lot of grave shapes, especially in the woods like that. If a tree tipped over fifty years ago, and its roots pulled up a hole in the ground, the radar'll see it."

Lucas looked at the screen. One word: *Processing.*

They all ordered pie and coffee, and Del leaned over and said, "Still processing."

"Takes a while," Lake said. He said that two months before, he'd been in North Dakota looking for a graveyard that was about to be flooded by a dam. "They knew pretty close where it was, but they thought it was a family thing. Five or six graves. Turned out that there were a hundred and seventy graves in there. They were pretty unhappy. They had like X number of dollars budgeted for moving graves, and they had to come up with like twenty X. People get pretty cranked up about moving Granddaddy's bones. On the screens, the graves looked like holes in one of those old IBM punch cards."

As he said it, the screen blinked: *Processing Complete.*

"Here we go," Lucas said.

Lake pushed his pie away, pulled the laptop closer, tapped a few keys, and a new message came up: *Generating Plot.* The new message lasted only a few seconds, then changed to *Plot Complete.* Lake tapped a few more keys, muttered, "There's Aronson's grave, that's the midpoint. Let's go up to the Number One point and scan east."

He manipulated the built-in pointing stick on the keyboard and began scrolling. "There's one," he said after a few seconds.

"A grave?" Lucas asked. He could see the deeper gray-shaded form on the plot.

"Don't know," Lake said. "Looks pretty small. This is all to scale, and it's less than a meter across."

"Pretty round, too," his assistant said.

They were all pressing in behind Lake now, watching the screen, which was showing a flat field composed of various shades of gray. The possible graves showed up as a darker gray in the background. They scanned across the hillside, then back, and across again, moving down the field in one-meter increments.

"Another one," Lake said.

"That could be one," his assistant said. "Let's get the co-ordinates."

"Let's just scan the whole thing first," Lake said. "That looked like a tree hole to me."

"There's one," Lucas said.

" 'Nother tree hole," Lake said.

"How can you tell tree holes?" Del asked.

"They got a certain kind of oval shape, egg shape, with the wide part uphill. . . . There's one," Lake said.

Two more scans, then Lake said, "Uh-oh."

"What."

He stopped the scan. "Look at this." He was talking to his assistant. "That looks artificial."

"Just like a grave," his assistant said. "Let me get the co-ordinates on this one."

He jotted the coordinates down, then Lake resumed scanning, stopping only a few meters farther along. "There's another one. . . . No wait, we're at zero, zero."

"What's that?" Lucas asked.

"That's the center point. That's Aronson."

"So the first thing you thought maybe was a grave, that was on this same level?" Lucas asked.

Lake nodded. "Yup. Five meters east."

"Goddamnit," one of the cops said. Marshall humped forward, pressing close to the computer. "A grave looks different from anything else?"

"Yeah. For some reason, people have always made them rectangular, even though the bodies don't go in the ground that way. You can pick them out by the squared corners." Lake manipulated the pointing stick, continued scanning, then stopped again. "Holy ducks, there's another one."

"Grave?"

"It looks artificial," Lake said. He looked at Lucas. "I'll tell you what. You can never tell what's underground, but . . . if that's not a grave, I'll kiss your aunt Sally on the lips."

He found a third, on the same line, a moment later, then

scanned back and found the lower portions of the three possible graves. "They're not only rectangular, they're just about five feet long. Something less than two meters."

"Keep going," Lucas said.

"Ah, look at this," Lake said a moment later. "We've got another one. Let me look at this. . . . Look, it's right between two of the graves above, but one level down. It's plotted out like a graveyard."

In the end, they found two dozen anomalies, including all the tree holes and natural gullies that had refilled with sediment. Six, Lake said, could be graves.

"Better get the sheriff right now," Hammond said. "If these things really are graves, it's gonna be a bad day at black rock."

Lucas looked at Del and said, "Six."

"Maybe they're tree holes."

Lucas looked at Lake, who shook his head. "I'm not saying for sure that they're graves, but they're artificial, and Aronson's grave fits right in the pattern."

THEY went back to the hillside site in a convoy, and within ten minutes, as Lake was setting up his total station, a half-dozen more cars arrived. Sheriff's deputies were scattered around the hillside in yellow rain slickers, four or five of them with shovels. Lake used the total station to guide his assistant across the hillside with the reflector pole. "There," he called. "You're standing on it."

Lucas stepped over to look: just another piece of hillside covered with leaves, with two small tree seedlings sticking out of it. Neither of the trees was bigger in diameter than his index finger. "No hole," he said.

A couple of cops had come over, bringing shovels. "Let us in there," one of them said.

He and the second cop began scraping at the surface,

cleaning away the leaves, and the air was suffused with the scent of wet spring mold. "Scrape it, don't dig down," Hammond said, standing off to the side.

"Take it real slow," Marshall said. "Ain't no hurry now."

Lake spotted the other suspected sites as the cops scraped at the first one, but they held off digging the others to concentrate on the first. Less than six inches down, one of the cops grunted and said, "This is a hole."

"What?" Lucas peered into the muddy gap in the ground. He couldn't see anything but dirt.

"I can feel it," the cop said. He looked at the other cop. "Can you feel the edge of the hole?"

"Right there? It feels . . ."

"That's it," the first cop said. "We're in the hole part here."

Still scraping, they defined the hole. "That looks like nothing more'n a grave," Marshall said to Lucas. Lucas nodded, and a minute later, Marshall stepped off down the hill and pulled a cell phone from his pocket. Lucas looked around the hill. All morning, the cops had been chattering as they took turns working down the hill with the radar set. Now there was nothing but the sound of the shovels and the occasional grunt of the diggers. Del caught his eye and shrugged.

Then: "Wait." One of the cops held out an arm to stop another, then knelt in the hole. "Is that a rock?"

He pulled off his glove and probed the soil with his fingers. A moment later he came up with a white object. "What is it?" Lucas asked, squatting next to the hole. Del moved in beside him, and the cop handed the white thing to Lucas.

Lucas turned it in his hand and looked at Del. "Finger bone," Del said.

"I think," Lucas said. He looked up at Hammond. "We better stop digging, and get the state crime lab down here. We gotta excavate these things an inch at a time."

"Ah, sweet Jesus," Hammond said. "Sweet fuckin' Jesus."

THE drizzle continued. The sheriff showed up and sent two deputies back into town to find some tarps to build tents over the supposed graves. Lake began working on a larger plot. The state crime people showed up at midafternoon and looked at the six sites that Lake had outlined.

The officer in charge, Jack McGrady, had worked with Lucas on another case. "We're gonna get some generators and lights from the highway department. We'll get some more tents up and get at it."

Lucas had shown him the bone in an evidence bag. "The question we all had . . . is it possible that it's not human?"

McGrady held the bag up to the sky, looked at the bone for a few seconds, then handed it back to Lucas. "It's human. A phalange—a little short and squat, so it's probably from a thumb."

"A thumb."

"Probably. Can't tell you what era. . . . Wish you'd picked a better day for this. You know, sunny and cool."

Lucas looked down the hillside and at the cop cars lined up along the gravel road, two at each end, with their light bars flashing. "Sorry," he said, and he was. Then: "What do you mean, 'era'?"

"Bones last a long time. This is kind of a pretty hillside, with a view. Maybe you've turned up a settler graveyard. Just by coincidence."

"I don't think so," Lucas said.

"Neither do I."

LATE in the afternoon, Lucas and Del went back into Cannon Falls, to the café, and ate open-faced turkey sandwiches with mashed potatoes. The café did a steady business, large quiet men in coveralls, coming and going, and smelling of wet wool, mud, and radiator heat.

"Mashed potatoes count as a vegetable?" Del asked.

"Not these," Lucas asked. "These are some kind of petroleum derivative."

They ate in silence for a moment, then, "If those are all graves up there, we've got a busy little bee on our hands," Del said.

"They're all graves," Lucas said. "I can feel it."

"In your bones?"

"Not funny."

"Okay, so we're looking for sources where he might have gotten the bodies for his drawings. If we can find those, maybe we can track back to his computer; we've got a photograph that he might have taken. We have a kind of physical description. We're putting together lists of everybody that all the drawings—what would you call them, victims?—we're putting together lists of everybody they know. What else?"

"Ware thinks he might be a priest."

"That doesn't make any sense," Del said. "A priest who was an art student? In Menomonie? Ware's either jerking us around, or we *really* don't know what's going on."

"But he didn't say for sure that the guy was a priest, just that something he said made Ware think he *might* be a priest."

"That's no help." Del picked up a glob of potato on a spoon and contemplated it. After a minute, he said, "Okay. Answer me this. You know the chick whose picture got pasted up on the bridge across the river?"

"Yeah?"

"Why was she picked out?" Del asked. "What'd she do to piss him off, that he went after her like that? Why was she treated different?"

Lucas leaned back in his chair and said, "Ah, shit. Why didn't we think of that before? Something's gotta be going on there."

"So we start pulling her apart," Del said.

"And maybe we check with the archdiocese, and see if they had any priests who were art students."

"In Menomonie."

A waitress came by with a pot of coffee. She was a pudgy young woman with heavily teased honey-blond hair. "Are you the cops digging up the Harrelsons' woods?"

Del nodded. "Yup."

"We heard you found a whole bunch of skeletons." Her jaw dropped open, waiting for the inside information.

"We don't know what we have," Lucas said politely. "We're still digging."

"That's a lonely place out there," she said. "Sometimes kids used it like, you know, a lover's lane. Park down there at the bottom, then get a blanket and go up on the hill. But it was always spooky."

"Really," Del said. "You ever go up there?"

"Maybe," she said. "And maybe not. You want seconds on them potatas? We got plenty more."

AT six, Lucas called Weather from the site and told her that he wouldn't be home until very late. "Trying to avoid your obligations, eh?" she asked.

"You sound like a fuckin' Canadian, eh?" he said. "Maybe I can get out of here a little earlier than that. . . ."

THE hill was lit by a half-dozen sets of powerful lights, plus lower-powered reading-style lights in an Army-surplus command tent. A diesel generator hammered away from the roadside, and the parking strip smelled like a bus stop.

Each grave had been covered by a broad tarp, and three of the six graves were being excavated by two-man teams; progress was slow, the excavation being done with small Marshalltown trowels. Along the road, three TV trucks were sitting in the rain, their crews warm inside, and un-happy: They would rather have been wet outside, with some close-up tape.

Lake came by just after dark, squatted next to Lucas, and said, "We've finished the next plot, going out another twenty-five meters in every direction, and I think you've got all the graves identified. There are two more spots that we're gonna stake out as possibles, but they're not as clear as the others."

"Good. Six is enough. If it is six."

Lake, with water dripping off the bill of his hat, said, "I'll tell you something, Lucas: You're gonna find bones in every one of those holes."

THE first grave, the one where the finger bone had been found, was the first to produce clothing—a polyester shirt that Marshall recognized as a brand sold at Wal-Mart. Mc-Grady, squatting next to the grave, looked up at Lucas and said, "So it's not a settler site." They went back to the command tent, and Lucas called Rose Marie to give her the news. He was just off the phone when one of the members of the excavation team called, "Jack: we got a skull," and as Lucas and McGrady recrossed the hillside, "And we got hair."

They got to the grave and looked into the hole. The skull looked almost like a piece of a dirty-white coffee cup. The guy in the hole touched the edge of the bone with the tip of his trowel and said, "Looks like blond hair."

McGrady got down on his knees to look, then said, "All right. Go to brushes and art knives. Careful with the hair."

Lucas nodded. "How long to clean out the graves?"

"We'll be working around the clock. We got TV now, so there's gonna be some pressure. These first three, if they're shallow, we'll have by midnight, I think. The rest by tomorrow. You heading out?"

"I'll stick around for the first three," Lucas said. "But we need to get working on the IDs as quick as we can. I've got a name for you, and there's some dental stuff available on her."

"If her jaw's intact, I can give you a quick read tomorrow morning, then," McGrady said.

DEL went back into town and returned with a thermos full of coffee. Lucas was drinking a cup when he saw a large man in a camouflage rain suit join Marshall on the hillside. The two bent together, and the new man put his arm on Marshall's shoulder as they talked; another Dunn County deputy, Lucas thought.

Clothing and bones were coming up in two of the three holes. Lucas had done a tour, spoke briefly with Marshall, looked curiously at the large man with him, but Marshall offered no introductions. Lucas wandered off to the command tent, where Del was talking with a group of coffee-drinking deputies.

"You got your two great families of wine," Del was saying.

"Yeah, yeah, red and white, which lacks something in the way of new information," one of the deputies said.

"I was talking about screw-top and cork," Del said,

"considering pop-top and bottle-cap as variations of the screw-top."

"You're talking about wine again?" Lucas asked. "You're turning into a fuckin' Frenchman."

"Am not. I use deodorant," Del said.

"Like that's gonna last," Lucas said skeptically.

Del turned back to the deputy. "As I was saying before the rude interruption . . ."

"Screw-top and cork, pop-top and bottle-cap," the deputy prompted. Now he was interested.

"Right. So among your screw-tops, you got your three basic families: fruit taste, Kool-Aid taste, and other."

"I think I've had some other," the deputy said. "I was once going through Tifton, Georgia, in a hurry. I was driving this 'sixty-three rose-blush Cadillac—"

Del interrupted. "You wanna hear about wine, or you wanna bullshit?"

"All right, fuck you, I won't tell you what happened."

"Good. Anyway, there's—"

At that moment, an anguished croak slashed across the hillside, the sound of a man who was having his eyes plucked out. The talk stopped cold and they all stepped to the edge of the tent, and Lucas saw the large man and Marshall on their knees next to the third grave. The two cops in the hole were standing up, unmoving, looking at the two men on their knees.

"Jesus Christ," one of the deputies said. "What happened to them?"

Lucas had an idea. He was on his way across the hillside, with Del a step behind. As they stepped into the harsh glare of the light, Lucas looked into the hole and saw a piece of reddish cloth. Terry Marshall put one hand on the shoulder of the large man and pushed himself back onto his feet. "It's Laura's shirt. We think it's the shirt she was wearing."

"It is." The large man sobbed. He had both hands to the sides of his head, as if he were holding it in place. "We hoped, we hoped . . ."

"Jack Winton. Laura's dad," Marshall said unapologetically.

Lucas was struck with a surge of anger. "Why'n the hell did you . . ."

"I couldn't keep him off; didn't even try," Marshall said. "He's family."

"Ah, jeez," Lucas said. "This . . ."

"This sucks," Marshall said. He patted the big man on the shoulder again. "Jack. Come on. Let 'em do their work. Come on."

LUCAS and Del left the site ten minutes later. With three graves producing bodies, there was little doubt that the others would, too. On the way back, Del said, "You getting pissed yet?"

"Getting closer to it," Lucas said. "Especially after that thing with Winton."

"Marshall should never have brought him."

"He's family. They're all family, and he couldn't say no," Lucas said.

"Yeah. . . . It's a good sign that you're getting pissed. Focuses the mind."

"I guess." They drove on a little way, listening to the heater, and then Lucas said, "I just hope it doesn't spill over on Weather."

"She knows what you do for a living," Del said. "I think it was just that one thing that fucked her up, when she was right in the middle of it. She's a good guy. I'm happy you're back together."

* * *

WEATHER was still awake, reading a Barbara Kingsolver novel. Lucas had hung his rain suit from a nail in the garage, kissed her on the forehead, and said, "I'm gonna get some soup."

"Guy called—a McGrady? He gave me a cell phone number, said you should call him when you got back."

"All right." Lucas got a can of soup out of the cupboard, dumped it in a microwave-safe bowl, stretched some cling wrap over the bowl, and stuck it in the microwave for two minutes. Then he dialed McGrady's cell phone; McGrady answered on the first ring.

"You know that first skull we pulled out of the ground?"

"Yeah?"

"We're down to the skeletal bones and so on. First of all, it's definitely a female. And we found the hyoid. It's in two pieces, and the break looks like it happened at the time of death. It's not a new break."

"So she was strangled."

"I'll let the medical examiner figure it out, but I'd bet on it," McGrady said.

"Check the others, if you find more."

"We're gonna find more," McGrady said. "We've got two more skulls coming up now."

LUCAS got the soup out of the microwave, stirred it, stuck it back in for another two minutes, and called Rose Marie to fill her in. He told her about Marshall, and she said, "You better keep an eye on him."

"Yeah. But it's his case, in a way. He put the file together."

"Sounds like he might be a little bit of a loose cannon, though," she said. "He can watch, but keep him out of trouble."

* * *

HE repeated the story to Weather as he was eating the soup. She dragged a chair around to sit behind him, and put an arm on his shoulder. "You look . . . forlorn."

"You should've heard that guy," Lucas said. "He sounded like somebody was . . . torturing him. Plucking his eyeballs out or something."

"Breaking his heart," Weather said.

They stayed up talking, since Weather wasn't scheduled to operate the next morning; talked about Marshall, about the killer, about the graveyard in the rain. Sat close together; eventually found their way back to the bedroom. Making a baby, Lucas thought later, is something you can do even after a day spent digging up a graveyard.

Maybe even a good time to do it.

10

THE TELEVISED DISPLAY of his drawings had been a hammer blow. As he sat in his office, peering into the depths of his computer, James Qatar would turn each and every time he heard footsteps in the hallway. He possessed a level of courage, but he was not immune to fear. The building was nearly empty during the study term, and the shoe heels of every passerby echoed through his office.

He was waiting for the police. He'd seen the television show on forensic science, how the police could track a killer with a single hair or a flake of dandruff or the imprint of a gym shoe. He knew much of that was exaggeration, but still: It produced a vision.

Qatar was an old-movie buff, and in his vision saw broad-shouldered police thugs with bent noses and yellow-tan woolen double-breasted suits and wide, snap-rimmed hats. They'd have eyes like bloodhounds and they'd jam into the doorway and then one would mutter to the others,

"That's him! Get him!" He'd stand up and look around, but there'd be no place to run. One of the cops, a brutal man with dry twisting lips, would pull a pair of chrome handcuffs from his pocket. . . .

The scene was all very retro, very thirties, very movie stylish—but that was the way James Qatar saw it happening.

Never happened.

The same night that he'd seen the drawings on television, he'd driven himself in a panic to a CompUSA, where he'd bought a package of ZIP disks and a new hard drive. At his office, he'd locked the door, dumped all of his lectures to the new ZIPs, then stripped the hard drive out of his computer. He also dug out every ZIP disk in the place, except those he'd bought that morning—some of the disks were unused, but he was taking no chances—and put them in his briefcase with the old hard drive.

He took an hour fussing with Windows, reinstalling it on the new drive, then began the task of reading his lecture files back in. The whole process would take time, but he got started. When he ran out of patience, he headed home, carrying his briefcase.

At home, he smashed the old hard drive, extracted the disks, and cut them to pieces with metal shears. He used the same shears to shred the ZIP disks. He could have dumped the mess into the garbage safely enough, but he was both frightened and meticulous. He put all the pieces in a sack, drove south down the Mississippi, found a private spot, and tossed the sack into the viscous brown water.

That was that. Let the cops come now, he'd thought, and do all their forensic work on the computer. They'd find nothing but a pristine drive and the usual academic software. No Photoshop, no photo files. Nothing but a bunch of paintings in a series of PowerPoint lectures.

* * *

THE cops never came. Qatar busied himself reinstalling software on the new drive, rebuilding his art files from the ZIP disks. He stayed off the porn websites, put away his drawing instruments. An overdue tidying-up; a good time to lie low, and perhaps do a little maintenance on his career.

A new book, perhaps. He'd been toying with the idea of a book on ceramics. He even had a title: *Earth, Water, Fire and Air: The Ceramic Arts Revolution in the Upper Midwest, 1960–1999*.

He bought a notebook and made some notes, and made more notes on his office whiteboard. Good for the image, he thought. Nobody here but us intellectuals.

THE one fly in this intellectual ointment was Barstad. She kept calling, distracting him. He'd destroyed all the images of her, but now found that under the pressure of the obvious danger of detection, his mind kept going to her.

The imp of the perverse, isn't that what Poe called it? The irrepressible impulse to do harm to oneself? He had put off another meeting with her, but that night had experienced the most intense fantasies involving Barstad, a camera, and his art.

All his work to this point had involved grafting women's faces to images from the 'Net. Now, it occurred to him, he didn't have to do that. He could get an image of a woman doing anything he wished—at least, he hadn't yet found anything that she wouldn't do—and create a genuinely unique work. An original. He needed to *work* with the idea. He needed to *manipulate* the woman to create a new vision.

His drawings continued to come up on the television with the better parts obscured—the TV stations couldn't seem to get enough of them—but after a day went by, and no cops came . . .

He began to feel safe.

Nobody *knew*.

If he was careful, he thought, he could begin working again. He began by making another trip to a CompUSA, where he bought a cheap laptop. That night, when Rynkowski Hall had gone dark, when even the janitors had gone home, he walked down the hall to Charlotte Neumann's office and slipped the door lock with a butter knife. All the locks could be done the same way; the professors knew it, as did the brighter undergraduates.

Neumann's office was a simple cube, with a bookcase along one wall. Her copy of Photoshop 6 was in the top left corner, and he lifted it off the shelf, pulled the door closed behind himself, and returned to his office. The installation took no time at all; in an hour, he was walking out of the building. He'd known Rynkowski Hall all of his life, all the nooks and crannies and hiding places. He would hide the computer after each day's work, he thought, and never again contaminate his daily work. . . .

BUT the next day brought bigger trouble; a dirty day, a grinding, bitter drizzle pounding down. Late in the afternoon, he'd gone down to Neumann's office on a routine errand—classes were about to resume, and a student who didn't have the proper prerequisites had asked permission to attend one of his classes. Qatar simply needed the permission form. Neumann's door was open, and she was sitting at her desk. He knocked on the door frame and said, "Charlotte, I need—"

She heard his voice and turned her head, and her arm spasmodically jerked across her desk, away from him. Her hand held a slip of blue paper; her face was locked with sudden conscious control, which produced a weak smile.

He continued without a break, "—a prerequisite waiver;

I don't seem to have any more. I'll need a permission number."

"Of course," she said. "Let me see . . ."

He looked unwaveringly into her eyes, but he was tracking her hand and the blue paper with his peripheral vision. She casually opened a drawer, slipped her hand in, riffled some papers, and said, "Where did I put those?" When her hand emerged, there was no paper in it. She opened the next drawer down, said, "Ah. Here," and handed him a half-dozen slips.

"The number?"

"Just a second . . ." She pulled down a file in her computer and said, "Make that 3474/AS."

"Okay," he said. He jotted the number on one of the forms and left the office. Stopped and looked back. Was she hiding something from him?

He was sensitive to the idea because of the discovery of the body, then the images on the television. He cleaned up some last-minute chores around the office, then headed home. He brooded about Neumann. What was she doing? Why did that slip of paper stick in his mind like a thorn?

BARSTAD called, and he put her off. "I'll try to get over later tonight, but if not tonight, tomorrow for sure. I've got a surprise treat for you."

"A treat?" She sounded delighted. She was a moron. "What kind of treat?"

"If I told you, it wouldn't be a surprise," he said, thinking of his camera. "I'll call you tonight if I can get away. If I can't, I know I've got time tomorrow afternoon. Can you get away?"

"Anytime," she'd said.

* * *

AT seven o'clock that night, with the janitors caucusing in the maintenance room, he went back to Neumann's with his butter knife and a flashlight. Her desk was unlocked, and he opened the drawer and looked inside. No blue paper. He checked the other drawers, nervous, listening for footfalls. Still nothing.

Checked her bulletin board, found nothing blue. Was about to leave, when he saw all the little tag-ends of paper sticking out from under her desk calendar. He lifted it up, one edge, deflected the beam of the flashlight beneath it. Still nothing; and he'd felt so clever when he lifted the pad, a sense of inevitable discovery.

Damnit. He let himself out of the office and walked down to his own, turned on a study light, swiveled his chair so that his face was in shadow, and closed his eyes. He knew that blue . . .

He might have dozed for a few minutes. When he opened his eyes again, they wandered, almost by their own accord, it seemed, to the bottom drawer of an old wooden file cabinet. Had he seen that blue in his own files?

He dropped to his knees and pulled the drawer out. A half-dozen fat files were stuffed with paper he hadn't expected to look at again until he retired and had to clean out the cabinet. He riffled through them, and the label "Planes on Plains" caught his eye. Notes, letters, comments on his cubism book. He pulled it, opened it, and saw the blue. He slipped it out, turned it, and recognized it instantly.

Jesus. Four years old, and somehow she'd remembered, long after he'd forgotten. An invitation to a publication party for *Planes on Plains*. The publisher, even cheaper than most of that notoriously penurious breed, hadn't been willing to pay for much of anything, so he'd done the party invitations himself. He'd done a quick little self-portrait for the front page of the blue invitation.

The drawing looked nothing like the drawings on televi-

sion, really. But his historian's eye *felt* the resemblance—
something in the technique, and the choice of line. Neumann was a historian herself. Qatar closed his eyes,
swayed, nearly fell, overcome by the image of Neumann
taking the paper to the police. They were that close.

Had she talked to anyone? Maybe not. To make this kind
of accusation would be extremely serious, and if she was
wrong, could end her career. She'd have to be careful.
Sooner or later, though . . .

"She's gotta go," he mumbled.

Right away. Tonight. He'd seen the logic of it in a flash:
If she'd talked to other people about the drawing, he was
finished. If he killed her, he might be finished, but then
again, he'd killed a lot of people, and the police had never
had a sniff of him. If he moved quickly enough, directly
enough, he might pull it off again.

He walked straight out of his office, down the stairs, and
out to his car. He'd been to her house, twice, and it wasn't
far away, just across the river and a little north and east. He
drove over, calculating. Park at her house, or down the
block? If he parked down the block, he'd have to walk, and
that would increase his exposure. If he parked in front,
somebody might remember his car when she came up
missing. He'd walk, he thought. It was raining. With a raincoat and an umbrella, nobody would recognize him.

Then he would . . . what? Knock on the door? Try to
grapple with her? She was a big woman. Even if he managed to take her down, there'd be a fight, there might be
blood—his blood—and she might even make it out of the
house. She might scream, she might wake up the neighborhood. There might be somebody else in the house.

Then he'd be cooked. . . .

Had to think. Had to think. Was thinking: His mind was
a calculating machine, and ran through the possibilities
with insane precision.

* * *

HE was cruising her house, a quick pass, when he saw the lights come on in the garage. The garage door started up, and a car backed down the driveway, into the street, coming after him. He pulled to the side and let her pass. Was it her? He could see only a profile, but thought the profile looked like hers. . . . He didn't know her car. Now what?

She turned right at the corner, and he followed, slowly. Another car went by, and he fell in behind it, watching Neumann's car—if it was her car—continuing ahead. They drove together for four blocks; then the car in front of him slowed and turned, and Neumann was directly in front of him. Down to Grand Avenue, to a supermarket. He pulled into the parking lot behind her and watched as she got out and hurried into the store.

There were only a few cars in the lot; if he had a gun, he could wait until . . . But then, he had no gun. No point in thinking about it.

She *should* be heading back home fairly quickly, he thought. Nobody buys groceries and then goes on to a movie. You take them home, put them away. Get the hamburger in the refrigerator. If she weren't getting a bunch of groceries, if she were just out for a pack of gum, she wouldn't have driven past a convenience store to a supermarket.

He decided. Wheeled the car in a circle and drove as fast as he could—without attracting police attention—back to her house. He parked a block down, got a collapsible umbrella from the backseat, turned up the collar on his raincoat, and got out.

He saw not a single person along the sidewalk: The rain was so cold and so enduring that the locals were all hunkered down in front of their natural-gas fireplaces, watching Fox, or whatever it was they did in these old houses.

Neumann's house was one of the prewar clapboard places that never quite slipped into the slums but had come close. It looked like a child's drawing: a peaked roof with a single window under the peak, a front door centered under that window, a window on each side of the door, a short stoop leading to the door. The garage sat to one side, originally detached, but now connected to the house with a breezeway.

Qatar turned smartly at the front walk, climbed the stoop, and rang the doorbell. Nobody answered. He pulled open the storm door and tried the doorknob. Locked.

All right. He hurried back down the steps and tried the breezeway door. Locked. He looked around, saw nobody, heard nothing but the rain. The house across the street showed a light at the front window, but the drapes were pulled. He left the shelter of the breezeway nook and walked back around to the front of the garage. Tried the main door: locked down. He continued around to the side of the garage. The next house was only twenty feet away, but a hedge ran between them. He could see no lights, so he lowered the umbrella and walked down the length of the garage, the wet leaves of the hedge flicking against his face and neck, chilling him.

Now he was in arrest territory, he thought. If somebody caught him here, they wouldn't listen to a story about dropping by for a cup of tea. He began to feel it in his stomach: the tension, the eager stress of hunting. . . .

The garage had a back door: locked. Cautious bitch, he thought. The breezeway also had a back door, and it was locked. The back of the house had a two-step wooden deck. He climbed the deck in the dark, tried the door: locked. A double window looked out over the deck, ten feet down from the door. He walked over and looked at it—and found a crack in the armor.

The window was positioned over the kitchen sink. Probably a replacement from some past remodeling, it was one of the triple-glazed kind that didn't take a storm window. It was cranked open about an inch, apparently to let some air into the house. A little cool air over the hot dishwater . . . He did it himself.

He looked around: He was safe enough, with the foliage in the backyard covering him. He grabbed the edge of the window and pushed it back and forth. It gave a bit, a bit more; in two minutes he'd managed to work it open far enough that he could reach inside to the crank, and crank it all the way open. With one last look around, he boosted himself into the window opening, clambered awkwardly across the sink, and stepped on a dish full of water when he dropped to the floor.

A dog?

He stopped to listen. Heard nothing but the hum of the furnace. He looked out the window, then reached over and cranked it shut and locked it. There were no lights in the back. Then a furtive sound to his right: He whirled and saw a cat, a gray-striped tiger. The cat took a quick look at him and sprinted for some other part of the house.

The kitchen lights were off; the illumination came from a couple of lamps in the living room and an overhead fixture in a hall that led back to a bedroom. He needed more light. . . . It'd be nothing but bad luck if she got back this quickly, he thought. He snapped on the kitchen light and looked quickly around.

As he suspected, he was leaving puddles of water and muddy footprints on the floor. He spotted a paper towel rack, rolled off a few feet of toweling, wadded it up, dropped it on the floor, and used his feet to push it around like a mop. When both his shoes and the floor were dry, he stuffed the dirty towels into his pocket. A box of garbage bags sat on the kitchen counter. He took one, turned off the light, and headed for the garage.

*   *   *

AFTER all that, the killing was simple, as it always had been. He found a spade in the garage and walked back into the breezeway.

He waited in the near-dark for twenty minutes, thinking about not much at all. Now that he was here, now that he was committed, there wasn't much to think about, and he relaxed. In the dim light he could just make out the reflection of his face in the breezeway glass; he looked dark, mysterious. The trench-coat collar cut him nicely along his jawline; he tried a smile, tried to catch a good profile. . . .

He remembered the time, a cold rainy night like this one, outside of Paris, or maybe it was Casablanca, 1941 or '42, standing in the shadows waiting for the Nazi to come in. He had a paratrooper's knife in one hand and could see himself in a mirror, a really design-o thirties woolen military trench coat broadening out his shoulders, a beret . . . well, a beret might be too much, maybe a watch cap, though a watch cap tended to make him look a little like one of the Three Stooges; not a watch cap, then, maybe a fedora, snapped down over his eyes, but you could still see his eyes in the mirror. . . .

He was working the fantasy when Neumann's car pulled into the driveway and the garage door started up. Qatar pulled himself back to the present, struggled to get out of vision mode and into the sharp mental state he needed to do the killing. He didn't want to chase her all over, like Elmer Fudd after the Thanksgiving turkey; there couldn't be a pursuit. The door opened into the garage, so he wouldn't have the cover of the door. He'd have to move quickly.

He heard the garage door start down again. The car engine hummed for a moment, then died. The car door opened, then closed; he lifted the spade. Then another car door opened, and he nearly panicked. She'd picked some-body up?

Wait, wait, wait. She's getting the grocery bags out of the backseat. A moment later, the door to the garage opened and Neumann stepped inside. She might have seen him—her eyes turned toward his in that fraction of a sec-ond before the spade hit her—but she had no time to react to his presence, or even flinch.

He swung as though he were chopping wood, and the back of the spade hit her on the forehead, crushing her skull like a cantaloupe. He hit her as hard as he'd ever hit a softball; grunted with the follow-through.

Neumann pounded back against the garage wall, then sagged and went down with a soggy thump. The bag of groceries she'd been carrying spilled around her with ma-jor brand color: Campbell's soup, Nabisco crackers, Swan-son TV dinners, Tampax . . .

Another furtive move, and again Qatar started: The cat was watching from the doorway to the house. It meowed once, then disappeared.

Goddamn cat.

He moved quickly now. He'd had experience with this part. Neumann was dead, there was no question of that. The spade had crushed her skull; he'd felt it, and kneeling by her head, he could see it. She now looked only a little like Charlotte Neumann. There wasn't much blood, but there was some. Before it could trickle onto the floor, he lifted her head by her hair, and fitted it into the garbage bag, then slipped the bag down the rest of her body; her head felt like a collection of bones and hamburger in an old sock.

The body went into the trunk of her car with the spade. He went quickly back into the house, got another garbage bag, filled it with the groceries. He had no intent to steal, but simply to obscure any sign of violence.

Now. Out . . .

But just a minute. There was no immediate rush. He could take a few seconds to look around. She talked all the time about her dead husband, letting you know about how well off they'd been. There might be something here in the house . . .

She had twenty-three dollars in her wallet, and he took it all. In her bedroom, he found nothing but cheap costume jewelry in her jewelry box. But in another, smaller box in the bottom of her chest of drawers, he found another three rings, a pair of earrings, and a necklace; they positively *thumped* with authenticity. These would be worth a few dollars.

In another drawer, he found two coin cards, and in each card, ten gold American twenty-dollar pieces from the nineteenth century. For the gold content alone, he thought, they should be worth close to three hundred dollars each; and if they were rare at all, maybe much more.

When he finished looking through the house, he thought himself perhaps fifteen thousand dollars richer.

A dream, he thought, to get so much by accident.

The dream quickly turned into a nightmare when he backed her car out of the garage and left for his disposal place. Getting into the countryside was easy enough; getting the body into the ground would be another problem, he thought, with the rain and cold. The leaves would be slippery and the slope was steep . . . although he'd enjoy the time on the hillside, there with his other friends. All the friends of James Qatar, gathered in the dark under the oak trees . . .

But when he crossed the creek and turned the corner, he was caught in a sudden blaze of light. There was no place to turn: He was stuck with the road. He slowed, but went ahead. They were right by his hill. What were they doing, police in the rain? A car accident?

As he crept up on the scene, a cop stepped into the road and waved him along. Qatar slowly moved past, lifting his hand to the cop as he went by, but turning his head, so the cop couldn't see his face. He turned it toward the hill and saw the men working on the hillside, saw a shovel held by a man in the road, saw three TV vans . . .

He was more stunned than panicked. They'd found his special place after all. The discovery of Aronson had made it possible, but when nothing had appeared in the papers, he'd thought they'd missed the others.

With his mind moving like mud, he wandered down a series of narrow blacktop tracks. Lights to the sides marked farmhouses; he passed a lonely Conoco station with two trucks in the parking lot, took a left, and faded into the dark countryside again. He finally crossed a highway with a north arrow, and took that: The Cities were north; he could hardly miss them. Then he passed the Conoco station again, and realized that he'd driven in a circle. He pulled in, went inside, and bought two packages of pink Hostess Snoballs and a Coke, and got directions from the kid behind the counter: "Go right straight up the road here, you'll cut 494 . . ."

He jammed the Snoballs into his face as he drove, chewing mindlessly through the sugar and chocolate—they *tasted* pink—and threw the packaging out onto the highway. The body in the back seemed to glow in the dark; he had to get rid of her. Had to.

That, it turned out, was as simple as the killing.

He cut I-494 south of St. Paul and took it back west, eventually finding his way to the Ford Bridge over the Mississippi. He parked at the end of the bridge, looked both ways, then carried the garbage sack out over the water and dumped the body into the Mississippi. He started to let the bag go with it, but caught it at the last minute. It was too dark to see the body hit, but it would soon be going over the dam.

And on the way back to Neumann's car, he realized what he'd done. He'd faked a suicide. She was certainly moody enough, dark enough. Lonely. Perhaps he could help the idea along.

He drove Neumann's car back to his own, took the groceries out, along with the spade, put them in the trunk of his car, then drove the car back to the bridge and left it parked illegally on Mississippi Boulevard. Then he started walking. Four miles to his own car. Four miles in the rain.

But he needed the time anyway—the time to think. Life was becoming complicated. He hadn't had any choice with Neumann, but he'd now done something he'd always carefully avoided in the past.

He'd killed somebody close to himself. The cops could stand in her office doorway and see his.

As he walked back, he began to weep again. Life was cruel. Unfair. A man like himself . . .

James Qatar walked along, snuffling in the dark and the rain.

And he thought about the friends of James Qatar, before tonight snugly buried on the hillside above the creek. Released now. He wondered if they would come to see him.

11

LUCAS GOT UP early, kissed Weather goodbye, and went to the telephone. The police in New Richmond knew the dentist used by Nancy Vanderpost, and the cop who answered the phone volunteered to run across the street to see if he had X rays of her fillings.

Next Lucas called Marcy, who was just out of bed. Del had suggested that there might be something special, or peculiar, about the drawings that were publicly posted, rather than mailed to the victim. Lucas told Marcy to get somebody prying into Beverly Wood's history. The killer, he thought, was back there somewhere.

He called Del and made arrangements to pick him up again, and while he was talking, got a beep of an incoming call. He rang off Del and took the incoming call: The New Richmond cop was calling from the dentist's office. The dentist had X rays, and was offering to scan and e-mail them immediately.

Lucas gave the dentist his e-mail address, got the dentist's phone number, then called Larry Lake at Lake's cell phone number. Lake answered after a single ring: "Mc-Grady decided last night that he wanted one more scan across the bottom of the hill. We think we found another grave. A seventh one. So we're doing another strip."

"Jesus. You sure it's a seventh? Anything come up yet?"

"They're just scraping the leaves off now. These crime guys are pretty fussy about how it's dug."

"Okay. See you in a bit."

He called Del back and told him about the seventh, then called Rose Marie. "We've got a seventh grave."

"Oh, boy. I'll tell you, the governor called first thing this morning. He wants a federal-state-local task force working on it."

"We're already moving slow enough."

"I suggested that he set up a federal-state task force to examine the forensic evidence, which is most of what we've got, and to coordinate between the local agencies."

"Tell me what that means," Lucas said.

"It means that we stay independent, but we send Xeroxes of everything to the task force, if there is a task force. But if there is a task force, it probably won't get started for a few days, so if we *really* want to look good . . ."

"We take the guy before that."

"Only a suggestion," she said.

"I'll keep it in mind."

LUCAS made a half-gallon of coffee and poured it into a thermos, got his rain suit off the nail in the garage, and tossed it into the back of the Tahoe. With little hope, he cranked up his IBM and looked at his e-mail—and found a message from a DocJohn. He opened it and brought up a page of scanned X-ray images. He sent the images to his laser printer and two minutes later had eight life-size X-ray images.

THE weather was better: still overcast, but dry. Del was waiting in front of his house. His wife waited with him, and when she saw the Tahoe coming, handed Del a cooler. Del said something to her, and when Lucas pulled into the drive, he sheepishly got into the truck. "No more meat loaf," Cheryl said to Lucas.

"I'll remember," Lucas said. "Don't let my meat loaf."

"Lucas . . ." A distinct threat hung in her voice.

"No meat loaf. I swear."

"Have Del tell you about his cholesterol."

Lucas looked at Del, who seemed to shrink down in his seat, then back to his wife. "We'll talk about it," Lucas promised.

On the way out of town, Lucas asked, "What's in the cooler?"

"Bunch of stuff. Mostly cut carrots. Fat-free water crackers."

"I like carrots."

"That's fuckin' great," Del said. "I'm happy for you."

"So are you gonna tell me about your cholesterol?"

Del shrugged. "It's been stuck at two fifty-five. The doc wants it down under two hundred, and if I can't do it by diet, he's gonna put me on Lapovorin."

"Uh-oh. Isn't that what . . . ?"

"Yeah. The guy who comes backwards."

Long pause. Then Lucas said, "Better than a heart bypass. Or dropping dead of a heart attack."

Del said, "Yeah. It kinda scares me, to tell you the truth.

The cholesterol does. My mom died of a heart attack when she was fifty-eight."

They rode along for a minute, then Lucas said, "So eat carrots."

Del cracked a grin. "I'm gonna love getting old."

AT the graveyard site, there were now a half-dozen TV trucks, along with the line of county sheriff's cars, state cars, a car with federal government tags, Marshall's Jeep, Lake's Subaru, and a few more.

"A simple cop convention yesterday. Now it's a full-scale cluster-fuck," Del said.

"In which nobody knows exactly who's doing what to whom, or with what."

"Or even why."

Lake was waiting on the hillside while his assistant carried the radar along the yellow string. Lucas headed that way first. "Any more?"

"Just the one I told you about this morning, the seventh one. They've got some clothing coming up now."

Lucas looked around the hill. "Where's seven?"

Lake pointed. "Those guys." He pointed farther along the hill. "And those guys, I think, are working on a tree hole, but it's big enough and defined enough that we thought we better dig it out."

"How much longer?"

"This is the last sweep. We'll have some data in a half hour."

Lucas and Del walked up the hill to the command tent. McGrady was still at work, but he looked beat. He peered over his glasses at Lucas. "You're pretty chipper."

"Good night's sleep, pancakes for breakfast, nice conversation with a pretty woman," Lucas said.

"Better'n this, huh?"

Lucas nodded. "You've got seven."

"Yeah." McGrady stumbled backward a step and sank into a canvas field chair. "You know what? The first six didn't bother me that much. The seventh, finding the seventh . . . that kicked my ass."

"I got some X-ray printouts for you. We can get the actual films if we need them. This is for the woman from New Richmond. Nancy Vanderpost."

Lucas handed McGrady the printouts, and McGrady looked at them for a long moment, then said, "Four."

"What?"

"They could be number four."

He walked across the tent to six long cardboard boxes. Inside each box was a stack of clear plastic bags, with the contents of each bag carefully tagged. He rummaged around in the box numbered four and came up with a bag. Inside, Lucas saw several separate bones, including a lower jaw. McGrady looked at the jawbone for a minute, then at Lucas's printouts, then at the jawbone, then at the printout. After a minute, he looked up at Lucas and said softly, "Hello, Nancy."

"You're sure?" Del asked.

"Ninety-nine percent." He dropped the bag back into the box, pulled off his glasses, and said, "Goddamnit. I'm so fuckin' tired."

"You oughta crash for a couple hours," Lucas said.

"Maybe tonight."

LUCAS called Marcy and told her about Vanderpost, then told her to start building a file with the cops from New Richmond. She said she would, and added, "Black was over at the archdiocese, and they're looking for a priest who studied art at UW–Stout in Menomonie, but this monsignor over there said they won't find one. He says he generally knows the background of all the priests in the area, and none of them went to Stout."

"That was thin, anyway," Lucas said.

"Yeah, but listen to this. After Black talked to the guy, he noticed that a bunch of these women listed 'going to Mass' as one of their social activities, and he started to add them up. Of the seventeen people who've gotten drawings so far, eleven are Catholic. That's way too many. Of the three dead women we know about, two were Catholic."

"Yeah?"

"Interesting, huh?"

"Push it."

"We are."

When he got off the phone, Lucas asked McGrady if he'd seen Marshall.

"He wanders around the hill," McGrady said. "He was right up on top the last time I saw him. Sitting on a log."

He was still sitting on the log when Lucas climbed to the top of the hill. He crossed the lip of the crest, and Marshall said, "More bad news." Not a question.

"McGrady says four is Nancy Vanderpost, from New Richmond."

"Ah, jeez."

"You did a hell of a job, man," Lucas said.

"I was nuts for all those years. That's the answer. I kept hoping she'd show up—you'd see those TV shows on amnesia. I knew it was all bullshit, that she was dead."

"You had the guy figured, and that's—"

"What the heck is this?" Marshall was looking past Lucas, down the hill. Del was climbing toward them at a dead run.

"What?" Lucas asked.

"Eight wasn't a tree hole," Del said, gasping for breath.

THEY were standing around hole eight, looking at a shoe with a dirty bone in it—with the combination of heavy soil and oak litter, the bones showed an irregular coffee color, with lines and pits of bone white. "We need to find a girl who wore red high-top Keds," said the cop in the hole.

"That fad faded a few years ago," Lucas said.

"Yeah, well, she's been here a few years."

Below, another federal car crept slowly past the cluster of cop cars on the road, parked, and three men climbed out. "Baily," Del said.

Lucas looked down the hill. Baily was the FBI's agent in charge at the Minneapolis office, a heavyset man who played a mean game of handball. "Better go get him, take him up to the command tent," Lucas told Del. "I'll round up Marshall and McGrady."

McGrady was at hole six. Lucas said, "The feds are here. Del's bringing Baily up to the command tent."

"Okay. . . . You think they'll come in?"

"Does a chicken have lips?"

Marshall had left his spot at the top of the hill and was wandering past hole three, where the diggers were getting into virgin earth. Lucas caught him by the arm. "Come on and talk to the FBI," Lucas said.

McGrady and Baily were shaking hands when Lucas and Marshall got to the command tent. Baily shook hands with Lucas and said, "Eight."

"Coming out of the ground now," Lucas said. "This is Terry Marshall, a deputy sheriff from Dunn County over in Wisconsin. He broke it."

Lucas explained, and when he finished, Baily nodded at

Marshall and said, "Nice piece of work. I'm sorry about your niece."

"I just hope we get the guy," Marshall said. "If he reads the newspapers, he might've taken off like a big-assed bird."

"Got nowhere to run," Baily said. "We've got enough bodies now that we should be able to pinpoint him with victim histories."

"Could be tougher than that," Lucas said. "We've been doing histories on all the women who got the drawings, and so far we've pretty much come up with zip. We got matches, of course, but nothing that looks likely."

"We're setting up a task force, Wisconsin–Minnesota, FBI. We'll run down every single possibility. We'll have all the manpower we need," Baily said. "I talked to the director this morning, and he made this the number-one priority nationwide. Nothing else comes first."

"Terrific," Del said. There was a *tone* in his voice, and when everybody looked at him, he said, "No, I mean it. I really . . . mean it."

LUCAS and Del left the site twenty minutes later: nothing to do that the professionals couldn't do better. McGrady promised updates by telephone, and Lucas told Baily that he would talk to Rose Marie about setting up a liaison to the task force. "Probably gonna be a sergeant named Marcy Sherrill," Lucas told him.

When they were on the road, Lucas looked at Del and said, "That was pretty swift of you, that 'terrific' you laid on Baily."

"Ah, the FBI's a bite in the shorts."

"Baily ain't bad," Lucas said.

"No, he's not. But I can see that he's building a machine, and I've never been much of a cog."

"You're more like a flywheel," Lucas suggested. "Or an air brake."

"You know what I think? I think we better get back and start cross-matching what we've got. I'm not saying this is a competition, but I'd like to be the ones to catch this asshole."

"I hope there's not a nine."

BACK at City Hall, Lucas spoke briefly with Rose Marie, filling her in on developments, then suggested that Marcy be made liaison with the joint task force. "Give her a little exposure," Lucas said.

"She could wind up getting her ass kicked," Rose Marie said.

"You don't know her well enough to know how unlikely that is," Lucas said. "But I'll tell you what—I really don't want to do it. If I've only got six months left in the job, I want to spend my time running around town, chasing this guy's ass."

Rose Marie got Marcy on the phone, told her to stop down. When she did, Rose Marie said, "You've been unanimously elected as our representative to the joint federal-state task force that's being set up. You've also got to coordinate for us, but I don't see how that could be much of a problem, since you'll mostly be doing the same stuff."

Marcy nodded. "Thanks. I'll do it. Anything else?"

"Go with God," Rose Marie said.

Out in the hall, Marcy said, "If you fixed this, I appreciate it." Lucas opened his mouth to reply, but she held up a finger. "You're gonna crack wise, but you don't have to. I appreciate it. Period."

Lucas shrugged. "So all right."

"If you're gonna spend all your time running around

town, why don't you figure out why we're up to our ass in Catholics?"

"Maybe I'll do that," Lucas said.

THE Aronson team had been compiling names and addresses, and cross-checking them. Out of a couple of thousand names, they'd found forty-four matches, and were trying to check the matches. "The problem is, there's only one person who comes up more than twice, and that's Helen Qatar, who runs the Wells Museum over at St. Pat's. She comes up four times."

"Catholic school," Lucas said.

"Helen Qatar's a semisedentary sixty-five," Black said. "She couldn't strangle a fuckin' gerbil. Even if she could catch one."

"Still a whole bunch of Catholics."

Black lowered his voice to a whisper. "And guess what? The guy directing the investigation for the City of Minneapolis is a Catholic."

"Lapsed Catholic," Lucas said. As he looked through the sets of matches, he saw nothing that looked like a pattern. Finally he asked, "Who talked to Helen Qatar?"

"I did."

"Show her the pictures?"

"A couple—she didn't recognize the style. She's pretty . . . old. I didn't roll out any of the vaginal extravaganzas."

"She's in art and she's named four times, and she's a Catholic."

"You want me to talk to her again?"

Lucas thought for a moment, then said, "Nope. I'll go talk to her. Get me out into town."

* * *

Sᴛ. Patrick's University was on the south side of Minneapolis, south of the Lake Street bridge along the Mississippi, and directly across the river from St. Thomas, its bitter intellectual, political, and athletic rival. Twenty buildings, mostly redbrick, sprawled along the west bank of the river under cover of six hundred oaks and a thousand maples, the maples replacing the elms that had dominated the campus before Dutch elm disease.

Lucas lucked into a metered parking spot a hundred yards from the Wells, got his file off the front seat, bought two hours of parking time, and walked across the street to the museum. The Wells was redbrick, a little newer than most. The floors inside were a shiny brown composite, but Lucas could hear the floorboards creaking beneath the brown stuff. It felt, he thought, like a college should.

Helen Qatar's office was at the far end of the building, behind a door with a translucent glass panel and a gold-leaf number 1. A heavyset secretary was reading a newspaper when Lucas stepped inside. She looked up and said, "Are you Mike?"

"No, I'm Lucas."

"Do you work with Mike?"

"No, I'm a police officer. I was hoping to speak with Miz Qatar."

"That would be Mrs. Qatar," the secretary said. She leaned toward an old-fashioned intercom, pushed a button, and said, "Mrs. Qatar, there's a cop here to see you."

A perfectly tinny voice came back: "Is he good-looking?"

The secretary looked at Lucas for a second, then said, "He looks like he probably cleans up pretty good, but he also looks like he's got a mean streak."

"Sounds interesting. Send him in."

Inside, Helen Qatar was also reading a newspaper. She had once been a very pretty blonde, Lucas thought, but her fine skin was now a dense map of tiny wrinkles. Her eyes were a perfect china blue behind a pair of small rectangular reading glasses. "Close the door," she said. "You're Lucas Davenport."

Lucas said, "Yes" and closed the door.

Qatar put down the newspaper and said, "Denise and I always read our newspapers at the same time in different rooms. She takes the news rather seriously." Lucas didn't know what to make of the remark, and smiled politely. Qatar took the reading glasses off and put them on the desk. "I talked to that nice gay man you sent over earlier. Is this about the same topic?"

Lucas frowned. "Black told you he was gay?"

"No, no, I surmised it. Is he still in the closet?"

"Technically. Everybody knows, nobody mentions it. Makes life easier."

"Do you have a lot of homophobes in the police department?"

"Probably about the usual number."

"Ah. Well. Is there something else I can help you with?"

"I can't say, really. Black explained all this about the drawings to you, and if you've been reading the paper you know about the burial ground down in Goodhue County."

"It's appalling," she said, turning her chin up.

"We believe the drawings and the killings are connected. We think that the killer has some special relationship with Catholics. We have one witness who might actually have met him, who said that he may be a priest—and this was without knowing that an unusual number of these victims were Catholic."

"Why would a priest kill Catholics?"

"Well, it could be something very simple—perhaps the overwhelming number of people he meets are Catholics. But we don't know that he's a priest: There's just one guy saying that, and he's not exceptionally reliable. There are other things that make it unlikely. . . . We think he may at one time have been associated with a state university, which would be unusual for somebody who not much later became a priest."

"Unless he already was, and was doing advanced study," Qatar said.

"We don't think that was the case. We think he was still pretty young. Anyway, what I'm here for—we're intensely interviewing these people who got the drawings, and we're researching the pasts of all the people who were killed. We're looking at address books and checkbooks and Christmas cards and everything we can find. Your name has come up four times. A lot of other names have come up twice, but you're the only four-time winner. So you have something . . . something in common with the killer."

That brought a moment of silence, then Qatar said, "Good Lord."

"Yeah. I'm sorry to put it that way, but there it is," Lucas said.

"But it may be something simple, like you said with the priest and the idea of killing Catholics. I'm a Catholic, and I know a lot of Catholics because of this school. Not all of my friends are Catholic, but most of them are, so that's probably why I came up four times."

"Probably. But there might be some other connection. I'm nowhere near smart enough to ask you exactly the right question that would give us the answer, so I was hoping you could mull it over and see if you could come up with something."

"Do you think he's connected to the university here?"

"We have no idea. None of the murdered women were, of the ones we've identified."

"Hmm."

"Since you came up four times, and you're an art museum, and he's an artist, apparently . . . although he may also be a photographer."

"We're not really an art museum," she said. "I mean, we don't have much in the way of paintings or sculpture."

"Really? I've never been here before. I assumed because of the name . . ."

"We have thirty thousand glass paperweights and ten million dollars' worth of Mayan pottery," Qatar said.

"Ah." But he was puzzled. "An unusual collection."

She smiled and said, "Our first graduate to become a bishop went off to care for the Indians in Mexico. When he died, the college got his money, which was considerable—he came from a rich milling family—and his pots. We couldn't hardly take one and throw the rest out. And eventually, people figured out that we had the best collection of authentic documented Mayan pots in the country, so we brought them out of the basement and now all sorts of scholars come to look at them."

"The paperweights?"

"Same sort of thing. Jemima Wells, whose son went to school here, left us one million dollars in cash back in 1948, and bequeathed additional funds to build this building, and also required that if we wanted the cash and the building, that we house her paperweight collection in perpetuity. We took the money. As it happens, the paperweights were a joke when we got them—they told terrible stories about us over at St. Thomas. But now we've gone full circle, and the thirty thousand paperweights are worth more than the Mayan pots. Scholars—"

"—come from all over to study them."

"Yes. They do. They shake them and watch the snow fall on the tiny villages."

Lucas stood up, took a card out of his card case, and handed it to her. "You will think about it?"

"Absolutely."

Lucas turned to go, then said, "Black showed you the drawings, I know. Did he show you a picture of the Aronson girl? She was not one of the Catholics, but she was from here in Minneapolis. She disappeared a year and a half ago."

"No. I only saw a couple of the drawings. Not the good ones, from what they say in the paper."

Lucas dug through the file, found the Aronson photo, and passed it across the desk. "This is the most recent photo we have of her."

Qatar put the reading glasses back on and peered at Aronson's photo. After a moment, she said, "A lot of young girls look alike to me now. They look so much the same . . . but I don't think I know her." She handed the photo back.

"Long shot," Lucas said. He was putting it back when he saw the Xeroxes of the Laura Winton photos. He fished a couple of them out. "How about these? It's possible that the killer took them himself."

Qatar said. "The killer took them?" She squinted at the top one, then shuffled once and looked at the next one. After a minute, she said, "No, I don't know her, I don't recall ever seeing her . . . but . . . Huh."

"What?"

"This background, the background here."

Lucas stepped around the desk to look over her shoulder. She had a finger on the rock wall in the background of the last of the photos.

"I thought it looked like it was along the river," Lucas said. "Here in town."

"I think it is. You know that big bronze statue of St. Patrick squashing a St. Thomas quarterback?"

"I thought it was a snake."

"Could be—they're easily mistaken. Anyway, I think this wall . . ." She tapped the photograph. "I think the end of this wall here is the beginning of the semicircular wall that goes out around the statue. It's on the south side of the statue as you come up toward it, along the bike path."

Lucas looked at the Xerox. "Really. You think?"

12

HELEN QATAR WALKED with Lucas down to the river. The ice was gone and a Corps of Engineers workboat was plugging along below them, a guy on the foredeck looking at the bank through binoculars. A cyclist went past, and, despite the cold, a redheaded jogger with bare tummy and a black jog bra. An eagle hung over the water, hunting for a tidbit.

The statue of St. Patrick looked as metallic as ever, staring blankly at the campus as though he'd forgotten something. He was, in fact, trampling on a snake; and the wall behind him was the wall in the photo.

"There," Lucas said to Qatar. "That little stack of rocks at the end of the wall. You were right."

"I can't see what possible good it will do," Qatar said.

"We have all these Catholics and now we've got a location. I don't know if he's associated with the college or if he just lives around here, but for some reason, they were *here*. You can almost see his shadow."

"An unusual thought for a policeman," Qatar said. "It could lead to poetry, or to country and western."

"God forbid," Lucas said, smiling at her. Then: "I *can* almost see the guy. One of the first women he killed said he looked like a movie star in an old movie, *Day of the Jackal,* about an attempted assassination of de Gaulle. The killer looked like the Jackal."

"That is grotesque, the coincidence is," Qatar said. "I'll have to rent the movie. You say it's old?"

"Sixties or seventies," Lucas said.

"Ah. I spent the fifties and sixties watching art films. They were very . . . bad."

Lucas laughed, and they walked companionably back toward the campus. At the corner of the Wells, Lucas said goodbye and started toward his car. Qatar called after him: "Mr. Davenport . . ."

Lucas turned. She was halfway up the walk to the museum, and now turned and walked back toward him. "I'm sure this has nothing to do . . . nothing to do with your case, but a professor in the art history department just committed suicide. Yesterday, or the night before."

"That's interesting," Lucas said, stepping back toward her. "What was his name?"

"It was a *her.*"

"Oh." Not what he wanted. "Huh. A suicide?"

"She apparently jumped off the Ford Bridge. She didn't show up for work yesterday, and then they found her car on Mississippi Boulevard. They thought . . . I don't know what they thought, but then her body was seen in the river. The St. Paul paper had an article that said the body's condition suggested that she went over the dam."

"Okay. Did the story say anything about depression?" Lucas asked.

"Nothing like that," Qatar said. "My son works in the department, and he said that she was troubled. Quite unpopular. I don't know if that leads to suicide."

"I'll tell you something, Mrs. Qatar: For depressives, *nothing* can lead to suicide. You get ink on a shirt and decide the only answer is to kill yourself. Unpopularity would be more than enough."

"I'll leave that for you to work out," she said. "In the meantime, I'll try to think what I might have in common with this monster."

THE killer and Aronson had been at St. Pat's, or at least along the bike path next to the St. Pat's campus. There hadn't been any bikes in the photo, which suggested to Lucas that they'd walked. If they were walking . . . they were on the wrong side of the campus to be casually shopping the college village. So they might well have a connection to the school.

He walked back to the truck and slipped the key in the ignition, paused, and then took out his cell phone. He got the number for the Ramsey County Medical Examiner from dispatch, and hooked up with an investigator named Flanagan.

"Can't tell you much, Lucas. We don't know exactly what killed her. She apparently went off the bridge fully dressed and in one piece, and then, after she went over the dam, she got caught up in some kind of tumbling current and it just beat the hell out of her. We kind of think that a massive blow to the head did the first real damage; looks like she hit a piece of abutment headfirst when she went over."

"Come on, Henry," Lucas said. "You're saying she dove off? Like saying goodbye with a big fuckin' swan dive? Nobody to watch? No audience?"

"No, I'm not saying that. I'm saying that somehow she smacked her head on something hard, and that might have been the first damage."

"You think suicide?"

"One of the things that weren't too damaged were her hands. No signs of defensive wounds. No blood in her car," Flanagan said.

"So are you carrying it as a suicide?"

"We're carrying it as unknown. I don't know if that'll change. Like I said, she was pretty torn up."

"Was she a big woman? Strong?"

"Large, but not especially strong. Pretty much a couch potato."

"Okay . . . but look, if you decide something different, give me a call."

"Is this about something?" Flanagan asked.

"I don't know."

"St. Paul has the file. We only got the body back last night, so everything is pretty intact. We notified a relative out in California . . . a sister."

HE was supposed to be rolling around town, and hadn't yet done much rolling. He looked at his watch, then called St. Paul and had the call transferred to Homicide. A detective named Allport took the call. "We don't want no davenports," he said. "We just got a new one, kind of a small classy-looking plaid with an ottoman."

"I'm calling to tell you that your wife wants a divorce. We're moving to Majorca to study oral sex."

"I'll tell you one thing for sure: You got the wrong goddamn wife," Allport said. Then: "I hope to hell this is a social call. I see you're working that graveyard case."

"Yeah. But I came across a really obscure, probably-nothing connection. The last woman killed—Aronson?—was over at St. Pat's just a few days before, maybe with the killer. We think the killer's an artist."

"I saw the drawings. And this chick who went off the bridge taught art at St. Pat's."

"Yeah."

"We got nothing on it, Lucas. She went through a meat grinder under that dam. We looked through her house, we looked through her car, no blood, no signs of a struggle. No nothin'. We talked to a couple of people in her department who said she was angry and aggressive and confrontational and maybe depressed. And maybe an unfulfilled lesbo. So . . ."

"No sign that she was strangled?"

"She wasn't *that* beat up. No, she wasn't strangled."

"Okay. Just a thought," Lucas said.

"Where are you at?" Allport asked.

"Over by St. Pat's."

"You aren't more than ten minutes from her house, then. Run across the Lake Street Bridge. She's practically right there. We had her car towed back to her place. You could look at it there, if you want."

Lucas looked at his watch, then said, "How do I get in?"

HE had to wait in the driveway for five minutes before the squad car showed. The patrol cop gave him the keys, and Lucas let himself inside. In ten minutes, he figured out that Neumann must have had a cat; not much else occurred to him. The house was ready for somebody to come back.

Her car was in the garage. He snapped on an overhead light, opened the door, and looked inside. She had not been particularly tidy about her transportation: The backseat was littered with old newspapers, memos, and empty diet Coke bottles, along with a few wadded-up translucent paper sacks of the kind that usually held bakery. Lucas looked through it, found nothing, looked under the visor and in the glove box. A couple of cash register slips lay on the passenger-side floor, and he picked them up and turned them over. One came from a Kinko's: She had apparently done some copying. The other came from a supermarket. Forty dollars worth of groceries, cat litter, Tampax, and lightbulbs. At the bottom were the date and time: ten o'clock on the night she'd apparently died.

Lucas scratched his head. The house inside had been fairly empty. . . .

He carried the slip back to the house and looked in the refrigerator and cupboards. Found a box of cat litter of the same brand, almost empty. Found a box of Tampax, almost empty.

He went back to the car and popped the trunk. No groceries.

"All right," he said. He called Allport with his cell phone.

"I just got back from lighting candles at the Cathedral. I was praying you wouldn't call back," Allport said.

"I found this cash register receipt," Lucas said.

He explained, and Allport said, "With the thing about the Tampax and the cat litter, it don't sound like she was taking food to a shut-in."

"No. She needed the stuff on this list. She got two quarts of two-percent milk, and there was an empty two-quart carton of two-percent in her garbage under the sink. She got bite-sized shredded wheat, and she had less than half a box of the same stuff in her cupboard."

"Goddamnit, where'd the fuckin' groceries go? I'll talk to the guys who found the car. Maybe they donated them or something."

"You think?"

"No. I don't think. Why don't you stay there for a few minutes. I'm gonna run over and get that cash register tape."

Allport showed up a half hour later, shaking his head. "The guys who found the car said there was nothing in it. No groceries."

"They're telling the truth?"

"Yup."

"Hard to believe that somebody knocked her on the head for her groceries," Lucas said.

"Stranger things have happened. You get some bums around that bridge—"

"Who knocked her on the head, threw her off the bridge, stole her groceries, but left her empty car in the street with the doors locked and two dollars in quarters in the parking-meter change holder."

"Probably not," Allport said glumly.

"Maybe the groceries depressed her and she took them with her," Lucas suggested. "You find any dead Tampax floating down the river?"

"Goddamnit."

WHEN Lucas got back to City Hall, Marcy Sherrill told him that the task force would meet the next day to get organized. "McGrady called. They think the hill's clean. They think they got all of them."

"So we're all done."

"Not quite. The feds want to resurvey the whole hill. They're bringing in a team from Washington."

"Lake is pretty good, I think. If he can't find any more, then there probably aren't any."

"Eight's enough. Nine would be excessive."

"Yeah. . . . All right, I got two things." He told her about the wall at St. Pat's and the professor found in the river. "What I want you to do is get a couple of guys working on St. Pat's connections. Get the names of everybody in the St. Pat's art department and run them. If you can't do it personally, get Sloan to do it. Black can be a little sloppy with that kind of thing. And do a background on this professor, the one who went over the dam."

"I'll do that. Are you off again?"

"Nope. I've got to make a couple of phone calls. Something just popped into my head."

He began by calling St. Paul Homicide and getting contact numbers for Charlotte Neumann, the art professor. She had no local relatives, so he started with the department secretary. After identifying himself, he asked, "Did Miz Neumann have any expensive jewelry?"

"Uh, a few pieces, I guess. She was a widow, you know."

"No, I didn't."

"Oh, yes, her husband was quite a bit older, a very well-known architect in Rochester. She had a nice diamond engagement ring—beautiful rose-cut diamond, a carat and a half, I think—and her wedding ring was gold, of course."

"Did she wear it?"

"Oh, yes. Not the diamond very often, but she wore the wedding ring, on her right hand. She also had an older woman's gold Rolex watch, which she liked because she worked in clay as her . . . artistic expression, I suppose you'd say. She said the dust didn't get in the Rolex like it did other watches. She also had a ring with a small green stone which might have been an emerald, but I'm not sure. Oh, and sapphire-and-diamond earrings. The earrings were very modest, but the sapphires were huge. A carat each. So blue they almost looked black. And, hmm . . . I think that was about it."

"No pearls?"

"Oh, sure, she had a string of pearls with matching earrings. I don't know how expensive they were. She wore them for routine cocktails sessions and so on. Social gatherings at the president's house."

"Listen: Thank you. You've really helped a lot." Lucas hung up and redialed St. Paul Homicide. "When you guys went through Neumann's house, did you inventory the valuables?"

"Sure. Want me to shoot you the list? There's not much on it."

Lucas felt the tingle. "You have it? The list?"

"Yeah, just a minute." The phone clunked on Allport's desk, and he went away. He was back in a minute, and he said, "She didn't accumulate a lot."

"She wore an older gold Rolex watch, had a diamond engagement ring, with a big diamond, maybe a carat and a half, pearls, a green-stone ring that might have been an emerald, and diamond-and-sapphire earrings. Big sapphires. Very expensive."

Long silence. Then: "You're really busting my balls, man."

"None of it's on the list?"

"No. I'll check with the guys," Allport said.

"She also wore a gold wedding band on her right hand," Lucas said.

"No wedding band. Nothing like that."

"What do you think?"

"I think I'm gonna wind up working overtime."

Lucas leaned toward his door and yelled, "MARCY."

She yelled back: "WHAT?"

"Do you have the number for Aronson's folks?"

She dug it out and brought it in. "What's going on?"

"Tell you in a minute," he said. She sat down, and Lucas dialed the number. Aronson's mother was named Dolly. She asked, quietly, "Did you catch him?"

"Not yet," Lucas said.

"I'm praying for it."

"Mrs. Aronson, did your daughter have anything expensive, especially jewelry, or anything small and high value like that, that might be missing?"

"Yes," she said positively. "We talked to somebody there about it, but we never found out what happened to it. We didn't want to seem like we were complaining."

"We think that the man who killed her may have taken the jewelry."

"Oh, no."

"But if he did, and we can identify it . . ."

"Oh, yes. I'd know these two pieces anywhere. An antique pearl necklace and an antique pearl wedding ring. They were my mother's, and her mother's before that. I had them myself for thirty years."

"Do you have photos or anything?"

"Actually, my insurance agent does, I believe. Shall I send them?"

"Yes . . . uh, no. What I would prefer is if you could take them to your local police department and have them make color copies and send the copies. Hang on to the originals in case we need them."

"I will do that. I will get them and make the copies and I will send them to you by Express Mail. Or if you need them immediately, I will have Dick drive them down."

"Express Mail would be fine," Lucas said.

When he got off the phone, he told Marcy, "We need a list of fences."

"I'll talk to the guys in property crime," she said. "If the guy is taking this stuff, you think he would be stupid enough to sell it here?"

"How many Minneapolis artists know fences in New York?"

"All right. I'll talk to them right now," Marcy said.

"How are the lists going?"

"We've got a couple more matches, but nothing hot."

"How about IDs from the graveyard?" Lucas asked.

"Just the ones we knew going in. The state guys are rounding up dental records for women reported missing, who are still missing, that more or less match the ones that we know—more or less blond, more or less interested in art, seventeen to thirty-five at the time of their disappearance."

"Bet we get a few," Lucas said.

"Ought to start getting some results by tomorrow."

"We want to get on top of them: Start making the lists as soon as we get a name."

She had a stack of papers in her hands, and she shuffled through them. "There was one girl from Lino Lakes, a Brenda . . . I think. Hmmm . . ." She was so intent that Lucas smiled and asked, "You like this? Running things?"

"Yes," she said, looking up. "Not only that, I'm pretty good at it."

"I thought you might be," he said. "I just hope you don't wind up spending too much time with this task force. Get your name known, but hang around here, not with them. It's always better to be with the winner."

"The winner?"

"Yeah," Lucas said. "The task force won't catch this guy. We will."

THAT night, Lucas made pasta with his special meat sauce—ground moose tenderloin with off-the-shelf vegetarian spaghetti sauce—with apple-onion salad and Chianti, and had it ready when Weather arrived. She came dragging in, her briefcase a half-inch off the kitchen tile. She sniffed the air and asked, "Moose?"

"Different this time. I've perfected it," he said.

"I suppose you've used the whole jar of spaghetti sauce."

"Nope. I knew you'd be chicken, so I saved some. You can sample the moose, and if you don't like it, we'll whip some of the straight stuff into the microwave." He picked up her attitude. "What happened to you?"

"I had a really bad day," she said. "Really bad."

"I thought you had the day off," Lucas said. "Paperwork."

"And a couple of office patients. Have I told you about Harvey Simson? The guy who runs the snowmobile and ATV shop?"

"No."

"He was cleaning out a carburetor a month or so ago with some kind of spray solvent, and it exploded. He got third-degree burns on his forearms, and after it was cleaned up, he needed a graft to cover the wound. I was up, so I took some skin off his leg and put it on his arm. No sweat. I saw him a couple of times, met his wife, she's this nice fat girl, one of the happy ones, and they've got a little daughter and another kid on the way. He's about thirty and he's finally got the shop going, and they're starting to make some money, but they didn't have a whole lot of insurance. So the question comes up, how are they gonna pay for the burn work? They're not poor enough to get aid, but they're not rich enough to write a check. So Harvey said not to worry, he'd cover it. He went to the bank, and the bank knew him well enough to give him another loan on his shop, and he's right up to date."

She put her head down and snuffled a couple of times, something Lucas hadn't often seen with her patients. "Well, Jesus, what . . ."

"So he came in today so I could take a last look, and I'm asking him how everything is, and everything's fine, and he's hoping we get an early spring so he can start moving the ATVs, and so on, and then he mentions he's got some kind of skin fungus going that he can't seem to shake, right in the middle of his back, and it itches. So I say, let me take a look. . . ."

"Ah, shit," Lucas said.

She bobbed her head. "Yup. A big fat melanoma. He's known he's had it for weeks, or maybe three or four months. God knows how long he had it before that. I sent him right over to Sharp, but . . . I think he's history. Just been too much time."

"Jeez." Lucas patted her on the back.

"Yeah. I can handle the ones where I know what's going on. But when it just jumps up like this, a guy younger than you are yourself, and he looks perfectly healthy and he's gonna be dead in a year . . . Man. I don't know. I'm wondering if I ought to have a kid at all."

"Hey. If everybody worried about what would happen to their kid if they died, nobody would have kids. You just do it."

"Yeah . . ."

"Tell you what's worse: If you have the kid, and the kid dies. That's worse."

"I guess." She sighed. "Fuckin' moose, huh?"

MARCY had photos of Aronson's jewelry when Lucas arrived at the office in the morning, as well as insurance photograph of Neumann's diamond and emerald rings.

"Aronson's parents came in this morning," she said. "They decided they didn't want to take a chance on the mail, so they drove down last night, stayed in a motel, and brought them in first thing."

Lucas looked at the photos. Both the necklace and the ring had been shot against a black background, and had been enlarged to show detail. "Better than I hoped," he said. "Get the property guys to run these around town. Paper the place."

"That's sorta under way," Marcy said. "We got some copies made, and Del's taking them around to people he knows, and he knows most of them. . . . Property's already doing some more."

"Okay. . . . Do you know if the state's still working the hill?"

"They are—McGrady called. They've got an ID on another one of the dead women. Ellice Hampton, from Clear Lake, Iowa. She disappeared four years ago, twenty-eight. She was unemployed and living with her parents when she disappeared. She'd been working with an insurance company in Des Moines, in the advertising and publicity department. She did advertising layouts for print media and was active in community theater. She'd been looking for work in both Des Moines and Minneapolis. Blond, good-looking, small, and busty. Divorced—ex-husband was a cop in Mason City, and he's in the clear."

"Another artsy type."

"That's the impression I get. I called down Clear Lake, but they've got nothing at all on the case—she vanished, and her parents didn't even know where she'd been planning to go that day, if she'd been planning to go anywhere. When they got home from their jobs, she wasn't there, though her car was. She just never came back."

"Is there any point in doing a list?"

"From what the Clear Lake cop said, her parents really didn't know too much about her friends either in Des Moines or up here. They don't even know if she had any friends up here."

"Goddamnit."

"He's careful about that. He cuts the woman out of her usual crowd, moves in, must feed them some kind of bullshit to keep them from talking, and then kills them."

"Maybe tells them he's married or something," Lucas said.

"Still, you'd think . . ."

"Yeah. *Somebody* would know."

They thought about that for a minute, then Marcy said, "So anyway, that's three people we've ID'd from the graveyard, five to go."

WITH nothing specific to work on, Lucas had to decide whether to drive down the graveyard—where he wouldn't have much to do—or review paper. The idea of reviewing paper bored him, and after a visit to Homicide to talk to Black, he noticed a shaft of sunlight out on the street.

"Sun's out," he said to Black as he left.

"Today only," Black said. "More rain or snow coming for the weekend."

The sunlight made the decision for him. He was out of downtown ahead of the rush, running through the sun-dappled countryside. The countryside still had the cold colors of winter, but when he cracked the windows, he could smell spring on the way. Still a little snow in the north shadows, along the shaded sides of the fence lines and the glacial hills, but the water was moving in the drainage ditches, and farmers had their tractors out of the machine sheds and the sun felt yellower and warmer than in the weeks just past.

On the grave-site hill, everything changed. The hill faced away from the afternoon sun, and under the oak trees, there was a river of mud, and men grubbing for bones. The hill, he thought, looked like an old browned photograph of a World War I trench site during a ceasefire, except for the brilliant blue slashes of a dozen plastic tarps.

McGrady had gotten some rest. He was sitting on a camp chair, reading a copy of *Maxim*, when Lucas climbed up to the command tent. "I always liked pictures of sexy women," he said, almost absently. "Like the *Sports Illustrated* swimsuit issue. But somehow, after all the liberation bullshit, we finally got around to the point where women have stopped being objects and have become products. Have you ever looked at this rag?"

"No." But he was amused.

McGrady flipped it over his shoulder onto the ground. "I'm just getting old, I guess. Couple of the younger guys were looking at it, thought it's great."

"Still eight bodies," Lucas said. He didn't care about *Maxim*, had never heard of it.

"Yeah, still eight. I think that's all it's going to be unless we find a whole new graveyard somewhere. We think one of them might be a girl from Lino Lakes, but we can't track down any dental records. I don't know what the hang-up is."

"Marcy said something about the parents moving a couple of times, and they're still trying to track them down. From what I saw of the records, I'm not sure how good a fit she is."

"Blond, busty, and missing."

"But some of her friends think she was about to run away to California; and she wasn't interested in art."

"If we find the parents, we could do some DNA and skip the dentals," McGrady said. He yawned, and then said, "Another day out here, I think. If we don't find anything new."

"You still got TV. . . ."

"Yup. But they're getting bored, I think. No new bodies." They both looked down the hill at the television vans. The crews were sitting along the edge of the road on blue tarps; two of the cameramen were playing chess and one of the reporters was sprawled out on his back, talking on a cell phone.

Lucas looked up the hill and saw Marshall sitting at the top, looking down. "But you still got Marshall."

"The guy spooks the hell out of me," McGrady said. "Good guy, but a little intense."

They talked for a few more minutes, then Lucas walked up the hill to where Marshall was sitting on a garbage bag. "How's it going?"

Marshall was smoking a Marlboro. He grinned and blew smoke and nodded. "Getting a handle on it," he said. "I got a little overworked there for a while. How's it going on your end?"

He sounded so mellow that Lucas couldn't help smiling back. "We're making some progress. We reviewed the cases we know about, and decided that our guy is stealing everything he can from the women he kills—everything small and worthwhile, anyway. Jewelry, cash, maybe small cameras. We've got photos of stuff that was taken from Aronson—and maybe another woman—and we're gonna run them around to every fence in town."

Marshall bobbed his head and then said, "I'm starting to worry about what happens when we identify him."

"That could be a while, yet," Lucas said.

"I know the kind of work you guys do—that *you* do—and I think that sooner or later, you're gonna figure him out. Am I right?"

Lucas shrugged. "I believe we will. We always have a few who slip past us, but once we get any kind of a handle on this guy, I think we'll be able to pin him with those drawings. Once we get a name, we can start connecting some dots, and we've got a lot of dots to start with."

"But what you'll get will be circumstantial: maybe really solid, but maybe not. He could beat it."

"That's always a risk."

Marshall blew more smoke, and his jaw worked. After a minute he said, "That would be . . . tragic."

"At this point, I don't think it'll happen," Lucas said.

"So tell me what you've got. I've been down here all the time. I keep meaning to come up to see you, but I can't get myself away from . . ." He looked down the hill, and his jaw worked again. ". . . all the holes."

Lucas ran the case past him, everything that they had learned. Marshall's eyebrows went up when he heard about the photo of Laura Winton at St. Pat's, and about the death of Neumann.

"You think they're all connected?"

"The Neumann thing . . . that's just not right. We know he was at St. Pat's, we know the art teacher died after the drawings were put on TV, we know that Aronson was missing jewelry, and so was Neumann. That's what we think. The St. Paul cops haven't gone public with it, but I think Neumann was killed as a kind of . . . cleanup. She figured something out."

"A cleanup," Marshall said. He pitched his cigarette down the hill. "The fucker ought to be skinned alive."

Lucas's cell phone rang a moment later, and he fumbled it out of his pocket. "Yeah?"

"This is Del. Where are you?"

"Talking with Marshall, down at the graveyard. What's going on?"

"We gotta break," Del said. "Get your ass back up here."

"What happened?"

Del explained quickly, and Lucas said, "I'm on my way," hung up, and to Marshall: "Gotta run."

"Something?"

Lucas was already headed down the hill, and he called back, "Maybe."

Marshall said, "I'm coming," and they both scrambled down the wet hill and hopped the ditch, Lucas hurrying to his car, Marshall jogging heavily to his, swinging then through U-turns and accelerating away to the north.

13

LUCAS WAS PORSCHE-TRAINED, and showed it, even in the hippolike Tahoe; he could see Marshall laboring to keep up as the Dunn County deputy tracked him across Dakota County toward the Cities. Once he was on the highway, he put the truck on cruise control to remind himself to slow down. Marshall got on his taillights and stayed there. Lucas led him into a parking garage downtown, called Del while the other cop parked, and after Marshall had climbed into the Tahoe, continued out. Del was waiting on the corner at City Hall.

"Tell Terry what you told me," Lucas said, as Del climbed in the back.

"I was running a picture of Neumann's and Aronson's jewelry around town," Del told Marshall. "There's a guy Lucas and I both know, Bob Brown's his name, he deals in estate jewelry. Tries to keep it as legit as he can. I showed him the pictures, and as he soon as he saw the Aronson ring and the pearl necklace, he recognized them. They came in six months ago. He'd sold the necklace, but the ring was still there, and it's got the 'Love Forever.' I gave him a receipt; it's back at the office."

Lucas said to Marshall, "The ring had 'Love Forever' engraved inside."

"So there's no question, then," Marshall said. "Where'd he get them?"

"Off a bartender named Frank Stans at the Bolo Lounge, a nudie bar out on Highway 55—that's just west of here, fifteen minutes," Del said. "Stans told him he bought the stuff across the bar from a guy who said he inherited it."

"What are the chances that Stans . . . ?"

"Stans is a black guy, and he's dealt with Bob on other stuff. So it's unlikely," Del said.

"And we know where he's at? This Stans guy?" Marshall said.

Del looked at his watch. "His shift started about ten minutes ago."

Marshall cracked a grin and said, "The big city."

"What?" Del asked over the seat back.

"Over in Wisconsin, the nudie bars don't get going until after dinner."

"I got a cabin in Wisconsin, up north," Lucas said. "I was going deer hunting a couple of years ago, and when I got up there, Friday night, late, it was snowing. So I'm in my cabin, checking everything out, and find out I'd picked up a box of varmint rounds for my .243. So I'm wandering around trying to find some place open that sells .243s, and I stop at a convenience store and they told me that the only place open that might sell them was this nudie bar. I went over, and sure enough, they had some decent loads, in about anything you wanted. And they had a grocery area and a bait operation in the back room. This chick up on the bar, dancing . . . I bet she went 180, and she was *not* a tall girl. Had bruises all over her, like she fell down a lot."

"Different culture," Marshall said. "We like something you can get ahold of."

"You not only could get a hold on this one, you could hardly avoid her," Lucas said.

"Bruises like she was getting beat up?" Del asked.

"Naw. Like she might start drinking martinis at breakfast," Lucas said. "She was definitely a . . . bruised peach. She could *dance,* though."

"Why'd you have to go through that whole thing about .243s to tell us a nudie-bar story?" Del asked.

Lucas shook his head. "The idea of hanging out in a combination bait shop–nudie bar looking at fat women dance at midnight before the deer opener . . . I don't know. It *does* feel different than what we got here."

THE Bolo Lounge was open but had no customers. A woman in a robe and plastic flip-flops was sitting on the edge of a table-sized circular stage when they came in, reading a throwaway real estate magazine. She looked them over, and Lucas shook his head. "Don't bother," he said. "Where's Frank Stans?"

She didn't answer, but she looked down toward the bar; a black man stood at the far end, looking down at the bartop. Frank Stans was older, in his sixties, Lucas thought, bald with a fringe of white hair. He did not look like anybody's grandpa—he looked like he'd once lifted a lot of weight, and from time to time some of it had fallen on his face. He was reading a Japanese manga comic book and drinking what looked like a Pepto-Bismol cocktail through a straw.

"Mr. Stans?" Lucas asked.

Stans looked up. "Who wants to know?"

"Minneapolis police." Lucas showed him his ID, and as Marshall and Del moved up beside him, pulled the photos of the Aronson jewelry out of his pocket. "We're told that you sold this ring and necklace to Bob Brown six months ago. We're wondering where you got it."

Lucas dropped the pictures on the bar, and Stans looked down at them without touching the photographs. "Don't remember," he grunted. "I sold things to Brown once or twice, but I don't remember this."

"It'd be really good if you tried hard," Del said. "The stuff was taken off a girl who was murdered and buried out in the countryside."

"We're not looking at you as an accomplice," Lucas said, trying to take the edge off.

"Not yet," said Marshall, putting the edge back on.

Lucas glanced at him—Marshall's voice sounded like chipped glass—then looked back at Stans and said, "So look at them again. Because it would be a rainy day in your life if you don't remember, and we find out later that you were bullshitting us."

Stans and Marshall had locked eyes, and neither was backing off. Del said, "This is particularly important to the deputy here, 'cause some of his family was killed by the guy who took this jewelry."

"You say Deputy Dog?" Stans asked, cutting his eyes over to Del.

"I . . ." Del started.

Marshall jumped in, talking to Del while he still looked at Stans. "He don't bother me. I deal with trash all the time. Sooner or later, something always happens to them."

"That a threat?" Stans asked, not quite looking at Marshall.

"No, I don't threaten anybody. I guess the good Lord just don't like accomplices. He winds up catching them behind the bar and taking them off."

Stans now looked at Lucas. "Listen to this shit. Listen to this . . ."

Lucas put up a finger, silencing Stans, then said to Marshall, "Shut up."

Marshall nodded. Lucas said to Stans, "So taking a second look, see if you remember better."

Stans had locked eyes with Marshall again, and this time, apparently saw something he didn't like. He looked back down at the pictures and said, "Yeah, I got it off some white boy. Never saw him before. Said somebody downtown put him on me, told him that I bought estate jewelry."

"What'd he look like?" Lucas asked.

Stans shrugged. "I don't know. Like a white boy. White face, skinny, maybe six feet or a little more or less, but about that. Brown hair. Maybe blond hair. No beard or anything."

"Nervous?"

"No." He looked at Marshall again, and then his eyes flicked away. "Doper. He was running on crack, I could tell by looking at him. He wanted the money, and he wanted it right that minute."

"What else?"

"Nothin' else. I had three hundred dollars on me, and that's what I gave him. I told him, take it or leave it, and he took it."

"Would you recognize him if you saw him again?"

Stans nodded. "Maybe. If he introduced himself, I'd remember."

They talked for another minute, but Stans insisted that the transaction had been quick and routine: Nothing had happened out of the ordinary, and the seller hadn't stayed for a drink or to look at the women. Lucas thanked him, and they headed for the door.

Outside, a little pissed, he said to Marshall, "That wasn't real cool, the way you jumped in there with the threats."

"Just being the asshole," Marshall said mildly. "Didn't mean nothing by it—and we got what we came for."

"You sounded like you meant it," Lucas said.

"I'm good at that," Marshall said.

Very good at it, Lucas thought.

They were in the truck when Stans appeared at the door and pointed at Lucas. Lucas ran the window down and said, "What?"

"Come talk to me a minute. Just you."

Lucas turned to Del, said, "Hold the fort," got out, and walked over to Stans, who held the door for him. They both stepped inside, and Stans said, "You gonna keep Deputy Dog away from me?"

"He was just being a hardass so I could be the nice guy," Lucas said. "You know how that works."

"So keep him off me," Stans said. Then: "I remembered one other thing about this white boy."

"Yeah?"

"He talked like a brother. I mean, you always running into white boys who see you're black and so they talk a little black, that's just bullshit. Fuckin' bigots. This boy, he talked like a brother like he didn't even know he was doing it. Sounded to me like he grew up in one of the projects."

"White."

"He was definitely white," Stans said.

"Did he look like he might've had a couple of fights? Fucked-up eyebrows, maybe a little loose in the nose?"

Stans thought about it for a minute. "Yeah, you know . . . he did," Stans said. "You know him? What happened to him?"

"I happened to him," Lucas said.

"Okay, forget Deputy Dog," Stans said, showing a grin. *"You* stay away from me."

When he got back into the truck, Del looked at Lucas's face and said, "What?"

"It's that fuckin' Randy Whitcomb," he said. "The fancy man."

"You *know* him?" Marshall asked.

Lucas nodded and said, "Yeah . . . it's not really that big a town. You hang around here long enough, and you get to know a lot of the characters."

"You think he could . . . ?"

Lucas shrugged. "Randy could do almost anything. He's a fuckin' pimp, we know he beats the shit out of his girls from time to time, and he's cut up a couple of them. Probably has killed somebody, or even a couple of people."

"Crazy motherfucker," Del agreed from the back. "But . . ."

"Yeah. Not really his style. The guy we're looking for is nuts, but he's under control, deliberate. Randy's completely out of control," Lucas said. "The other thing is, he would have been too young when your niece was taken. Randy's still gotta be in his early twenties. Twenty-one, twenty-two."

"So maybe he was just passing the jewelry along."

"If he only took three hundred for it, for the necklace and the ring, then he probably got it for free, or the next thing to it. If Randy didn't do it, the guy who gave him the jewelry knows who did."

"So we look up this Randy," Marshall said comfortably. "We find him, we're right there."

"Trouble is, the word was going around that Randy moved to L.A.," Del said. "He's supposedly been gone for a couple of months."

"Gotta find him," Lucas said. "He's a key."

"Somebody's gotta find him," Del said. "Not you."

Lucas nodded. "Okay."

Marshall picked up the interplay. "What happened?"

"I once arrested Randy a little too enthusiastically," Lucas said. "It created a situation."

Del snorted. "Shit. It got your ass fired, is what it did. Randy looked like a carpet that had been beat with an ax."

"But you're back," said Marshall. "You got unfired."

"Just about took an act of God," Del said. To Lucas: "But I'll get him. I'll look up some of his pals tonight and confer with them."

"I'm coming," said Marshall.

"You don't have any—"

"I don't give a shit," Marshall said. "I'm coming."

Del nodded. "Okay. You can watch. Gonna catch us a fancy man."

14

RANDY WHITCOMB, HIS clothes aside, resembled a photograph of a Civil War soldier: pale, rawboned, head slightly misshapen—not distorted, exactly, but simply lopsided—thin nose, broken a time or two, thin lips, crooked teeth, the skin of his face touched with pocks, the result of an early and violent encounter with acne.

He looked like a mean white hillbilly. He didn't let that stop him.

Randy Whitcomb was a fancy man. He liked blackthorn walking sticks with gold-nugget heads, big broad-rimmed llama-felt hats, gold chains, and red sport coats with black collars spiked with gold threads. Tall boots made of alligator skin, with three-inch heels. Moleskin pants. Not just cars: *motorcars*.

He'd driven a crimson Jaguar for a while in L.A.—a short while, before both the car and L.A. got too hot—and carefully called it a "Jag-u-war," a pronunciation he picked up from a radio advertisement. Randy thought he was a black pimp, though he was, in fact, a white boy from the suburbs of Minneapolis. His background didn't keep him from talking ghetto-black and laying down lines of hip-hop when he had a little crack rolling through his veins.

Randy was twenty-two but looked forty-two, with lines in his forehead, at his eyes, slashing down his cheeks. Cocaine, speed, PCP, all that shit will make you old. Randy sold dope, ran an occasional whore, and was James Qatar's fence.

Through some process that Qatar didn't totally understand, Randy would exchange jewelry and other high-value stolen goods—handguns, mostly—for dope out of Chicago. He would peddle some of the dope and eat the rest.

The stolen jewelry sold in Chicago for half of what it was worth, Randy said, and the Chicago people gave Randy only half of what they could get for it. So Randy could only give Qatar half of what he could get from the Chicago people—an eighth of the real value. But that was crime, Qatar thought. That's the way things worked.

"You get me guns instead of this other shit, I get you real money," he said. "None of this half-and-half-and-half shit with a good nine-millimeter." But Qatar wouldn't touch handguns: Handguns could be traced with minute precision.

Qatar had met Randy through an improbable accident: A hip marketing professor who did a little cocaine had put them together on the back porch of his house during a Fourth of July barbecue, dropping a broad hint that Randy was a criminal friend. Then Randy and Qatar had embarked on a complicated, circumspect conversation, which ended with Qatar asking about underground jewelry sales.

"I can do that," Randy said. "I got the connection down to Chicago."

"Chicago."

"That's where the boys are," Randy said.

"Okay. . . . Do you have a card?"

Randy's forehead furrowed, and Qatar thought he might have blushed. "You think I should?"

"Well, I'd like to get in touch with you, maybe," Qatar said. "Nothing stolen, but I would like to get rid of it quietly."

"If it ain't stolen, you'd be stupid to sell it to me. You could just take it to a jewel store. Get a lot more for it."

"I need to keep it very quiet. If a jeweler up here ever put it in an estate sale, and my in-laws ever saw it, I'd be in real trouble."

Randy saw through it—the stuff was stolen—but if Qatar wanted to bullshit, that was his problem. "I give you my cell phone number," he said. "By the by . . . where would I go to get a card?"

The next time they met, Randy had business cards, and Qatar had gotten $1,500 for what he supposed was ten or twelve thousand dollars' worth of mediocre jewelry he'd taken off a woman from Iowa.

What Qatar didn't know was that Randy really didn't have a fencing connection in Chicago; he sold it on the street in Minneapolis, to whoever would take it. What Qatar didn't know wouldn't hurt him, Randy thought. Besides, why should he give a shit about Qatar?

QATAR had called Randy's beeper in the afternoon and had gotten an address in St. Paul, on Selby. He wouldn't be home until late, Randy said. After midnight.

Qatar looked at his watch when he arrived outside Randy's. Ten past twelve. Randy lived in a yuppie-looking town house, gray and white, in a long line of town houses that looked like they'd had government design input. The place was not what Qatar expected.

But Randy answered the door. He was wearing a red silk dressing robe and had a brown-tinted joint stuck in an onyx cigarette holder. His mouth was an angry slash. "Who d'fuck are you?" he asked.

"Uh, Randy, I called . . ." Qatar stepped back, half turned.

"Shit you called. What'd you call about?" Randy's eyes seemed fogged; he was wrong, and it was more than a little hash. Qatar backed away another step.

Randy took a step after him, and Qatar looked quickly up and down the street. He didn't need this. "This afternoon I called. I've got some jewelry."

The fog seemed to lift an inch. "Jim," he said. "You're Jim."

"I better go. . . . You look like you need some sleep."

Randy suddenly laughed, a long, deep rolling peal, as though he were an aged blues singer doing a cameo in a white movie. "Don't need no sleep. I *don't* need no sleep." He turned angry. "You sayin' I need sleep?"

"Listen . . ."

"C'mon. In." Randy had stepped close, and he caught Qatar's arm just above the elbow. His hand felt like a mechanical claw. "Got the slick crib. Wait'll you see inside. You're Jim, Jim."

Qatar was dragged along, afraid to protest, into the town house and up a flight of stairs. "Mostly garage down there," Randy said. At the top of the stairs, he said, "Check it out."

Qatar whistled, genuinely amazed.

Scarlet flocked-wallpapered walls were punctuated by three faux-antique mirrors with foam-plastic frames painted to resemble gilded wood. A fifty-two-inch widescreen TV was pushed against one wall, sitting on a black furry rug in front of a white furry couch. On the wall to the left of the TV was a fireplace with a steel surround. Erté graphics hung everywhere.

Randy must have found a frame shop, Qatar thought. One that was big with faux everything. "Pretty amazing, Randy."

Randy backed up to the railing next to the stairs, steadied himself, and studied the room as if suddenly puzzled. Something missing? He took it in for another few seconds, then shouted, "Hey, bitch, get out here."

A minute later, a too-thin blond girl padded out of a back hallway. She might have been sixteen, Qatar thought. She was round-shouldered with defeat, and barefoot, and said apologetically, "I just had to pee, Randy."

"Yeah, well, get me and my friend a beer. Make it fuckin' quick. And wash your hands first."

"You want it in glasses?" The question came out as a whine.

"Of course we want it in fuckin' glasses. And they best be clean." He said to Qatar, "I ain't got her fully broke yet."

Qatar nodded and tried not to look embarrassed; and in fact, he wasn't much. "I've got some stuff for you."

"Let's see it . . . Jim." Qatar handed him the little bag of jewelry, and Randy shook it out into his hand; the hand was suddenly steady. "What's it worth?"

"I've been checking the jewelry stores. I should get three thousand. You should get six from Chicago. Both the diamond and the emerald are real."

"Okay. I got no cash right now. I get it to you day after tomorrow." He put the jewelry back in the bag, slipped the bag into his pocket, and said, "Hey, look at this." He picked up a T-shaped remote control and pointed it at the fireplace. A fire sprang up. "Just like TV: real fire. Even looks like real logs in there, but it's gas. But it looks like real logs. You can get some shit that you sprinkle in there, and it smells like burning wood."

The woman came out of the kitchen with two glasses of

beer and two bottles balanced on a round tray. She did it well enough that Qatar thought she must've worked as a waitress somewhere, though she looked too young.

"Beers," she said.

"Look at this," Randy said. He turned one of the bottles. " 'Special Export.' "

"You're doing well, my friend," Qatar said.

"I am doin' well." Randy looked at the woman and said, "Sit on the floor." She sat, and Randy and Qatar both had a sip of beer, and then Randy said, "You got any cash on you?"

Qatar's eyebrows went up. "A little, not much."

"How much?"

"Fifty dollars, maybe."

"Got a cash card?"

"Well . . ."

"What's your limit?"

"Four hundred," Qatar said, mentally kicking himself the moment the words were out of his mouth.

Randy looked at him for a moment, then said, "I tell you what happened. I started partying at six o'clock and I run out of cash. So I went to a cash machine and I partied some more and then I run out of cash again, and I was at my daily limit. So then I borrowed some, and pretty soon I ran out of that, and then nobody would give me no more even though I just gotta wait until tomorrow before my cash card works again."

"Hmm," Qatar said. He thought about asking for the jewelry back, but Randy was pretty coked and had a tendency to get excited.

"So . . . I ain't asking for a loan. I want to *sell* you something," Randy said.

"What? I mean, I really don't need—"

"Her," Randy said, nodding at the woman on the floor. She looked at Qatar but said nothing.

Qatar said, "I don't fool around with prostitutes. I mean, I've got nothing against it, but I worry about AIDS and syphilis and gonorrhea and herpes."

Randy put a hand to his chest, offended. "Randy ain't gonna give you the clap, man. Randy ain't gonna give you the clap. You ain't gonna get the clap sticking your dick down her throat. No way you're gonna get the clap from doing that."

"Well, I . . ." Qatar looked at the woman again and shook his head. She *was* his type, he couldn't deny that—although a little dirty-looking, like she should use some cleanser on her feet. The thing was, Barstad was wearing him out. He hadn't had a random sexual thought in days.

"She'll do anything you want, Dick." When Qatar turned to look at Randy, Randy nodded and said, *"Anything."*

"Man, I appreciate it. . . ."

Randy couldn't believe he was being turned down. He turned to the woman and said, "Stand up, bitch. Take off the clothes and show the man what you got."

The woman stood up and started shedding her clothes. Pulled her sweatshirt over her head, pulled off her jeans, popped off her bra, peeled off her underpants, and then stood in front of Randy, looking at his face. Said nothing. All her pubic hair had been shaved off, and Qatar noticed that she was developing a rash. Ingrown hair, he thought, almost sympathetically. Something about that part—the rash—stirred him. She seemed so helpless. Unformed.

"She do anything," Randy said again.

Qatar noticed that Randy now had a sheen of sweat on his face. His physical condition seemed to change from minute to minute, and when he picked up his beer again, he picked it up with both hands. "I'll make you a deal," Qatar said. "You may not like it."

"What is it?" Randy asked.

"If you give me give five thousand for the jewelry, plus my four hundred dollars back—five thousand, four hundred dollars total, next week—I'll get the money out of the machine right now."

"You fuckin' kike," Randy shouted. He laughed, excited, and jumped up. "You got it, Dick. You got it."

"But you gotta get me the money, Randy," Qatar said. "Honest to God, it'd really hurt me if I didn't get it. I'm in a jam, too."

"You'll get it, baby," Randy brayed. Spit flew out of his mouth. "I never let you down. You a fuckin' client. Five thousand, four hundred dollars. You get it in two days, soon as the delivery boy comes from St. Louis."

St. Louis? They looked at each other for a moment, then Qatar shrugged. "All right."

"Yes," Randy shouted, pumping a fist. He didn't seem to notice that he was shouting.

"Can I come with you?" the woman asked.

"Shut the fuck up," Randy screamed. He pointed a trembling finger at her. "You can't go outside until you gots a name, bitch, and you ain't got one." To Qatar: "I ain't figured her name out yet."

"Okay. . . . So . . ."

"So let's go, Dick. Let's get the fuck outa here."

Qatar was now Dick—because Randy had used "dick" in a sentence? He wasn't sure, but looking at Randy leaning against the passenger-side window blubbering to himself, he was very sure that Randy had gone over some unseen edge.

They went to a cash machine at a branch bank on Grand Avenue. Qatar took out four hundred dollars in twenties, and as he pulled it out of the machine, Randy snatched it away from him and then backed away, said, "Get the fuck away from me. Get the fuck away."

"Randy, Randy . . ."

Randy jammed the money into his pants and asked, "You know who you're fuckin' with, motherfucker? I'll hunt you down like a dirty dog, you fuck with me."

"Okay, okay . . ." Qatar held up his hands. He was leaving. "I'll see you in a couple of days."

Then Randy came back: "Ain't you gonna drop me?"

"I thought, uh . . ."

"You can't leave me out here on the fuckin' street, man. Where's my money?"

"In your pocket."

Randy dug in his pocket, found it. "Sonofabitch. I had it all the time. Let's go."

On the way, Randy pressed his hands to his temples, looked at Qatar, and blurted, "I made a garland for her head and bracelets too and fragrant zone. She looked at me as she did love and made sweet moan."

"What?"

"I made a garland for her head . . ."

Randy's brain was missing a few links, Qatar thought. Even so, he knew where he was going. He would point at corners and say, "There," and "There, that way." He said, "Over there, Richard. . . . Can I call you Richard?"

In five minutes they were idling in front of an apartment on Como Boulevard. Randy hopped out and said, perfectly rationally, "You can come in if you like, but they mostly brothers. They don't like white boys that good."

"That's okay. I gotta get home anyway."

Randy slapped the car roof in reply, then darted into the apartment's dark front entry, never looking back.

QATAR rolled away from the apartment. Instead of cutting back onto I-94 to Minneapolis, the car seemed all by itself to roll back across the interstate to Randy's place. He'd been thinking about the woman since they left the apartment—not the possibility of sex, but the other possibility.

He sat outside for ten minutes, unable to make up his mind. He was sure that Randy had no idea who he was; he might never get the money from the jewelry, but he ought to get something. He could feel an artery in his neck, beating harder, a thick, ropy pounding. He wanted her; he could feel her. He fished the starter rope out from under the front seat of the car and tucked it into his hip pocket.

Randy's brain was fried. He wouldn't remember this. . . . Did he really know who Qatar was, anyway? And Qatar was suffused with courage. He was competent, hard, athletic. He went to the door and rang.

The blonde had gotten dressed again, though her feet were still bare. At the door, Qatar said, "Randy talked me into giving him five hundred. But he said I get you, any way I want."

The blonde looked past him, unsure, and then asked, "Where's Randy?"

"He's back at the apartment, partying. When we're done, I'm supposed to take you over there."

A misstep: Now she was suspicious. "I can't go outside 'til I got a name."

"He thought of the name," Qatar improvised. "You've got a name."

"I do? What is it?"

"Tiffany. Like the jewelry store."

"Tiffany," she said aloud. She tasted it. "That's pretty good. Tiffany." She looked him over again, then said, "Okay. Come on in."

She was a hooker, and it didn't take long: He got her on her hands and knees, in front of the couch, waiting for him to enter her. He'd rolled the condom down, positioned himself behind her. His pants had been tossed on the couch, and he fished the rope out of the back pocket. Touched her back with it; trailed it her down her spine.

She asked, "What's that?" and turned her head.

"Nothing, nothing . . . keep going."

Formed his loop; touched her neck again. Held the loop open, smiled, dropped it around her neck and . . .

Snap! He tightened it like a hangman's noose, and her hands went to her throat and she tried to turn, flailing like a caught crow, but he pressed her down with his weight. He didn't want to see her eyes; he used the power of the rope to bend her sideways and down, and she continued to flop and twist and struggle, her feet banging against the couch, smashing the back legs of an La-Z-Boy, and then he half stood, and lifted her, held her suspended above the floor like a billfish on the deck of a big-game boat. Held her and shook her and watched her hands flailing, watched them weaken, felt the power surging through his arms into his heart. . . .

As her struggles slowed and weakened, he straddled her and lowered her to the floor, her hands scratching along the furry carpet. He knelt over her, then sat on her buttocks, keeping the pressure on, his teeth showing now in a slashing grimace, squeezing, squeezing. At the end, she arched her back and her hands fluttered in a terminal dog-paddle, and she died.

God, that felt good.

When she stopped moving, stopped the shuddering that came with brain death, Qatar released his grip, sat back on her hips. He was sweating, just a bit, and wiped his forehead with his shirtsleeve, then rolled her over. Her eyes were open, staring sightlessly up at the ceiling, her mouth touched with blood; and a puddle of blood pooled on the rug beneath her neck. She'd bitten her tongue, he thought. He rolled her. "Tits not bad. Soft and warm," he said.

No response. After a minute with her, he sighed and stood up. "Gotta get going," he said. "The clock is running.

Gotta go." He didn't feel rushed; if anything, he felt lan-guid.

And his lip hurt, he realized. He wandered into the bathroom to look at it in the mirror. He had a full under-lip, usually pink, now bruised. Sometime during the strug-gle, she must have hit him, but he didn't remember it. Hit him hard, judging from the split lip. There was no swelling yet, but he could taste the blood in his mouth. "That was completely fucking unnecessary," he said. He probed the cut with his tongue, winced at the pain. The lip would get big if he didn't get some ice on it, but the swelling would be disguised by his thin beard. "Unfuck-ing-necessary."

He had to stay focused. He got dressed, flushed the con-dom—surprised to find it full of semen; he didn't remem-ber that part—straightened his shirt, tucked it back in his trousers, got himself neat. Got a chunk of toilet paper and walked through the apartment, wiping everything he could remember touching. Another flush, and he was done.

"Thank God for toilets," he said to himself.

Money. There wouldn't be any cash, but there should be something. . . . Randy had stuck Neumann's jewelry in his pocket, so that was gone. Qatar walked through the apart-ment, looking. And found almost nothing small. Randy had apparently sold everything that could be peddled on the street.

"Moron," he said aloud. He stepped over the woman's body on the way out. Queen for a day, Tiffany for a minute. Nice tits, though.

RANDY got back at dawn and pounded on the door, because he didn't want to go through the whole business of finding his key. He was not in any shape to find it. So he beat on the door until somebody shouted, "Go away or we'll call the police."

Some fuckin' neighbor. But he didn't need the police, so he took five minutes and finally found the key, and another five minutes and he fit it into the lock and the door swung open. He shouted up the stairs, got no answer. Climbed the stairs in the dark—there was a switch at the entrance, but he was too fucked up to use it—and in the living room, in the dark, tripped over the woman's body.

"Fuckin' . . ." He groped around on the floor, felt a breast. Knew what it was and knew it was too cold. Randy started down, the cocaine strength dissipating like a fart in a thunderstorm. He crawled across the floor to a lamp, climbed the lamp like a monkey, turned it on.

Looked down at what's-her-name. Who was she? What had he done? He pressed his hands to his temple, trying to squeeze out the memories that must be there somewhere. When had he done it?

"Motherfucker," he said.

15

WEATHER HAD SPENT the night at her own place. "If we haven't rung the bell yet, I don't think we'll get it done this month," she'd said. "Plus, my house is getting stale. I need to air it out."

Lucas didn't remember that when he woke up. Still drowsy, he reached out for her shoulder, came up with air, and bumped up, quickly awake, looking for her. He remembered the question he'd asked the night before. Pregnant? Not pregnant? When would they know?

"In the bye and bye," she'd said cheerfully. "It was fun working with you, Davenport. Maybe we can do it again next month. Then again, maybe we won't have to."

He half-smiled at the thought, punched his pillow back into shape, and drifted off again. Lucas liked to stay up late, but didn't like early mornings. A good day, he believed, generally started around ten o'clock.

* * *

TEN o'clock was just coming up when the phone rang, and continued to ring. He recognized Del's style. "Yeah?"

"Randy's around, but I can't find him. People say he ran into some shit out in L.A. Ambition combined with stupidity, probably."

"Probably," Lucas said. He yawned. "Who'd you talk to?"

"The Toehy sisters. They said he was running a hooker named Charmin until a couple of weeks ago, but—"

"Charmin like the toilet paper?"

"That's what they say. Anyway, he wandered off in a cocaine blizzard, and she transferred to DDT and that's where she's still at. Thing is, I can't find DDT right now. I got a couple of people looking for him and also for Randy."

"DDT, huh?"

"Yeah. Thought you might be interested."

"I am. Did Marshall ride with you?" Lucas asked.

"You know: That's how it goes," Del said.

"He's standing next to you?"

"You got it," Del said.

"Careful with him. I hate to say no, that he can't come along—but if he starts stepping on you, I'll pack his ass back to Wisconsin."

"We'll figure something out," Del said. "We're okay for now."

"You want me to come along if you find DDT?"

"If you don't mind. He owes you big, and he don't owe me shit."

"Gimme a call," Lucas said.

Lucas shaved and spent ten minutes in the shower, working on a sound he'd heard on a David Allen Coe album, from a song called "The Ride"—twisting the word "moan," trying to get three syllables out of it. He agreed with himself that he sounded particularly good that morning, got dressed, looked out the window—patches of blue sky and the street was dry—and loaded into the Porsche.

He was carrying a red apple and whistling when he pushed into the office. Marcy was talking on the phone, twisting a ring of her dark hair around her index finger, her feet up on her desk. She stopped playing with her hair long enough to raise a hand to Lucas, then started talking into the phone again. Lucas paused and looked her over: Marcy tended to be a little too tense all the time, and when the tension was suddenly relieved, it showed.

She noticed him studying her and turned away. Lucas continued into his office, a little pissed now: That goddamn Kidd had gotten into her pants. He knew the look too well to be mistaken. And they hardly knew each other, Lucas thought, and Kidd was a lot older. He retracted that a bit: Not too old—actually, he was probably a year or two younger than Lucas, so he couldn't be *too* old, because Lucas himself had . . .

"Goddamnit," he said. He flipped the apple up at the wall and caught it on the rebound, leaving a small pink patch behind on the wall. If Kidd and Marcy . . . He didn't want to think about it. But it sure as hell was going to reduce her efficiency at a critical moment in the case, and—

"I don't want to hear the first fuckin' word from you." Marcy was in the doorway.

"I just—"

"Not the first fuckin' word," she said, holding up a finger. When he opened his mouth again, she said, "No! Bad dog."

Lucas dropped into his chair, looked away from her, then said, quickly, "You don't know him that well."

"Shut up, Mr. Why-don't-we-screw-Marcy-Sherrill-on-the-office-carpet."

"We *knew* each other," Lucas protested. "For a long time. That was *spontaneous.*"

"So was last night. And I'll tell you what, he's a good guy," she said.

"You spend the night?"

"He did. At my place. We were just coming back from dinner, and it happened."

"He bring his toothbrush?"

"No, he didn't bring his toothbrush. And that's all I'm telling you," she said.

"What'd he brush his teeth with?"

"His finger."

"That's *so* unsanitary," Lucas said sourly.

Marcy put her hands on the top of her head and started to laugh, and a moment later Del came in, with Marshall trailing behind, and asked, "What's so funny?"

"He is," Marcy said, pointing at Lucas.

"I ain't even gonna ask," Del said, looking from one to the other. To Lucas: "We found DDT."

DDT stood for Dangerous Darrell Thomas. Thomas had given himself the name when he was riding with a motorcycle club and was interviewed for a public radio magazine. The magazine writer got it wrong, though, and referred to him as TDT—Terrible Darrell Thompson—which lost something of its intent when expressed as initials; and since the writer got the last name wrong, too, Thomas never again trusted the media.

Darrell wasn't much of a pimp. He didn't solicit customers and he wasn't particularly interested in sex, money, or any kind of fashion. His only pimping qualification was that he liked to fight, and when a girl wanted to leave her former sponsor, or was having trouble with a customer who expected fidelity, she might move in with Darrell.

He would grudgingly take care of her, and if she wanted to chip in a few bucks every once in a while, and maybe clean house and cook a few meals, that was okay. And if she didn't, that was okay, too. They tended to drift away when they discovered that Darrell really *didn't* care.

At all. About anything.

Except cars.

Darrell was a professional house-sitter.

"Can't believe he got a gig in Edina," Lucas said, as they pulled into his driveway. They were driving a city car, a dented Dodge, and they all peered through the windshield at the house. The house was long and white and two-storied, with double faux-marble pillars on either side of the front entry. "Wonder what the neighbors think about the whores going in and out all the time?"

"Maybe they think it's colorful," Del said.

They got out of the Dodge, and Lucas took a second to look around the neighborhood. Nothing moved: The place was one large bedroom.

When Lucas caught up, Del and Marshall were already looking at an enormous wrought-iron knocker on the front door. "Use the doorbell," Marshall said. "You'll knock the door down if you use that thing."

"How about a nice-knocker joke?" Del asked.

"None of those either," Lucas said. Del leaned on the doorbell, and after three long buzzes ten seconds apart, a woman with power-frizzed hair, wearing a pale blue quilted housecoat, stuck her head out, looked at the three of them, and snarled, "What?"

"Time to get up, sleepyhead," Del said, showing her a badge. "We're friends of DDT. Is he home?"

"Yeah, but he's in the spa," she said.

"That's something I wouldn't want to miss," Del said. He stepped forward and the woman stepped back, a good enough invitation, they thought, and they all trooped inside.

"It's outside, on the deck," the woman said, pointing at faux French doors at the far end of the living room.

Del's nose was working. "Something smells like dog shit," he said.

"We got a new puppy," the woman said. As she passed the table, she picked up a bottle half full of white wine and started working the cork loose. "We're paper-training it. You guys want some wine?"

Lucas said, "No, thanks," and she took a pull on the bottle, and Del and Lucas walked over to the French doors and out onto a deck.

The spa was big enough to seat eight, but in this case, sat three: DDT, a large, balding, and mildly fat man with scant chest hair, who was reading a folded copy of *The New York Times;* and two women, both with short mousy brown hair. Steam rose out of the spa into the cold air, but they all seemed comfortable: None of them were wearing any clothing at all, and when Lucas, Del, and Marshall pushed through the doors, one of the women said, "Better turn on the bubbler, Marie."

"Hey, Lucas, how they hanging, man?" DDT said, looking up from the paper. "Del, you fuckhead. What's happening?" To the girls he said, "They're cops."

"We got a problem, Darrell," Lucas said. "We're looking for a girl named, uh . . ." He looked at Del.

Del said, "Charmin."

DDT pointed at one of the mice, who said, "Jesus Christ, it's Charmin', like in Charming, you asshole. It's not *sharmin,* like the toilet paper."

"We thought maybe it came from Please Don't Squeeze The," Marshall said. The crow's-feet around his eyes compressed a little, and the corners of his mouth may have turned up. He was being funny, Lucas realized.

"No, it don't," the woman said frostily.

"You guys want to get in? Plenty of room. Water's hot," DDT said, nodding at the bubbling surface.

"Ah, we're kinda running," Lucas said, looking at

Charmin'; she was the larger of two women, and her breasts were floating on the top of the water, her nipples pointing straight out like the prows on a couple of fancy powerboats. "Charmin', you were working for Randy Whitcomb until not long ago, and we need to find him."

"What's he done?" she asked.

"Nothing. We're trying to figure out where he might have bought some jewelry. This was back before he went to L.A."

"Yeah? I wasn't with him them. I didn't join up until after he got back."

"I know that," Lucas said patiently. "But we need to find him now."

"I don't know if I oughta talk to cops," she said. "Randy's a crazy motherfucker."

"Tell them," DDT said.

She looked at him and said, "You're supposed to be on my side."

"I owe him," he said. "Big-time. So you can tell him or move the fuck out."

She looked at DDT for a minute, then at Lucas, and said, "He's in St. Paul, one of them gray apartments on Sibley. I don't know the number." She gave them a few details, and Lucas nodded: He knew exactly where she meant. "Thanks."

"You be careful. The crazy fucker's been smokin' crack since he got back—he ain't got any brains left. And don't tell him where you got this."

DDT said, "So what're you driving?"

"C4," Lucas said. "Bought it new last year."

"Yeah? But you're not right now. . . ." He raised his eyebrows and looked at the three large men.

"Not with me. I'm in a company car," Lucas said.

"Whyn't you bring it around sometime?" DDT asked.

"I will," Lucas said. "Probably when it warms up a little. We'll take it out for a run."

"Do that," DDT said.

On the way out of the house, Marshall said, "That was pretty smooth. Why'd he owe you so big?"

"Last fall, I found him a four-fifty-five Olds engine. He was really hurting for one," Lucas said.

Marshall looked at him strangely and said, "You pullin' my weenie?"

"No . . . I mean, it was absolutely *cherry*."

LUCAS called St. Paul from the car, got Allport and filled him in on the jewelry and the connection to Randy Whitcomb.

"I thought that cocksucker had moved to San Diego or something," Allport said. "I'll check with the condo association and see where he is."

"We're on our way right now," Lucas said. "If you or one of your guys wants to hook up with us."

"Need some help?"

"We could use a warrant and somebody to block the back."

"Warrant's no problem, not with this case. I'll get a couple of squads and come up myself," Allport said. "What, half an hour, forty-five minutes?"

"About that," Lucas said.

They were out on I-494, one of the outer-loop highways around the Cities. Marshall, in the back, leaned forward and asked, "What are we doing?"

"St. Paul's going to block for us," Lucas said. He explained the layout of the apartment complex: a rectangular block of two-story town-house condos, facing the streets on all four sides of a city block. The interior of the rectangle was a common lawn, with marked but unfenced private patio areas behind each town house.

"Can you get a car in back?" Marshall asked.

"Not without trying pretty hard. There're arched entrances to the big lawn on all four sides, but they're not used for vehicles. Not regularly, anyway. I think they're more like an emergency thing if there was a fire or something. St. Paul guys'll have to go in on foot."

"Think this guy'll run?"

"Can't tell what Randy'll do," Del said. "He's a rattlesnake and a crazy motherfucker. Comes from a decent family, and they just should have snapped his neck when he was a baby. Would have saved everybody a lot of grief."

"Known a couple like that myself," Marshall said. He thought about it for a minute, then said, "Farm kids, usually. When it happens like that."

AFTER another phone call to Allport, they agreed to meet three blocks from Randy's to coordinate. Six St. Paul uniformed guys arrived in three squads, including one guy who was the designated hammer. They were all in their thirties—veterans—and Lucas guessed that it was not by chance: Allport was taking it seriously.

"The problem is that the door is at the bottom of a set of stairs—the downstairs part is basically a garage and workshop, or extra bedroom, and the living quarters are upstairs. So we're gonna be squeezed onto the stairs if we have to kick the door," Allport said. He looked around at his crew. "Lucas and Del and I have known this asshole ever since he came downtown six or seven years ago. He can be bad news, so be careful. He's not that big, but he's crazy and he's tough as a goddamn hickory tree. He's a biter. He'll bite your goddamn fingers off if you get too close."

The uniforms weren't worried. "Give us a couple of minutes to get close," one of them said. "He won't run away from us."

"We've never found a gun on him," Lucas said. "But he's carried one from time to time. He's been doing a lot of crack, we hear, and maybe some other shit. So . . . if you've got to tackle him, tackle him hard. Don't hurt him—we need him to talk to us."

They were all starting to breathe hard, feeling the rush: a critical point on the case, and with a crazy.

"Come in last," Del told Lucas. "If there's no trouble, it won't make any difference. If there *is* trouble, maybe it won't rub off on you—but if there's big trouble, you'll be in position to lay some shit on him."

Lucas nodded. Randy had been a new guy on the block when one of his girls had spent some time with Lucas, talking. Randy had heard about it. He'd learned from the cheaper TV shows that the girl had to be taught a lesson for her disrespect, or he'd be disrespected himself. He'd taught her the lesson with a church key, cutting an average-looking hooker into a scholarly paper in a plastic surgery journal.

Lucas had felt pressured by street ethics to repay the attack. He and Del had gone to arrest Randy at a bar, but everybody had known it would come to a fight—and it had. Lucas had gone a little further than he intended, had lost it a little, and Randy had ended that particular day in Hennepin General's critical-care unit.

After a long tangled series of arguments and legal maneuvers, Lucas had left the department under the cloud of possible excessive-force charges. He'd been back for a while, but Randy Whitcomb still could be a political problem.

The hooker had left the streets after she got out of the hospital, and now worked at a Wal-Mart checkout. She looked okay from three feet, though a close inspection showed a plaid pattern of scars across both of her cheeks. She didn't talk to Lucas anymore.

They went to Randy's door by walking along the face of

the apartment building, five of them, led by Allport, followed by the hammer, then Del, then Lucas, with Marshall trailing. At the door, Allport spoke into a handset: "Ready?"

The uniforms were in position, and Allport slipped his gun, nodded, and pushed the doorbell. No answer. He pushed it again and they heard feet on the stairs, and then the bolt rattled and the door opened, just a crack, with a chain across the crack. Through the crack, Lucas saw a slice of Randy's face and one eye. Randy jerked back and screamed, "Shit," as Allport stepped forward and Lucas said, "Watch it!" The door slammed and the bolt slammed with it, and Allport said, "Hit it."

Lucas stepped out of the way, and the uniform swung his sledgehammer at the doorknob. The door blew open with the sound of a Cadillac hitting a picket fence. Allport did a quick peek, pulled back, said, "Let's go," and burst in onto the landing. He was turning for the stairs, Del two steps behind him, when the first shot BANGED overhead and Allport screamed, "GUN," and he and Del both went down and scrambled back off the stairs and out the door.

Lucas did a quick peek, saw nothing, and heard Allport screaming, "Gun," into his handset, and at the same time saw Del rolling off the porch and onto his feet, and then he was onto the stairs, moving up, felt Del behind him as a shadow, shouted, "Watch along the railing, watch . . ." And they both watched the railing at the stop of the stairwell. . . .

From up the stairs Lucas heard glass break, then another shot BANGED through the apartment, and he flinched and looked back and it wasn't Del behind him but Marshall, a trooper's long-barreled .357 revolver in his fist. He had no time to think when Marshall said, "I'll go to the top, you peek over the rail," and then Marshall was past him to the top of the stairs, and Lucas did a quick peek between the rails at the top and couldn't see anything.

Marshall scrambled out onto the carpet at the top, and he was shouting, "Living room is clear, I don't see him."

Another BANG from the back, and Lucas shouted, "He's in the back, it sounds like he went out." He heard somebody screaming, "Watch it, watch it, coming your way, watch it . . ."

Allport, he thought, and then he was at the top of the stairs and saw Marshall, now up and moving in a crouch, headed toward a hallway leading toward the back. He did a peek as Lucas came up and said, "Clear, I think."

Lucas did a peek and heard more shouting from the back, and ran down the hallway just in time to hear a fusillade of shots, and more yelling. He was coming up on a room to his right and a closed door on his left. He did a quick peek into the bedroom, saw nothing, continued through a small kitchen, saw broken glass, shouted back, "Watch the rooms, they're not clear, they're not clear," saw Del behind Marshall, got to the window, and looked out.

Randy Whitcomb was lying faceup, spread-eagled on the grass below the back deck. His shirt was soaked with blood and one hand was flapping convulsively, as though he were fanning himself with a broken arm.

Lucas turned, saw Del and Marshall in the hallway, and said, "He's down out back. Check the rooms." Allport and the hammer cop loomed from the living room. To Allport, Lucas said, "Get an ambulance moving." Then he was out and down the stairs onto the lawn, where the St. Paul uniforms, guns still drawn, had gathered around Randy.

Randy had been hit four times, twice in the legs, once in the stomach, and once in his left forearm, the arm that had been flapping. One of the uniform cops was now holding it to the grass so he couldn't flap it. Randy wasn't saying anything, not a sound: no whimpers, nothing. His eyes rolled, rolled, rolled, from this side to the other, up and down; and his mouth strained, not to say something, but as if it were trying to escape his face.

"Got an ambulance coming," Lucas said to him. He didn't hear it.

One of the St. Paul uniforms said, "He had a gun."

"Yeah, he let go a couple of times inside," Lucas said.

The cop said, "He had a gun. Up there, we heard it."

"Yeah, he did."

One of the other cops said, "I think it's in the bushes. He had it in his hand when he came out."

"Find it," Lucas said. "Don't touch, just find it."

Del came out on the deck. "Nobody in the house. But, uh . . ." He looked back into the condo, and Lucas could hear Marshall talking. Then Del turned back to Lucas and said, "There's a lot of blood up here."

"Nobody shot at him up there."

"No, no, I mean, somebody else's blood. He was trying to clean it up with paper towels, but it's kind of splattered on the couch and there are little droplets on the wallpaper."

Now Randy moaned, just once. Lucas looked down at him and said, "What'd you do?" But Randy didn't hear him; he just rolled his eyes again.

From the corner of the house, one of the St. Paul uniforms said, "There it is." To Lucas: "Got the gun, Chief."

"Just stay right next to it. Keep an eye on it until the crime-scene people get here. Don't let anyone get near it."

Allport came out on the deck and asked, "Everybody okay?"

"Everybody except Randy. He's hit pretty hard." Lucas looked down at him again. Randy's shirt was soaked with blood, and Lucas noticed that even with the convulsions running through his upper body, his lower body never moved. Spinal, he thought.

Allport yelled at one of the uniforms: "Freeze everything, John. Don't let anything move." Then, to Lucas: "You oughta come up and look at this mess."

Lucas said, "Okay," then looked down at Randy again. "What the fuck did you do, you little asshole? What'd you do?"

16

MARSHALL AND DEL came down from the apartment to watch the paramedics working over Randy. Whatever they did brought the pain on, and the kid started a cowlike lowing that seemed to inhabit all the air in the common area. He was still doing it when they strapped him on a gurney, ready to move him.

Two dozen kids, half of them white, the other half Hmong or black, most of them serious but a few cutting up, milled in a wide semicircle around the shooting scene, kept back by uniforms. Somewhere in the crowd was a young girl who'd periodically call out in her high-pitched TV-whore voice, "That motherfucker dead?" or "You shoot that motherfucker?" When the paramedics started wheeling the gurney toward the ambulance, she cried out, "Put him in the 'fridge, he dead."

When he was gone, the cops on the original blocking squads were isolated to make statements, and Randy's revolver was photographed, measured, and carefully plucked out of the weed bed where it had fallen. The crime-scene guy who lifted it popped the cylinder and said, "Four rounds fired."

"That's about right," Allport told him.

"Can't tell when," the crime-scene guy said.

"About a half an hour ago, dickhead," Allport said.

Lucas, Del, and Marshall clustered around the bottom of the apartment steps. Marshall said, "He doesn't look that bad, considering."

Lucas nodded. "If they get him to Regions alive, he'll make it—as long as he doesn't have too much shit in his bloodstream."

"I told the paramedics about the crack," Del said. "They'll watch out for it."

"I want to know what the heck happened," Marshall said. "Why'd he open up? Because we took the door down?"

Lucas rubbed his head, looking up at the apartment, and said, "I don't know. He's always been a crazy sonofabitch, and he never worried about getting hurt. Not brave, just nuts. I never really thought about him being suicidal."

"It's that blood," Del said. He looked up, where Lucas was looking, and continued, "Something happened up there."

"He couldn't be our guy," Marshall said. "You didn't have any goddamn twelve- or thirteen-year-old traveling around the countryside picking up women in their twenties. I mean, I don't know what it means."

"He was probably just a connection," Lucas said. "But he knows our guy."

"We could get a name tonight, then," Marshall said. "They sew him up—"

"If he'll talk," Del said. "He's a little asshole, and he'll be pissed."

"More pissed than you might think," Lucas said. "His legs weren't moving when he was on the ground. The slug that took him in the stomach might have clipped his spine."

Marshall winced, and Del said, "Ah, shit."

The crime-scene people were taping the apartment when the three of them climbed back up the stairs and tentatively stepped inside. Allport spotted them, shook his head: "Quite a bit of day-old blood. We don't think it was his."

"Is someone dead? That much blood?" Lucas asked.

Allport relayed the question to somebody out of sight. A second later, a cop in a tweed jacket and golf slacks stepped into the hallway and looked down at Lucas and said, "Not that much. I'd say it's gotta be maybe a pint, give or take. Of course, we don't know how much he cleaned up."

"Doesn't look like he'd done much cleaning," Del said. "There was still some blood on the wallpaper."

"You find any jewelry?" Lucas asked. "Good stuff?"

"Haven't looked yet," the cop said. "Would that be a priority?"

"Yeah, it would be," Lucas said. "Get the sequence of events on the entry nailed down first, though. We don't want that to get confused."

The cop nodded and dropped back out of sight. Allport said, "Give us half an hour. Then I'd appreciate if you could slow-walk through the place, see if anything catches your eye."

Lucas nodded. "We'll be back." To Del and Marshall, as they stepped back out onto the deck: "The day started so pretty that I drove the Porsche."

"Still not a bad day," Marshall said, looking up at the sky. "Still pretty. Even smells good, once you get away from the blood."

*   *   *

THEY wasted the half hour and a little more at a bagel shop on Grand Avenue, drinking coffee and trying to figure out the next step. They were still shaky from the shooting: talking too fast, digressing into stories, arguing the Aronson case.

"The woman over at the Catholic school, the museum lady—we gotta talk to her some more," Marshall said. "She comes up four times on our lists, and she takes you right over to that wall in Laura's pictures. That place has gotta be involved, and it's gotta be somebody close to her. Maybe somebody who works at the museum. People come to see her, and he picks them up there."

"Black's running down all the names in the museum and the art department—everybody over twenty-five," Lucas said.

"I'm supposed to go to this task force meeting tomorrow with Marcy," Marshall said. "I'd rather hang with you guys, but if you want, I could go over there and tell them about St. Patrick's and what we've seen so far, and maybe . . . I don't know, maybe we could get them to do research on everybody in the whole *school*. Everybody. Maybe there'd be some way to hook up the records from the school computer with the FBI, and run them all off in an hour or something."

"That's a thought," Lucas said. "I just can't figure out what a guy at St. Pat's is doing with a pimp like Randy."

"Just a fence," Del said. "The guy's a sex freak, so maybe they got hooked up that way, and then he started fencing stuff through Randy."

"You know what we should have done?" Marshall said. "When we had that woman over at DDT's place this morning, the one that used to work with Randy, we should have showed her the picture of the guy from the movie."

"Goddamnit," Lucas said irritably. "I should have thought of that."

"I'll get back to her," Del said. "Maybe I can hook up with some of Randy's other girls, too."

Still cranked, they all went back to Randy's. Allport was in the living room with two other cops, and said, "We gotta guy coming down with a recorder and some forms, if you guys could make a preliminary statement before you take off."

They all nodded, and Lucas asked, "Anything new?"

"Can't find his stash."

"Gotta be one," Lucas said. "He was weird about all that English shit—he had a walking stick, and he used to stroll around in riding boots and breeches and hats with feathers. You oughta look behind mirrors and paintings and check for hollowed-out banisters and all that. Look in the clocks."

He was standing at the top of the entry stairs, next to a banister knob, and tried to turn it; it was solid.

"What'd you hear from the hospital?" Del asked.

Allport shook his head. "He's in surgery, and they're giving us about the usual: Nothing, fuck you very much."

"How about the spine thing?"

He shook his head again. "I haven't heard a thing."

The crime-scene people found Randy's stash in a hardbound copy of *Bulfinch's Mythology,* one of a line of what looked like decorator books in a built-in bookshelf over the television. The pages of the Bulfinch had been haphazardly glued together, and then a hole cut out of the middle. The hole was just big enough to hold a couple of ounces of grass—it didn't, but it did hold a chamois bag.

The cop who found the book shook the bag into the palm of one hand, and out tumbled two rings, one diamond and one emerald. Lucas, Del, and Marshall had seen pictures of them.

"Sonofabitch," Del said.

"Now we know for sure," Lucas said. "He's the link."

They spent another hour at the apartment, giving brief

statements to a St. Paul investigator who would be looking into the shooting. When they were done, Marshall asked, "Where can I hook up with this Anderson guy? He's never around when I come through your office."

"He basically works with the computer system," Lucas said. "I'll take you around."

"Got an idea?" Del asked.

"No. I just want to look at all these lists he's making. Have we called these women up, the women in the drawings, to see how many of them have a connection with St. Patrick's?"

"Yeah. Many of them do—I mean, everybody in town is gonna know somebody from the place; it's a big school. But direct connections are pretty thin."

"Four hits with this old lady Qatar is a lot," Del said.

"Gotta be something there," Marshall said.

"Just like there is with Randy," Lucas said. "But how do you connect an elderly museum lady with an asshole like Randy? I looked at her, and I couldn't tell you."

BACK at City Hall, Lucas dropped Marshall with Anderson, the computer guy, and Del headed back to DDT's: "I'll show her the pictures, and maybe Charmin' can give me the name of some of his other girls," he said.

Lucas went back to the office, where Marcy was talking with Lane and Swanson. "Did you hear about Randy?" she asked.

"What?" He stopped in his tracks. "He died?"

"No, but he won't be walking anywhere for a while. Allport just called and said the surgeons are trying to fix his lower vertebrae so he doesn't do any more damage to his spinal cord, but there's already been some damage and they don't think he's gonna have full use of his legs. Not right away, anyway. He'll have to do rehab, and you know how that goes."

"Ah, shit." Lucas shook his head and said, "Nobody knows what happened. He just opened up."

"You don't look too shook," Marcy said.

"I didn't even see anything, until it was all over," Lucas said. "We came in the front, he ran out the back and opened up." He told them the story in detail, and about the rings.

"Allport told me about the rings," Marcy said. "Christ, if Randy hadn't had a gun, we'd have the guy now."

"Did Allport say if he was conscious?"

"Docs have really cut him up—they figure it'll be the day after tomorrow before he makes any sense, and maybe longer than that. They had to go into his gut and he's gonna have a lot of pain, so they're pouring the drugs into him." They all looked at Marcy: What happened to Randy seemed like a replay of what had happened to her. She picked up the vibration and said, "I didn't get the spine. But he's gonna be hurting, I can promise you that."

Swanson had been sitting with his head propped on his hands, and now he looked up at Lucas and said, "Damn good thing you weren't doing the shooting."

"Yeah. The thought's occurred to just about everybody," Lucas said. He looked at the three of them, huddled around Marcy's desk, and asked, "What's going on? You got something?"

"Just trying to figure out this Catholic and St. Patrick's business," Lane said. "To tell you the truth, we've got too many names. We've got connections running all over the place. We've got so many, we don't know what we're doing anymore."

"On the other hand," Marcy said, "I looked at the *Minnesota Almanac* and guess what? There's a whole bunch of Catholics among the women who got drawings and the dead ones we've identified, BUT . . ." She dug around in a mess of paper and pulled out a slip with penciled numbers. "We don't have a lot more than the percentage of Catholics in the Minnesota population as a whole. In fact, if the rest of the dead ones turn out not to be Catholics, we'll be a Catholic short."

"In other words, the Catholic thing just went up in smoke," Lucas said.

"There's still St. Patrick's," Lane said.

Lucas pulled up a chair. "Let me look at this stuff, okay? Where're the names of the people on the faculty? Have you run them past the women who got drawings? We're gonna have to do that."

THEY were still deep into the papers when Marshall came back, with Anderson a few feet behind. They were an odd pair: Harmon Anderson, an aging computer geek, pale as a boiled egg, and Marshall, as weather-beaten and brown as last year's oak leaf. "Might have something to look at," Marshall said gruffly. "Maybe you already thought of it."

"I don't think so," Anderson said. To Lucas: "Terry's smarter than he looks."

Marshall grunted, maybe in amusement, then pushed the paper at Lucas. "I wanted to know which women named Mrs. Qatar as an acquaintance, so Harmon wrote them down for me. He has a chart on his wall that shows when the women got the drawings, and when he wrote down the ones who knew Mrs. Qatar, I couldn't help noticing that they were all listed next to each other on the chart. They all got their drawings over a two-month period, a year and a half ago."

Lucas said, "Huh. So what . . . ?"

"They say they don't know each other, but they seem to be connected somehow with Mrs. Qatar. I started to wonder, could they have been at the same place, at the same time—like just before the first drawing came in? Some kind of public event? These four drawings were just about two weeks apart, so if it takes two weeks to do one, is it possible that they were at an event two weeks before the first one came in?"

Lucas leaned back in his chair, thinking about it. Then he looked at Lane, who said, "Could be something."

"I wonder if Helen Qatar's secretary keeps a calendar," Lucas said. "Let me check." He stepped into his office, rummaged through his collection of business cards, found the card he'd collected from Qatar's desk, went back to the main bay, and used Marcy's phone to make the call.

Qatar's secretary picked up and said, "Wells Museum, Helen Qatar's office."

"This is Lucas Davenport, the Minneapolis police officer who was there the other day. . . ." He explained what he needed.

"Let me check with Mrs. Qatar," she said.

Qatar picked up a moment later and said, "We're looking. You think this could be significant?"

"It would explain a lot," Lucas said. "We can't figure how *you* hook into it, but if you were all at the same place, especially if you were one of the main people . . ."

"A year and a half ago? In August?"

"August, early September . . . couldn't be any later than September fourteenth," Lucas said. He heard the secretary talking in the background, and then Qatar came back.

"I think . . ." Then she was gone again, talking to the secretary. A moment later: "We had a preterm gala for alumni and friends of the museum, to try to raise a little money for our museum fellowships." She was gone again, then back. "August twenty-ninth. We invited six hundred people. We don't know how many came, but all the food was eaten, and the party was crashed by a number of students coming back to school."

"These other women who identified you as an acquaintance. Would they have been invited?" Lucas asked. Marcy whispered: "Guest list." "Do you have a guest list?"

"We wouldn't have a guest list anymore," Qatar said, a tingle of excitement in her voice. "But we invited everybody on our contacts lists, and I think all four of them are on it. When Officer Black gave me the four names, I knew three of them as acquaintances, but the fourth one didn't ring a bell. When I looked in our files, though, there she was."

"If you could find a guest list, that would be a mammoth help to us," Lucas said.

"We'll look. I don't think we'll find one, but I bet we could reconstruct it."

"That would be terrific, Mrs. Qatar."

"We'll try to get something for you tomorrow," she said. "I never did get a chance to look at that film. Maybe I'll do that tonight."

"Anything you can do, we'd appreciate," Lucas said.

"Just like Miss Marple," she said, with relish.

17

WEATHER SLEPT OVER—not for the sex, she said, but because she missed him. "I think we're settling in," she said, as she lay on the bed with a book on her chest. "Are we going to talk about the house?"

"What about the house?"

"Do we want a bigger one?" she asked.

He looked around: He'd been in the place for better than ten years, and it fit him reasonably well—but if there were children and a wife, things might be a little tight.

"Maybe."

The talk kept him up even after Weather was sleeping: night thoughts about big changes. The idea of a change didn't worry him much, he realized, somewhat surprised at himself. When he really thought about it, he didn't think as much about this house as he did of the house he might have.

More space; a media room and a workshop. A real study,

instead of a converted bedroom. A nice master suite, extra bedrooms for the kids. Kids. What all would they need? With Weather committed to surgery, maybe they ought to think about a full-time housekeeper. . . .

He liked the neighborhood, and the neighbors. He would miss it, and them, if they moved. How about this: Maybe live in Weather's place for a while, and remodel this place, or even take it out and design and build something new?

There was plenty of room to expand into the backyard. He'd need a bigger garage, for sure, maybe with four places. A bigger basement workshop would be nice, and maybe they could build a completely dry basement this time.

When he went to sleep, he was thinking about table saws. He didn't have much use for one, but he'd been looking at them in hardware stores. Interesting tools. Lots of parts. You could sit in the basement and fool around with a table saw for hours. Big table saw, and maybe a planer/jointer. He could make furniture. . . . *Zzz.*

WHEN the phone rang, it was still dark. Weather moaned, "I'd forgotten about this part. The calls in the middle of the night."

"Five-thirty," he said; the clock's green numerals glowed at him through the dark. He found the phone, picked it up, groggy. "Yeah?"

"Chief Davenport?" He could hear traffic in the background.

"Speaking."

"This is John Davis, I'm a St. Paul patrol sergeant. Lieutenant Allport said I ought to give you a call."

Lucas sat up. "Yeah, John, what's going on?"

"I'm with a garbage crew out on East Seventh, out at the Kanpur Indian restaurant? They pulled a body out of the

Dumpster an hour or so ago. We don't have an ID, but she's young, small, blond, naked, and she's been strangled with a rope. It might not have anything to do with your case, but Allport says to tell you that she fits the profile of all them women you been digging up . . ."

"Ah, jeez."

". . . and she fits the description of a woman who was supposed to be living with Randy Whitcomb. We don't know for sure yet, but we're taking some blood samples and oughta know pretty quick. We're trying to find a neighbor of Whitcomb's who saw her a few times. One of our guys supposedly talked to this neighbor, but we don't have her name yet."

"All right." Lucas thought for a minute, felt the power of the bed pulling him down. "If I came down, would there be anything for me to see?"

"Well, just the body, like they found it. We're giving it the full routine, so it's gonna be here for a while. You could look at the tapes later. Maybe if we get the neighbor down here . . ."

"Ah . . . Listen, keep working. I'm gonna try to make it over."

"You know where it is?"

"Yeah. And listen, let me give you a number. . . ." He gave the cop Del's number and said, "He was looking for some other women who worked for Randy, and they might have seen this chick, too, if you can't find the neighbor."

"All right to call him in the middle of the night?"

"Oh, hell, yes. Del's an early riser—I wouldn't be surprised if he was up already," Lucas said.

HE took the Tahoe for its cup holders, stopped at a Super America and got two big cups of coffee and a box of powdered doughnuts, and pulled into the Kanpur's parking lot a half hour after the call from the St. Paul cop. The back of the store was dimly lit by two distant orange sodium-vapor security lights, a variety of lights from the cop cars, and the light from a video camera. Several cops turned to look when Lucas pulled into the lot, and when he got out, a sergeant broke away from the group and walked over.

"John Davis," he said, and they shook hands. "She looks pretty bad." The Dumpster was against the back wall of the store, and they walked over together. "She might have gone right into the truck, except that the Dumpster was overfilled and the driver got out to toss a couple of bags before he hooked it up."

"She was right on top?"

"She was down a way. The driver threw a couple of bags off and saw her arm."

"Pretty dark," Lucas said.

"They have lights on the truck so they can see to hook up the Dumpster."

Lucas looked in. The dead woman was naked, as advertised, her face innocent but gray, her eyes half open. She had deep ligature wounds on her neck, a rime of blood around her mouth. One arm was bent sideways and disappeared under the garbage bags to her right. The other was sitting on top of her chest.

"She does fit the profile," Lucas said. "You got a flashlight?"

Davis handed him a flashlight and he pointed it at the visible hand, and bent farther into the Dumpster.

"What?" David asked.

"She's got a broken fingernail . . . two broken fingernails," Lucas said.

"Trying to defend herself."

"We've got a guy with a theory," Lucas said. "If he's right, we gotta take a close look at the rug up at Randy's."

As Lucas pushed back from the Dumpster and handed

the flashlight to Davis, Del pulled into the lot and got out of the car. He didn't look much like a cop, and he held up a badge to the St. Paul cops who started toward him.

"Coffee in the truck," Lucas called.

Del swerved over to the Tahoe, opened the door, and a moment later continued across the lot to where they were standing and introduced himself to Davis. To Lucas he said, "I was planning to kill you for having them call me, but with the coffee . . ." He slurped at the cup.

"There's a possibility that she's Randy's girl," Lucas said.

"John told me," Del said. "There's one chick living with DDT—not Charmin', but the one named Melissa? She might have seen her last week at a party up on Como."

"You called DDT?"

"Yeah. There was a game last night over at the Target Center, and Melissa was working it. She didn't expect to get back last night, and she didn't."

"So she's shacked up somewhere downtown with a fuckin' basketball player."

"Yeah, and I hope one of the Chicago guys," Del said. "She didn't look that healthy."

"Does he have any idea when she might get back?" Lucas asked.

"He thought maybe midmorning."

"Goddamnit. Be nice if he could have tossed her in the backseat and dragged her ass over here."

"Early enough to miss the rush, too," Del said, taking another hit of the coffee.

Davis said, "We rousted the guy who talked to Whitcomb's neighbor, and we got her name and sent a squad over. I haven't heard back yet." He turned and looked across the lot at a couple of St. Paul cops who were blocking the parking lot but not doing much else. "Hey, one of you guys call Polaroid and ask him if he's found that neighbor."

One of the cops lifted a hand and fit himself inside a squad. A few seconds later, he slid out of the car and said, "They're on the way back here. They got her."

Lucas nodded. "All right."

"These other strangled chicks . . . were they on the corner?" Davis asked.

"The idea came up, but it doesn't look like it," Lucas said. "This is"—he waved a hand at the Dumpster—"out of whack."

"And Whitcomb can't talk."

THE neighbor was named Megan Earle. She'd put on her red parka for the trip across town, and walked over to the dumpster with the hood up. "Do I gotta look?"

"You gotta," Davis said. "Just a minute, though." He turned to one of the crime-scene cops and said, "Put one of them empty bags over her. You know."

The cop covered the dead woman's body and neck with an empty plastic garbage bag, nodded, and Earle shuffled over to the dumpster and stood on her tiptoes and looked in. "Oh, God," she said. She stepped back, looked at Davis, and said, "That's Suzanne."

"Her name's Suzanne?" Lucas asked.

"That's what she told me. I only talked to her once or twice when she was taking garbage out."

"You're sure it's her."

Earle nodded. "It's her. Oh, God . . ."

The cop who'd been with her peered into the Dumpster, then took a camera out of his pocket and fired it into the Dumpster—a Polaroid, Lucas realized when the photo whirred out of the front of the camera.

Lucas stepped over to Del but didn't say anything for a moment. Del said finally, "Randy's too young to have done the first ones."

"What if there are two of them, working separately? But then the graveyard doesn't make any sense, does it?"

"What if this is just a big fuckin' coincidence?"

"Then what about the jewelry?"

Del scratched his head. "We got all these pieces, but they don't fit."

"Randy can make them fit," Lucas said.

"If he will."

"He's looking at a murder rap if he doesn't. If this girl's blood is all over his apartment."

"Maybe I ought to go baby-sit him. Just sit there until he wakes up," Del said.

"Not be a bad idea," Lucas agreed. "First guy who talks to him probably gonna break the case."

They hung around long enough to make sure there was nothing under the body. When it came out clean, and the medical examiner's people were bundling it away, Davis said, "We'll do some quick processing, and I imagine we'll know if we've got a blood match by the middle of the morning. Take a while to get people going."

"Gimme a call?" Lucas asked.

"I'll be off. Allport will know, though."

"All right. I'll call *him*."

"How many murders have you had this year, City of St. Paul?" Del asked.

"I think this is five," Davis said.

"Jeez. We got ten in almost three months," Del said. "Nobody's killing anybody anymore. Even ag assault's way down."

"Same here. Drugs are down. Rape's still cooking along."

"Yeah, rape's a bright spot," Del agreed.

"We're talking about consolidation—moving guys out of violent crimes and hitting property crimes a little harder," Davis said. "Some of the new plainclothes guys are sweatin' a transfer back to patrol."

"No offense, but I couldn't go back," Del said. He shivered. "Patrol, man—I feel for you guys."

"Ah, we like it. Not as many assholes."

"You mean on the force, or on the street?" Del asked.

"Whichever," Davis said, and they all laughed, and Lucas said, "I resemble that remark."

LUCAS went back home, unplugged the bedroom phone, closed the door, and fell facedown on the bed. The next time he moved, it was after ten o'clock. He groaned, pushed himself up, shaved, showered, and headed downtown.

Marshall was talking with Marcy. He saw Lucas and stood up and said, "I heard about the girl in the Dumpster. What do you think?"

"Gotta call St. Paul. They were gonna try to match her blood to the blood at Randy's—but I'd say the chances are about ninety-five percent that it's the right woman. Let me call Allport and see if they've got anything."

Allport had the tests. "She was killed in Whitcomb's apartment, that's her blood on the wall," he said. "It makes me feel a little better about what happened—the docs are pouring on the steroids, but that spine thing is looking worse. They don't think he's gonna walk again."

"Is he gonna be able to talk?" Lucas asked.

"Probably not today. They're keeping him sedated until they get the spine managed. They're going back in this afternoon to try to consolidate it, and now they think they might have some outside soft tissue in the spinal cord itself, which they didn't pick up on the X rays the first time around. Like some of his skin got blown into the cord and they couldn't see it."

"Tomorrow?"

"I don't know. He may be dead tomorrow."

"Not really."

"No, not really, but . . . man, they aren't saying much. He is pretty fucked up, and they really don't know when we can talk to him."

"It's like a goddamn TV show," Lucas said. "The next thing is, he's gonna fall out of the bed and hit his head and get amnesia."

He told Marshall, and Marshall shook his head. "I'd give a thousand dollars if we could take back what happened yesterday," he said. "That boy getting shot."

"He's a major asshole," Lucas said.

"I don't much give a shit about that. That's your problem," Marshall said. "My problem is, I want a name out of him. He gives me the name, and after that, he can get run over by a steamroller. But I want the name first."

"Did you look at that event over at St. Pat's?" Lucas asked.

"Yup. Copied out every one of Miz Qatar's names into a laptop, gave the disk to Harmon, and he ran them late last night," Marshall said. "Didn't come up with much—except that we figured out one more thing. They got a college alumni magazine called the *Shamrock*. Some pictures from this get-together were in there, and it was all these women out on a lawn and they were all wearing name tags. So if our guy was there, taking pictures, he could take a shot and know who the woman was, without even asking her name. Or even talking to her."

"Goddamnit. That doesn't help us much," Lucas said. "How many guys on your list?"

"Maybe a hundred and fifty. Harmon's running them against the sex-offender files right now."

Del called from Regions hospital: "They let me in to see Randy, and he is seriously fucked up. He makes a little goddamn noise once in a while, and that's it. His folks got a lawyer and they gave me some shit. . . . I don't know, it's getting tangled up over here."

"Might as well come back," Lucas said.

"Yeah. Nothing's gonna happen today, unless he bites it."

"Allport says that's not much of a risk."

"I dunno," Del said. "The docs say he's got so many weird drugs in him that they're fighting withdrawal symptoms along with everything else. He's got heroin in him, cocaine, maybe some PCP—he was using inhalers. . . . The little prick."

MARCY and Marshall left for St. Paul, the first meeting of the interagency board on what the papers and TV stations were now calling the gravedigger case. The label was created by a Channel Eight anchorman, was picked up by Channel Three, which began using a graphic of a hillside grave with its stories, and finally by the papers. The name looked like it would stick.

After they'd gone, Lucas continued to read through the accumulating paper in the case, without any penetrating insights. When he went out for lunch at midday, he found the clouds had closed down again and a miserable cold drizzle was whimpering through the streets. Cold and damp, he loafed around City Hall, talking with Lester and Sloan, then went through the secret tunnel to the medical examiner's office and talked to an investigator there about strangulation.

At two o'clock, he was back in the office, when Weather called. "Why don't you invite the Capslocks and the Sloans over tomorrow night. We'll get some lobsters."

"All right. Short notice, though," he said.

"They never do anything. And it's been a while since we all got together."

"Who knows," he said. "Tomorrow night—maybe it'll all be over by then."

But he didn't really think so. The case felt like it was slowing down. Everything was pinned on Randy, and Randy had gone to never-never land.

18

THE KILLING OF the unnamed hooker at Randy Whitcomb's brought a temporary semblance of peace to Qatar's soul. He mentally replayed the scene every few minutes, especially the last part, when he hung over her and she began to quiver. . . .

It's the killing, stupid.

He'd always thought it was the sex, that the killing was punishment for the sexual disappointments the women had inflicted upon him. He knew better now. Any sexual practice he'd ever remotely considered he'd now tried with Barstad. He'd found it, ultimately, to be boring. It was the killing, he thought, and it felt fine—*fine*—to have that clarified.

He searched for a metaphor. His realization of the exact nature of the beast was, he decided, the psychological equivalent of the first taste of a great French white wine, properly cool, properly tart; a bit of an intellectual tangle, perhaps, but there was a wonderfully clear, clean response at the sensual level.

He wanted another one.

Barstad.

They were meeting twice a week and the sex had gone past strenuous, lurching off into the weeds of intricate variation. He was not so much entertained as amazed, he thought. The last time they met, he'd spanked her with the Ping-Pong paddles until her ass was fiery red, yet she seemed to feel that he'd done an inadequate job. The pain, she said, had been on the very periphery of her pleasure, rather than at the center, where it should have been. She sounded, he thought, like a French literary theorist writing on sex.

Today, he thought, things would be different. He had the starter rope in his back pocket when he arrived at her apartment, and a duffle bag and spade in the backseat of the car. He would bury her so far out in the countryside that she would never be found. If the police wanted to attribute her disappearance to the gravedigger, he thought, let them do it.

He no longer cared. The power was in him. He even enjoyed his new media appellation: "the gravedigger." All right. He whistled as the elevator took him up to Barstad's.

SHE was nude when she met him at the door: propped it open with one arm and posed, her eyelids drooping. "James," she said. "I've already started."

"I see that," he said.

"And I've got a new movie," she said. "A DVD. I pushed the couch back so we could put the futon in front of the TV."

Sex first, he thought. First the sex, and when he'd been emptied out of all the stray emotions that sex seemed to dissolve, he could better appreciate the clear, cool strangulation. There was, he thought, an aesthetic to it all.

They began with the movie and masturbation, moved on to oral sex, and then the intricacies. He found his mind wandering in the middle of it all, and he looked down at her neck below him and then around for his pants. They were out of reach, and he was unable to detach himself at the moment. He continued, looking down at her neck and the fine groove of her spine, thrilled already by what was coming. . . .

She finished, and he did, and they lay side by side, her head on his shoulder. She always wanted a long second bout, had even urged him toward chemical reinforcement. He *would* have another opportunity with the rope. What, he thought, would it be like to strangle a woman who was at that moment in the throes of orgasm? Would she stop? Would he?

"James," she murmured into his neck, "I am going to make you very, very unhappy. If you want to punish me, I would accept that. But I want you to hear me out first."

He pulled back, said nothing. What was this?

"It's time to enter a new stage of exploration," she said. She'd always been formal about the sex, as though she were filling out a lab book. What would she do when she got to the end, when she'd exhausted all the possibilities? Build hot rods? Write haiku? "I've been talking to a woman that I've known for several years. She has had some sexual relationships with other women, and we have decided that we would like to explore that together. Intergender sexuality."

He looked down at her, flabbergasted again. "You want to try women? Lesbianism?"

"Maybe the first time . . . but we've talked about it and I'd like you to meet her. We're discussing the possibility of the three of us . . . if you and she can be friends."

The three of them? He sat up. "You told her who I am?"

"Not exactly. Just that you were a professor. I had to do that much. She wanted to know your bona fides. She wouldn't have wanted to sleep with a street person, or a musician or something."

"You told her." He was enraged.

"Yes."

"Goddamnit, I told you I can't be brought into this. I teach at a Catholic school. My whole career, my whole livelihood . . ."

She put a finger out to his lips to shut him up, and said, "She's very discreet. She understands all of that. She's married, and her husband has no idea."

"You fuckin' moron. You fuckin'—"

She said, "Hit me, James. In the face. Hard. C'mon, hit me."

He said, "You're nuts."

"I'm a seeker, James." Her face was placid, lit from within. "Hit me."

He slapped her.

"Harder, James."

The second time, he hit her hard. He'd counted on killing her, but that was now an impossibility—impossible, at least, until he had time to better figure out what she'd told the other woman. He hit her with an open hand, hard enough to knock her flat. She looked up at him, blood on her lips, her eyes glittering. "Rape me."

He shook his head: "Listen . . . I . . ." He looked down at himself: He was shaking like a Jell-O mold.

"James. C'mon, James, please . . ."

HE was at home that evening, eating a bowl of Froot Loops, reading the back of the box, when his mother called. She sounded ill: "James, I need to see you."

"Something wrong? You sound . . . afflicted."

"I am afflicted," she said. "Sorely. I need to talk to you immediately."

"All right, then," he said. "Let me finish my cereal and I'll be over."

She rang off and he sat down again, but rather than go back to the text on the box, he began considering the tone of her voice. She had definitely sounded ill—and there was an unaccustomed urgency in her tone. Maybe she really *was* ill. Her mother had died of pancreatic cancer at a younger age than she was now. . . .

His mother, he thought, all those years with a good salary; a woman born at the end of the Great Depression, of parents who'd suffered through chronic unemployment and the loss of a house, who had inflicted her with the fear that she'd wind up alone and penniless and too old to help herself. That fear had kept her working beyond the normal retirement age.

And kept her piling money into her Fidelity account and into her 401(k) plan. She had a half-million in Fidelity, God-only-knew-what in the 401(k), and the college provided excellent medical, so the estate wouldn't be soaked up by medical costs or nursing care.

A half-million. His mother, gone. He put his head in his hands and wept, the tears streaming down his face, his chest heaving, a catch in his voice box. After a minute, he gathered himself.

A half-million. A Porsche Boxster S could be had for fifty thousand.

The image of himself in a Boxster, a tan leather jacket—not suede, he thought, suede was passé, but something reflective of the suede idea, with light driving gloves of a darker brown—lifting a hand to a small, blond, admiring coed on a street corner: The image was so real that he nearly experienced the reality itself, sitting in his kitchen chair. A cool clear fall afternoon, leaves scuttling along the street, the smell of yard smoke in the air, a day perfectly fitting for the not-suede jacket, the girl in a plaid skirt and white long-sleeve blouse, a cardigan over her shoulders. . . .

His mother had said she was afflicted. He hurried out to his car.

HE parked in the driveway, climbed the stoop at the side door, and stopped for a second to look at the house—he hadn't even considered the house, but in this neighborhood, in this condition, the house itself had to be worth a quarter-million. And they had done no estate planning: none. The thought of losing it, even a piece of it, to taxes, again brought the welling tears. He squared his shoulders and rang the doorbell.

Helen came to the door, pushed open the storm door, said curtly, "Come in." She didn't sound ill, he thought.

"Are you okay?" he asked.

"No." She led the way back to an L-corner where she had her television, and sat in her rocker. Qatar trailed along, and when she sat down, perched on the couch. She took a remote control from her reading table, pointed it at the television, and a moment later Qatar found himself looking, with some puzzlement, at an old movie. The movie ran for two or three seconds, and she paused it. A nice-looking actor was caught full-face.

"The police have come to see me three times," she said. "It has to do with this man who buried all those girls on that hill. They have learned that this man had some training in art; that he spent time at Stout, in Wisconsin; that he has some connection with St. Patrick's and myself; that he probably murdered Charlotte Neumann . . ."

Qatar had tightened the grip on himself as she began to speak. He was an exceptional liar, always had been, his face loose and observant, questioning, wondering where the speaker was going, ready with the surprise and denial.

"And," his mother concluded, "they have learned that he looked like this man."

"Yes?"

"James. That is you, ten years ago. Even five. That is you," she said.

His chin dropped. Then he said, voice rising, "You think, you think . . . Mother, you think it's me? My God, this man is a monster. You think it's me?"

Her head bobbed. "I'm afraid that's what I think, James. I want you to convince me that it's not true. But I remember all those poor cats, with their heads twisted."

"That was not me. That was Carl Stevenson, I told you then it was Carl."

She shook her head, "James . . ."

"What can I tell you?" He was on his feet. "Mother, I did not do this."

"Convince me."

He shook his head. "This is crazy. This is completely *crazy.* Lord, I hope you haven't told anybody about this. It's my life, my career. I had nothing—nothing—to do with any of this, but just the accusation or even the suggestion would finish me. My God, Mother, how can you think this?"

She looked at him, tears in her eyes now. "I want to believe that, but I don't. I knew about the cats. I hid it even from myself, but I saw you one day, going out in the garage, and I found the cat later."

And suddenly she broke down and began to cry, a series of breath-catching moans—a sense of agony that brought tears to Qatar's eyes, not because of his mother's pain, but because of the injustice and the lack of understanding, that she should betray him by her lack of belief.

"That was not *me,*" he insisted. "Mother, who have you talked to about this?"

"Nobody," she said, shaking her head. "I know the effect

this could have on your life. I took care—but now I have something to pray over. My own flesh and blood."

"Ah, man . . . Mother, I don't want to have to deal with this, but I have to say it: I think you are `. . .` afflicted. You've made this up. Created it. The man on the television is *not* me; I *saw* the drawings on television. You really think I could draw those things? C'mon, Mother."

But it wasn't going to work. He could see it. "I need something to drink—water," he said. "Don't go away."

He walked past her, through the living room and into the kitchen, opened a cupboard, got a glass, let the water run for a moment as the calculations flew through his mind. With the glass overflowing, he turned the water off, drank a sip, exhaled, poured the rest of the water down the drain.

Well, she knew. He had to act.

SHE was still sitting in the rocker when he walked back into the room; the actor's face was still frozen on the TV screen, watching them. Helen seemed in despair, but without a touch of fear.

"The best thing to do—" she began.

She didn't finish. He caught her one-handed by the hair and pulled her straight forward onto the carpet. She yelped once and went facedown, and he dropped on top of her, pinning her with his weight. She grunted, desperately, "James," and turned her head, her eyes rolling wildly, looking up at him, unbelieving, and he slipped one hand around her face and cupped her mouth in the palm of his hand and with his thumb and forefinger, pinched her nose. He took care: He didn't pinch tightly enough to bruise, only to stop the flow of air. She struggled, she tried to get a breath—he could feel the suction against the palm of his hand—but it was all over quickly enough. He held her until he knew she was dead, then held her a minute longer.

* * *

ALL right. That was done. They were four blocks from St. Pat's. She walked most days, so moving her car would not be a problem. She was always the first one to work, so finding her there would not raise any eyebrows.

He would have to change her, find something appropriate for work. He went to her bedroom, found a rack of business suits still in their plastic clean bags, found one that he knew she favored. The change itself was distasteful: She was like a withered bird, no muscle left, barely sexed. He hurried through it, but made sure that she was neat, just as she was in life.

He turned off the porch light, stepped outside, waited for a moment in the dark, scanning the strip of visible street. This was all familiar enough, and he was good at it. When he was sure, he quickly moved her to the backseat of his car.

Purse and keys. He got them.

Money. She had fifty dollars in her purse; he took forty, left ten. And she kept money under the cup in the flour canister in the kitchen. He opened the canister, lifted the cup, and found three hundred and fifty dollars in tens. The money lifted his heart, and he hurried up the stairs. She accumulated money in a variety of ways—maybe even stole some of it from the museum, he thought—and squirreled it away. He didn't know where, exactly, but he thought the bedroom. . . .

And it was in the bedroom, in the closet, under the carpet, in a hole in the floor. He would never have found it if he hadn't been on his hands and knees, checking her shoes. A corner of the carpet was pulled up, just enough that he reached over and gave it a tug. A square of it came away, too easily, and when he looked . . .

A wad of cash. He pulled it out, and his heart leapt when

he saw that most of the bills were fifties and hundreds. There must be thousands. He rolled out of the closet and counted, eyes bent close to the cash, stopping to wet his index finger on his tongue, the better to count. He counted once, could not believe the total, and counted again. Eight thousand dollars?

He closed his eyes. Eight thousand. Everything he wanted, all right here. . . .

Back down the stairs. He found a flashlight in a drawer by the sink, turned off all the house lights, and headed out.

The night was cold and moonless. He drove the four blocks to the museum and parked on the street. Sat watching, letting an odd car pass by. A few minutes before nine, he got out, walked once entirely around the museum, then tried her key in the side door. It slipped in easily, and he was inside.

There were safety lights at either end of the hall, and in the deadly silence he walked down to the office, let himself in, walked carefully past the secretary's desk into his mother's private space. Okay, he thought. This would work.

He left the door unlocked and walked back out to the car, took a look around, then lifted her out and carried her across the lawn under one arm, as though he were humping a rug into the building. Inside, he put her in her chair.

Got her cup, in the light of the flash, went down the hall to the men's room, filled it with water, found a pack of instant coffee next to the microwave in the secretary's office, and stirred the coffee into the cup. When it was all ready, he sat her in the chair, put her fingers around the cup handle, then pushed her onto the floor.

She went over easily, dragging the cup with her.

He looked around. What else?

Nothing. Simple was better, and anything elaborate would take more time. And it really looked good, he thought; she was on her side, as if she'd gone to sleep. There was no trace of violence, just a little old lady who'd gone to sleep. The way she'd have wanted to go. . . .

With a last look around, he left the building, locking the door behind him. Out to the car. A nice night, he thought. Money in his pocket.

A half-million in Fidelity?

Too bad about Mom.

But she was old.

19

LUCAS WAS TALKING with Rose Marie Roux the next morning when her secretary poked her head in the door, looked at Lucas, and said, "A hysterical woman is on the phone, looking for you. She says it's an emergency."

"Switch it in here," Rose Marie said. The secretary backed out of her office, and a few seconds later, Rose Marie's phone burped. She took the receiver off the hook and handed it across the desk to Lucas.

"Lucas Davenport."

"Officer Davenport, this is Denise Thompson. . . ." The woman seemed to be falling apart, her voice pitched high and wobbly with stress.

"Denise . . . ?"

"Thompson, Helen Qatar's secretary. You know she died—"

"What?" He stood up, scowling, astonished. "She died? How'd she die?"

"She died at her desk. I don't know, I don't know, she just died. She was at her desk with a cup of coffee and she must have had a stroke or something."

"Did she call out or—"

"No, no, I wasn't here, it was before anybody got here this morning. I saw her door open and her light on and so I went in, and I just saw her legs on the floor and I went around to see . . . she was gone. I called 911 . . ." Now she did break down and began a breathy weeping.

Lucas let her go for a few seconds, then said, "Okay, okay, Mrs. Thompson. Police came?"

"And the ambulance, but it was too late. I could see it was too late."

"Okay."

"I don't know why I'm calling you except that you'd been to see her and she was joking about being Miss Marple and now she's gone."

"I'll talk to the medical examiner and make sure there was nothing improper," Lucas said. "We'll make sure. Are you the contact on that, or . . . ?"

"Her son is, really, if he's not too wrecked. He was pretty wrecked this morning. I called him, and he ran right over. He went a little nutty."

"All right. Well, thank you for calling," Lucas said.

"Mr. Davenport . . . I don't know, I'm not sure I should even bring this up. . . ."

"Bring up anything you want," Lucas said.

"Well, I'm sure it was a stroke or something, something regular, she was an older woman . . . but—she didn't bring her newspaper."

"I beg your pardon?"

"Every day for years, as long as I've worked here, she would carry her newspaper in. She told me that she would get up, she would eat raisin bran or bran flakes and a cup of yogurt, and she would make her list of things to do for that day. She wouldn't get the newspaper until she had her list. Then, when she left for work, she'd pick up the newspaper from the front porch and carry it in. If the carrier didn't bring it or something, she would stop at a box on the corner and buy one."

"Every day."

"Every day. When she got here, she would put the paper in her in-basket and make a cup of coffee, and then she would answer all of her e-mail and write e-mails to people she corresponded with. I would come in with my paper and we would work on her to-do list until break time, and then we would read our newspapers at the same time. But to-day . . . she didn't bring her newspaper."

"So what do you . . . ?"

"It's just strange. Of all days . . . I'm sure it's nothing, but it's just strange. I wanted to tell somebody."

"Thank you. We will look into it all," Lucas said.

WHEN Thompson was gone, he looked at Rose Marie and said, "Shit."

"It didn't sound good from here."

"A little old lady is dead—Helen Qatar, down at St. Pat's. It's possible that she was taken off by the gravedig-ger. Goddamnit. She joked about being Miss Marple, and we think the guy may be around there somewhere, and I never told her to back off or be careful."

"Try not to get too deep into the guilt," Rose Marie said.

"I won't. But I liked her. One of those active old birds. Smart. Still working. Goddamnit." He ran both hands up through his hair, then locked them behind his head. "Just wish . . . I don't know. There's something going on that we don't see. We're a lot closer to him than we think, and somehow we dragged her into it."

On his way out of Rose Marie's office, he stopped at the

secretary's desk and dialed the number of an investigator at the ME's office. "Yeah, we got her in," the guy said. "I can't tell you much, except that there's no sign of violence and she was older and was taking some heart drugs."

"Could you do everything?" Lucas asked. "There's a chance that somebody took her off. I've been told that she died while she was drinking coffee, so check for poison, or weird drugs, anything like that."

"You say everything, we'll do everything," the investigator said. "I'll tell the doc, and get him to push it a little."

"Thanks. Let me know."

"Sure. Hey, you know she's got a son, right? He's here now, somewhere, I think. I haven't seen him leave. Probably doing papers."

"Hold him, will you?" Lucas said. "I'm gonna run over."

He was going out the door when he saw Anderson and Marshall talking in a doorway. He went that way instead, and when Marshall looked up, said, "You hear?"

Marshall pushed away from the door. He was wearing a hip-length rough-leather coat lined with fleece, and with his rough face and hands, looked like a Marlboro ad. "I guess not," he said. "It must not be good, from the way you sound."

"Helen Qatar's dead. She was found dead this morning by her secretary. She's over at the ME's office, and her son's there. I was just heading over."

"I'm coming with you," Marshall said. He turned to Anderson and said, "Catch you later, Harmon."

On the way through the secret tunnel, Lucas said, "You and Anderson seem to be getting along."

"Yeah. Can't tell you why. He's just a good old boy, though he looks like an old geek or something."

Lucas nodded. "Smart guy. A pretty damn good street cop, when he was on the street."

"That's what I see," Marshall said. "I'm a pretty good

street cop myself, and I'll tell you what—if I make it to heaven, I wouldn't mind spendin' part of eternity sitting in a tile room with a bunch of street cops, drinkin' coffee and tellin' stories."

"Well, goddamnit, Terry, you oughta be a poet." Marshall shut his mouth and seemed embarrassed by Lucas's reaction. Lucas picked it up and said, "I know exactly what you mean, though. That would not be a bad way to spend some time. Let me tell you what happened when Del ran into this chick with these pinking shears. . . ."

They were laughing when they got to the ME's, and stopped just a minute to sober up before they pushed through the door at the end of the tunnel. Lucas stuck his head into the investigator's office and asked, "Where's the son?"

"He's down talking to the doc . . . right there, second door."

QATAR was a small man—not short, but willowy, and bald, with a narrow face. His baldness seemed to push his features too far down on his oval head, so that his deep-set eyes, delicate nose, full lips, and rounded chin were all pressed into the lower half of the oval. His face was pink as a lamb chop; he'd apparently been weeping. The doc was behind his desk, and a remote, smooth-faced blonde was perched on a swivel stool next to a drawing table; she was wearing a white blouse and a skirt the precise pale green color of her eyes. She had long legs, and most of their length was visible.

After Lucas knocked, the doc invited them in and said, "Mr. Qatar is having a hard time with this."

"I'm sorry," Lucas said. "I only met your mother a few days ago, but I liked her. She seemed like a really nice woman."

"She was," Marshall said. "I liked her a lot too."

"Jeeminy Christmas," Qatar said. "I knew, I knew, I knew . . ."

"Mr. Qatar," the doc started.

Qatar got it out on the fourth try: "I knew this could happen anytime. She had the heart problem, but she seemed, no problem, yesterday, no problem. She looked perfectly good. I saw her at three o'clock and I had to rush off I don't even think I said goodbye I just said, 'Look, I gotta go,' and I took off and just left her standing there and I never thought . . ."

He started sniffling again, and Lucas and Marshall both looked quickly at the woman, who didn't appear to work there, but neither was she comforting Qatar. When tears appeared in his eyes, Marshall slapped an arm around his shoulder and said, "I dealt with a lot of these things in my life, son, and the best thing for you to do is go home, find someplace comfortable, and put your feet up. Let it all out when you have to."

Lucas jumped in. "Did she tell you anything about talking to the police over the last few days? Of looking around for somebody who might have been at a museum event a year ago last fall? Anything . . ."

Qatar was shaking his head. "No. No, nothing like that. Everything we talked about, it was just so . . . inconsequential. I still have so many things to say to her. . . . God, I've got to do something about a funeral, I've got to call somebody . . ." He flapped his arms around, looked all around himself as if disoriented, and said, "I've got to get going, I've got . . ."

The blonde hopped off the stool. "I can help for a while," she said. "This gentleman is right," she said to Qatar, tipping her head at Marshall. "Why don't I take you back to your place, and, you know, I'll hang around."

"You're a friend?" Lucas asked.

The woman patted Qatar on the shoulder and said, "Yes. James and I have been seeing each other. . . ." She looked at Lucas a little too long, a full extra beat, and down in his heart Lucas thought, Hmm.

"Take care of him," Marshall said, and the doc added, "We'll get back to you about your mother sometime this afternoon, so you can make arrangements."

Qatar had started leaking again, and the blonde led him out of the room with a quick backward glance at Lucas. The door shut behind them, and they gave them time to get a decent distance away, then the doc shook his head and said, "Guy was losing his shit. I was glad to see you guys."

"Was it real, or was it bullshit?" Lucas asked.

Both Marshall and the doc looked at him. "That was real, as far as I could tell," the doc said. "He was freaking out. You think it might be something else?"

He thought about the bald man. "Nah, not really. He seemed a little overcooked," Lucas said. "On the other hand—do the chemistry."

"Wanna watch?"

"No, thanks. A nice clean piece of paper would be fine," Lucas said.

On the way back to City Hall, Lucas said, "This is it— we pull everybody off everything else, and we take St. Pat's apart. The guy is over there somewhere."

"Unless she had a heart attack."

"Maybe she did, but you know what? The photograph down by the statue, Ware remembers talking to somebody who might have been a priest, you dug up that thing about the lawn party, Neumann getting killed, now Qatar gone: This shit is telling us something."

"Hope it's not a priest," Marshall said.

"So do I." He stopped and looked back at the ME's door. "What?"

"I don't know. I should have figured something out from this, but I didn't," Lucas said.

"There's so much stuff."

"That's not what I mean," Lucas said. "I mean, I know something, but I missed it. You ever have that feeling?"

"Yeah. Street-cop stuff. It'll come to you."

"RANDY'S awake," Del said. He caught them walking back toward Lucas's office. "He's hurtin', but he's up."

"You going?" Marshall asked.

"Yeah." Del nodded. "I got any company?"

Marshall nodded and said, "Me," and Lucas said, "I want to come, but let me talk to Marcy first."

Marcy, Black, and Swanson were drinking coffee and looking at paper when he walked in with Del and Marshall trailing. "All right, people, we're ripping everything up and turning it around. We're gonna look at nothing but St. Pat's. The guy is over there somewhere." He told them about Helen Qatar.

Swanson said, "Whoa," and Black said, "Wasn't her heart—I got a hundred bucks says it wasn't. Goddamnit, she was a nice old bat."

"I'm with you," Lucas said. "I think she knew the killer, and somehow tipped him off. Marcy, I want you to get everyone you can find over there with copies of the artist's sketch. I want you to interview all of her old friends. I want you to go through her house. Check her mail. Look at her e-mail, first thing."

"We got all the lists we need," Marcy said. She looked at Black and Swanson. "Now we need complete bios. Let's start cross-interviewing people. Not about themselves, but about people they know who do art."

"All we need is a name," Lucas said. "If we get a name, Randy should be able to identify him. I want a name."

* * *

RANDY was in the ICU at Regions Hospital in St. Paul. There was a uniformed St. Paul cop outside the door who nodded at Lucas and said, "His lawyer's in there."

"Who is it?"

"I don't know. Somebody from the public defender's."

Lucas knocked, stuck his head inside. Randy was lying almost flat, his head elevated two inches; his shoulders seemed narrow and ratlike in the hospital gown. An IV drip was fastened into one arm. He looked like a deflated version of the Randy they all knew and hated. The lawyer sat next to him, a man Randy's age, early twenties, in a battered black suit and too-narrow tie. A Samsonite briefcase sat next to him on the floor.

Lucas said to the lawyer, "I'm with the Minneapolis police. I need to talk with you."

"Later," the lawyer said. "I'm talking with my client right now."

"Do you know how much later?"

"Whenever I'm done," the lawyer said. "Wait in the hall."

"Better be pretty quick," Lucas said. "We don't have a lot of time here—"

"Hey! When I'm *done,"* the lawyer said.

Lucas backed out, and Del said, "Oh, boy."

"Officious little prick," Lucas said. He took his cell phone out of his pocket and called the Minneapolis dispatcher. "Could you get me Harry Page's number over at the Ramsey Public Defender's Office?"

She came back a minute later with the number, and Lucas poked it in. Page, the number-two man in the PD's office, came on the line a moment later. "Lucas Davenport. I think you still owe me three dollars for that egg-salad sandwich I bought you when we were on that panel up at White Bear—Century College, whatever it was."

"Yeah, yeah. Christ, you been whining about it for months," Lucas said.

"I need the money. I'm thinking of getting a divorce."

"I'll send it tomorrow. I'd hate to see your wife starve," Lucas said. "Listen, I'm over at the hospital and we've got a situation."

"What's the situation?"

"You got this officious little prick over here talking to Randy Whitcomb, and if Randy gives us the help we need, it'll get him out of a lot of the trouble he's in."

"Uh, Whitcomb is the guy the cops shot. . . ."

"Yeah. And we found blood all over his apartment, which he was trying to clean up with paper towels when we broke in. Then the St. Paul cops found the body of his girlfriend in a Dumpster behind an Indian restaurant, and her blood matches the blood in his apartment. So he is in a shitload of trouble, but we might be able to get him off the murder charge if he gives us a little help."

"How?" Page sounded as if he was eating a sandwich between words.

"The killing looks a lot like the killings by this gravedigger guy, and we know that Randy has been in touch with him. Randy sold some jewelry that came off one of the victims. If we can get an ID from Randy, we think the murder charge'll go away. There's a good chance, anyway. But your officious little prick won't even let us in the door."

"Which officious little prick did we send over there?" Page asked.

"Real young. Black suit looks like it was run over by a tractor. He's got a plastic briefcase bigger'n your dick."

"It's a wonder he could lift it," Page said. "The little prick's name is Robert call-me-Rob Lansing, like in Michigan. You say you're in the hallway?"

"Yeah."

"Stand right there. He'll come talk to you."

Lucas hung up, and ten seconds later, they heard a cell phone ring inside the room. A minute after that, Lansing popped out into the hallway.

"Which one of you assholes called Page?" he asked.

"I did, you officious little prick," Lucas said. "You want to talk about the welfare of your client, or you want to play status games?"

THE legal matters took five minutes to straighten out. Lansing told the cops that they could not ask any questions directly about the killing of the woman or the shooting at the apartment when the cops broke in. They were allowed to ask about the gravedigger and show Randy the artist's drawing.

When they went into the room, Randy seemed to have gone back to sleep. But when Lansing said "Mr. Whitcomb," his eyelids lifted slowly and his eyes drifted over the four of them as they stood at the end of the bed. Then they drifted back and stopped at Lucas.

"You fuckin' asshole," he said, his voice as arid as the hum of a paper wasp.

"Yeah, yeah, blow me," Lucas said. "Randy, you are in a shitload of trouble, but God help me, I'm here to try to get you out of some of it. Do you know the man who killed your girlfriend? Killed Suzanne?"

"Not me," he whispered.

"Who did?"

"Some fuckin' asshole."

"You got a name?"

Randy shook his head. "Can't remember. Head's all fucked up."

"Look at this picture," Lucas said. He showed him the artist's sketch of the actor from *Day of the Jackal*. "Is this the dude?"

Randy looked at the picture, his eyes drooped and his head turned away, and a moment later he seemed to pull himself together and he whispered, "No, man. I don't know the dude."

"You don't know him," Lucas repeated.

"He doesn't know him," Lansing snapped.

Del said, "You *want* him to know the guy. You got the concept here?"

"Hey, listen, you—"

"Shut up," Marshall said to Lansing. And to Randy: "A first name, a last name, somebody else who knows him, anything?"

"I gots to think," Randy said. "I'm all fucked up."

They came at the question nine different ways in the next ten minutes, but Randy shook his head as hard as he could and finally seemed to doze off.

"That's all," Lansing said.

Lucas looked at Marshall and Del. "It's a problem."

"Maybe tomorrow," Del said. "He's still got a lot of shit in him."

Randy came back, looked at Lucas. "Can't feel my legs, dude."

"They're working on you, Randy. You got good doctors," Del said.

"Yeah . . ." And he was gone again.

Out in the hall, Lucas said to Lansing, "I got a few words of advice for you. When cops want to talk to you or your client off the record, ninety percent of the time, you oughta do it. If you don't, you've got your head up your ass. We're not going to try to get somebody to incriminate himself off the record with his lawyer standing there. If we say we think he can help us and we can help him, we're telling the truth."

"To quote the famous Lucas Davenport," Lansing said, "blow me."

* * *

LUCAS led the way out to the car, with Marshall and Del trailing. Halfway across the parking lot, Lucas heard them start laughing and looked back and said, "What?"

"We were talking about your interpersonal relations technique," Del said. "Terry thinks you might need a course."

"Fuck Terry *and* his course," Lucas said. "The officious little prick."

Marcy was the only person in the office when they got back. "We've got everybody down at St. Patrick's," she said. "We got some chemistry back from the ME's office: They think maybe she was smothered."

"I knew it," Lucas said. "Might have been spontaneous rather than planned . . . but if it was spontaneous, it had to be somebody who knew her well enough to get her back to her office. What was her kid's name? James?"

"Yeah."

"Doesn't fit the picture, but the picture could be crap," Marshall said. "He doesn't look like the right movie star. He looks more like Yul Brynner."

"You think he could kill his mother?"

"The gravedigger could because he's crazier'n hell," Lucas said. "But we saw him over at the ME's office and he was pretty fucked up. Marshall had to hold him."

"I'm always pleased when strong men allow themselves to show a little tenderness," Marcy said to Marshall.

"Fuck you, little lady," Marshall drawled. He'd caught on to Marcy's act. "I just patted him on the back."

"What happened with Randy?"

"We ran into this officious little prick . . ." Lucas told her the rest of the story, while Del and Marshall found chairs.

"Gotta get back to him," Marcy said. "He's still got the key."

"I know, I know. . . . Goddamnit, it looked like it was gonna be easy. Instead, it's like counting votes in Florida."

A lot seemed to be happening, but there didn't seem much to do—the trouble was sweeping them along, and they couldn't get a handle on it. "So what do we do?" Del asked Marcy.

"There're plenty of people to talk to down at St. Pat's."

"Ah, shit," Del said. "All right, I'll do it."

"I'm gonna go talk to Harmon," Marshall said. "Maybe the computers will spit something out."

"They did, this morning. Those names Ware gave us—remember those—we got two hits. One guy for dope, possession of cocaine after a traffic stop, the other guy for crim sex III, problem with his wife. I pulled the mug shots, and they do sorta look like our picture."

Lucas shook his head. "Keep them in mind, but they're not our guy. Not even Ware thought so. I'll go on down to St. Pat's with Del, and we'll hook up with the other guys. He's down at St. Pat's."

THE rest of the afternoon was tedious. They all stopped at two o'clock to catch a cup of coffee and a sandwich, then went back—looking for professors, talking with students, pushing to find friends of Helen Qatar. At the end of the day, they'd struck out.

"I got one possible, an anthropologist who took drawing lessons so he could draw signs and statues and shit like that. He's a little crazy and he looks sorta right, but he claims he got his Ph.D. from USC six years ago and never set foot in Minnesota before then . . . and other people in his department say that's right," Del said.

"Better'n me," Swanson said. "I didn't find anybody."

"I got a guy who looked like a very distant possibility,

but, uh . . ." Black turned away and said, "I need another sandwich."

"But what?" Lucas asked. "What about the guy?"

"He sorta came on to me," Black said. "He, uh, isn't oriented toward women at all—and I got that confirmed from his department."

"Maybe something repressed," Swanson said. "Maybe when he's pushing fudge, all he's thinking about is killing women."

They all sat chewing for a moment, then Del started to laugh, and then both Lucas and Swanson. Black, who was gay, said, "Fuck all of you bigots."

JUST before they quit, Lucas said to Del, "You and Cheryl are coming for lobsters tonight, right?"

"Hell yes. Gotta keep this mass-murder shit in proportion."

20

"I HAD NO idea that you could show this depth of emotion, even about the death of a parent," Barstad said as they left the ME's office. "It's a side of you that I haven't seen before, James. I'm encouraged and . . ."

And blah-blah-blah, Qatar thought, tuning her out. There were still tears in his eyes, crouched at the corners, but they were quickly drying.

His mother. There *had* been some good times: Learning to ride a bicycle. Christmases come and gone. The first drawing materials she'd bought for him, and how, when he'd wanted to learn to paint, she'd gone down in the basement, and with his father's tools and a bunch of boards, laboriously put together a professional-quality easel. His first drawing lessons; his first life lessons; his first live naked woman, a redhead.

And some bad times.

He could remember Howard Cord, a history professor

who wore red bow ties and seersucker suits, and smelled of tobacco and chalk, and how he would come over late in the evening, after he'd been sent to bed, and bang his mother's brains loose. She must've known that he could hear it all, in his bedroom right above hers, all the groaning and mumbled pleas for this or that. Must have suspected that he'd lifted a floorboard and cut a hole in a heating vent so he could watch. Watch her doing all that . . .

And not just Howard Cord; there had been ten or fifteen men from the time his father left, and then died, and he went off to school. Academics, mostly, his mother passed from hand to hand through the University of St. Patrick's and then St. Thomas; a priest or two, he thought.

But they were *only* bad times. In analyzing his own craziness, which did not come without psychological penalty, he really couldn't blame his mother's galloping sexuality for his problems. They went much further back. He remembered still the intense pleasure of burning ants with a magnifying glass when he was not yet in grade school; remembered even the acrid scent of the little puffs of smoke. He drowned gerbils in grade school, put them in the aquarium during recess, while Mrs. Bennett was out in the schoolyard; and he still remembered the quiet of the schoolroom, and the distant shouts of the other children, barely audible through the windows, and the frantic paddling of the gerbils. They looked like they might last a little too long, so he pushed them under, both of them, one at a time, and watched their slowly diminishing struggles through the glass walls. . . .

He'd already known enough to hide himself and his impulses. He'd slipped out of the room in time to have a few words with the teacher on the playground, to establish his presence there.

And when the gerbils had been found, he'd happily helped plan the funeral.

His personal craziness had been there all along, the

cross he must bear. Bear it he did. His mother was *not* to blame.

". . . Blah-blah-blah?" she asked.

He hadn't heard any of it. He had, in fact, brought her along as a prop. His woman, should any of the cops think there might be something odd about him. They had been all over campus. "What?"

"What now? There's not much to do until you know when . . . she'll be released," Barstad said.

"I don't think I can deal with it right now," he said. "I'll call the funeral home this afternoon. Let them handle it. We weren't religious, so there won't be any church services." The tears were gone now. "Why don't we—I don't know—should I take you home?"

"We could walk around for a while."

"I haven't eaten. I don't know if I could eat," Qatar said "Maybe a little something."

They walked to the Pillsbury Building, went up the escalator and through the warren of shops in the Skyway. "It's really like a Middle Eastern bazaar," Barstad said. They were in the back of a coffee shop, eating baklava and drinking strong coffee. "You could get exactly what we're eating and drinking anywhere between Istanbul and Cairo, in the same circumstances, except the people are polite there and the coffee isn't as good."

"Never been there, the Middle East," Qatar said vaguely. Then: "Have you ever noticed that men with a certain shape of skull don't look good with high collars? They need flat collars?"

"What?"

"Would I look right in a turtleneck, do you think? Or would it come so far up my neck that my face would look like . . . that I'd look like, like a Renaissance burgher?" He crossed his hands, thumbs under his chin as though he were strangling himself, to show her the line of the sweater. "It frames the face, you see, but it also isolates it."

"I see," she said. "Well, if the person were tanned or sunburned, I think there's a possibility that the head would look wooden. You'd look like a wood carving on a pedestal."

"Hmm," he said. Actually, that sounded interesting. "Let's walk some more," he said.

In fact, he had the money in his pocket from his mother's house; and Saks and Neiman Marcus were right around the corner. On the way to the mall, he stopped and looked in the window of a jewelry store, where they were featuring small men's rings set with star sapphires. He'd never considered a ring, but they had a certain look.

"In here," he said. "Just on a lark."

He paid two thousand dollars for a gold ring that perfectly fit his right pinkie. "My mother's favorite color was blue," he told her. He teared up again, wiped them away, and they mushed on to Saks.

The men's store was on the first level. He led her down to the first level—and there they found the most marvelous thigh-length leather jacket, smooth-finished with kangaroo-hide details, on sale, $1,120.

He looked at it and said, "Oh my God, forty-long." Her eyes were on him, and he said, reverently, "It's exactly my size."

"Oh my God," she said.

21

WEATHER SAID IT was no big deal, just friends getting together for a beer and a little seafood, but she got to Lucas's place early and spent three hours dusting and vacuuming, and made it smell like nobody lived there but forest elves and evergreens. She was also wearing the engagement ring.

"Sort of stinky right now," she said, "but when you cook up the wild rice and mushrooms the spices'll make this place smell like . . ." She couldn't think of anything. "Good," she said. "You don't have enough beer, by the way, and when you're at the store, get a couple bottles of pinot noir—everybody drinks that, right? Something nice and buttery."

"Buttery," he said.

"Yes. Ask the clerk. Maybe three bottles. You better get some paper towels, and some regular napkins—you're all out of those."

"Never had any," he said.

"What'd you use?"

"Toilet paper," he said.

She put her fists on her hips. "I'm not exactly, precisely, in the right mood for humor, with the house being the wreck that it is. You wanna go to the store?"

SLOAN had traded his usual brown suit and wing tips for khakis and a brown sweater with oxblood loafers. Del did his best to look neat, in jeans that had been ironed, brothel-creeper boots, and a blue fleece pullover. Their wives looked like cops' wives: carefully dressed in sweaters and slacks, a little too chunky, with skeptical eyes.

Lucas had set up the charcoal grill in the back, heaped it with charcoal and a half-pint of starter fluid, stood back, and touched it off; he and Del and Sloan all smiled at the *foom* the fluid made when it ignited, and the resulting fire-ball. When the charcoal was going, he put the iron pot on top and poured in enough water to cover the lobsters.

"Teach the little fuckers to come back to life as lobsters," Lucas said.

"The only problem is, he's too chicken to put them in. I've got to do that," Weather said.

"Damn things bite," Lucas said. "Did we get some crackers?"

"Those little round ones?" Del asked hopefully.

THEY talked about cases, but not the gravedigger case. They talked about medicine, but not Randy. Weather talked about a skull reconstruction that she was working toward, and how image-manipulation technology allowed her to image a skull three-dimensionally, work out the recon-struction to the millimeter, and fit all the bones together at the end. "Of course, it doesn't always work out that way, and there's some fudging, but it's light-years past five years ago. . . ."

Del's wife had a story about another plastic surgeon who got into an instrument-throwing fit. "He's usually a nice guy—must be something going on."

Weather knew him and pitched in. "He was talking about quitting surgery and going into investment banking—he got really deep in investments. I think it was pretty risky. He told me if I wanted to kick in a quarter-mil, he could make it a mil in a year. I told him I couldn't afford it, but what I really think was, the risk must have been terrific. Maybe he took a hit."

They batted it all around for a while, and finally Cheryl, Del's wife, watching her husband crack a lobster claw and dip it in butter, asked, "I wonder if lobster has as much cholesterol as shrimp?"

"Both are sorta like bugs," Lucas said. He got up and said, "More beer?"

Cheryl looked at the other two women. "Is Del the only one with high cholesterol?"

"Ah, shut up," Del said.

"No, really."

"Sloan's is so low that it's like a race with his blood pressure, to see which one can hit bottom first. I'm sorta borderline," Sloan's wife said.

"I'm okay. Lucas has to think about it, but he's basically okay, if he'd just cut out the doughnuts," Weather said.

"Del's ought to be better with this Lapovorin stuff." Cheryl poked her husband with her elbow. "That doesn't mean you can eat everything in sight. Go back on those terrible pig rinds."

"Shut up. You gonna eat those claws?"

She pushed her plate toward him. "Mr. Sophisticated has been worrying about what that guy told you in the bar," she said to Lucas.

Lucas had to think a minute: the Cobra. "Oh, yeah. Lapovorin makes you come backwards."

"What?" Sloan was interested.

"Ah, Jesus," Del said.

"This guy told us that this woman who got killed by the gravedigger, that the only thing that she said about him—she was laughing about it—was that he was taking Lapovorin and was afraid that he was gonna be screwed up sexually."

"Like he isn't," Weather said.

"Yeah, but this is some kind of real physical thing," Lucas said. "Some kind of ejaculation thing happens, and . . ."

He hesitated to say it, but Del didn't. "You come backwards. Nothing comes out."

They were all mildly amused, and Weather said, "Del, that's nonsense. I know a little about Lapovorin, and there are no side effects like that at all. You've got to have your liver function checked every once in a while, a blood test—"

"Really?" he said, brightening. "I got the blood test."

"You mean the guy was talking through his ass?" Lucas asked. "I was planning to pimp Del with this for the next ten years."

"Not Lapovorin. What he was talking about is a situation that you see in a certain percentage of men who use that baldness drug," Weather said.

"What?" Del asked.

"You know. It's on television all the time," Weather said. "It's got enough weird hormones in it that they recommend that women never handle it. Not even get dust on them."

* * *

THE three cops did the dishes while the women talked in the living room. They filled Sloan in on the gravedigger case, and talked a bit about Terry Marshall.

"Tough guy," Del said. "You get that way, I think, when you're one of those country guys. Around here it's all lawyers and shit, but out in the country, a lot of times it's just you, and you got to fix it."

"Know what you mean," Lucas said. "But he's got this soul-brother thing going with Anderson."

"Anderson."

They spent the rest of the evening gossiping about friends and acquaintances. Cheryl Capslock asked Weather if they'd made any decision about children, and when they were going to get married, if they were. "We haven't figured out a wedding date," Weather said. "We're still working on that. We're working on a kid at the same time."

"Good luck," Sloan said. "Let's see, Lucas, you'll be about, mmm, ninety-four when the kid graduates from high school. . . ."

WITH all the talk, nothing tripped with Lucas until the next morning. Weather had already gone, and he was in the shower.

Weather, he thought, might have been slightly irritated with Sloan's crack about Lucas's age, especially since Weather wasn't *that* much younger. The thought of aging, and the thought of the whole group getting gray, and that they were worrying about cholesterol and reverse ejaculation . . .

He was grinning into the shower head, thinking about the coming-backwards discussion, when it struck him.

"Sonofabitch," he said. He stepped away from the water and looked down at his feet. Weather said it was the baldness remedy that made you come backwards?

So the guy was bald, or getting that way. He didn't look like the Jackal actor—that guy was all teeth and eyes and hair. Take away the hair . . .

He'd just met a young bald guy from St. Patrick's who was close to Helen Qatar, and who—was he remembering this right?—Mrs. Qatar had said was in the same department as the Neumann woman. He closed his eyes and pictured Qatar with hair. Holy shit.

Could be a coincidence. Didn't feel that way.

"Fuckin' James Qatar," he said aloud. He started to get out of the shower, then jumped back in to rinse the soap off his legs. Saw James Qatar in his mind's eye. Saw James Qatar's girlfriend in the corner—young, blond, fairly small, arty-looking. She could have been a model for the women who'd been murdered.

"Fuckin' Qatar," he said wonderingly.

MARCY was immersed in a pile of paper; Del hadn't made it in yet, and Marshall was drinking coffee and reading a copy of *Cosmopolitan*. The magazine cover promised to reveal hitherto-unknown love secrets that would win back the man who dumped you, and Marshall appeared to be deep into it.

Marcy looked up and said, "Hey. Black and Swanson are getting nowhere, but we're piling up a shitload of data. The FBI just came in with a revised sexual profile, plus backgrounds on all the members of the St. Patrick's faculty that they have files on. A lot of the older ones had to have clearances because of government work back in the bad old days, and—"

Lucas interrupted. "Doesn't matter."

"Doesn't matter?" She stood up. She knew the tone. "Why doesn't it matter?"

Marshall had stopped reading as Lucas continued to his

office and pushed open the door. Before he went inside he said, "Because when I was in the shower this morning—I was soaping up my hard, washboard abs at the time . . ."

Marcy was following along behind him. "Before washing your socks on them."

"When I realized that the gravedigger is none other than . . ." He paused, letting them guess. Nobody guessed, but they were both paying attention. ". . . James Qatar, Helen Qatar's son."

Marshall looked at Marcy, who looked at Marshall, then they both turned back to Lucas and Marcy said, "I'd like to know why."

"I could explain it, but instead of wasting the time right now . . ." He looked at Marshall. "You know anybody at Stout?"

He nodded. "Yeah. A few people. I know the president. Most of the vice presidents. And all the coaches, and—"

"Call somebody who might know. Ask them if they show a James Qatar as a student when Laura disappeared."

Now Marshall was intent: He could see Lucas was serious. He said, "I can sure as shit do *that*," picked up the phone, put it back down, dug a card case out of his jacket pocket, pulled out a stack of cards, shuffled through them, then picked up the phone again and punched in a long-distance number.

A minute later, he said, "Janet? This is Terry Marshall with the sheriff's office. . . . Ah, God, thank you, it was pretty terrible. . . . Yeah, I've been over there every other day. . . . Yeah. Listen, I'm working on the case, I'm over in Minneapolis. Could you look in your computer and see if you show a student there, ten years ago—be good if you could look a couple years on either side of that, too—by the name of James Qatar? Yeah, Qatar, Q-A-T-A-R. Yeah, like the country."

As they watched, he said, "Yeah," then doodled a minute

on the front of the *Cosmo,* looked at them, rolled his eyes and shrugged, doodled some more, and then said, "Yeah? What years? Uh-huh. Could you print that whole thing out and fax it to the Minneapolis police department if I give you a fax number? Uh-huh."

Marcy jumped up, scribbled a number on a piece of paper, and Marshall read it into the phone. He said "Uh-huh" a couple of more times, then "Thanks" and "Listen, keep this strictly under your hat."

He hung up. "You oughta take more showers," he said. "Qatar was there."

Lucas told Marcy, "Get everybody back here—and don't let any of this leak to the goddamn interdisciplinary group, or wherever it's called. I don't want a bunch of feds in blue suits running all over the place. Let's just keep it quiet, but point everybody at Qatar."

She said, "Right," and started doing that.

"They told me that sometimes you do this kind of shit," Marshall said. "But *how'd* you do it?"

Lucas told him, and when he finished, Marshall rubbed his chin and said, "I believe you. But basically, it's all bullshit and lies held together with baling wire."

Lucas said, "I wonder if that chick he was with knows him very well? I wonder if she signed in yesterday when they were at the ME's office—I think if you're gonna officially look at a body, you wind up signing something. Don't you? Maybe we ought to look her up."

Marcy looked up from the phones. "Now that we got a name, there's about twenty things we can do. There're so many things to do, I don't know where to start."

"The woman with the pictures on the bridge," Lucas said. "Let's start there."

22

WHILE MARCY WAS calling in Black, Lane, and Swanson, Lucas got on the phone to Del and caught him at breakfast. "What the hell are you doing up?" Del asked when he took the phone from his wife.

"I need the name of the woman you talked to, the one whose pictures were posted on the bridge."

"Beverly Wood. But I talked to her a couple times, and there's not much there. She has no idea."

"You got a number?"

"Yeah, just a minute. Did something come up?"

"I solved the case this morning," Lucas said modestly. "Maybe talking to her again will give us another confirmation."

"Jeez, that's good," Del said. "Here's the number." He read off Wood's phone number and then said, "I'm not getting any big wry-humor vibrations. You didn't really solve the case, did you?"

"We're meeting here as soon as Marcy can get the other guys back. Probably an hour. Tell you about it when you get here."

"Gimme a hint," Del said.

"I ejaculated backwards," Lucas said.

HE called Beverly Wood, was told that she was in a class-room. "Her seminar on women expressionists," he was told. There was no phone in the classroom, but he was no more than ten minutes away. He caught a squad about to leave the building and commandeered it as a taxi.

"Who's gonna protect Washington Avenue from speed-ers if we've got to haul some deputy chief all over town?" asked the guy at the wheel.

"I can fix it so you have extra traffic time, if you want," Lucas said.

"I don't take shit from guys who drive Porsches," the cop said. "You're speeding when you're sitting in the park-ing ramp."

BEVERLY Wood's class involved eight people slumped around a pale maple table looking at Xerox copies of mag-azine articles. Lucas stuck his head in, and they all turned to look at him. "Beverly Wood?"

"Yes?"

"I'm with the Minneapolis police. I need to talk to you somewhat urgently. Just for a minute."

"Oh. All right." She looked around at her class. "Nothing scandalous, I can assure you. Lily, why don't you begin the discussion of Gabriele Munter, since I've already read your paper and know your views. I'll be back in a minute"—she looked at Lucas—"I assume."

"Maybe two minutes," Lucas said.

He got her out in the hall and said, "You've talked to Officer Capslock a couple of times about the drawings . . . but let me ask you—you've got to keep this confidential, by the way—do you know of, or have you heard of, a man named James Qatar?"

She cocked her head. "You've got to be kidding."

"You know him?"

"Not exactly. He published a ridiculous paper on what he called 'riverine expressionism,' in which he suggested that European expressionism found its way into the Midwest during the 1930s by way of the great river valleys. I'm afraid I ridiculed it in my reply."

"You ridiculed him personally?"

"Everything's personal when you're talking about scholarship," she said. "I suggested that the riverine influences probably weren't that great since we had radios, newspapers, books, museums, trains, automobiles, and even airline service at the time."

"But he would have felt ridiculed personally?" Lucas asked.

"I certainly hope so. . . . He's the one who did the drawings?"

"We don't know. His name came up, and we were wondering if you might have had some contact."

"Just that article. I've never laid eyes on the man, as far as I know," she said.

"How long between the time you published the article and when the drawings were posted on the bridge?"

"Let me see. . . ." She looked at the floor and muttered to herself, then looked up again. "Four months? I would have told Officer Capslock, but to tell you the truth, the whole thing was so trivial to me—the review, I mean—that I'd completely forgotten it."

"What if the shoe were on the other foot, and you'd writ-

ten an article and it was criticized in the same way. . . .
Would you have remembered the criticism?"

"Oh, yes, probably forever," she said. "Maybe I
shouldn't have, but I had a pretty good time with him."

"Thank you," he said. "Please don't tell anybody about
this talk. We don't know who this man is for sure."

"The gravedigger . . ."

"If he is, we figure it's best not to attract his attention."

THE cop was waiting in the squad with the motor running.
Lucas opened the door and climbed in, and the cop said,
"Four speeders. They passed me with impunity."

"Impunity, huh? You in a vocabulary class?"

Del was waiting when he got back, and he took two minutes to explain it. Marshall added, "We got that fax from
Stout. He was there for two years, then went to Madison
the year after Laura disappeared. He majored in art at
Stout, and from Madison, they tell me that he was in art
history."

"So he's gotta be able to draw," Lucas said.

Marshall asked, "I wonder what he was doing with that
pimp?"

"We can ask Randy," Lucas said. To Marcy: "We need to
get somebody from intelligence to track him down, Qatar,
and take a picture of him without him knowing it."

"Lane can do that," Marcy said. "He's got a darkroom at
his house. He's a good photographer."

"All right, that's good. Let's get Lane going."

When they were all assembled, Lucas laid out what they
had: Qatar had been at Stout when Laura Winton disappeared. He'd grown up near St. Pat's, where his father had
been a professor and his mother an administrative em-
ployee and later head of the Wells Museum. He fit the im-

age of the man described by Winton, or, at least, he would if he had hair. He had art training. His office was just down the hall from Neumann. His mother died shortly after saying that she'd snoop around a bit. And his current girlfriend was the spitting image of all the women who'd been killed.

"Her name is Ellen Barstad," Marcy said. "Believe it or not, there are two Ellen Barstads in Minneapolis, so we're sorting that out now."

"We know he steals valuables from his victims—they're not souvenirs, though, he's apparently doing it for the money. Once we get in his house, we've got to look at everything with a microscope, in case he keeps anything else. If we could find one thing that comes from the victims, that would be enormous."

"We gotta get in and grab his computers," Lane said. "If Marcy's artist friend is right, and he's drawing from computer photos, then maybe they'll have everything we need."

"Good," Lucas said. He made a note on his legal pad. Then: "I would like to know why we weren't onto him sooner, with all the time we put in at St. Pat's."

Black said, "Because we were looking for people connected with art, and the art department and the museums. That's hundreds of people. And after that, we were just asking around. Qatar and Neumann were in the history department." He shrugged. "We never looked in history."

THEY'D all gathered at the desks in the work bay, but as the talk continued, they'd pulled chairs around until they were in a rough circle, facing each other, intent. When they'd talked out all the possibilities and probabilities, Lucas said, "Check me on this. I see two keys: We need Randy to identify him as the guy who sold him the jewelry, and maybe—maybe—we can do something with his girlfriend."

"I can get a headshot," Lane said. "It might take me a day or two if we don't want him to spot me."

"Push it hard," Lucas said. "I'd love to get something today, so we can get it over to Randy."

"How about the girlfriend?" Del asked.

"That's you and me," Lucas said.

Marshall said, "And me."

Lucas nodded and turned to Swanson and Black. "You two, I want you back at St. Pat's. See if there's any way we can nail down whether he was at that museum reunion party—but keep it tight, undercover. I need a bio on him. Something that could put him with the other dead women that we've identified."

"Are we gonna track him?" Marcy asked.

"I'll get some guys from intelligence. We don't need a full team, I don't think—that's too dangerous. We'd have to talk with his neighbors and college faculty people to pull off a team, and the word might get around. So maybe just one guy at a time, keeping a light tag. No reason to think he's gonna run."

Marcy asked, "What about me?"

"Go talk to the county attorney. Tell him what we've got and find out what we need—how bad we're hurting and what we can do."

"I think we're hurting a little," she said. "Like Terry said, we've connected a lot of dots but nothing really critical."

"Except Randy."

"Who we managed to cripple," she said.

"Yeah . . . the little prick."

BEFORE they went looking for Ellen Barstad, Lucas stopped at Rose Marie's office to tell her what they were doing.

"What are the chances?" she asked after he gave her a quick summary.

"I think he's the guy. Proving it is gonna be harder. The problem is, except for the first one, they were coming to him—he seemed to be picking on women from out of town, or women who just got to town, so her friends would never see him. Who knows, they may never even have known his real name. . . . We think he gave a fake name to the Winton girl."

"Are we watching him?"

"Yeah. I need you to talk to the intelligence guys. We're not gonna climb all over him, but we want to know where he is."

"I'll talk to them," she said. She made a note on her desk pad. Then: "New topic: If you had a chance to take a job with the state, would you take it?"

He shrugged. "I sorta like it here."

"But if you couldn't stay here?" she pressed.

"What are you working on?"

She leaned across the desk. "The guy running the department of public safety? The governor doesn't like him. He *does* like me—and he should, since I did most of his homework for him when he was in the state senate. We get along on a chemical level."

"So you're thinking of moving up."

"The possibility's out there," she said.

"Well . . ." He rubbed his forehead with his fingertips. "That's a different kind of work."

"Not for you, it wouldn't be. You'd be doing the same thing you do here—working on your own, big cases, intelligence. Figuring things out. Maybe some political work. You could bring along Del, if you wanted."

"I don't know if Del would go. Maybe he would."

She leaned back. "Think about it. I don't know if the

whole thing is gonna work out, anyway. A couple of things have got to fall just right."

"But the governor likes you," Lucas said.

"He does," she said. "What's even more important, he's gonna be reelected, if he doesn't fuck up the tax thing, so we'd have at least seven more years. We'd be like *Hawaii Five-O.*"

"Jesus, *Hawaii Five-O.* All right. I'll think about it."

"Keep in touch on this Qatar thing," she said. "It wouldn't hurt our image if we nailed this down. Politically, it's just the right time."

HE picked up Del and they got a city car and went looking for Barstad. Marcy had straightened out the confusion on the two Ellen Barstads—one of them was an elderly resident of a nursing home—and so they had an address and phone number, but nothing else.

The address turned out to be in another one of the faceless business parks, not far from the nearly identical one where Ware had his porn studio.

"I thought it was her home address," Del said, as they pulled into the parking area. Thirty or forty cars were scattered down the length of the narrow, block-long lot.

"Maybe she lives here," Lucas said.

"There's a sign on the door."

The door was heavy silvered glass, and the sign was in gold stick-on letters: "Barstad Crafts." The door was locked, but they could see a light in the back. Lucas knocked, then cupped his hands on the glass to peer past the reflections. He knocked again, and a woman stepped into the light in the back, then started toward them. When she got close, Lucas took out his ID case and held it up so she could see it.

She turned the lock and said, "Yes?"

Lucas recognized her from the ME's office. "Ellen Barstad?"

"Yes?" A worried, tentative smile.

Lucas introduced himself, and then Del, and said, "We have a serious problem, and we need to talk to you about it. Would you have a few minutes?"

"Well . . ." She looked carefully at Del and then said to Lucas, "You're the man who was at the medical examiner's office."

"Yeah."

"Okay." She opened the door all the way and stepped back. "Come in. Let me lock the door behind you."

The front of the store was an open bay, with quilt frames made out of brightly painted one-by-two lumber leaning against the walls, and another lying flat on a series of saw-horses. All held quilts in various stages of completion.

"I give classes," she said.

"This is a *really* nice quilt," Del said, and he meant it. The quilt was a traditional log-cabin style, but the colors had been carefully chosen and placed, so that light seemed to be falling across the quilt from one side to the other; it was almost as if the quilt were spread across a bed by a sunlit window.

Barstad picked up on his sincerity and asked, "Do you have quilts?"

"Two of them," Del said. "My sister-in-law makes them. Nothing like this, though."

They spent a moment looking at the quilt, bonding. And then Barstad, flattered, said, "What can I do for you? Is there a problem?"

Del said, "Let's get some chairs." There were several chairs scattered around the room, and he reached for one.

"Why don't you come in back," she said. "I can make some coffee, if you don't mind microwave."

She did live in the place. The back part of the commercial space had been carefully divided into small rooms with drywall partitions. She might have done it herself, Lucas thought: A green Army-type tool bag and a drywall square sat in one corner of the main room, on a white-plastic bucket of drywall compound.

He could see one end of a bed in a side room, and a toilet and sink in a corner between the bedroom and the living room space. A kitchen had been carved out of another corner and equipped with a half-sized office refrigerator, an old electric stove, and what once had been a standard industrial sink. Shelves and cupboards were fashioned from chromed industrial kitchen racks. Altogether, he thought, it looked snug, artsy-craftsy, and even a little snazzy.

As she got cups, Lucas said, "You were at the ME's office with James Qatar."

"Yes. James and I have been dating."

"We are doing . . . research . . . on Mr. Qatar," Lucas said. "He's basically the guy we want to talk about."

"Do you think he killed his mother?"

Lucas looked at Del, who shrugged, and Lucas asked, "Where did that question come from?"

"I don't know," she said. "His mother's dead in a weird way, and the cops show up and ask questions. Was she murdered?"

"We think she may have been," Lucas said. "Was there anything in particular that caused you to ask the question?"

"Yes," she said. "James is a would-be clothes horse. He *loves* to get dressed up. When I was studying fabric I did quite a bit with fashion, you know, and I never met anybody with as much need to project himself through clothing as James does. . . . It's like when he tries to picture himself, the main thing he sees are clothes, but he never has enough money to get the really good ones." She reached out and touched Lucas's jacket. "He would love something like this."

"Uh . . ."

"Just a minute, I'm getting there," she said. The microwave beeped, and she took the three cups out and passed them around. Watching her talk and move around, Lucas had concluded that she was an attractive woman hiding behind a plain facade—part of the curious Minnesota female ethic of dressing down. She went on: "Anyway, he called me after his mother was found, said he needed moral support to look at her body. So I went with him, and we identified her, and he was all weepy when you showed up. I felt like I was a prop. But I'll tell you, the weeping stopped one minute after we left, and we went on a shopping spree. For him. He paid two thousand dollars for a *pinkie ring,* for God's sake. Probably three thousand dollars more in Saks and Neiman's, and he just doesn't have that kind of money. I think it came from his mother's house."

"Huh. Not a lot of grief," Lucas suggested.

"Not when he wasn't around the medical examiner's or you police," she said.

Del said, "Look, we don't want you to betray a friendship—"

"Of course you do," she said. "What do you want me to do?"

Lucas cocked his head. "I get the impression that you're not all that friendly."

"We've been sleeping together for three weeks—but it's just about to end, to tell you the truth. He's not exactly the package I was looking for. I think . . ." She paused, and actually seemed to think about it. "I knew he might have been a little freaky in some ways, right from the start. He had that shine in his eyes. But I had some things I wanted from him, too, so that was okay . . . and he's clean and everything. But after that deal with his mom, he sorta scared me."

Lucas looked at Del and said, "I guess we tell her about it."

23

BARSTAD HAD NOTHING to contribute but impressions. Qatar was capable of violence, she said, "Sometimes we have pretty rough sex," she said, but she added that there had been no hint of anything else.

"When you say rough sex, you mean he forces you?" Lucas asked.

"No, usually I have to suggest it," she said. "He's not very creative."

"Oh." Lucas carefully didn't look at Del.

She said, "How about if I asked him about it? Killing people. Don't you guys bug apartments and stuff? I could get him here and ask him and you could record it."

"That might be a little crude—just coming out and asking," Del said. "Especially if it pissed him off and he picked up a steam iron and popped you on the head with it. We could get in quick, but not that quick."

"But I'm not stupid," Barstad said. "If he looked like he

was getting ready to do something, I'd scream my head off. He doesn't carry a gun. Believe me, I know that for sure. He doesn't even carry a pocketknife."

"You seem pretty willing to get into this," Lucas observed.

"Hey. It's interesting," she said. "You think he might have killed his mom, I'm willing to help out."

"There's more to it than that, about Qatar," Lucas said.

Del said, "If you've seen the TV stories on this guy they call the gravedigger . . ."

She straightened. "You're kidding me," she breathed. "Oh, man."

"A violent guy—if he's the right guy," Lucas said.

"Well, let's get him," Barstad said enthusiastically. "I can bring him over here. We can work out something for me to say, either leading him on or just putting it right to him."

Lucas nodded. "We can work on it," he said. "We appreciate this."

She said, "Those women the gravedigger killed. They said he likes a type. I thought about it, because . . ." She looked down at herself.

Del said, "Yeah. You're the type. Exactly."

They talked a while longer, about the possibilities of bugging the apartment. "If it worked . . . we're really looking for every scrap we can find, so it would be very helpful," Lucas told her. "We don't want you to get in over your head."

"But this guy is some kind of maniac," Barstad said. "You've got to catch him. If this is the way to do it . . . I can help. It sounds . . . neat."

Del shrugged, looked at Lucas, and said, "I think it's worth a try."

They agreed to try, as quickly as it could be done. Lucas suggested that until they could work the trap, Barstad stay out of her apartment and out of touch with Qatar. "Maybe call him right now and tell him you have to go somewhere—Chicago—to see about a quilt show. Tell him you'll be back tomorrow."

She agreed, and while Lucas and Del looked, she called Qatar's house, got an answering machine, and left the message. "Listen, I really, *really* need to get together tomorrow, though. Could you come over tomorrow after your one o'clock class? Then maybe we can go wine shopping. I got out some more money—might as well do it right. . . ." She hung up.

"That was fine. And now, get out," Lucas said. "Get some clothes together—we'll take you with us and find you a place to stay."

"What about this place?" she asked. "When are you going to bug it?"

"If we decide to go ahead, probably this afternoon or tomorrow morning. Otherwise, we'll just keep you out of sight until we pick him up. Don't want to take any chances with you," Lucas said.

"I work at a bookstore in the evenings. Could you call them and fix things?"

"Yeah. We can take care of it."

She got a bag, took ten minutes to pack it, and they left together in the city car. On the way back, Lucas called Marcy, who set up a room in the Radisson Hotel. They checked her in, warned her about going out, and left her.

"That's the goddamn ditziest woman I've met since forever," Del said on the way out of the hotel. "What are the chances that she's gonna stay in that room?"

"She says Qatar doesn't like to go out, so . . . I don't know. She oughta be okay," Lucas said. They rode in silence for a minute or two, and then Lucas added, "I hope."

"Maybe we ought to put somebody with her."

"I'll talk to Marcy. Maybe tonight . . . She *is* a little loose in the hinges, isn't she?"

WHEN they got back to the office, Lucas asked Marcy, "Hear anything from Lane?"

"He said Qatar's got a class. He'll try to spot him, then figure out a photograph. If he can't get him at the school, he'll try to get him at his house."

"He can't be seen," Lucas said.

"I told him that. He knows," she said. "Towson called. He wants to talk to you. And Weather called."

"Towson's got a problem?" Randall Towson was the county attorney.

"I told him everything," she said. "He's a little worried about going with an identification by Randy. Randy's pretty impeachable, he says."

"Sure, but we've got the hard evidence: We found the earrings in his apartment," Lucas said.

"Call him," Marcy said.

"I will—but I need you to check out a surveillance deal. . . ." He told her about Barstad and her apartment, and the possibility of using Barstad as bait in a trap.

"All right, I'll get on it. I better talk to her first, find some place we can do the monitoring from."

Lucas looked around. "Where's Marshall?"

"He went home. He'll be back, but he had some stuff to do."

"Okay. And I'll call Towson." As he was dialing, he could see Marcy moving around the office. She was moving well, the pain receding from her face, although on occasion she would *ease* herself past a piece of furniture or up a step, still feeling the damage to her side and rib cage.

But maybe the artist was good for her, Lucas thought. She'd been cheerful for the past couple of days, the first time he'd seen that in a while.

RANDALL Towson wasn't a bad county attorney, as county attorneys went; still, he had his own priorities, like reelection. He did not enjoy losing court cases that were heavily covered by the movie people, who might imply that he'd let a multiple murderer slip through his incompetent fingers. With evidence, he always wanted more.

"Look," he said, "Marcy laid it out pretty well, and I appreciate the circumstantial stuff and the supportive evidence like his college record. But at this point, if you don't get Whitcomb you don't get Qatar. And Whitcomb is not reliable. When he figures out that he could be in a wheelchair for the rest of his life, he might be pretty unhappy with our side. And what's Qatar ever done to him?"

"I know. We're working on one more thing," Lucas said. He described the relationship between Barstad and Qatar. "She's cooperating. We're gonna wire her apartment, and if we get him talking, maybe we won't need Randy as much."

"Good. The more the better," Towson said. "You still want to get Whitcomb, but this Barstad—if we can get him on tape, and Whitcomb comes through, he's toast."

"If he doesn't say anything?"

"Well, shit . . . Wait for Whitcomb, and if Whitcomb comes through, take Qatar. Once we get him and we get into his house, get at his computer and all his other stuff, there's a chance we'll find more."

"That's what I was thinking," Lucas said.

" 'Cause there'd be one thing worse than losing the trial—and that's having him kill somebody else while we're jacking around."

"Especially if the TV people found out about it."

"That's what I was thinking," said Towson.

WEATHER had called to see if they were going out for dinner. Lucas said, "Things are happening. I'll get back if I can, but you better not count on it."

"There. You sound as cheerful as you have all winter," she said.

"Yeah, well . . . it's getting intricate." He liked intricate. They talked for a few more minutes, and then he saw Marcy hold up a finger, and he said, "I gotta go. Titsy calls."

"Then you gotta go."

Marcy moved quickly on the surveillance. "We've got Jim Gibson free. He's going up to the Radisson to get Barstad's keys, and then he's gonna go over and look at her apartment right now. Barstad says there's a place next door called Culver Processing Sales that's a good possibility as a place that we can hide out. I just talked to the owner, it's a Dave Culver, and he says he wants to talk to the guy in charge—you—before he says yes."

"I'll get a bite and then I'll run back up there," Lucas said. "Is Gibson on the way?"

"Pretty soon."

Lucas walked across to the cafeteria, got a tapioca pudding and a cup of coffee, glanced at the morning papers, and then headed out again. At Barstad's, he saw Gibson standing in the parking lot behind his van; when he swung past to park, he saw Barstad using her keys to open the door. "Goddamnit." What was she doing here?

"She told me she was supposed to come along," Gibson said when Lucas got out and asked him. "Is that wrong?"

"It would be if Qatar swung by for an afternooner," Lucas said.

Inside, Barstad said, "I needed to come back anyway. I

forgot some stuff—I refuse to wash my hair with hotel shampoo. You never know what's in it."

"We need to keep you out of sight."

"James is teaching," she said. "He'd never come all the way here without calling, so . . ." She shrugged, then smiled and said, "C'mon. I'll introduce you to Dave Culver. He's a nice guy."

"What does he do?"

"Sells big meat cutters and grinders and so on to restaurants."

Culver was a heavyset man in his late fifties with a square dark face with a Stalinesque mustache. He was in the back of his business, ripping cardboard boxes, when they pushed through the front door. A buzzer went off in the back, and Barstad shouted, "Hey, Dave, it's me. And the cops."

They were standing in a small reception room, with three easy chairs and a coffee table. The coffee table had three deer-hunting magazines, a four-wheeler magazine, a battered copy of *The New Yorker,* and sales literature for automated meat cutters.

Culver came out of the back, said "Hi, sweetie" to Barstad and "Dave Culver" to Lucas. Lucas shook his hand and introduced himself, and outlined what they hoped to do.

"Is Miss Crazy Quilt gonna get her ass in trouble?" Culver asked.

"That's why we need to be close," Lucas said. "We don't think he'll pull anything, but just in case . . ."

"All right," Culver said. "My only other problem is, I don't want to be dealing with some gang or something that's gonna be coming by here afterward and tear up the place. I've got a quarter-million bucks' worth of new equipment in the back."

"It's one guy," Lucas said. "He's not connected to anyone. If we take him off, he won't be out of Stillwater for thirty years minimum."

Culver nodded. "So, use the place. You got any friends in the restaurant business, give them my card."

CULVER'S shop was divided into three: a front reception area with the coffee table, only a few feet deep; two offices behind the reception area; and a big warehouse area behind that. Gibson looked at it, measured it, walked over to Barstad's, did some more measuring, and wound up in one of the middle offices. "I can go right through the wall here, and here, no permanent damage," he told Culver. "Is that okay?"

"Fine with me. . . . Get some of my stuff out of your way."

"How good will the sound be?" Lucas asked.

"Should be great," Gibson said. "When I get done miking the place a goddamn cockroach couldn't sneak through on its hands and knees. We won't need any transmitters— we can hard-wire everything. Digital sound. You want a camera?"

"I don't know. Is there a problem with a camera?" Lucas asked.

"It's a little more intrusive," Gibson said. "I think we could fix it so he couldn't see it—in the big room, anyway; there's no good place in the bedroom or the bathroom—but there's always the chance that he'll spot it. If the camera can see him, he can see it. The lens, anyway."

"See what you can do," Lucas said.

"There's also a privacy question," Gibson said.

Barstad was there, and said, "What's that?"

"If you are . . . luring him . . . and if you've slept together, then he may expect some physical contact. Sound is one thing, pictures are something else."

She shook her head. "Go ahead. I'm not body-shy."

They both looked at her. Lucas shook his head and said to Gibson, "Whatever you can do."

When they were done, and the equipment had tested out, Lucas looked at his watch and said, "We're all done for the day. Jim, if you'd drop Ellen off at the hotel on the way back, I'd appreciate it. We all gotta be back here, in place, at noon tomorrow. Ellen, you and I can talk about your approach to Qatar when we're back here tomorrow—think of some possible things you might say, and I'll think of some, and we'll work it out tomorrow. Okay? Everybody know what we're doing?"

Everybody knew.

LANE called later, about Qatar: "I missed the sonofabitch—there're just too many doors here, and I don't know where the hell he's gotten to. He's not home. But I've seen him, I know who he is, and I'll wait outside his house. If he comes in too late, I'll get here early tomorrow. I'll get him tomorrow for sure."

"Soon as you can, man."

"I know, I know."

24

Marcy called Lucas at eight-thirty and caught him still in bed. He picked up the phone and said, "What?"

"The docs had a talk with Randy late yesterday afternoon," she said. "They told him he might not walk again and all the rest of it. He freaked out. I called over there today, to this Robert Lansing guy, to set up a rush-rush deal to get the photos over there when Lane gets them . . . and Lansing says it's all off for now. He said Randy won't talk to anyone—he won't even talk to Lansing. He screams at everybody who comes in the room. He ripped out all his IVs—the nurses had to tie him into the bed."

"Jesus."

"Well, you know, if it was one of us . . ."

"Yeah." If it was him, Lucas thought, he might sooner or later stick a gun in his mouth. "What about Lane? Do we have anything to work with?"

"Not yet. We're still on hold. He got Qatar in the parking lot, but just couldn't get around in front of him enough. The whole problem is getting in front of him. He's gonna sit on the car all day, and get him coming in."

"Goddamnit, Marcy. Tell him to push it," Lucas said.

"Even if he takes a chance on being seen?"

"No, no, no . . . He can't be seen. That'd mess up everything."

"Then you gotta be patient, Lucas," she said.

"No, I don't. I'm the fuckin' boss."

QATAR was sitting at his desk, trying to get through a deck of photographic slides he used in lecture. He didn't like to use more than twenty per class—they couldn't be absorbed, he felt, and forced him to rush the analyses; when all was said and done, he *was* a decent teacher—and they had to be arranged in a certain aesthetic order. He hated to have light, bright slides immediately before or after dark-colored slides. That was like serving heavy, strong-flavored food with light, delicate wine; you couldn't appreciate either one.

Beyond that, as a buzz in the back of his mind, lingered the fear created by the growing media spectacle of the gravedigger. The state forensics team was still working on his hillside, and there were daily alarms, later retracted, of more bodies. And speculations about the ogre who could have killed so many women. Two of the stations had paid retired FBI agents to profile the killer; the profiles were generally similar, with one of the agents specifying a "fastidious dresser" who would be as meticulous in his personal habits as he was in his graveyard.

All of this was humming in the background of his slide-sort, when the phone rang. He picked it up, thinking, *Ellen,* and it was.

"I'm back," she said. She seemed uncharacteristically breathless. "Did you get my message?"

"Yes. This afternoon would be fine. How much do you have for the wine?"

"A thousand. I sold a huge star quilt, the rippling light. I thought with a thousand, I could get a really good start."

"A fine start," Qatar said. "I'll bring my book and we can work through the list before we go."

"Listen . . . I don't want to give anything away, but . . . have you ever heard of sexual asphyxiation?"

"What?"

"I saw it in a movie last night. Some art film. A guy hanged himself—not completely, but enough to choke off the air—and when the police asked him about it, he said you have the most wonderful orgasms."

"Well . . . I've heard of it, but it sounds painful. I understands it's often done with silk neckties, but I think it might be dangerous. I mean, brain damage."

"Oh. But, if you were *really* careful . . ."

"Ellen, I don't know. Let's wait until I get over. We don't want to go *too* far."

"Okay. I'll see you this afternoon." Again, a little breathless. She must've been busy. "But, James . . . *think* about it."

He couldn't stop thinking about it. He kept thinking about it as he finished sorting, and developed an erection so intense that it was almost painful. He might have done something about it immediately, but for his class. And during his class . . .

One of the young virgins in his Matrix of Romanticism class was nearly perfect: blank, clueless blue eyes, fine slender body, punky blond hair. She would be perfect, he thought, except for her incessant gum-chewing, and the constant presence of an earphone in one ear. She even tried to listen to music during his class, until he questioned it. She unplugged, annoyed, and told him that she was only listening to background music for his lecture and the art. She always tried to find something appropriate.

Like what? he asked. Beethoven?

"Enigma," she said. *"The Screen Behind the Mirror."*

"Please . . ."

But today she was sitting there with her virginal legs stretched out in front of her, and a little into the aisle, nicely encased in nylon; and she wore a thin white sweater like a fifties movie star.

He thought of sexual asphyxiation and tried to talk about Géricault's *The Raft of the Medusa,* and also keep his sports jacket appropriately draped as the erection came and went. He could imagine this blank-eyed blonde on a bed, the long groove of her spinal column leading up her back to her neck, her head arched in orgasm and the rope in his hand . . .

By the time he left for Ellen Barstad's studio, he was in a hurry, his worries about the gravedigger investigation pushed to the back of his mind. He needed to see her now.

In his hip pocket, he carried his rope.

LANE called: "Lucas, I got him coming out of the building, heading to the car. Good shots. I'm gonna take it over to a one-hour place—I oughta have big prints by the time you get out of there."

"Good, but have you talked to Marcy? We're a little hung up on Randy," Lucas said.

"Yeah, I talked to her. They haven't worked anything out yet, but having the pictures can't hurt."

"Okay. You just do the pictures. You say he's out of the place?"

"He is, and he's moving in your direction. He's in a hurry."

Lucas, Del, Marshall, and Gibson were huddled in the middle office with two TV monitors, both hooked to the same camera and each with its own tape deck; a couple of Bose speakers; two tape recorders; and four separate cell phones.

Lucas picked up his phone and called Barstad next door. "Ellen, he's coming. Now, if it doesn't work, if it gets uncomfortable, throw his ass out. If he won't go, yell for help. Are you okay?"

"I'm fine," she said. "Don't worry, Lucas. I'm going to hang up now. . . ." And she did.

"Crazy chick," Gibson said.

They couldn't see her: She was in the bedroom, and there had been no place for a monitor. Even if there had been, Lucas was worried by the privacy problem: A camera pointing at the bed didn't seem right, though Barstad hadn't seemed bothered by the concept. They'd finally decided that the room was simply too small and sparsely furnished. Qatar had been there several times, Barstad said; they didn't want to change the style just to hide the camera. The only camera was hidden behind the grille of a return-air vent at the front door, from where it could sweep the room.

Gibson could change the sound from one mike to the next with a simple slide switch. The microphones were sensitive enough that they could hear Barstad moving around, could hear the refrigerator open, could hear her flush the toilet.

"One more mike, we could hear her pee," Gibson said.

"That's what we want to put in front of a jury," Del said. "Our witness taking a leak."

Marshall disapproved. "I worry about this girl. She thinks she knows what she's getting into, but she doesn't. She ain't a hell of a lot more than a child."

"She says he doesn't carry a gun, he doesn't carry a knife. If he goes to get a knife, she'll scream her head off and we'll be there in twelve seconds."

The twelve seconds wasn't a guess. They'd timed it.

"That's a long goddamn time if somebody is cutting your throat or hitting you on the head with a ballpeen hammer," Marshall said.

"Yeah, well . . . So I'm worried too. This is what we've got, and I think we're ninety-seven percent okay," Lucas said.

DEL had moved out to the front while Lucas and Marshall argued; Qatar drove a green and silver Outback, and from the silvered window, Del could see the entire parking lot. The waiting grew uncomfortable as they listened to Barstad moving around in her apartment. Then Del said, "He's here."

Lucas was speed-dialing Barstad. She picked up, and he said, "He's here. You know how to call us."

"I know. I'm ready." She was gone.

"He's out of the car," Del said. He stepped away from the window and headed back toward the office. "Here we go."

"Oh, shit—look at this," Gibson said. He was staring at the monitor. They'd heard Barstad step away to the bedroom after she hung up the phone, and now, five seconds later, she was back—and she wasn't wearing a stitch. She was walking toward the door and the camera.

"Jesus," Lucas said.

Del picked up the tone and bent around the monitor to look. "She must have goose bumps the size of watermelons," he said. "You know . . . she's . . . jeez. She's not bad. All natural."

She glanced up at the camera as she got to the door, and Lucas thought she might have been smiling. "Fuckin' crazy goddamn . . ."

* * *

BARSTAD opened the door and said, "Come in quick. It's a little cool."

"Mmm," he said. He fitted a hand around her hip and they kissed, long and carefully. As they broke apart, he said, "You look nice. The cold is nice for your nipples." He reached out and gently pinched one, and the slight pain caused her to breathe in, sharply, quickly. She said, "James, I really need something here."

"So do I," he said. He had the cord in his pocket, but for now, forgotten. She had taken his hand and was pulling him back toward the bedroom.

"Wait," she said. "The bedroom's so dark." She went to the wall, where a futon unfolded over a couch rack. "Help me," she said.

Together they pulled the futon off the rack and threw it on the floor, and she began tearing at his clothing. He was saying, "Wait, wait wait . . ." as she pulled at his shirt and then at his belt. He was staggering around with his pants down around his ankles when she caught him in her mouth, and he started to laugh and tried to push her away and finally collapsed on the futon.

"GOD help me," Gibson said. "Look at this."

"This could be a problem," Lucas said. "This could be a problem. Christ, the defense attorneys will put this on and they'll impeach the shit out of her."

"I don't know," Del said. "She's so up front about it. Maybe she'll just tell them she likes . . . Oh, Jesus."

"Maybe she likes it, but on television?"

Marshall backed out of the office. "This is over the edge."

"The guy's kinda hung," Gibson said.

"You think so?" Del asked. "I was gonna say he was a little small."

As sex always does, it ended, with Barstad and Qatar lying on the futon. The camera wasn't good enough to tell, but the cops imagined that both of them were covered with sweat and out of breath; they thought that because everybody in the monitoring room was sweating and out of breath. Lucas could smell them all.

BARSTAD, nearly recovered, said, "James. You *were* ready. What have you been doing? You were really *excellent*."

Qatar smiled at her, but his ears tingled: There was a false note there, a kind of patronizing overtone. He'd never heard it before. He said, "Thank you. You can get me . . . seriously turned on."

"Do you like slapping me?" she asked. There it was again, that *tone*.

"If you like it," he said. "I think I like the Ping-Pong paddles better."

She made a little moue. "That just made my bottom hurt, and I didn't get to see it."

"But *I* got to see it," he said. "And it more than made your bottom hurt."

"We're past that," she said. "Moving on."

"Moving on sooner or later," he said. He stood up. "I'm going to run back to the bathroom. Back in a sec."

FROM Culver's office, they could hear him in the bathroom, the water running in the sink. On the television monitor, Barstad lay with her back to them, but once or twice peeked over her shoulder in the direction of the camera.

"She's really getting off on this," Del said.

"So am I," said Gibson. "I wonder what her date calendar looks like."

"Ya oughta keep your goddamn mouth shut," Marshall

snapped at Gibson. Lucas said, "Hey," and Marshall said, "Goddamnit, Lucas, she's the spitting image of Laura. If I'd known this—"

Gibson interrupted. "Here he comes."

QATAR walked back toward the camera, much diminished now. He was carrying a blanket from the bedroom, and when he dropped beside her, put it over his shoulders and around hers. "Did you ever talk to that woman again? The lesbian thing?"

"Not yet. There's no point, if you don't want to go along."

"All right." He was satisfied—clear on the lesbian front. He could *hear* the rope in his pants pocket, calling to them. "You know, I can see why somebody like you might be interested. But I . . ." He sighed and stopped.

"Tough day?" she asked.

"Oh . . . with Mom gone . . . I mean, with the medical examiner and everybody looking at her. They're saying that the cause of death is undetermined, which I don't know—it means they might think it's not natural."

"James," she said, "when we left the medical examiner's the other day . . . we went shopping and that kind of freaked me out. I mean, it seemed almost like you'd forgotten her somehow."

"What?" His forehead wrinkled. "Ellen, that's just what I do when I'm upset. You know I like to shop, and I was just very upset and I . . ."

His words were coming faster and faster, and finally she held up her hand and said, "Okay, I'm sorry." She wrapped her arms around her knees. "I just, I don't know. I've been reading about this gravedigger guy, and he seems so . . . cruel. I thought *you* seemed a little cruel."

He heard the false note again. He was a historian and a

critic, and he could pick up a false note as quickly as anyone. He said, "You're comparing me to this gravedigger person?"

"No, no. I just want people not to be cruel." Then she smiled at him and her hand wandered to his groin. "Well, maybe a little cruel sometimes," she said. "Have you been thinking about my call?"

His mind was clicking over now: She was interrogating him. But was she doing it on her own, or was there somebody with her? Could somebody hear them? For Christ's sakes, could somebody *see* them? He didn't dare look. He said, "I thought this afternoon, because of my mother . . . something gentle. Something that takes a long time."

She seemed disappointed, and that was, in his mind, confirmation. Something was going on, and he didn't know what it was. "Why don't we do something excessively oral?" He slipped his fingers between her legs. "I haven't been in here yet."

"HE sorta walked away from that question," Del said.

"Doesn't look like she'll be asking any more for a while," said Gibson.

"Goddamnit," Marshall said to Gibson. "Somebody ought to kick your ass for you."

"Take it easy, pal," Gibson said. "When we get finished with this, you wanna take it outside, I'll go with you."

"Nobody's taking it outside," Lucas said. To Gibson he said, "Another comment about Barstad and you'll be directing traffic at a construction site." And to Marshall: "You keep your problems to yourself or I'll ship your ass back to Dunn County." And to both of them: "Everybody know where I'm coming from?"

* * *

LATER, when they finished with a second round, Barstad asked, "What do you think of the gravedigger?"

"Well, I guess I think what everybody thinks," he said. "He's a crazy man. He needs care."

"I think they just ought to take him out and dump him in a hole somewhere, and cover it up and not tell anybody where he is," she declared. "That would teach him."

"That would," he said. "You're right." Qatar stood up and gathered his clothes. "Everything's getting wrinkled," he said fussily. "Let me go hang them up."

"The rack in the bedroom," she said lazily. "Hurry back."

"You are far too young for me, m'dear," he said.

Qatar was in a panic. She'd mentioned asphyxiation sex twice; she'd mentioned the gravedigger three times—she was interrogating him, he thought, but then . . .

Was it possible that it was all a symptom of her craziness, with her whole sexual experimentation regime? Was it possible that the gravedigger turned her on? That all of this was innocent?

Then why the false notes? And they were false, clanging like a leaden bell. And now some of her smiles seemed false, and her sexual commentary too dramatic.

The biggest problem, he thought, was that he'd stupidly brought his rope. If there were police around, if they were watching him, they would hang him with it. He didn't know the details of DNA, but he had a general idea of how it worked. And the rope *looked* dense: It must have soaked up blood—there had been blood almost every time—and skin, and who knows what else.

In the bedroom, he looked around quickly, but there seemed no place to hide anything. He carefully hung his clothes on the rack, then took the rope out of his pants pocket, coiled it tightly, and stepped out of the bedroom and into the bathroom. She had a large rack of towels, washcloths, and other bathroom equipment on a stainless-steel kitchen rack, pushed against one wall. He turned on the water, then slipped the rope under the bottom pile of towels. He washed himself, dried, and went back to the front room.

A camera? Who knew? It might even excite him if he knew. . . .

She was waiting and asked, "What next? You don't want to try the necktie thing?"

"Some other time," he said. "It really makes me nervous, thinking about it."

Again the shadow of disappointment—but exactly how was she disappointed? Because a conspiracy was failing, or because she wanted a loop around her neck?

"James, you can be such a pill," she said.

A little after three o'clock, Qatar left.

"I thought we were gonna go wine shopping," Barstad complained. "I got some money out, I got a book on it—"

"Ellen, you have absolutely destroyed me. I couldn't go wine shopping today without risking a stroke. Next time, we'll go wine shopping *before* we start the sex. Honestly, you're a little bit . . . over the top."

"A pill," she said. "You really can be."

"NOTHING here," Del said, as they watched him leave.

Marshall said, "But I think that little girl could use treatment."

Lucas said to Gibson, "I want the tapes—I'll take them with me. I don't want any copies made, I don't want any editing. I'll tell you guys, we're all playing with our jobs on this. If it turns out that Qatar is innocent, and he believes we set him up to make this tape . . . our gooses could be cooked."

"Hey, I just did what you told me," Gibson said.

"I know. But you'd be cooked anyway. That's why I'm taking the tapes. They're going in a safe, and if we don't need them in this case, I'll burn the sonsofbitches." He shook his head. "Little Miss Muffin may have fucked us up."

THEY stood by the silvered window and watched Qatar walk across the parking lot and get into his car. He seemed a little beaten, and Lucas almost sympathized with him: Barstad was definitely, distinctly, too much. Lucas collected the tapes, and said to Del and Marshall, "We're back to Randy."

25

LUCAS BROUGHT IN the intelligence cops to watch Qatar. Since Qatar didn't know he was being watched, only one man was assigned at a time: one man to watch the car, get him to work, monitor the classroom and his travels during the day. "If he gets erratic, we'll get you help," Lucas told the first guy up. "Basically, at this point, it's baby-sitting."

The baby-sitter took Qatar through the night and then to work; a new guy picked him up at work, took him out of his office to a classroom, out to lunch, shopping, a visit to a funeral home, back to his office.

Lucas stayed in touch all day, but focused on the problem with Randy. He finally decided the best way to handle it was with Marcy. "He relates to women. He may relate to your getting shot."

"You want me to show him the bullet hole?"

She didn't have a bullet hole; she had a scar that looked like the star shape made when a pebble falls in mud, with a string leading out of it, which was the surgeon's entry cut. She was being tough, and Lucas recognized it: "If you think it'll help. You've got to read him."

Lucas applied some pressure on Randy's attorney by calling the public defender and explaining the deal. The PD went to Lansing and told him to take it, and to talk to Randy about it. The bureaucratic hassling took all of the morning and a piece of the afternoon, and finally an assistant county attorney got back to Lucas.

"We've been talking with the Ramsey county attorney and the Ramsey PD, and this is the deal: If Whitcomb can positively identify the picture, and give us details surrounding his contacts with the suspect . . ."

"Qatar."

"Yeah, Qatar. If he can do that, Ramsey'll reduce the ag assault to simple assault and drop the drug charge down to misdemeanor possession—and he takes a six-month to two-year sentence, which he spends in the hospital, because that's how long the docs think rehab will take. In other words, he takes an easy fall and we pay for medical."

"We'd have to pay it anyway, one way or another," Lucas said. "So the deal is done?"

"Everybody's agreed but Randy. The idea is, you show up with the pictures and see if you can get him to move."

"I'm sending Marcy Sherrill in to talk to him. He has a personal problem with me."

"Whatever you think. We need him if we're gonna have a chance with Qatar."

Lucas and Marcy drove to Regions together, and talked about approaches. "He's a pimp," Lucas said. "You oughta show a little street balls, like a hooker, but basically back off when he comes on to you. Gonna have to play him."

"That's the bullshit I don't like," she said. "That's why I

never was a good decoy. I always wanted to go straight for the throat."

"Aim a little lower this time," Lucas said. "If you can get a grip on his dick, we can put Qatar away this afternoon."

Lansing was waiting outside Randy's hospital room. Lansing looked at Marcy and asked Lucas, "Who's this?"

"Why don't you ask me? I'm standing right here," Marcy said.

Lansing stepped back. "All right. Who're you?"

"I'm a Minneapolis police sergeant and I'm a little fuckin' cranky this afternoon, so if you don't want me to pull your nose off, I'd suggest you be polite. I'm the one who talks to Whitcomb."

Lansing looked at Lucas, who shrugged. "*I'm* always polite with her."

Lansing nodded abruptly, as if he'd had enough of the Minneapolis police show. "All right. I'll tell Mr. Whitcomb why we're here, and then you can make your pitch. It's all fine with us, if he goes for it—but he's pretty angry."

"I can relate," Marcy said.

Lucas waited in the hall, holding the door open just enough to hear. Lansing started the introductions, and Randy said, "Get her out of here. Get her the fuck out of here."

He sounded like he was trying to scream, but his voice was a cross between a whisper and a croak, as though he'd been shouting in whispers all day.

Marcy said, "I know what you're feeling, Randy. I got shot myself last year. I'm still in rehab."

"Tell somebody who cares, you fuckin' cunt," Randy croaked. "I wish they'd hit you in the fuckin' head."

Lansing said, "Randy, you've got to listen to this. This is a deal that's the best you could hope for, this is—"

"Fuck you. You're fired. I want another attorney. I got no fuckin' legs. . . . You hear this?" Lucas heard a whacking sound and peeked through the door. Randy was flat on his back but flailing at his legs with one free hand. "Nothing here, nothing here . . ."

Lansing tried to grab his arm, said, "C'mon, stop it, Randy, gotta stop, you're hurting yourself."

A nurse burst past Lucas and into the room and shouted, "What's going on here? What's going on?"

Randy subsided, looked at the nurse, and said weakly, "Get them the fuck outa here. Get them the fuck out."

"NEVER had a chance," Marcy said, as they left the hospital. "Never let me get going."

"He was a little excited," Lucas said.

"Ah, man. I felt sorry for the guy," Marcy said. "Makes me think . . . I got lucky last year. A couple inches to the left, and I'm just like that."

"Nah." Lucas shook his head.

"Sure I would've been."

"Nah. A couple inches to the left with that rifle, and you would've been deader'n a mackerel," he said.

She stopped. "I'm not riding back with you if you're gonna pout about this."

"Who's pouting?" He looked back at the hospital. "Miserable little shit."

AFTER Qatar left Barstad's apartment, he'd driven home and buried himself in his bed, sick with apprehension. But nothing had happened. Was it simply paranoia?

He relived every moment of the afternoon's sexual seizure with Barstad—it had been more like a seizure than play, he thought—and he worked through it, eyes closed, in the silence of his bedroom.

The false notes were there. Everything she'd done had

been dramatized. In their other meetings, she'd been the sexual technician: do this, do that, do the other. This time, she'd been a movie star: a bad actress.

He was worried about his rope. If she looked in the closet, she'd find it. She was sure to come across it sooner or later. He had to get it back, and hide it someplace where it would never be found. If the police were on him . . .

If the police were on him. That was the question.

He pushed himself up, steeled himself, got a drink of water, took a couple of aspirins, and went out to his car. He had an hour of light, he thought. If the police were there . . . He thought about it for a few minutes, then headed over to the Minneapolis Museum of Art. The museum was a reasonable destination for an art historian; even better, most people parked along the narrow streets, around the museum, and finding a space wasn't all that easy.

As he drove, he watched his rearview mirror. He assumed that any police car would not be right on his tail, so he tried to look three or four cars back. By the time he got to the museum, he was watching a gray American car. The car was a few years old and completely nondescript. He cruised up to the museum and slowed, looking for a space; stopped when he found one, a small one, tried to maneuver into it. Got it wrong, deliberately, and pulled back into the street.

The gray car, as far as he could tell, had disappeared from view. He tried again, messed it up, then gave up and drove past the museum, around the corner, around another corner, down the back of the museum, moving quickly now. As he reached the next corner, the gray car appeared in his rearview, and his heart jumped.

He was right: They were onto him.

He turned the corner, found another parking space halfway down the block, between the museum and a park.

He began maneuvering into it, and with his arm over the backseat of the car, saw the gray car stop at the corner before coming around it. He was sure the man inside was looking at him. He got the car into the space, locked it, and, never looking back, walked around the corner and down the block to the museum entrance.

He visited the Impressionists and post-Impressionists. Forced himself to take some time. Looked long and hard at a van Gogh, but saw nothing in it. Walked slowly around the gallery, and the paintings might as well have been Snoopy cartoons. A few people wandered past, but none of them met his eye or seemed interested in him. After a half hour, he could stand it no longer, and headed for the exit. He still had some light.

He maneuvered the car out of the parking space and headed home; never saw the gray car, could never find a car that seemed to be tracking him. Had he been wrong? He stopped at a grocery store, bought some sliced turkey and bread, more milk and cereal, finished the drive home. Nothing. Where were they?

By early evening, he was exhausted and bored at the same time. He had convinced himself again that he was being watched, and was afraid to leave the house in the night. He ate cereal again, munching through three bowls of the stuff, and lurched away from the table with a sugar high. He tried television, tried music, tried reading. Nothing worked, but the hours passed.

At midnight, he went to bed. Couldn't sleep, got up and took a pill. Still couldn't sleep, got up and took another one. And slept, but poorly.

But the next morning, on the way to work, he found them again.

"There you are, moron—there you are," he said, as the gray car nosed around a corner two blocks back. They weren't staying tight, but seemed content to follow at a distance. Was it possible that they had put a tracking device on the car? It was possible, he guessed. He went to work, taught a class, went to lunch; went to Marten's Funeral Home to talk about caskets for his mother. The funeral home would arrange to retrieve her body from the medical examiner.

He did it all on remote control. Most of his mind was busy worrying about the rope.

She'd find it; it was only a matter of time. And she'd know who put it there. And if she didn't do something silly, like play with it—if she just called the cops and told them about it—they'd find his prints all over the excellent rubber handle.

He had to get it back.

LUCAS and Weather went to a new French restaurant called Grasses. At the door, Lucas discovered that the owner was named Grass and that they served beer, and felt better about it. "I was afraid we were gonna have a choice between rye and Kentucky Blue," he said. "Fuckin' French."

"Behave yourself. I know you like new restaurants."

It was true, he decided, and he even liked French food, if it wasn't of the two-crossed-carrots-and-a-fried-snail variety. They got menus and looked them over, and Weather said, "Nothing sounds good."

He looked at her over the top of the menu. "You're pregnant."

"No . . . that's not it. I'm just not particularly hungry," she said.

"That's a first, in a French restaurant. And it looks pretty good to me."

"Maybe a salad," she said. "A glass of wine."

They talked about Randy over the meal. "We've got to

get him," Lucas said. "I'm going in tomorrow morning and give it another try."

"What about Miss Porno Queen? Are you going back?"

"Maybe—if Randy doesn't work out, we've got to find something to make him move. But this thing with Barstad . . . She was a hell of a lot freakier than he was. He was along for the ride."

"I *need* to see that tape," she said.

"Never happen," Lucas said. "If we ever go into court with that, I'm going to have a line of custody that nobody can shake. The word's gonna get out, and I told the guy at the evidence locker that if I ever see or hear of a piece of that tape getting out, or being played by anyone, he's going to jail. I made him believe me."

"Like that."

"Yeah. We could get murdered if that tape is ever shown to anybody. It'd be like the Los Angeles cops beating up those guys on tape. Can't you see some talking head during the sweeps, screaming about how we used this young woman to do *that* to get a confession out of the guy? We didn't know what she was going to do, but once she was into it, there was no way to back out. But nobody would believe us if we said so."

"You told Rose Marie."

"Of course."

"What did you say to the girl?" Weather asked.

"I yelled at her a little bit, but we've got to stay on her good side—we may need her again."

"To do the same thing?"

"No. No way. If she did it again, I'd kick the door and take Qatar right there. We won't be doing this again."

As they were talking, Qatar was leaving his house.

The decision hadn't come easily. As far as he could tell,

there'd been only one car with him during the day. He couldn't imagine that he had a large network around him—probably just somebody to keep track of him. If that was the case, and if he was very, very careful, he might be able to walk away from them. And he'd have to walk: There might be a locator device on the car, and he had no idea of what it might look like or where they'd put it.

He dressed carefully for the trip—in gray and black, with a watch cap. He left the television on, and changed his answering machine so that it would answer on the first ring. If someone were to call, that might leave the impression that he was at home, on the phone. He put a lamp in the study on his vacation timer. The light would go on at eight and go off at nine-thirty. He would have to be back before midnight.

He got his city map, slipped it into his pocket, checked his supply of small bills, said to himself, "This is crazy," and went out through the garage. He could have gone through the garage door into the backyard, but to do that, he would have to put himself in the open, against the white clapboard siding on the house. But a hedge ran down the side. . . .

The garage interior was pitch black. He pulled the door closed behind himself and groped toward the window. He found it, unlocked it, slid the window slowly up, and stepped over the sill into the side yard. If the police did have a network, or whatever they called it, watching from the upper floors of the back neighbor's house, then they might see him: But they would have to be watching closely, because the night felt as black and dense as velvet.

He pulled the window down and stood and listened; he heard nothing but cars. After two minutes of listening, he walked along the hedge all the way to the alley in back. Still heard nothing. He walked down the alley, the long way out, across the street at the end of the block, and into the next alley.

They might be following him, he thought, but he really didn't know how. He could hardly see *himself* in the night. He turned north, toward a shopping area. He needed a phone and a taxi.

The phone and taxi came easily enough, and Qatar marveled at his own courage as they went north through town to a strip mall above Cleveland Avenue. "There," he said, pointing. "The golf store."

"Want me to wait?"

"No. A friend will take me back," he said.

He made one fast run around the golf store to let the taxi get out of sight, then went back outside himself. He was a mile or two from Barstad's; he didn't know the exact distance, but it didn't matter. He started walking.

What would he do when he got there?

He didn't know, exactly. Love her up? Get the rope afterward? Tell her he lost his ring? He could feel the pinkie ring on his little finger. He could take it off, tell her he lost it, look around, then borrow the bathroom, retrieve the rope. Even get her to drive him back home . . .

He smiled at the idea: That would take some balls. Have her drop him off on his doorstep. The cop outside would have a heart attack.

He walked, thinking, What to do?

She'd betrayed him, that was for sure. He intertwined his fingers, flexed his hands. All right, he was a little angry. She'd betrayed him and she had that neck. . . . She had that neck and she'd taken him to the cops. . . . A little angry. She'd pretended to love him, had *used* him, and then had gone to the police. . . .

What to do?

26

MARCY AND MARSHALL were waiting when Lucas got in the next morning. "You better get over to Regions," Marcy said. "The public defender called and he said Randy's calmed down—but he wants to see you, not me."

"Did he say why?"

"Randy said he wanted to deal with the boss," she said.

Lucas shrugged. "So let's get together a spread and take it over."

"It's ready," Marcy said, holding up an envelope. "There're pictures of the jewelry you got out of the place, and of the dead girl, Suzanne. I've arranged for a court reporter—we're gonna share one with the PD's office. A guy from St. Paul Homicide will be there."

"And I'm coming," Marshall said.

On the way to Regions, Lucas called Marc White, the intelligence cop baby-sitting Qatar. "Where is he?"

"In his office. Craig Bowden watched him into the

building, and I picked it up from there. I haven't actually seen him yet, but he's due for a class in a half hour."

"Stay close. We might be about to get an ID, and if we do, we take him."

When he got off the phone, Marshall asked, "Are we gonna get an ID? Or is this Randy guy too crazy?"

"Randy's crazy, but he's not stupid. If his head is working, he'll do it if the deal's good enough. That's what he's all about: deals."

"I always hoped I'd see the day, but I didn't think I would," Marshall said. His voice grated like a rusty gate.

Rob Lansing was waiting in the hall with his briefcase, a stocky black woman who carried a court reporting machine, and a St. Paul Homicide cop named Barnes. Lansing said nothing at all, but pointed at Randy's room and pushed through the door, followed by the court reporter. Lucas trailed behind, with Marshall and Barnes a step back.

Randy's head was up, and he had some color, but every minute of a hard twenty-plus years was etched into his forehead and cheeks. "You guys really fucked me this time." None of the hysteria of the day before.

"I feel pretty bad about it," Lucas said. "You know I don't like you—and I know you don't like me—but I wouldn't have wished this on you."

"Yeah, yeah," Randy said. He looked at the court reporter and said, "Who's this?"

"This is Lucille. She's going to take down what we say, so there's no question about what the deal is," Lansing said. The reporter had unfolded her machine and was waiting.

Randy looked at Lucas and Marshall. "Is this deal straight? You guys take care of the medical and cut all the rest of the charges?"

"That's the deal," Lucas said, nodding.

"Let me see the picture."

"I've got six pictures. We want to see if you can pick one of them out as the guy who sold you the jewelry." Lucas took the manila envelope out of his pocket and shook two groups of photos into his hand and pulled the paper clip off one group.

"You have a name on the guy?" Marshall asked.

"I mostly called him 'dude,' but I think his straight name is James."

"James," Lucas said. He looked at the court reporter, who was taking it all down.

"One more brick," Marshall said.

Randy took the first group of photos from Lucas, shuffled through them quickly, cocked his head at one, and said, "This is the dude. James."

Lucas took it, showed it to Marshall, and then passed it to Lansing. To the court reporter he said, "Make a note that Mr. Whitcomb indicated the photograph of James Qatar and that officers Davenport, Marshall, and Barnes, and attorney Lansing are witnesses." She nodded, and typed.

"Now I'm going to give Mr. Whitcomb another group of photos, and all of these are of James Qatar. This is to confirm his initial impression."

Randy took the photos, again shuffled through them, and said, "Yeah, that's the dude."

"Did he kill Suzanne Brister?"

"Who?"

"Suzanne Brister was killed in your apartment. We have all the evidence, Randy—her blood was all over the place."

"Dude . . ." Randy scrubbed his face with both hands. "I can't remember. I was partying that night, and I come home and she was dead. I freaked out."

"Did you do it?"

"No, man, that's what freaked me out. I *didn't* do it; I'd

remember *that*. I walked up the stairs in the dark and I stepped on her and I felt down and here was this cold titty, and I almost jumped out the window. Then I turned on the light and there was this blood . . ." He shuddered. "Felt her up in the dark. I didn't know she was *dead."*

"So when was James last over?"

He scrubbed his face again. "I can't *remember."*

Lucas went back to the envelope of photographs, shook out the shots of the two rings found at Randy's, and handed them to him. "We found these at your place—in your hideout. They came off a woman professor at St. Patrick's University. You remember where you got them?"

Randy looked at them and scratched his head. "You got them at my place? My stash?"

"Yeah."

"Must've been when I was wrecked, because I don't remember."

"What do you remember?"

"Well, that night, I was partying. I partied all night. I ran out of money and I went home and I got some more money, and then I partied some more and then I ran out of money again. . . . I kept running out of money and I kept going home and getting some more. . . . That's what I remember, going back and forth, and then feeling this cold titty."

"Who were you partying with?"

Randy rolled his eyes at Lansing, who nodded. "Dude named Lo Andrews."

"I know him," said the St. Paul Homicide cop. "Got a place off Como. There's usually smoke coming out of the windows."

"That's the dude," Randy said.

"You don't know when Suzanne was killed or when you last saw James."

"If James gave me those rings, he must have come over when I was wrecked," Randy said.

They talked a while longer but got nothing significant. Out in the hallway, Lucas asked the St. Paul cop for Lo Andrews's address, and the cop made a call to St. Paul Narcotics and get the number on Como.

Back in the car, Lucas called Marcy and said, "We've got a positive ID on Qatar. We're gonna pick him up. Get started on a warrant for his house."

"That's great—I'll get the warrant started right now. Del wants to talk to you."

She handed the phone off to Del, who said, "Can I come with you?"

"Sure. He's down at St. Patrick's. Meet you there. Is Lane around?"

Lane came on the line, and Lucas gave him Lo Andrews's address. "Find the guy—St. Paul Narcotics will give you a guy to walk around with—and ask him about that night. If anybody went home with Randy, if anybody saw anything . . ."

"Talk to you this afternoon," Lane said.

"NEVER thought I'd see it," Marshall said. "Goddamnit."

Lucas looked at him, and Marshall seemed to be sweating. He'd gotten a Coke from the hospital waiting room, and when he lifted it to take a drink, his hand was shaking. "You feel all right?"

"Well, uh, I'm not having a heart attack or anything, but my blood pressure's probably nine hundred over nine hundred. I want to drag that sonofabitch out of that schoolroom. . . . He's a goddamn teacher, Lucas. A *teacher*."

"Teachers . . . They're about as messed up as anybody. We've had a few of them over here."

Marshall sat staring out the window, his lips moving, as though he were saying a silent prayer, but he'd heard Lucas, and suddenly smiled and seemed to unwind a notch.

"Yeah, you're right. Did I ever tell you about this weird old white-haired teacher from River Falls? I got a friend who's a deputy in the county next door, and he swears it's a true story. . . . Did I tell you this, the story about the guy and the llama and the golf club? No? Anyway . . ."

He had Lucas laughing in two minutes. But Lucas, glancing sideways, could see what seemed like despair hanging in his eyes over the storytelling smile.

THE arrest happened almost exactly as Qatar had seen it in his nightmares, give or take a snap-brimmed fedora. He was in his office, and heard the voice and footsteps in the hall—the bustle of people moving, a voice that was hushed. He turned his head, sat up straight, listening. A second later, the door opened and a dark-haired, dark-complected man in a gorgeous charcoal suit opened the door and asked, "James Qatar?"

Behind the man in the suit were two other men, and Burns Goodwin, the college president.

Qatar stood up and tried to look puzzled. "Yes?"

"HE sorta freaked," Lucas told Marcy. "He denied it all and then he started crying—I mean, really weeping. Sobbing. I think it bummed Marshall out. He wanted resistance, and all he got was this mud puddle."

"Where is he? Marshall?"

"Still over at the jail talking with the county attorneys about Wisconsin stuff. If we find anything in the house, there may be a Wisconsin claim."

"What difference does it make? He's gonna get thirty years."

"If we get him. If we don't, but if we have something from Wisconsin, that could be another trial."

After talking to Marcy, Lucas walked down to tell Rose Marie about the arrest.

"Another notch," she said.

"If we get him. Towson is worried that Randy's identification might be a little shaky."

"Ah, we got him," she said. "With Randy and the jewelry, with Qatar's access to all the victims, with the Wisconsin school record . . . we've got him."

He went back to Marcy. "I'm gonna go over to Qatar's house, see what's going on there," he told her. "Then I'm gonna go home and take a nap. Fuck around the with car. Let me know."

The phone rang, and she held up a finger, picked it up, listened, and said, "Just a moment. I'll see if he's in." She pushed the hold button and asked, "It's that Culver guy. He says he really needs to talk to you."

"Let me have that." He took the phone and said, "Lucas Davenport."

"Chief Davenport, listen, did you take Ellen somewhere? I mean, do you know where she is?"

"No—she was at her place the last time I saw her. What's going on?"

"I haven't seen her. Usually she comes over for a cup of coffee or I go over to her place, but it's all locked up. Now a bunch of women are milling around outside. They were supposed to have a quilting class, and they say whenever she's had to cancel a class she's called them. She doesn't answer her phone. I can't see inside very well because of the one-way stuff, but I can see a little, and it looks like some stuff has been tipped over or thrown around."

"Stay right there," Lucas said. "I'm on my way." He dropped the phone, looked around for Del, a little wild-eyed, said "Fuck," and headed for the door.

"What? What?" Marcy yelled after him. "Where're you going?"

"Call the dispatcher and tell them I want a squad, right now, out front. . . . Right now," he shouted back. He was running down the hallway when he saw Marshall carrying a carton of yogurt and a cup of coffee.

"Terry, c'mon, Terry . . ." He kept running, and Marshall ran carefully after him, calling, "What happened, what happened?"

A squad was cutting across the street toward the front entrance, the driver waving at Lucas. Lucas caught the front door and Marshall piled in the back. Lucas said, "Go that way, across the Hennepin Bridge, lights and siren." The driver nodded, and they took off, slicing through the traffic like a shark. When they were moving, he turned to look at Marshall in the backseat and said, "Nobody can find Ellen Barstad. The Culver guy from next door says it looks like the place is a little torn up inside."

"No, no." Marshall was shocked. "Not that girl—we've been following him, he couldn't have."

"Maybe it's nothing."

Lucas began giving directions to the driver as they made the turn onto Hennepin, and then Marshall said, "But this feels really bad. This feels bad."

"She's from outstate somewhere. Maybe she got freaked and went home."

"No, I don't think so. This has got that bad feeling about it."

Lucas nodded. "Yeah, it does."

THEY were halfway there when Del called: "What the hell's going on?"

Lucas told him in three sentences, and Del said, "I'll see you there."

*   *   *

THEY pulled into the parking lot in front of Culver's shop ten minutes after Lucas and Culver spoke on the phone. Lucas hopped out, spotted Culver talking to two elderly women, and walked over, Marshall a step behind. "Is there a landlord? Who has the keys?"

"There's a manager, but he goes around between buildings. I've got a cell phone."

"Call him and see where he's at," Lucas said.

Culver hurried into his shop. Marshall was already pressing his face to the silvered glass on the door. "He's right, it looks like some stuff is turned over," he said.

Lucas pressed his face to the door and cupped his hands around his eyes. One of the quilt frames had been knocked onto the floor. "Goddamnit." He stepped back, and over to the door of Culver's place. Culver was walking toward him with a cell phone to his ear. He was saying, "Where're you at? We need to get in."

Lucas asked, "Where?"

Culver said, "He's in Hopkins. He can be here in twenty minutes."

"Fuck that," Lucas said. "Have you got something we can break the glass with?"

"Here," Marshall said. He reached under his jacket and produced a large-frame .357 Magnum. He pointed the weapon to one side, as though he'd done this before, stood close to the glass, and punched it with the butt of the gun. The punch knocked a dollar-size hole in the glass. He gave it another light whack and a piece of glass broke out. Marshall carefully reached through the hole and flipped the inside lock.

Lucas led the way in. The frame was on the floor and . . .

"Step easy," he said sharply. He pointed at the track of blood.

"Ah, no, ah, man . . ." Marshall turned to the door, where

Culver was standing, and said, "Stay out of here. Keep everybody out."

They walked carefully through the blood spots— "Looks like an impact spray," Lucas muttered—to the door of the living quarters. Lucas put one finger high on the door, muttered "Don't touch" to Marshall, and pushed it open.

ELLEN Barstad was lying by the sink. She was fully clothed and she was dead. No strangulation, this: Her head lay in a puddle of congealed blood, with patches of dried blood around it. The back of her head appeared to be torn off. Lucas said, "All right, let's get some people on the way." He glanced at Marshall. Marshall's eyes were closed and he had one hand pressed against the middle of his face, the heel of his hand under his chin, the fingers pressed against his forehead. "Terry?"

"Yeah, yeah . . . Goddamnit, Lucas, I think we did this to her."

Lucas swallowed once, trying to get rid of the sour taste in his throat, shook his head. Looked down the length of the kitchen and saw a hammer. "Weapon," he said.

Marshall took his hands away from his face. "Had to be something like that to do the damage." He was closer, and stepped over next to it. "It looks like it's been wiped. I can see streaks, like . . . paper towel."

"Let's get out of here before we fuck something up," Lucas said. "Get the lab guys going."

Del arrived five minutes later and saw them outside, duct-taping a piece of cardboard over the hole in the glass door. They were just finishing as he came up, and he looked from Marshall to Lucas and said, "Don't tell me."

"She's gone," Lucas said. Del stepped toward the door

and Lucas said, "Watch the blood in the work area. Don't touch the door going into the back."

Del disappeared inside, came back a minute later. His face carried the same expression as Marshall's.

"When did he do it?"

"Looks like last night," Lucas said. "The blood puddles had started to dry out. Maybe we can get a temperature and tell that way. We taped over the door to try to keep the ambient the same inside."

"Christ, he looks like he freaked out," Del said. "Looks like he chased her from the front door, maybe picked up that hammer off the frame—"

Lucas interrupted. "Sure it was hers?"

"Yeah, I'm pretty sure—I saw it sitting there the other day, and the one I saw isn't there anymore. Picked it up, took a swing, cut her, but she made it into the back."

"Hope the motherfucker pushed that door open with his hand," Lucas said. "That's the way you'd do it—run right in there and push it back with your hand."

"Problem is, he's been here," Marshall said. "We got movies of it. If he hit the door with his hand, he could say he did it some other time."

"Yeah, but if there one's big brand-new print on the door, it'll be a brick. Goddamnit to hell, why didn't we get her out of the way? Why didn't we get her out?"

"Why'd he do it? This isn't anything like he did the others."

"It's like he did Neumann," Lucas said.

"If he did Neumann. That could be hard to prove by itself," Del said.

"Hey, who the fuck's side are you on?" Lucas asked, the anger surging up.

"I'm on your fuckin' side, but I'm thinking about the trial," Del snapped. "That's what I'm worried about. We've got Randy the coke freak, and we've got these unconnected killings at St. Pat's that are all close to him, but none of them are in the style of the gravedigger's, and what's worse . . ."

"What's worse?" Lucas snapped back.

"What's worse is, we had a guy watching him when he had to be over here killing her," Del said, jabbing a finger at Lucas. "How'd he do that, smart guy? What's gonna happen when they get *that* into court, with a second-man theory? If you take Randy out of the equation, we ain't got squat, and Randy has a good reason to tell us anything we want him to. You think Qatar's lawyer won't make a big deal out of that?"

"Ah, Jesus," Lucas said.

"That *is* what the lawyers will say," Marshall said. "We can't lose this guy. There's no way."

"We won't. Gonna hang the motherfucker," Lucas said.

THEY all stayed, all the way through the crime-scene work, through the removal of the body, snarling at each other from time to time, all of them in dark moods. Lucas talked to Rose Marie twice, by phone, keeping her up to date, and to Marcy. When it seemed as if nothing new would be found at Barstad's, Lucas asked Del, "You got a car, right? Didn't you?"

"Yeah."

"Let's go on over to Qatar's house. They oughta still be working on it. Let's see what they got."

"I'll tell you one thing—he maybe cleaned up after himself pretty good over here, but he had blood on him when he left," Marshall said. "Bloody coat, bloody pants, bloody shoes—there's gotta be something."

ON the way to Qatar's, Marshall seemed to shrink in the back. "You all right?" Lucas asked.

Marshall started talking, rambling. "My old lady died the second year we were married. She was pregnant at the time. Hit a bridge one day, there was some snow on the road, just a little bit. She was racing my sister to see which one was gonna have a kid first; they both got pregnant at the same time, and it was neck and neck . . . 'cept my old lady never got to the finish line."

"Never remarried?" Del asked.

"Never had the heart for it," he said. "I still talk to June every night before I go to bed. When Laura was growing up, she was just like a daughter to me; I was over there just about every day. When she got taken off, there wasn't a goddamn thing I could do about it. Big cop in town, knew everything about everything, couldn't find my own goddamn daughter. . . ."

He went on for a while, and Lucas felt Del glance at him just as he looked at Del. Unspoken thought here, as they listened to Marshall ramble: Whoa.

QATAR'S house was neat and beautifully decorated. A crime-scene specialist named Greg Webster was running the crew who were looking at the house, and when he saw Lucas, Marshall, and Del on the walk leading to the porch, he stopped outside and said, "I heard."

"You got anything useful?"

"Not much. We did find a set of women's earrings in his chest of drawers. They look pretty good, so they might be a possibility. We have to check with all the victims we've identified so far. . . . Have you talked to Sandy MacMillan? I heard she got something up at his office."

"What?"

"I don't know. One of the guys just said she was pretty excited—some computer shit."

"We need to get his phone records as far back as they go," Lucas said. "Check him for cell phones. . . . We need to look at picture albums, any loose photographs lying around, any negatives, anything that could be a souvenir."

"We know," Webster said patiently. "We're looking for it all."

"Did you look in the washing machine?"

"Yeah. It's empty. Nothing in the dryer."

"Is Sandy still up at his office?"

"I don't know—she was an hour ago."

MACMILLAN had moved downtown. When Lucas finally found her, she was in Lucas's office, talking with Marcy.

"Greg Webster said you found something in his office computer," Lucas said.

"No. We didn't find anything—that's what was so interesting. He put a new hard drive in his machine the day that the story broke on finding Aronson. He pulled some files off an old hard drive and reinstalled them on the new one—the dates are right in the machine. The thing is, why would you do that? If you could pull the files off, the old drive was still working. It could have been full, I suppose."

"Bullshit. He was getting rid of evidence. Bet he had Photoshop or one of the other photo programs on it, and some of those drawings."

"Not on the new one."

"Check and see if you can find any software," Lucas said.

"No software except Word and some other minor bullshit. He *is* hooked into the 'Net, so we're gonna try to track that. Gonna go out to his ISP and see what they have in the way of records."

"Sounds like he's a half-step ahead of us," Lucas said. "Keep digging around. That date will be useful, though."

He told Del and Marshall about it, and Marshall said, "Another brick in the wall."

"No wall so far," Lucas said. "Just a lot of bricks."

THEY were standing on Qatar's front sidewalk, ready to leave, when Craig Bowden showed up. He parked down the street and jogged back to them, a small man in a yellow windbreaker. Lucas noticed that down the street, two women were sitting on their front porch, watching. Everybody knew. . . .

Bowden looked scared; he was the intelligence cop assigned to watch Qatar overnight.

"I even took notes," he said. "Lights on and off, all that. Television on and off."

"Could he have gotten out the back?"

"Yeah, sure—not with his car, of course, but if he'd wanted to sneak, he could have. There was just one of me, and he wasn't supposed to know we were interested in him."

"What about this morning? Was he carrying anything when he left?"

"I couldn't see when he loaded the car, because it was in the garage. When he got out at St. Pat's, he had a briefcase and a sack."

"A sack?"

"Like a grocery bag."

"Clothes," Marshall said.

"You didn't see him do anything with the sack?"

"No . . . he went inside and that's the last I saw him. Marc White took over from me."

THEY called White. He had never seen Qatar with a sack. "I never really saw him at all—I just sat and waited and then you guys showed up and busted his ass."

They called Sandy MacMillan again, the crime-scene cop who'd been working Qatar's office. "There were a couple guys there with me—they might have found something and didn't tell me, but I didn't see any sack. I'm sure I didn't see any clothes. I would have heard about it."

"Sack's still gotta be in the building," Lucas said. "Who wants to look for a sack?"

They all rode to St. Pat's together, but hope was dwindling. They'd been run around too much, with too little to show for it: one of those days when nothing was going to work right.

They found a janitor, an elderly man with a drinker's nose, who told them that all the trash cans in the building had been emptied. He didn't remember any brown sacks, and certainly no sacks full of clothes. "I could have missed it, though. I put them all out in the Dumpster, and I'd be happy to go out and rip them apart, if you want. Aren't that many, really."

They all followed him out to the Dumpster. He got a stepladder, climbed the side, jumped in, and began throwing sacks out. There were fifteen of them, one from each of the built-in trash receptacles in the building. The janitor got a new box of bags, and as they broke open each bag, they shifted the contents to a new one and tossed it back into the Dumpster.

"Shit," Del said when they finished. "All we got was a bad smell."

"What the hell would he do with them?" Lucas asked.

"Tell you what I would have done," the janitor said. "I would have taken them down to the furnace room. It's a gas furnace, but it's got big gas bars and you could cremate a hog in there. A pair of pants would go up like a moth in a candle."

"Show us," Lucas said.

He did, and as they looked at the flames roaring away, Marshall said, "God almighty."

"Would James Qatar know about this place?" Lucas asked the janitor.

"The little fart grew up here. He was in and out of every corner of this college since he was a baby. Nothing here that he doesn't know. Got all these little hidey-holes— probably knows the place better'n me."

"Okay. Let's get this fire turned off. We'll send somebody around to look underneath it, see if there're any remains of zippers or buttons or whatever."

"What an asshole," the janitor said.

"You didn't like him?"

"I didn't like him from way back. Sneaky little fart. Always sneaking around. Scared the piss out of me more than once—I'd be doing something, and all of a sudden, there'd be Jim, two inches away. You'd never see him coming."

"You know he's been arrested?"

"Yeah. I think he probably did it."

O N the way out of the building, Lucas said, "We ought to check trash cans all around Barstad's place, see if we find any blood. And the cab companies—if he figured out we were watching him, and snuck off, he had to get there somehow. Let's see if we can figure out taxi dispatches from around his place to around Barstad's. What else?"

"I'd get with the FBI again and really push the Internet thing," Del said. "If we can show he was on those porno websites, and cleaned out his computer the day Aronson made the papers, that'd be strong."

"Another brick," Marshall said. Then: "What if he didn't do it?"

Lucas thought about that for a minute, then asked, "What do you think the chances are?"

Del said, "Two percent and falling."

Marshall: "One percent and falling."

"One fucking bloody fingerprint or piece of clothing with her blood on it—that's all we need."

Marshall said, "We can't lose him now. We just can't."

Lucas said, "Hey . . ."

Marshall looked at him for a couple of seconds, then wearily pushed himself up. "I think I'll go home. Say hello to my sister, check in with the office, fix the garage-door opener."

"We'll get him," Del said.

"Sure," Marshall said. He glanced at Lucas, then quickly away. "See you tomorrow, maybe."

"Let it go," Lucas said. "We're doing what we can."

27

WEATHER FOUND HIM sitting in front of the television, watching the PBS national news, a beer in his hand. "That kind of a day?" she asked.

"Much worse," he told her.

She took off her coat and said, "Start from the beginning."

He started from the beginning, and he finished by saying, "So we might have gotten Ellen Barstad killed and it's possible that the guy is gonna walk. I think we got enough—and we didn't feel like we could leave him out there any longer, not after Neumann and his mother were killed. He's freaking out. He's killing everybody. He's on some kind of psychotic run."

Weather was shocked about Barstad. She had nothing to say except, "You'll get him."

"Yeah. . . . But you know what the county attorney's gonna wind up doing. If they can't cut some kind of deal with him, they'll go for a something-else conviction, and that's always risky."

A something-else prosecution rolled out every scrap of evidence, no matter how shaky or distantly circumstantial, teased out every possible murder scenario, threw in a variety of psychiatric testimony, and used the whole show to make an unstated argument that even if the particular murder couldn't be proven, the defendant had surely done something else he should be in prison for, and should be convicted simply as a matter of public safety. The perfect juror was both frightened and timid; one skeptic on the jury could screw the whole thing. And something-else convictions always left a bad taste with everybody. Not a clean kill.

"You need a smoking gun."

"We've been so close in so many ways," Lucas said. "If we could find just one picture. One piece of clothing with blood on it. Anything . . ."

LUCAS got in late the next morning, found Marshall already at the office. "I thought you might take a day or two off."

"Can't stay away," Marshall said. "But my ass is kicked."

"Lane wants you to call him at home," Marcy said to Lucas. "He left a voice mail, said call anytime."

Lucas called and Lane answered, his voice thick with sleep. "I just got to bed. I wound up chasing that Lo Andrews guy all over the metro," he said. "I finally caught up with him about the time the sun was coming up."

"He have anything?"

"Yeah. He was carrying a little coke and we took him down to Ramsey county jail. He's on hold until we get a statement. The bust is probably bad, though."

"Yeah, yeah. What happened?"

"He says he was with Randy the night Suzanne Brister was killed and that Randy ran out of money and so they took him to an ATM and he maxed out his card. Then he ran out of that, so they went back to Randy's place and they got a compact sound system and sold that on the street, and they ran out of that, so they dropped him at his place—but an hour later he was back with four hundred dollars that he said he took off some white dude."

"Yeah? You think it was Qatar?"

"I used our warrant and went over to the bank and we looked at Qatar's ATM use. He took four hundred dollars out of an ATM on Grand Avenue, about eight blocks from Randy's, at 12:38 P.M. same night."

"Goddamnit, Lane."

"What can I tell you? I'm good," Lane said.

"You *are* good. You gonna nail this down?"

"I'd like to get a little sleep first, but we're gonna get with Lo Andrews's attorney at three o'clock this afternoon. Probably drop the charges on the drug bust, and get the statement."

When Lucas got off the line, Marshall, who'd taken up residence at Lane's desk, said, "Another brick?"

"A decent one. We can put Qatar eight blocks from Randy's house the night Suzanne Brister was killed. That's not all. . . ."

He explained the rest of it, and Marshall said, "That's good, but you know what I'd do if I were Qatar's attorneys? I'd make the case that Qatar smoked pot, maybe even a lot of pot, and maybe used a little cocaine. He's an artist, right? So they say that's how he knew Randy. And that Randy was attracted to Qatar by the people Qatar knew—and that's how Randy met Neumann and Qatar's mother and all those other people. That Randy was the killer. We've got a dead woman, strangled in the style of all the others, in Randy's apartment, with his fingerprints all over the place, in blood, and he tried to shoot a cop when he busted out—"

"He was too young for the first ones."

"Well, who knows?" Marshall said. "To get like he is now, he must have been a monster when he was young. He would have been, what, twelve or thirteen when Laura disappeared? How many twelve-year-old killers do you think are running around the Cities?"

Lucas shrugged. "So you make a case. Do you believe it?"

"Of course not. For one thing, the guy was supposed to be dating Laura."

"If that's the guy who killed her," Lucas said.

"C'mon. We know who killed the girls. But I'm worried about a trial."

"Always worry about a trial," Lucas said. "But we're piling stuff up."

"Need a smoking gun, like your girlfriend says," Marshall said. "With everything else, if we had the gun, I'd be satisfied."

QATAR'S preliminary hearing had been set for the following Monday. Nothing more turned up. Lab techs searched the debris tray on the furnace at the St. Pat's museum, found various bits and pieces of metal, but nothing that could be specifically identified as coming from clothing. Lane identified three cab trips from the general area of Qatar's house to the general area of Barstad's, but none of the drivers could identify Qatar as a passenger.

Lo Andrews made his statement, but, as an assistant county attorney pointed out, it was a statement by another heavy doper. Thirty cops were recruited to look inside every trash can and behind every fence within a half-mile of Barstad's. They found all kind of clothing and shoes, but none of it the kind that Qatar might have worn. It was all old and obviously abandoned, or was identified by the people who owned the trash cans.

"What if Qatar didn't do it?" Swanson asked.

"He did," Lucas said.

"I think we're in trouble," Marshall said. Marshall had begun to brood. "I'm not sure we should have taken him when we did," he said. "We could have thrown a net over him, done a full-court press. Sooner or later, he would have fucked up."

"By the time we might've done that, he'd already have spotted us," Lucas said. "And the longer we went with a full team on him, the more innocent he'd look."

MARSHALL stayed in town over the weekend. He got permission to enter Qatar's house under the warrant, and spent most of the time taking the house apart. He unscrewed every power outlet, dug through all the loose fiberglass insulation between the ceiling joists, looked up and down the chimney, and took the flue mechanism apart.

He called Lucas late Sunday afternoon. "You know what I got?"

"Something good?"

"I got a face full of glass splinters from the insulation, and I'm covered with soot. I look like I just crawled out of a Three Stooges movie, if somebody'd only hit me with a cream pie. There ain't nothing in the house."

"My fiancé is about to make some meat loaf with gravy and Bisquick biscuits," Lucas said. "Why don't you drag your sorry ass over here—we'll throw your clothes in the washer and give you something to eat."

"I'll do that," Marshall said.

* * *

MARSHALL liked the food, and Weather liked Marshall.

"You know what we really wanted for Laura was not re-venge," he told her. "All we wanted was justice. I don't think we're gonna get it. I think we're gonna get a lot of bureaucracy and treatment programs, and Qatar's probably gonna sue everybody in sight and get them all running around like chickens, and nobody's gonna want to hear about Laura. Nobody misses her but me and her folks and her family. She hadn't done anything; hell, she might've turned out to be a cook or something, though I think she woulda been better than that. But nobody misses her. If we could just get a little justice for her . . ."

"HE was just like all the good old guys back home," Weather told Lucas after Marshall left. Weather had grown up in a small town in northern Wisconsin. "They want to keep everything simple and right. I really like that, even if it's a fairy tale."

"Problem is, it *is* a fairy tale . . . at least mostly," Lucas said.

EARLY Monday morning, Lucas took a phone call at home from the county attorney's secretary: "Mr. Towson would like to talk to you as soon as possible, along with Marcy Sherrill. What would be a good time?"

"I'll come down right away—is he in now?"

"He's on his way. Would nine o'clock be okay?"

"That's fine. You'll call Marcy?"

Randall Towson, his chief deputy, Donald Dunn, and Richard Kirk, head of the criminal division, were waiting in Towson's office when Lucas and Marcy arrived. Towson pointed them at chairs and said, "The Qatar case. You know J. B. Glass is handling it?"

"I heard," Lucas said, and Marcy nodded.

"He's pretty good. We're wondering what the reaction would be if we talked to them about a plea—guilty to one count of second-degree with confinement at the mental hospital instead of Stillwater. He'd have to do his time if he were ever found competent."

"Uh, I think people would be pretty unhappy."

Kirk said, "But the guy's gotta be crazy, and our priority has to be to get him off the street. If we get the judge to do an upward departure, and he gets twenty, by the time he got out he'd probably be past it as a killer."

"Oh, bullshit," Lucas said irritably. "Most of them might stop killing when they get older, but not all of them do. He could come back out and start killing again in a month. If you get him twenty, and if he only had to do two-thirds of it, he'd be out when he's about fifty-one, fifty-two. If we take him on a first-degree, he has to do a minimum of thirty. Then I'd feel pretty safe. He wouldn't get out until he was in his late sixties."

"We'd do that, if we didn't feel a little shaky on the case," Dunn said.

"You gotta take some risks sometimes," Lucas said. Cops hated the conservative prosecution policies: The county attorney's office had a near one-hundred-percent conviction rate—which looked terrific on campaign literature—mostly because they prosecuted only the sure things. Everything else was dealt down or dismissed.

"We're not just risking a loss," Kirk pointed out. "If we lose him, he kills somebody else."

"But I'll tell you what," Marcy said. "If you go to J. B. with that kind of an offer, he's gonna smell blood. He'll turn you down. If you make an offer, it's gotta be tougher than that."

Towson shook his head. "How can we make it tougher? If we go up one notch to first degree, the way the mandatory sentencing works now, he'd go down for the max—same thing he'd get if he fought it. Without a death penalty, we've got nothing to deal with except dropping the degree of guilt."

"Why don't you talk to Wisconsin?" Lucas asked. "They have a couple of counts on the guy, they think. Work out a deal where if he takes one count of first degree over here, he serves his time, and Wisconsin drops out. If he doesn't agree, he goes to trial in both states. One of us'll get him."

Towson was drumming on his calendar pad with a yellow pencil. "That's an option," he said to Dunn. "Weak, though."

"The problem is, I've looked at the Wisconsin cases, and they've got less than we do. About the only thing that connects him to Wisconsin is that he was at Stout."

"And Aronson's pearls and the method of the murders and the fact that they were buried together. There's really a lot there," Lucas said.

"Tell you what," Towson said. "We won't make any move on a deal until we're through looking at everything. If you've got anything else, roll it out. And maybe J. B. will make the first offer."

"Who's handling the preliminary?" Lucas asked.

"I am," Kirk said. "We're just gonna sketch the case, put Whitcomb up and get a statement about the jewelry, and that pretty much ought to do it. You coming?"

"Yeah, I want to look at him again," Lucas said. "He's a strange duck."

MARSHALL was back for the preliminary hearing, dressed in a brown corduroy suit and fancy brown cowboy boots, his hair slicked down.

"You look like Madonna's boyfriend," Marcy told him.

"Aw, shoot, you get off my case," he said. He didn't quite dig his toe into the tile.

The hearing was routine—Qatar in a dark suit and tie, but his face drawn and white, his eyes ringed as though he'd been weeping—until Randy Whitcomb was rolled in.

Randy, strapped into a wheelchair, looking out at the chamber under a lowered brow, scanning the rows of press people and gawkers, finally found Lucas and fixed his gaze. Marcy, sitting next to Lucas, whispered, "Is he looking at you?"

"Yeah. And he looks pissed," Lucas whispered back.

Kirk took Whitcomb through the preliminaries.

Yes, Randy said, he'd bought the pearls from a man who said he was from St. Pat's. Yes, he'd bought the diamond rings from the same man. He'd sold the pearls on the street, he said. He didn't know who had them now.

"Do you see the man who sold you the jewelry here in the courtroom?" Kirk asked.

Randy looked around for a full minute, scanning up and down each row, then said, "No. I don't see him."

Kirk took a step back. "Look at this man here at the defense table."

Glass, Qatar's defense attorney, surprised as anyone, struggled to his feet, but before he could object to Kirk's direction, Randy leaned toward the microphone and said, "I never seen him before in my life."

A moan swept the courtroom. Marshall said, "What happened?" and Marcy said, "The little jerk."

Lucas didn't say anything, because he could feel Randy staring at him and knew he wasn't finished. "How do you like that, asshole?" Randy bellowed into the microphone. He pointed at Lucas and yelled, "You cocksucker, how you like them apples?"

The judge was beating on his desk, but Randy kept shouting, and finally the judge told the bailiff to wheel him out. Randy went, screaming all the way, and Lucas stood up and said, "We gotta find out what happened. We gotta get the little sonofabitch. Where's Lansing? Did anybody see Lansing?"

Lansing was in the hallway. As soon as Lucas and Marcy stepped outside, Randy, whose outburst had subsided, began screaming again: "You keep that motherfucker away from me; you keep that motherfucker away."

Lansing came over and said, "You heard him."

Lucas reached forward and pinched a piece of Lansing's coat lapel between his thumb and forefinger. "It's not up to me to give you advice, but I will, because you're so young and dumb. You better find out what happened, or you could be looking at the end of your legal career. You cut this deal, and we've got the case hanging on it. We're all in shit city now—you not the least of us."

Lansing swallowed and stepped back. "I know. I'll find out what happened."

"Get back," Lucas said.

MARSHALL came out and said, "Well, shit. That really put the dog amongst the cheeseburgers."

"What's happening in there?" Lucas asked. He took a step back toward the door.

"They're talking about bail," Marshall said. "They're gonna give it to him."

28

"Somebody called Randy last night and talked to him," Lansing said. He was on the phone from his office in St. Paul. Lucas and Marcy had just gotten back from a meeting with the county attorney, where Kirk and Towson began laying the lines of a deal offer for Qatar. "Randy's not the most coherent guy, but the basic story is, whoever talked to him told him that the word on the street is that you turned him. That you own him, that you're running him, and that you're going around town bragging about it. It's supposed to be all over town."

"That's bullshit," Lucas said.

"Who've you talked to?"

"Outside of this office, nobody. My social life is my fiancé, and we haven't been going out that much. I have been nowhere, I've talked to no one."

"How about other people?" Lansing said.

"I'll ask around, but it smells like bullshit."

"Randy doesn't think so."

"Get Randy on the line with some of his pals—or if he doesn't have any, some of his acquaintances. Have him ask," Lucas said.

"Well . . . let's see what happens."

"I'll tell you one thing that happens. The deal he made was predicated on honest testimony. He either lied to us in his statement—and I know he didn't do that, because he picked the pictures out without having seen them before— or he perjured himself this morning. You can tell the little cocksucker two things for me: First, I never talked to anybody; and second, he can kiss his ass goodbye. He's on the train to Stillwater, and when he gets out, he'll be ten years older than I am now."

"Wait a minute, wait a minute. . . ."

"I'm not gonna wait a minute. I'm gonna take a couple of days off, and if Randy decides he wants to change his mind, he'll have to change it with somebody else. I'm finished with him. He can rot in fuckin' Stillwater."

Marcy, who'd been listening, said, "Wow. Really?"

"Really. If anything urgent happens, call me on my cell phone. I'll keep it on, but don't call unless you've got no choice."

"Marshall took off?" she asked.

"Yeah. His head must have been about to blow up."

"I don't know. He just shook his head and that was that. He was a hell of a lot calmer than you were. More like he was amazed. You want to put a team on Qatar? Just to make sure?"

Lucas shook his head. "He's got to wear an ankle bracelet, he doesn't have any access to money, and J. B.'s already told him we're whipped. Why would he run? What would he run with?"

"All right. See you when? Wednesday?"

"Or maybe Thursday. I want to take a little time with Weather. . . . Goddamnit."

LUCAS spent the evening thinking about the phone call from Lansing—and about the phone call *to* Randy. He and Weather ate in, Weather watching him, and when they were done she said, "I'm going to let you brood," and got out her laptop to do some office catch-up. Lucas wandered around first the house and then the garage, cleaning nothing out of the Porsche, then the yard, and back into the house again, working through it. Weather fired up a DVD movie, but he couldn't focus. "You haven't figured it out yet, whatever you're figuring out?"

"I hope not," he said.

They finally went to bed at midnight, and just before she went to sleep, Weather asked, "Are you really going to stay home all day?"

"Nah. Probably not. May go for a run in the Porsche. Knock around a little."

"I'll try to get home early. Why don't we go out to the marina and take a look at my boat?"

"Okay."

She went quickly and softly to sleep, as she often did. Lucas lay awake, waiting for the phone to ring. He thought it might ring sometime after three o'clock, but it didn't. He never heard Weather leave, and when he opened his eyes, it was eleven in the morning.

He ate breakfast, went out and got in the car, took it out on the Interstate across the river to Wisconsin, jumped on his favorite blacktop road to River Falls, and let the Porsche engine out of the box. For the next hour he looped along the backroads, surprised that the golf courses were already open, looking for but not seeing any more snow in the woods—it had melted away in a week. Sometimes, after a long winter, the snow stayed back in the trees into May. Not this year.

He thought about Qatar, about the bloody clothing from Barstad's. At three o'clock, he pulled the lightly breathing Porsche into the parking lot at St. Patrick's, walked across the lawns to Qatar's office building, and found the janitor with the whiskey nose.

"If you were gonna hide something in this building where you could get at it quick and whenever you wanted, safely and without anybody seeing, but you didn't want to hide it in your own office . . ."

"You mean like if Jim Qatar hid some evidence."

"Yeah. Where would you hide it?" Lucas asked.

The janitor thought for a couple of minutes, then said, "I personally might hide it anywhere, because I can go anywhere in the building and nobody looks at me twice. But if I was Jim Qatar . . . Let me show you. You know about the skeleton cases upstairs?"

"No."

"Next floor up from Qatar's office. Just up the stairway. Let's take the elevator," the janitor said. On the way up, he said, "You think maybe he didn't burn the clothes?"

"I don't know. It seems a little risky. . . . What if somebody saw him down there?"

"Yeah, but if you know your way around, like he did, you could do it. It's a little risky, but hell, what're we talking about? You think he murdered—what, a dozen people?"

They got out at the top floor. The hallway outside the elevator was lined with glass cases, each holding reconstructed skeletons or stuffed birds or animals—thirty or forty of them, Lucas thought, lining both sides of the narrow hall. The ceiling hung low overhead, a checkerboard of darker and lighter wood panels.

"This originally was book storage and supplies, but when that moved out, they put these cases up here for the art students," the janitor said. "They're supposed to draw from them, and some of them do. Human skeletons down that way, and some muscle things, full-sized."

"So Qatar . . ."

"I'll show you." There were hard-backed wooden chairs between cases. "They sit on these, drag them around. . . ." He pulled a chair out, stood on it, and pushed one of the wooden ceiling panels. It lifted easily. "There used to be a higher ceiling—way high, to the top of the building—but dirt filtered down all the time, and there wasn't any way to clean it, so they put this drop-ceiling in. Years and years ago. Maybe in the sixties, maybe. Anyway, all the kids know about it. There's a ledge right inside, and sometimes, if they're working, they'll just push one of these things up and leave their stuff in here."

"All right." Lucas looked down the hall. There were probably a hundred panels per side: He could spend the rest of the afternoon looking, and probably not finding anything. On the other hand . . .

"You want to look? Glad to give you a hand."

"Nah, you go on," Lucas said. "I might push up a few of them."

"Are you sure? Glad to."

"Nah. I can take care of it."

Lucas looked him back into the elevator, and when he was gone, and the elevator cables stopped grinding, he dragged a chair out and began pushing up panels in the silence of the long hallway. He found he could place the chair beneath one panel, lift it and the panels on both sides, and so cover three with one move of the chair. He went left down the hall from the elevator, spent twenty minutes, found nothing but an old lunch—very old, maybe a decade.

Instead of working back down the other side of the hall, he carried his chair back to the elevator and started the other way. On the second panel, he saw a plastic sack stuffed on the ledge. But Qatar had been carrying a grocery sack. . . .

He had driving gloves in his pockets. He pulled them on, then tugged at the plastic bag. Heavy and hard. He lifted it down carefully and peeled back the garbage bag.

A laptop: not what he'd been expecting. He stepped down carefully, sat on the chair, and opened the laptop's cover—found the switch and turned it on. A green light came up instantly: still charged. A student? Windows came up, and then the icons on the left side of the screen. Halfway down he spotted the eye-in-the-square of Photoshop.

"Sonofabitch," he muttered. He brought Photoshop up, found a file listed as "B1," opened it. A photograph of a woman, but skeletonized, reduced to a skein of fine lines. He maneuvered it awkwardly around the screen, unfamiliar with the Photoshop protocols, but finally got a face. Barstad. "There you are," he said. He maneuvered the pointing stick, brought up another one. A woman he didn't recognize, but he recognized the pose: It had been lifted from a porn site. He scanned the list of files. Found an A1, A2, and A3.

Opened A1, found the face.

Closed his eyes for a moment, then said, "Gotcha."

Aronson stared back at him.

There had to be prints on the bag or the laptop. Nobody could be *that* careful, *that* paranoid . . . and the surfaces were perfect for prints. But now, what to do? He sat thinking for another five minutes, vacillating, then stood on the chair and put the package back on the ledge.

Hesitated, then put the panel back in place.

Went down in the basement and found the whiskey-nosed janitor. "It's taking longer than I thought, and I can't see well enough, all the way back," he lied. "I'm gonna bring in a crime-scene crew tomorrow. Don't let anybody go up there, okay? You don't have to guard it, but don't let *anybody* mess around up there."

"I'll keep everybody out. I'll block it off, if you want."

"It doesn't look like there are many people around . . . why don't you just keep an eye on it? There might be fingerprints somewhere, and we wouldn't want to mess them up."

The janitor nodded. "Never thought of fingerprints. Whatever you say—I go home at seven, but I'll make sure that everybody knows it's off-limits."

HE spent that evening thinking about the phone call to Randy and about the laptop. Did the laptop assemble the bricks into a wall? Or was it just another half-assed brick? Even if they could demonstrate that Qatar did the drawings, and therefore knew Aronson before she died, what if Qatar argued that he met her through the second man— Randy—or vice versa, that Aronson had met Randy through him. After all, only one of the dead women was associated with a drawing. And there were more than a dozen women still alive who'd got them.

Weather said to him, "You've been in never-never land again. What's going on?"

"Working on a little puzzle," he said.

"Want to talk?"

"No. Not right now." He looked at her. "Maybe tomorrow."

She was mildly offended and a little stiff after that, but

that had happened before. She always got over it. Again, Lucas lay awake after she slept.

The phone call, when it came, would probably be a little after three o'clock, he thought. The pit of the night. . . .

Three o'clock passed, and he dozed. Woke up briefly at four, then dropped back asleep, more soundly now. The problem may have resolved itself, he thought as he went under.

He really wasn't prepared when the phone rang at five o'clock.

He was awake instantly, rolling off the bed, Weather waking and saying, "What? What?"

Lucas picked up the phone. "Yeah."

"Chief? This is Mary Mikolec over at the Center. You asked to be called. We've sent a car over to Qatar's place. He's running."

"Okay," he said. "When did he walk?"

"About fifteen minutes ago."

"Thanks. . . . Thanks for calling."

"What's happening?" Weather asked.

"Qatar's gone," Lucas said.

"Are you going?"

"No . . . nothing for me to do," he said.

"Lucas, what's going on?"

He sat on the bed and said, "Jesus. I dunno—I might have screwed up, but there's no way to know. That's what's been worrying me."

"Tell me," she said. She sat up and put a hand on his shoulder.

He thought about it for a minute, then said, "It was that call to Randy. You gotta ask yourself, who knew the direct-line number into his room? After they moved him out of the ICU, they put him in this little room by himself where he'd be away from everybody else, and you could see the door from the nursing station. The switchboard was told not to switch any calls without an okay from Lansing. I asked the nurses: He didn't have any visitors. . . . And then you've got to ask why somebody would do that. Make that call, even if he could?"

Weather was puzzled. "Well, why?"

"Because he wanted Qatar turned loose, or at least let out on bail. If he was in jail, and if he cut a deal on a plea— second-degree with psychological evaluation, whatever— he'd be out of reach."

Weather thought about it for half a second, then her hand went to her mouth. "Oh, no. Oh my God."

"Yeah. I think Terry Marshall probably picked him up. It's about sixty-forty that Qatar's dead already."

"Lucas . . . why did you . . . ?"

"Because I wasn't *sure*. And even if I thought so, I'm not sure it's not the right thing. What if Qatar gets out in ten or twelve years and starts killing again? That could happen."

"Yes, but Lucas—this isn't right. This is awful."

"But Qatar—"

"Lucas, this is not about *that* asshole. This is about *Terry*. If he's done this, it's gonna be terrible for *him*. The heck with Qatar, it's *Terry*."

He looked at her and said, "It's only about sixty-forty that Qatar's dead. If he's not, it's about sixty-forty that I know where they're going."

Weather said, *"The graveyard."*

"That would fit with the way Terry's mind works, I think."

"Lucas, you've got to call somebody," she said. "Lucas, you can't let this happen."

Lucas put his hands to his head, sitting on the bed, frozen. Then, suddenly, looking up: "All right. I'm going. I can beat them down there. The alarm went off fifteen minutes ago. Maybe I can work something, maybe I can, if there's time, maybe . . ."

He was out of bed, pulling on his pants, boots. "Gimme my sweatshirt, give me my sweatshirt . . ."

They stumbled all the way through the house, Lucas pulling on clothes, out to the garage. He climbed into the Porsche as the garage door rolled up, and she shouted, "Go! Go!"

29

LUCAS FUMBLED HIS flasher up on the dash and plugged it in, and with the harsh red light cutting holes through the night, he followed it down along the Mississippi, across the river by the airport, across the Minnesota River at the Mendota Bridge, and then south on Highway 55, all the time running the numbers. Marshall wouldn't be driving more than a mile or two over the speed limit, to avoid any possible traffic cops—it was early for traffic cops, but the first trickle of the rush was beginning, and Marshall wouldn't want to take any chances.

And that gave Lucas a chance. Giving Marshall a twenty- or twenty-five-minute head start—Marshall was starting farther into town than Lucas was, and facing more traffic—he and Lucas should arrive at the graveyard about the same time. What would happen there, Lucas didn't know; and if Marshall wasn't there, if he'd just decided to drop Qatar out in the woods somewhere, in some predug hole, then it was over.

Cell phone, he thought. Maybe he should call the Good-hue County sheriff, get them to send a car. But then, if Marshall wasn't there, they'd know that Lucas knew who had taken Qatar. . . . He touched his jacket pocket for the phone, still thinking about it. The pocket was empty. The phone was back on the charger on his desk.

One option gone.

He touched his belt: The .45 was there. He'd taken it without thinking. But what for?

THREE people would know about all of this—he and Weather, and Marshall—and Del would probably figure it out if he ever sat down to think about it. There would never be any proof. Marshall would be too careful for that. What to do if he got there too late, with Qatar already dead? Just keep going?

He had to run. . . .

He went through the suburbs, through the red lights and around shying cars, watching for movement along the sides of the roads, of people unaware. If he hit another car at this speed, the Porsche would be flattened into a hubcap; if he hit a wandering human, he would instantly convert that human to hamburger.

All the way, calculating, wondering: He hadn't told Weather or anyone else about the laptop. If he'd taken the laptop downtown after he found it, had processed it, they could have rearrested Qatar on the Aronson charge and he probably wouldn't have made bail. Marshall's whole con-cept would have been short-circuited.

But then what happens to justice? Ten or fifteen years in jail, with Qatar coming out all clear, even more careful, to kill again? Some of them, some of the Qatars, *never* stopped. Lucas was still uncertain of the equities. If it weren't for Weather, he might have let it go. . . .

H E hit the blacktop north of the Pine Creek crossing with enough daylight to see it clearly. He slid through the turn and jumped back on the gas, then cut out on the gravel road. Close now; more light. He saw the DNR parking area coming, and sitting in it . . .

"Goddamnit." Marshall's red Jeep Cherokee.

Lucas screamed into the lot, braked down beside the Cherokee, and hopped out.

Looked around . . .

Marshall and Qatar were up on the hillside. They had stopped walking, and both were looking down at him. Qatar was dressed in pajamas, and his feet were bare. He had been gagged for a while, Lucas thought: Several coils of duct tape were looped around his neck, as though they'd been pulled down from his face. He was shivering, either from fear or simply from the cold.

Marshall was wearing jeans and a tan barn coat. He had one hand on Qatar's jacket, and in his other, the big-frame .357.

Qatar shouted down, "Help me, please. He's crazy, he's going to kill me." There was a catch in his voice. His hands had been cuffed, and he held them out toward Lucas as though he were praying.

"Terry, goddamnit," Lucas called. "Don't do this, man."

Marshall called back, "I was about half afraid you'd show up here. I didn't think you'd be this quick. Ten minutes later and we'd have all been fine."

"Terry, we got him," Lucas shouted, moving closer. "I found his laptop computer. It was in the ceiling in the museum. Me and the janitor found it. It's got pictures of the

women on it, it's gotta have prints—we got him for everything, man."

"Little too late for that," Marshall said. "This is better
anyway. Takes care of a couple of problems: his and
mine."

"Shoot him," Qatar screamed at Lucas. "Shoot him."

Marshall jerked him another step across the hill, dragging him by the loops of duct tape.

"Terry, goddamnit, stop it. Stop it." Lucas was walking
up the hill toward them.

"You gonna shoot me and save this asshole?"

"No. But you gotta listen. We can still smooth this out:
You turn him in, we tell everybody you freaked, you talk to
a shrink for a couple of weeks . . ."

He was fifty feet away. Marshall had gotten Qatar to the
dug-over area where the graves were.

"Oh, horseshit, Lucas, you know better'n that," Marshall
drawled. He might have been smiling. "Minnesota's the
same as Wisconsin: They'd hang me by my nuts. They'd
make an example out of me. Cops can't do this shit."

Forty feet. Qatar's eyes were wide, his shoulders twisting away from Marshall. "Don't let him . . . You can't just
shoot me," he shouted at Marshall. "I can't die today. I
can't . . . I have *classes* today. I have *responsibilities*. The
college is *expecting* me."

"I don't think so, pal."

Thirty feet. Lucas could see that Qatar's bare feet were
bleeding, apparently from dragging over the rocks and
roots of the hillside. Marshall lifted his pistol so that it
pointed directly into the back of Qatar's head. "Stop right
there," he said to Lucas.

"Terry, please, man, you're a good guy. And listen to
this—one last thing." Lucas was begging for time.
"There's not much chance, but what if he is innocent?
What if we've screwed this up somehow?"

"That's right," Qatar said. "This is completely illegal. My lawyer—"

"Shut up." Marshall snapped the pistol barrel against the back of his head, and Qatar stopped, his mouth open in midsentence. Marshall said to Lucas, "There's a tape recorder on the front seat of the car. When I got him in the car, I pulled the duct tape off his mouth and told him what I was gonna do, but I told him that maybe I wouldn't if he'd tell me about the women. You listen to that tape, you'll get all the names, and pretty close to the dates, and the places he picked them up. He even says there are two more down in Missouri, some godforsaken place down there."

"You promised me," Qatar said. He tried to twist out of Marshall's grasp, but Marshall played him like a fish. "You promised."

"I lied," Marshall said.

"All right, I'll go to trial, I'll confess," Qatar said. "You got me. All right? All *right?* Just stop this, stop this now. You win. *Okay?*"

"On the other hand, I could always shoot you, too," Marshall said to Lucas, but he was showing a grin again. "How'd they ever prove it was me?"

Lucas shrugged. "They would. Tire tracks, the slugs, nitrites when they picked you up. There's probably a parade on the way here now."

"Yeah, I know, I guess," Marshall admitted. The smile, if it was ever there, faded away and he took a deep breath and looked around the hillside, tipped his head back to look up through the oak branches. Again he cocked the gun up against Qatar's head. "Well, I guess there ain't gonna be any big ceremony in this."

Qatar looked at Lucas, his voice level but desperate. "Help me."

Lucas said, "Terry . . ."

"You want to say a couple of words, this is your last chance. You're gonna be in hell in ten seconds," Marshall said to Qatar.

Qatar turned his head away, trembling violently. And then he stopped. Maybe the finality of the situation had finally hit him, maybe he was embarrassed by his pleading, maybe this was simply the real Qatar—Lucas didn't know. But he reached down, carefully brushed some mud off his pajamas as well as he could with his cuffed hands, and then looked Marshall in the eyes.

"Your niece—she was a tasty little cunt," he said. "She took a long time to die."

"You cocksucker," Marshall screamed, and Lucas shouted, "Terry, goddamnit . . ."

The pistol shot was an earsplitting BANG, and Lucas flinched away from it. Qatar's face had a bloody hole in it where the hollow-point had exited; his legs went out, and he pitched down onto one of the refilled graves. He twitched once; he was dead. He didn't look like Edward Fox anymore, not even a bald one.

"Terry . . . Jesus Christ, Terry . . ." Lucas said. He was twenty feet away.

Marshall was talking, but talking to Qatar. "I didn't think you had the guts for that," he said. "You got to me. You did that."

He shook his head, looking down the slope at Qatar's crumbled body, but now talking to Lucas. "I had a little time to think on the way down here," Marshall said. "Time to think. I spent ten years of my life looking for the miserable shit. Ruined my life, what was left of it, after June was killed. Took Laura . . . I just wish Laura would have had a chance in life, you know? Where's Jesus when you need him?" He put the pistol under his own chin and turned his head to look Lucas in the eyes. "But you know what, Lucas?" He took a last look around and a deep breath. "Today's a nice day for this. You might want to look away for a second. . . ."

"Terry!" Lucas screamed.

DEL arrived twenty minutes later, pounding into the parking lot in his wife's Dodge. He jammed the transmission into park and jumped out of the car. Lucas was sitting cross-legged on the hood of the Porsche.

"Weather called," Del said. "I got here as soon as I could. Thought maybe I should call somebody, but I didn't . . . not yet." Lucas didn't respond, and Del looked up at the hill. The bodies were out of sight, untouched, except for the handful of dried oak leaves that Lucas had dropped over Marshall's half-open eyes. "Too late?"

Lucas sighed, rubbed his forehead with his fingers, eyes closed. "Just in time to say goodbye," he said.

30

LUCAS AND WEATHER were working on her boat, an aging S-2. The sky was a perfect blue, and the sun felt as if it wanted to burn down on the back of his neck but didn't yet have the horsepower.

"The thing is made of fiberglass—you wouldn't think you'd have to sit around and sandpaper and varnish," Lucas grumbled. "What the hell is fiberglass for, anyway? Why did they make the goddamn hatch cover out of wood when they had a fiberglass factory?"

"Shut up and paint," Weather said.

"Aren't you supposed to have, like, croissants and wine when you're working on a sailboat? And some friends come by and the guy has got a square chin and the chick is really good-looking and has loop earrings? And they're both wearing turtlenecks and you get this little vibration of possible group sex?"

"The more you talk, the sloppier you get. Just paint and

shut up and let me scrub." She was down below, scrubbing what appeared to be chemically hardened chipmunk shit out from under the sink. Lucas was sitting in the cockpit, working on the slip-out hatch board. He secretly believed it was makework to keep him out of the way while she did the real cleanup.

Around them, in the marina, two dozen people were working on boats, and from where he sat on top of the boat, which was on top of the trailer, he could see a mile across Lake Minnetonka to one of the season's early regattas.

"Glad we're not out there racing," he said. "Those guys gotta be freezing their asses off."

"Best time of year," she said. She stepped into the companionway, stepped up, and looked toward the racers. "Nice and dry, too—couldn't be much wind over there."

"Love sailboat racing," Lucas said. "No wind, they still race."

"That's Lew Smith way out on the end—look at him, he must think something's coming."

Lucas leaned back and closed his eyes. It all smelled good: the day, the lake, the marina, even the varnish. If everything were like this all the time . . .

Well, he'd go nuts. But it was nice to be like this every once in a while. He opened his eyes and looked at Weather. She was still talking, but it was all about racing and who was being lifted above whom, and who was looking at a header, and he really couldn't care about any of it. What he did care about was Weather, and he smiled, watching her enthusiasm.

Sailing.

FOR two frantic days after Qatar and Marshall died on the hillside, Lucas had shuttled between grand juries in Goodhue and Hennepin counties. The papers and television stations were wild for the story, and that might yet go on for a while. They all wanted to know why Lucas had gone down to the graveyard. Lucas could only say that it had been a hunch that came to him when he got the call from the 911 Center.

Why didn't he call Goodhue? Because he had no real knowledge that Marshall was involved and didn't want to damage a friend if he was wrong, and had been so disturbed by the possibility that he'd launched himself onto the road without his cell phone, and once on the way, it seemed best to continue . . . blah, blah, blah.

Cops and lawyers came and went, but as long as Lucas's story stayed simple, there were no seams to cut onto. On the day after the shooting, he sent a crime-scene crew to St. Patrick's to talk to the janitor, with instructions to search the overhead on the skeleton floor, and anything else the janitor suggested. The crew found the computer an hour into the search, and the laptop had Qatar's prints all over it. The computer forensics people did their work, and up popped drawings of Aronson and another woman from the graveyard.

At the same time, an illegal copy of the tape recording that Marshall made of Qatar found its way to Channel Three, and then to every TV and radio station that wanted it. Lucas didn't know who leaked it—he suspected Del, but Del professed to be mystified, as did Marcy, Sloan, and Rose Marie. Qatar's babbling confession, and his naming of names, led to quick IDs on the unidentified bodies from the graveyard, and to a new search in the countryside a few miles east of Columbia, Missouri.

The usual Minnesotans were shocked by the police misconduct that had led to Qatar's killing, but Rose Marie had a quiet word with old friends in the Democratic Party's political-feminist hierarchy; with that, and with the constant playing of the tape across nine-tenths of the electromagnetic spectrum, the controversy withered. There was some expected grumbling from the Minnesota Civil Liberties Union about police-sponsored lynchings, which everybody agreed was the MCLU's perfect right. Free speech, and all that.

That cleaned up the case.

Del had wondered, privately, just how early Lucas had suspected Marshall. Lucas shook his head and walked away from the question. Avoided the lie, but Del knew him well enough to understand the walk.

Rose Marie also had a few questions that she didn't ask. She did take Lucas aside and said, "The governor was impressed. I gave him ten minutes on what a great crime-detection bunch we have over here, and you know what he said?"

"What'd he say?" They were in her office, and she was looking more cheerful than she had in weeks.

"He said, 'I don't care about how good they detected—what *I* liked was the way they *handled* it.' "

"So that's good," Lucas said.

"That's very good."

TIDYING up the loose ends on the case hadn't tidied up Lucas's head. A vague melancholia settled over him, a mood that Weather picked up. She began arranging events and talked to Marcy behind his back; Marcy began arranging events, and suggested that Lucas and Weather and she and Kidd go out to dinner. Lucas said "Sometime," and kept wandering around town.

He could have stopped the whole train, he thought. He'd never made up his mind; he'd never gotten clear on what he should do. He could have made a decision, but he hadn't—a private failing, and a serious one, he thought.

* * *

THAT night, after the sailboat, after a salad of roasted chicken breasts and walnuts and lettuce, after a bowl of wild rice soup, after a beer or two, he was puttering in his study, the whole case still tingling at the back of his brain. After a while, he sighed and walked down to the bathroom. The door was shut and locked.

"Weather?"

"Yes. Just a minute."

"That's okay, I can run down—"

"No, no, just a minute." He could hear her moving around, and tried the door. Locked.

"What are you doing?"

"Uh . . ."

"Okay, I'll run down to the—"

"No, no . . . I'm, uh, I'm just, uh, peeing on a stick."

"What?"

"Peeing on a stick."

"Weather? What . . . ?"

"I'm peeing on a stick. Okay?"

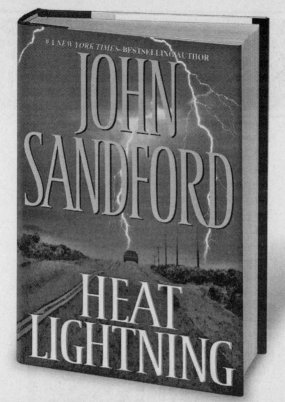

NEW FROM #1 *NEW YORK TIMES*–BESTSELLING AUTHOR

JOHN SANDFORD

www.JohnSandford.org

A member of Penguin Group (USA) Inc.
www.penguin.com

M303JV0608

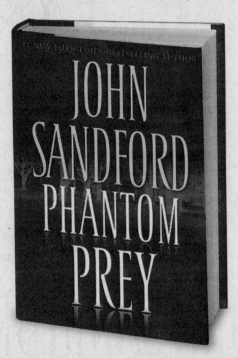

DON'T MISS

BROKEN PREY

"Riveting."
—*Richmond Times-Dispatch*

"[A] sexy, bloody thriller."
—*Publishers Weekly* (starred review)

"Blistering."
—The Associated Press

From "the best thriller writer working today"*

#1 *NEW YORK TIMES* BESTSELLING AUTHOR

JOHN SANDFORD

*San Antonio Express-News

penguin.com